Maeven:
Dragon Thief

by
Margaret Gregory

Tried And Trusted Indie Publishing

Also by Margaret Gregory

TYMOREAN TRUST SERIES:
Book 1 - Power Rising
Book 2 - Great Ones
Book 3 - The Return to Earth
Book 4 – Earth Mission
Book 5 – Alien Contact
Book 6 - Invasion

ATAPI SORCERESS SERIES:
Prequel – Korvu: The Beginning
Book 1- The Wild One
Book 2 – Atapi Sorceress

THE THIRD GENERATION SERIES:
Wanda – Early Days (anthology)
Wanda - Risking Life to Live

Cover designed by msgdragon
Cover Image Credits: © Can Stock Photo Inc. / fmarsicano
Cover Image Credits: © Can Stock Photo Inc. / amelislam

For permission requests, address the request to the author c/o
Permissions,
Tried and Trusted Indie Publishing
PO Box 2728
Rowville, Victoria, 3178
www.tatindiepublishing.com

CHAPTER 1 – THE QUEEN DIES

"I wish I had a dragon and could fly away from here…"

Maeven, youngest Princess of Thulor, heard the soft tones of her voice echo from the vaulted roof of the stone tower. She turned away from the view from the large square opening in the stone wall and continued, "Some place where my mother didn't die."

Through eyes filled with unshed tears, the dragon figures etched and painted on the underside of the roof seemed to move sinuously.

An icy gust of rain-scented air caused Maeven to glance at the dark grey clouds that seemed close enough to reach out and touch. Any moment now, the clouds would dissolve into rain.

The clouds reflected her mood but she was determined not to dissolve into tears. Instead, she watched the long line of shuffling peasants waiting for permission to enter the grounds to see the King.

"Don't those peasants know anything?" she said aloud, simply to hear a voice speak, albeit shakily. "No one is seeing the King. Not even me!"

She strode to the second opening and perched on the knee high ledge, and picked at the plate of pastries she had put there. On the ledge were weathered etchings that could have been more dragons.

"If I had a dragon – I'd show them…"

"What?"

Maeven felt the question in her mind and thought it was her own. Her resentment with everyone supplied an immediate answer.

"I'll teach them all that they can't ignore me. I'll have a dragon. They will have to do what I want or be turned to cinders."

"*Why?*"

Was that her conscience talking to her?

"Why? Because nobody wants me. I don't think Rhovert knows I exist and Leane and Finora have each other and don't want me around. Father never seems to pay us any attention… and I haven't seen a servant in three days."

"*How?*"

"Well – I'd have to find a dragon's egg," Maeven said aloud. But you didn't see dragons scratching around like chickens and laying their eggs just anywhere. "And if I did – I'd hatch it and train it and… I'd love it and it would love me!"

What was the use? Dragons were only myths anyway.

"Are they?" Was the thought hers?

"Nobody I know has ever seen a dragon," Maeven told the voice in her head. "I might only be nine years old but I've listened to Mama's ladies talking. If any of them had ever seen a dragon – they'd have told everyone about how smart they were to escape the terror."

"Dragons protect people," the strange voice stated.

Where did that idea come from? Every tale she had heard about dragons said they were greedy for gold and jewels and that they would kill humans to get them.

"Mama?" Maeven asked aloud – wondering if the strange voice was that of Queen Rheanna. Her mother had said something like that once – what was it?

Maeven stared at the painted dragons and tried to remember. The words came back to her as if they had just been spoken moments past – not years ago.

"Thulor is the Dragon's realm. Dragons protect Thulor and keep it safe and prosperous."

Maeven glared at the paintings, focussed on a silvery one and spoke to it.

"If you exist – where the hell were you when my mother – the Queen of Thulor – needed protection? Where are you now? When my father – the King – is skulking in his chambers – seeing no one – ignoring his duties – ignoring his children – ignoring Me!"

No voice answered her, just the echoes of her own words.

Tears threatened to overcome her, but she held herself in check, clenching her fists until her nails dug into her palms. The pain cleared her mind. Her hand moved to the last of the dainty pastries she had pilfered from the kitchen. Once consumed, she threw the china plate across the tower, sending it smashing against the stone wall – with all the force of her resentment.

"At least those things tasted better than that servants' glop that they expected me to eat these past two days," Maeven muttered.

Movement below caught her attention. Below was the Queen's garden, her mother's favourite place. Small figures dressed in brown tunics and trousers were scrambling through the branches of the old oak trees. Servant's brats! Anger rose in her for a moment. How dare they desecrate her mother's garden?

Tempted though she was to tell on them, she made no sound. She did not want to betray her hidey-hole either. She was no more allowed in the tower, the dragon's tower, than the brats were allowed in the garden. At least they didn't seem worried about getting their clothes dirty, or skirts snagged.

She scowled; her own clothes were none too clean right now. No one had laid out clean clothes for her for the last three days, so she had to dress herself without help in the old dirty ones. No one had helped her with her hair, either. The part of her that detested being forced to be a lady actually enjoyed the situation, but the other part that was beginning to like fancy gowns as a sign of rank was not impressed. At least the boring lessons had been stopped, too.

Lightning flashed from cloud to cloud.

Maeven drew back a bit from the open window as a gust of wind blew her long light brown hair around her face.

Then unexpectedly, a shaft of sunlight broke through the clouds and lit the hill beyond the palace walls. Caught in the light was a horse and rider, racing to the palace as if a demon was chasing them. The rider, wearing royal blue, was unhelmed – an officer of the guard then.

"Maybe it's…" Maeven began to say. The person had blonde hair. Perhaps it was her uncle, Prince Esmond, returning. She watched as the rider slowed near the gate, paused briefly to speak to the gatekeeper and then was admitted.

"It is him. Now, something might get done around here."

Maeven stepped down from the stone window seat, and left the tower as quietly and quickly as she could, skipping down the tight spiral stairs. She wanted to be near her father's private suite before her uncle got there. Maybe she could slip in behind her uncle. The guards had not let her go in on her own.

CHAPTER 2 – CHANGES

The dark clouded sky looked like it would soon teem with rain as Prince Esmond slowed his sweating mount to a walk. He maintained the slow pace as he passed the long line of petitioners trying to enter the palace grounds.

"I'm sorry, Good Sir," the King's Seneschal was saying politely to a well-dressed merchant. "His Majesty is not seeing petitioners today. You will have to come back tomorrow."

"That's what you told me yesterday and the day before! I insist that I be allowed to speak to His Majesty today!"

"Sir, you may not be aware… Please make way for Prince Esmond, Sir."

The merchant glared at the rider of the grey horse who was wearing the dark blue livery of the King's Own Guards.

"Trouble, Kensan?" Prince Esmond asked quietly as he drew level with the sturdy, grey-haired Seneschal.

"Nothing I can't handle, Sir," Kensan assured the Prince Esmond nodded and urged his tired beast into a trot.

As he rode on, the Prince tried to determine what was wrong. The faint feeling of dread that had hastened his return was much stronger now.

There were serfs tending the palace vegetable gardens but they seemed like puppets. The movements were there but the usual chatter was not. Some looked up as he passed but none waved and all returned stolidly to their task.

The depression he sensed might have been due to the impending storm but that would not explain why someone was out in the archery field, using a sword to dismember the man shaped, straw filled targets. Esmond slowed his mount again. From the finery adorning the swordsman, it had to be his nephew, Prince Rhovert.

The dread intensified further. Esmond spurred his mount again as the rain began. In the short distance to the stable courtyard, he became soaked. He dismounted near the palace door and handed the reins to one of the stable serfs, a grizzled old man with red watery eyes.

Without a word, he strode into the palace, his boots clattered on the flagstone floor. The sound echoed in the unnatural hush as did the water dripping from his blue dyed leather cloak. No servants greeted him so he hurried his steps in the direction of his brother's audience chamber.

The chamber seemed deserted. The King was not on his throne, but as he turned to leave, he saw his brother's scribe and Court recorder, slumped miserably over his normal bench.

"Where is the King?" Esmond demanded.

The scribe, a young man relatively new to his position, looked up. He too had bloodshot eyes.

"Sir, His Majesty is in his private apartments. He won't let anyone in, not even the servants. He won't even eat."

"Jays, what in the name of the Dragon has happened around here?"

"Haven't you heard, Sir?" Jays said, his eyes going wide. "It's Queen Rheanna, Sir, she's … dead!" The young man seemed about to cry again. "Three days ago…"

"Do you mean to say that my brother hasn't eaten for three days?"

Jays nodded.

"Pah!" Esmond said involuntarily, controlling his anger. It was not Jays's fault.

"Jays, go down to the kitchen and tell them to prepare a tray for His Majesty. Then, have someone bring Prince Rhovert in from the practice field before he gets sick. Where are the girls?"

"Princess Leanne and Princess Finora are with their tutor. They have been haunting that little alcove near the King's apartment. Princess Maeven is being… a little difficult."

Prince Esmond frowned. The fourteen year old twins had always relied on each other, but the baby, nine year old Maeven, had been closest to her mother and Rheanna had been the only one capable of making her behave in a civilised manner.

"Bring the food up when it is ready," Esmond instructed Jays, who seemed to have more life in him now that there was someone giving orders.

Esmond removed his wet cloak and left it on a bench outside the Audience Chamber for a servant to deal with, then strode in the direction of the Royal Apartments. He stopped briefly to speak to his twin nieces. The tutor was not in sight.

"I'm sorry about your mother," he said gently. "Now she is gone there will be changes around here…"

"You will teach me to fight, Uncle?" Leanne broke in, her eyes brightened, anticipating his answer.

Esmond nodded. "And I will have you all tested for magic talent – it runs in the family. We are going to have to use whatever talents we have."

Finora jumped up and hugged her uncle. "Thank you, thank you, thank you."

With a smile, Esmond left the girls talking earnestly to each other. The misery had gone from both sets of blue-green eyes.

Further down the passage his smile faded. The sounds of a tantrum were growing louder and as Esmond turned the corner to come in sight of his brother's door.

"Why - can't - I - see - my – father?"

Esmond winced at the shrillness of Maeven's voice.

"We are to let no one in," was the stolid reply of the dark haired guard.

"I'm not no-one! I'm his daughter and I want to see my father."

This time Maeven stamped her foot. "And I will tell him you were rude to me."

The other guard answered her, "Princess Maeven, you should be with your nurse."

"I'm not a baby. I don't need a nurse. I – want - my - father!"

Maeven saw him coming and stopped screaming at the guards. They did not hide their relief as she moved off down the passage. She watched as her uncle spoke quietly to the guards.

The guards bowed and stood back in their usual guarding positions. They said nothing as Maeven sidled in after her uncle. Her father or uncle could tell her off.

Inside, King Westron sat in his favourite chair, staring at the grey-stone walls of his private chamber. His eyes were red as if he had been crying or had not slept for three days.

"What happened?" Esmond demanded, walking in to stand in front of his brother.

"A spooked horse ran her down," the King said in a hoarse voice. "She was walking back from one of her visits to town."

Esmond knew Queen Rheanna had often spent time with the commoners, either helping the poor or visiting with those she knew when she was still a merchant's daughter.

"Two of her ladies were injured as well, but what I can't understand is why she left her talisman here."

"Perhaps she had a premonition of her own death," Esmond suggested.

"Then why didn't she tell me?" Westron demanded.

Esmond felt a surge of fear. The death of the Queen had turned his confident and arrogant brother into a wreck. If an enemy had done this, they could attack now and the realm would be leaderless.

"Every time she foresaw a death, be it noble or merchant, we were able to prevent it," Westron said with passion. "If she'd said something…"

"She always wore the talisman," Esmond said slowly, an idea forming in his mind. He teased it into the open. "I know we have thought that many of those – accidents – might have been more than that but what if she saw only that someone wanted her talisman?"

"Who?" Some life came back into the King's face as his mind focused on the problem. "She might have left it here to be safe – but why didn't she say anything?"

"You might have been with Prince Malokin, the envoy from Vatarik," Esmond suggested, aware of that visit. "If the premonition came then, she would have planned to tell you later. I remember her saying that she didn't like Malokin, something about the way he looked at her at your wedding. Who found her?"

The King looked searchingly at his brother, his mind grasping the innuendo.

"Tormore and his son, but they were too far away to save her! No one else was close."

Esmond considered the notion of Barstow Tormore wanting to kill the Queen. It was simply too incredible. He and Westron had grown up with the man who had proven his loyalty to the King many times over. Moreover, Tormore's son, Col, and Prince Rhovert were friends.

"It looks like an accident," Esmond agreed. "But what if it was a clever attack on you? Your cousin, Merlie, had very little that was good to say about the Vatarins."

The King began to look more like his normal self, calculating and considering. He straightened in his chair.

"Prince Malokin was long gone by the time the accident happened. The guards had already returned from escorting him as far as Mayfield. They brought back the serving wench, Jilli. The one the Steward assigned to Malokin. She had tried to leave with him," Westron commented thoughtfully.

Esmond snorted. "They should have let that man-bait go! Where was she at the time?"

"I had her put in the dungeons for two days." Westron dismissed the subject as unimportant. He moved on to more important matters. "You got what I sent you for?"

"I've got Merlie's talisman and Carolona's," Esmond confirmed, noticing the King was idly playing with the one that had been Rheanna's.

Esmond went on to say, "My little shadow, Leanne, will get mine, of course. Merlie's is for Finora and Carolona's for Maeven. I had no trouble with Merlie; he was ready to pass it on. He has some form of progressive sickness and not as active as he was. I met trouble with his sister. She is a possessive, acquisitive crone. She didn't want to give up her talisman but finally accepted a hundred silver coins for it."

The people under discussion might have been strangers for all the interest the King showed.

"Give the girls their talismans," the King instructed, his mind on something else.

"With respect, Westron, you should be the one to present them," Esmond insisted. "Your children need you!"

"I gave you an order!" Westron snapped. "Leave me!"

Esmond glared for a moment. "There is a tray coming from the kitchen! See that you eat!" he said as he turned on his heel to stalk out.

As he passed the wooden door to the King's bedchamber, he heard it close softly. Intrigued, he opened it and went in. Maeven was there, near the carved wood drawers and the reflecting glass, hiding something from view.

"What are you doing in here, little lady?" he asked kindly.

"Nothing!" she said with a flash of uncertainty in her eyes.

"Show me," Esmond insisted. He caught her eye until she brought her mother's silver hairbrush from behind her back. Silent tears ran down her cheeks.

"You wanted something of your mother's?" he asked gently. Maeven gave a little nod.

"I'll tell your father you have it. I think it will be alright."

Esmond felt compelled to offer her comfort with a hug. She stood stiffly, not returning the gesture.

"I have something to give you," he said after a moment.

The tears vanished, replaced by a flash of interest. The hairbrush had disappeared into Maeven's pocket.

Leanne and Finora sat close together on a low stone wall in the small kitchen garden, comparing talismans and sharing a plate of cakes. The servants were, in their way, trying to cheer up the grieving princesses.

Hearing a slight noise behind her, Leanne turned suddenly and saw her youngest sister walking quietly between the rows of herbs.

"Go away you sneaking little brat!" she said loudly.

Maeven's eyes filled with tears but the tactic had no impact on her sisters. She began to shriek as if badly hurt. Leanne jumped down on that side of the wall and slapped her.

"Stop it you wretch. There is nothing wrong with you!"

Finora twisted around and kicked her sister in the shin when her twin had dragged Maeven closer.

"You may as well have something to scream about," she said sweetly.

The commotion drew the King's attention. He had finally emerged from his chambers and had been deep in conversation with one of the kitchen women.

"Leanne! Finora!" he said sternly taking in the scene. "Both of you will spend the rest of the day in your separate chambers."

They hid glares of resentment by looking at the ground.

"Go on!" their father insisted.

To his youngest daughter he simply said, "Stop your noise and go clean yourself up!"

Maeven stopped shrieking and watched him through narrowed eyes. Other servants were around so she went and sat on the stone parapet next to the cakes, sniffing miserably. She pretended to ignore the plate but when she left, ten minutes later, all the cakes had gone. With a smug smile, she wandered back into the palace, edging in through the kitchen door, to try to hear what her father was discussing. She scowled, when she heard him organising a dinner for her mother's closest friends.

Col Tormore, son of King Westron's Chief Advisor, found his long time friend Prince Rhovert, walking aimlessly around the palace grounds.

"My condolences, Rhovert. Your step-mother, Queen Rheanna, was a wonderful person," Tormore said quietly to his friend.

"Thanks," Rhovert replied listlessly.

"How are your sisters taking her death?"

Rhovert shrugged. "You know how they are – Leanne and Finora have always preferred each other's company and Maeven is doing everything she can to get attention." He sounded disgusted. "Just this morning, I caught her hiding Father's Rings of State. Little wretch, she was going to have the servants waste their time looking for them."

"Perhaps I could talk to her," Tormore suggested diffidently. "I know what it's like to lose a mother – I might be able to help her."

"I'd forgotten about your mother," Rhovert apologised. "It hasn't been that long, has it? Still, if I were you, I wouldn't bother. You would play right into her hands."

"Perhaps. But she might listen to me and perhaps I could convince her to be less of a spoilt brat."

"Good luck!" Rhovert wished him, shrugging. He continued his aimless walk around the inside of the castle walls.

Tormore was twenty-four, the same age as Prince Rhovert, and in spite of his voiced concern he also considered Princess Maeven a nuisance. So, she wanted attention. Well he would give her that all right, and he would find out why she had pinched something from his chamber that morning and where it was.

He was tall, with long, gingery blonde hair pulled into a braid that came to his collar. His attire showed him to be well proportioned and obviously a nobleman. He spoke with no trace of a common accent in his voice.

It took him a while to find her, but like most women he met, she was impressed by his interest in her. Her childinsh chatter, was annoying, but letting her talk was a minor matter, and when he ordered some drinks and cakes for them, she was enjoying herself so much that she had no suspicions of his intentions. After eating, he suggested a walk, and he let her wander aimlessly through the Queen's Garden until they reached a quiet corner near the castle wall, and hidden by a huge weeping willow.

Turning unexpectedly, and catching her wrist in a strong grip, he spun her to face him and demanded, "I want what you pinched from my room this morning!"

"I didn't take anything!" she denied automatically, shocked by the sudden accusation.

"A silver comb and cloak clasp," he said fiercely. "I saw you, girl!"

As he saw the tears start, he appeared to relent. "You liked them, did you?"

Her watering eyes turned calculating as she considered what to say.

"I'll let you have them in exchange for…" he seemed to ponder. "Oh, that piece of commoners' frippery your uncle gave you."

It was the wrong thing to suggest, Tormore saw at once. Maeven had begun to back away and try to pull her wrist free.

"Rigidus!" he said in a commanding voice, smiling as the wizard trick froze the girl in mid-step.

He released her wrist, which remained stretched out and walked closer to her. One hand felt in his pocket for a slab of soft wax. The other groped down her bodice for the talisman. Her eyes widened in indignation but she could neither scream nor move to stop him. He made an impression of the talisman in the wax, then deliberately returned the talisman to its hiding place. He enjoyed the girl's discomfort and the angry and impotent glare she gave him. It was a pity that she was not a few years older. Then, to give her something to think about, other than what he had done with the wax, he unclasped his belt and gave her two hefty thwacks on the buttocks. He smiled and released his spell. He watched with amusement as Maeven turned and ran.

As he refastened his belt, thinking that she would think twice about stealing from him again, he savoured the thought of how she would be hurting. That thought aroused him in a different way and he began to walk after the princess, until he spotted one of the maids watching him.

The story would soon be all over the palace. No matter. He would tell his father he had done it because she had stolen from him. His old man already thought the girl deserved a good beating. If the brat told her father, the King, of the incident, his advisor would tell him the reason.

Tormore turned his attention to the maid. He recognised her – he had taken this one within her first week in the castle and often in the two years since then. She liked men, the bitch; liked them to hurt her a bit, too. She was just what he wanted right now.

Maeven did not know that her new maid had been watching. She ran until she reached the castle's keep, pausing only to throw two silver objects into the midden. Then she continued to the audience chamber, entered by the back way the King used and crept next to the carved throne to hide in the folds of his robes of state. She did not see him glare down at her, being too busy crying genuine tears of indignation and pain.

The petitioners did not miss her arrival and assumed the young Princess was still grieving. They looked kindly on the King for letting her remain there. It reminded them of the King's own now controlled grief, and they did not demand all the concessions they had wanted.

The King sensed the change of heart and chose not to berate his daughter for her unseemly conduct. So long as she was content to stay hidden in his robes, he would say nothing.

Maeven was glad her father had let her stay with him. She was more than relieved that he did not ask what caused her behaviour. In her mind there was no doubt that her father would agree with the action of Col Tormore. He had a fierce hatred of thieves.

CHAPTER 3 – NEW DIRECTIONS

Three years later.

Maeven was enjoying herself immensely. The servants were busy making her a new gown. They thought that she was to attend the Solstice Ball that was to occur in two days' time. It was amusing to act annoyed at the fittings and fuss and the need to rush. The servants worked very hard to please her, fearing dismissal if they did not.

In fact, at age twelve Maeven was too young to go the ball. She was playing with the idea of sneaking in amongst the guests and seeing if she could tell how many of the unmarried ladies were vying for her father's attention. He'd made no secret that he was looking – having paraded a different one each month since her mother had died. Anyway, that was why she wanted a new dress – only this time she had not been allowed to go into town to get it made by one of the seamstresses there.

The servants had her standing on a low table so that they could adjust the hem of the gown. From that position, Maeven could look out through the window of the room that had once been her mother's solarium. She watched her sister Leanne, dressed as usual in long sleeved tunic and breeches, striding towards the palace with an armful of weapons. As she came closer, Maeven could see that her face was reddened with exertion.

Leanne was pushing herself harder than ever this past week, as if she blamed herself for the freak training accident that had killed their Uncle Esmond.

Maeven halted the fitting session and quickly redressed in her older gown. Of course, half way around the hem was an awkward time to stop – even if the servants were grateful for the respite.

"Did our Uncle turn you into a man?" Maeven asked, leaning against the doorframe to Leanne's chamber and blocking her sister from entering. She gave her elder sister a deliberate appraisal from head to boots. "Are you going to the ball dressed like that, or like a Princess?"

Leanne began to reply and then changed her mind. Three years of intense tuition had taught her to rein in her temper while developing the unladylike muscles.

"If I had to act like you to be a Princess – I'd rather be a man," Leanne said instead. "Move out of my way! I have more important things to do than listen to a child."

Maeven smirked and decided to obey. She sauntered down the passage towards her own chamber. A large ball of glowing energy suddenly appeared in front of her. It forced her to stop and made her head itch. It vanished again after a few seconds and just as quickly, Maeven controlled her expression. It was not her intention to let Finora know how impressed she was by that demonstration of magic.

"I don't know why you must be so horrid to Leanne," Finora said coming out of her chamber. "She misses Uncle Esmond dreadfully."

Maeven was convinced that her sisters shared each other's thoughts. How else did Finora know what she had been doing?

"She wouldn't be allowed to go around looking like a man if Mother were still alive," Maeven said without thinking. "And you would never be allowed to do magic!"

Finora, a more delicate version of her twin, looked frail but the hand that gripped Maeven's slender wrist was like steel. She laughed softly and said with equal malice, "Do you think that you would be allowed to be a spoilt, indulged and altogether useless court decoration if Mother were still alive?" She was rewarded by seeing the flash of pain that crossed her sister's face. "Unlike you, Leanne and I intend to do something useful with our lives."

"Stupid little parlour tricks!" Maeven retorted.

Finora suddenly laughed. "You're jealous. You haven't got any magic talent and I have!"

Maeven forced a smile. "Who'd want it? What use is it?"

Finora merely smiled. "You are such a child!"

With a scowl, Maeven stalked away, wishing for a way to get her back for that remark. It was frustrating to admit, but Finora had been right. She did wish that she had some magic talent. A trick like that light would be preferable to having to liberate candles from the storeroom.

Why in the name of the dragon had her Father suddenly decided to stop her trips to town? What would he consider an essential reason if getting a new dress wasn't?

Well, the servants may have instructions not to take her but she had discovered a secret way out of the palace. She could go by herself – but the tunnel was dark and had not been used in countless years; hence the candles.

Maeven had a sudden idea, and turned back. Finora was out of sight – probably in Leanne's room. She went to the door to Finora's chamber and slowly opened it. She had no particular plan, just the desire to annoy her sister.

The room was vacant, and extremely neat. How to mess it up…?

Maeven went to the wooden chest that Finora used for her clothes, intending to pull them out onto the floor, but her eye caught sight of some green ribbon and she went to look at it.

The ribbon was threaded through Finora's dragon amulet, and Maeven realised that she had never seen Finora wear it, though Leanne wore hers all the time. Suddenly she giggled and took her own talisman from her pocket. She'd stopped wearing her own because it seemed to give her a headache, but that didn't matter – she would swap Finora's for hers, and see how long it would take her sister to realise the switch. Oh, but the idea was priceless: a big fat juicy secret.

Three days later, as Maeven was returning from the stables after a riding lesson, she saw her brother Rhovert leaning casually against the trunk of a tree in the Queen's garden. He was dressed in a fancy creation made of gold satin and emerald green silk flounces.

"You've been into town again," was his challenging remark as his sister drew level with him.

Maeven stopped in her tracks.

"I distinctly remember Father forbidding such trips!"

"He doesn't care what I do! And if doing these lessons wasn't better than being bored, I wouldn't and he'd still say nothing."

"The Seneschal's wife seems to think that you are picking up too many common habits," Rhovert commented.

"That's rubbish – Leanne has run around with the soldiers for years and Mother used to spend a lot of time in town. What I do is hardly a scandal! How did you know anyway?"

"I saw you! You walked right past me." Rhovert watched as his sister's expression went blank.

Maeven thought back to her most recent trip – her second through the secret passage.

She didn't remember seeing Rhovert. Those clothes he wore would make him hard to miss, and she had been wearing servant clothing! She smirked as the answer came to her. She would have to learn to pay greater attention to details.

"Why were you down there?" she quizzed her brother.

"Why shouldn't I be? I am not a naïve, twelve-year-old girl. Why were you?"

"Father has no right to keep be cooped up here! He's treating me like a prisoner."

Rhovert, with a faint smile, shook his head at her. "If you don't agree, take it to a higher authority," he said mildly.

"Like who?" Maeven snapped – their father was the King!

Rhovert answered her by inclining his head slightly to the right, tacitly confirming that she had caught his point.

Maeven scowled and changed the subject. "Does Father say anything about you going about dressed in such highly decorated clothes like a…?"

Rhovert didn't even blink when his sister repeated a very rude word for 'effeminate'.

"Oh, these old things?" he pouted and spoke in a high pitched, whiny voice. "I look so handsome in them, don't I?"

Maeven smirked again as Rhovert posed, acting as he did at court. Then he dropped the pretence.

"As with you, Father doesn't care how I act, so long as my official duties are performed. You would be wise to remember that even if Father seems not to care about us, it is for his own reasons. Just as he has his own reasons for every unfathomable order he gives us."

Maeven only shrugged.

Rhovert sighed as if he thought his youngest sister was being particularly dense.

"However, that wasn't the only reason I came out here. You might be interested to know that Leanne and Finora have gone."

"Gone! Where?"

"Leanne is apprenticed to Shuggan, a Sword Master of the Order of Swords. Finora is apprenticed to Ermytrude, a member of the League of Sorcery. All nice and legal. Father, thanks to his own convoluted laws, can't touch them."

Maeven shrugged again. "Good riddance if they want to be exploited and overworked! What did Father say? I assume he knows."

"Oddly enough, he hasn't said anything," Rhovert said with a serious expression. "It is almost as if he knew they were going to leave and it suited his purpose to let them."

Rhovert pushed himself upright and began to walk away. After a few paces, he stopped as if a thought had occurred to him. "I wonder why he did forbid you to go into town." He shrugged as if it wasn't important and continued walking.

Reminded again of her recent discontent, Maeven muttered to herself.

"What Father doesn't know, he won't care about. He's just a pigheaded, arrogant old man who likes to indulge himself. He certainly doesn't care about anyone else."

Maeven continued on her way, thinking of her two solo trips. It was fun, pretending to be a commoner, dressing like them, eating what they ate, joining their games. Most of all it was exciting to sneak out on her own.

Life was good!

"Lord Tormore! You want me to marry him? Father, you have to be joking," Princess Maeven insisted, having to look up at the King sitting in his huge gilt throne. He had the Kingdom's heraldic banner, with a dragon in the sky over green hills, hanging from the roof behind him.

"As his late father used to be, Col Tormore is my most trusted advisor," King Westron said evenly. "You are a mere child. I will not allow you to marry someone totally unsuitable."

"He's old! He must be fifty at least," fifteen-year-old Maeven spluttered. "He looks like a toad and he gives me the creeps!"

"He is only thirty and has asked to marry you; I have accepted," King Westron spoke as if he would not change his mind. Maeven had recently come to recognize the futility of arguing with that tone!

"I won't marry Lord Toadface!" Maeven insisted with a look of disgust mingled with stubbornness, but she met her Father's equally obdurate look. *Maybe that was why her sisters had gone off to be apprenticed.*

"Have you someone else in mind?" he asked with a mildness that was quite provoking and not at all deceptive.

"No, dammit! You've kept me cloistered in the palace since I was twelve – just because my sisters had the sense to leave."

"Elvira Tormore is an excellent hostess. If you marry her brother you won't have to do that task if you don't want to."

The King was waiting for a reaction from his daughter and was not disappointed. Maeven's face went a deep red that clashed with the oranges of her outfit; she almost squirmed with embarrassment. The fiasco of her first, and so far only, stint as Hostess for her father was still a vivid memory. She had not wanted the job in the first place. In her opinion, it was servants' work. However, her father had made it a condition for continuing to receive an allowance. A very unsatisfactory state of affairs.

"You should let those – women – of yours have the job," Maeven retorted. "They enjoy acting like a Queen and ordering the servants around."

"The few so privileged have done an excellent job," King Westron pointed out. "However, you are my daughter and you are now old enough for some responsibility and Royal Duties. Your mother was an excellent hostess."

"My mother is probably turning in her grave!" Maeven flounced so that her orange skirt flicked up revealing the multiple petticoats below. "Were you also sampling every woman you saw back when Mother was still alive?" Maeven continued imprudently, deciding to straighten the skirt over the annoying petticoats once more.

"You have no right to criticise me," the King said with controlled anger. He started to rise from his seat then settled back.

Even without his formal regalia, he was a tall and imposing presence. At sixty-four, he had steel grey hair, grey eyes and a powerful physique. Of his children, only Maeven had not inherited his height, and only Leanne had inherited his solid build. In all other appearances, the King's children took after their mother.

"No? Fine! I will simply despise you!"

"I am simply trying to find a woman the equal of your mother!" he sighed as if his womanising was a chore of mammoth proportions.

Maeven looked at him with disbelief. Then she spoke again. "Is that why you let them wear Mother's Dragon Talisman until you discard them like so much trash? Do you like having them display your mark of ownership?"

Servants entering with the King's formal robes and his jewel studded golden crown interrupted the argument. Others brought refreshments for him to have before the audience session began.

The King stepped down from his throne and sat in a chair near the low table that was in an area normally used by waiting petitioners.

"We will need to continue our discussion later," he said firmly, pretending that he had not heard his daughter's last insults. "Have something to eat and drink with me."

Maeven stared at her father in disgust. She considered walking out but the sumptuous pastries on the plate looked so much better than the ones the servants gave her.

Sitting in a second chair, in a very unladylike posture (one leg over one arm and her back against the other) she snatched at a cream filled pastry and ate it in large, messy bites. The King watched her without comment until the plate was empty.

"Instruct my daughter's servants to bring her something to wash with," King Westron commanded the servant clearing the tray. "She will be playing during the Audiences."

He might have been daring her to object.

Maeven began to protest but snapped her mouth shut. This was another Royal Duty, which if performed well would permit her some Royal Allowance.

Well, at least she enjoyed playing the great harp. She was an unusually adept musician and while her nimble fingers plucked well-known tunes, her mind was listening to her father making decisions.

As much as she disliked his recent authoritarian stance, she had to admit that her father was skilled at settling disputes between his subjects. He also gave due consideration to all requests – even if ultimately denying them. But then, Maeven thought cynically, if he wants to continue to enjoy all those little luxuries, he has to make his subjects think they are getting value for their taxes!

"And he was recognised by the men at the smith's shed as the man who ran out of the inn after the robbery," Maeven heard the King's herald report.

As the King listened to the list of charges against a thief, Maeven found her fingers plucking a tune she had heard recently. It suited her mood of rebellion and from the occasional glances from her father, he was finding the music most inappropriate.

He had officially outlawed the Thieves Guild some years ago, but obviously they still existed in hidden enclaves. This thief, surprised with his hand in some merchant's money chest, was guild-bonded.

Maeven shook her head. Guild-bonded thieves usually got sent to the dungeons for a very long time. The King saw bonded thieves as men who made a living preying on other people. The pathetic-looking, un-bonded thieves usually received a lesser sentence such as working for the guardsmen for a time.

Once the Audiences had finished, the King came over to her. "Where did you learn that disgraceful tune?" he demanded. Seeing him resplendent in his formal robes of deep crimson edged in some kind of white fur, reminded her that he was the ultimate authority in Thulor.

She opened her mouth to ask, "What tune?" but subsided under the stern glare. "I must have heard it somewhere and liked it. Maybe in the kitchens, when I was learning about housekeeping?" she said meekly.

The plausible lie hid the truth and the King maintained his glare for a long moment, distrusting the meekness.

"I will be dining out tonight. You and Rhovert will be accompanying me. I expect you to be ready and suitably attired by dusk."

"Where are we going?" Maeven looked interested until the King answered.

"Lord Tormore's town house," he told her. "He is inviting a number of important people to dinner, and since you feel so strongly about being cloistered in the Palace, I decided to accept his invitation! I will be confirming my acceptance to his suit and officially announcing your betrothal. He will be leaving on a trip for me early tomorrow and you will accompany him. You will spend the night at his house. I will have the servants pack what you will need. It is time you learnt how to be a useful wife."

There was mutiny in Maeven's face as the King threw her complaints back in her face.

"May I go now, Father?" she asked, managing to control her revolt under a thin veil of politeness.

King Westron waved his daughter out and she did not see his thoughtful expression.

Maeven fumed as she threw open all the cupboards and drawers in her luxurious bedroom that had, until now, been her haven.

"Three hours! My life ends in three hours."

From deep in one wardrobe, behind a row of expensive dresses, she pulled out a traveller's pack that had been 'lost' by one of her father's guests. A false floor in another wardrobe hid two sets of common worker's clothes that had been 'misplaced' over time by the laundry staff and used every time she snuck out of the Palace alone. These she stuffed into the pack. It was well that some women of low station affected men's clothes for work. Skirts with their voluminous petticoats served only to control women!

Various drawers yielded "trinkets and baubles" that were quite valuable and several pouches of coins that her father did not know she still had. He thought she was a complete simpleton with respect to bargaining for her new clothes for she always told him the prices were twice what she actually paid. The servants, when they escorted her, had received a silver coin to confirm her claims.

There were only a few other items that she decided to pack – traveller's cutlery, tin plates and mugs, a blanket that would look less out of place in a stable, some candles and fire starters; there was nothing that would identify her as Maeven, Princess of Thulor.

She had just finished tidying her chamber and hiding the pack back in the chest when her brother Rhovert entered unannounced.

"Congratulations!" he said without preamble. He lounged in the doorway, dressed in his usual foppish style, which was his way of baiting the King. Maeven did not underestimate him. He may have the same slight frame that she had but he was a skilled duellist and stronger than most people expected from the way he presented himself. He was also extremely well educated.

"I'm not getting married," Maeven muttered, taking from around her neck the triangular amulet and throwing it onto her dower chest. Rhovert moved to pick it up.

"You should keep it with you," he said seriously. "It's a Dragon Talisman – it protects the wearer from all sorts of danger. I have one too – it's saved my life at least twice."

"I won't wear a symbol of Father's ownership!"

"It isn't that," Rhovert assured her. "The amulets don't look valuable, but they have been in our family for generations. I got mine when Grandfather died."

He pulled his out – it was 'V' shaped like the King's, not triangular. "I heard once that the pieces fit together to make a really powerful protective charm."

Idly he tried to fit the two pieces together but they wanted to slide apart; he put his sister's amulet down.

"I find it nauseating to see that progression of women Father brings through the palace wearing Mother's talisman. For as long as he chooses to sample their delights, that is!"

"Oh, I don't know, some of the leftovers are quite … tasty!"

Maeven gave her brother a thoroughly disgusted look.

"So, are you coming tonight?" Rhovert asked, watching her reaction.

"I haven't much choice!" Maeven scowled.

"Our sisters made another choice!" he said mildly.

"Yeah and where did it get them? They're still indentured for another five years!" Maeven sneered.

Rhovert merely shrugged.

"Why don't you leave?" Maeven challenged her brother.

"I have my reasons."

"Father's lackey!"

Maeven turned to review mentally the contents of her rooms for the last time.

"I said I had reasons. Mine – not his!"

"Well, you can tell Father that I will be ready by dusk." Maeven smiled to herself when her brother could not see. Rhovert shrugged again and turned to leave.

It was Rhovert's turn to smile when dusk arrived but Maeven did not.

After waiting half an hour, the King's face was unreadable as he ordered his guards to search the palace.

In spite of the guardsmen searching the palace grounds and the village – Maeven slipped like a shadow in the wake of the royal party.

It wasn't hard to be ignored. She was now dressed like the serfs that tilled the fields within the bounds of the castle. Her face was dirt smudged and her hair was tightly coiled under a coarsely woven woollen cap. All she had needed to do was follow a group of serfs who were returning to the village outside the walls.

When the King's retinue began to walk towards the town, she simply followed at a greater distance.

The pair of mounted guardsmen that questioned her presence accepted her respectful claim of having a message to deliver. Only then did they ask her if she had seen a missing girl, dressed in an orange dress. In the darkness, they must have thought her a boy, so she deepened her voice as much as she could, and told them that she had not seen any girl. After they had ridden off, she allowed herself a laugh before hastening to keep her father in sight.

Once she identified which of the fancy stone houses belonged to Tormore, she drew back into the shadows. Lighted lamps were spread at intervals in the streets where the nobles lived and one was not far from Tormore's house. She did not want to be seen by the guards who were spreading themselves out around the house. Once they had stopped at their posts, Maeven dodged between them and found a position under a window where light streamed out. It was a very small space between three big pots with bushes growing in them. If she stayed still and silent, no one would notice her.

Just as she began to think that the dinner would be in a different room, she began to hear voices. The window was unshuttered, probably to let in the cooling night breeze – so the voices carried clearly to the outside. Most of the talk was about trade. She heard her father's voice occasionally, asking probing questions. She didn't understand most of the discussion, but her mind grabbed one piece of information. Tormore was leaving in the morning on a journey into Declanor, the kingdom to the south of Thulor. It might have been interesting to go there – but not with HIM.

The food smells wafting out of the window made her glad she had eaten already. Only bread and cheese, but they had tasted deliciously of freedom. After a long period of time with quiet murmurs and the sounds of metal eating tools on expensive baked clay plates, the gentle chiming of something striking a crystal goblet jolted her wandering attention.

With the silence within the room, she could hear the gravel moving under the restlessly shifting feet of the nearest guard. She risked a peek through the window. Her father stood at the head of the table, facing the window but looking at the other guests. Tormore sat beside him, with his attention on the King – smiling slightly and anticipating the announcement.

Maeven quickly lowered herself, desperately hoping her father had changed his mind. It was a vain hope and she heard the announcement of her betrothal to Col Tormore. The other guests clapped quietly and murmured their congratulations to their host. Tormore, his voice sounding unmistakably smug, simply replied with his regrets that Princess Maeven's indisposition had prevented her from attending.

"A passing phase," her father had assured him. "My daughter is still too young to appreciate that wiser heads need to choose her life partner."

Maeven risked another peek. Tormore's grin was malicious – he was probably envisioning his new fiancée being punished for discussing him so nastily. She had known that the creep was listening in to her private audience with her father.

She stayed out of sight for the rest of the dinner. When King Westron had apologised to his Chief Advisor for Maeven being unable to travel with him on his business trip, Tormore had graciously agreed to take her at the next opportunity.

There won't be one, Maeven vowed, as she waited for the guests to leave.

When she had first thought about running away – she had only thought ahead to the little shack in the village that she had bought off an elderly woman. That's where all the things were that she had taken when she left. Though if her father was looking for her, and no doubt Tormore would be soon – was it a safe place anymore? Probably not – but where else could she go? She had money – but how long would that last before she had to work like a serf to survive? She shuddered. It might be fun pretending to be a serf – but not to actually be one.

Then resentment set in. Tormore, as her promised husband (the words left a horrid taste in her mouth) should have given her a betrothal gift. He had not even mentioned such a thing. Suddenly she chuckled quietly. Tormore would be away the next night – why didn't she just go and pick her own? Jewels perhaps, or even coins?

A sense of delicious irony made her writhe in amusement. Doing that would make her a thief. Her father didn't seem to care about her, so she would become what he hated – a thief. *A damned good one,* she added.

How to proceed with her plan occupied her mind whilst she waited for the last of the guests to leave. She studied what she could see of the shutters. They could be secured from the inside by a latch that dropped into a slot. The wood was new looking so that there would be no gaps, or only a very slight one between them. What could she find to fit such a gap?

The breeze tickled her face with a loose hair and gave her an idea. In the darkness, she let her hair down and pulled out several hairs. They were long enough for her purpose. As she twisted the strands together, she watched the departing guests from between the pots. She made a loop in the hair, to go around the latch and waited until no one was looking her way to stand up and slip it in place. With the aid of a sharp edge of a stone, she nicked the wood, enough to catch the hairs on the outside of the shutter. Then she ducked out of sight again, and just in time to avoid being seen by two of the guards.

The King was the last to leave. However, instead of walking back to the palace, he waited outside. When his carriage arrived, Maeven ignored it; her mind was occupied by her exciting new plan.

She would have to cut her hair – maybe even colour it. Her mother's maids had something they used for that. Then she would need something to prise open the chests or what ever Tormore stored his valuables in. Where would that likely be – his bedchamber? The idea made her shiver. Even the thought of embracing him made her feel sick.

"Damn. I'll have to sneak back into the palace," Maeven said to herself. That shouldn't be a problem – except that she had finally made the break.

She waited until the king's carriage was out of sight and the extra guards had marched off towards the palace. When she peeked out, she could still see some of the locals staring at the house, though the regular guards were telling them to move on.

Just when she was about to leave, she heard voices in the room again.

"No matter, Rolliver," Col Tormore spoke in a moderate tone. "The wench likes her little luxuries too much to hide out for long. She'll turn up – probably in the town. What with the King's guards looking for her and our friends as well – I will have her in time. Then I will insist that the wedding be as soon as possible. Once she is mine she will learn to obey me."

"As it should be, My Lord. Have you any instructions for your absence?"

The voice was a particularly unctuous one and Maeven knew she would recognise it if she heard it again.

"If the wench is found, they will bring her here," Tormore said with assurance. "See that she stays."

"In the cellar, My Lord," Rolliver suggested.

"No, the wench is likely to touch things," Tormore mused. "The attic will do. I will set a mage lock on it – it will activate when you close the door. I will put one on the cellar too. I do not want my sister to be tempted to look down there either."

"A wise precaution, My Lord," Rolliver agreed.

"As always, Rolliver, I expect you to watch things here until I return."

"Naturally, My Lord. Will I send for the Lady Elvira to clean up?"

"No need. My sister knows her place."

The voices ceased, leaving Maeven considering what she had heard. The light stayed on, and a short time later it sounded as if servants were clearing dishes away. She risked another glance. Only one person was in the room – Elvira Tormore – and she was dressed like a noble guest, but was scraping dirty plates into a bucket.

The sight confirmed in Maeven's mind her hatred of Tormore.

He's going to lock his cellar, is he? Well, guess what, Maeven thought to herself. I'm going to look there. As she began to move away, sneaking from shadow to shadow. Some of the street lamps had already burned out.

Before she returned to her shack, she would sneak into the palace one last time. To do that though, she would have to return to the village that nestled in the protection of the palace walls. More precisely, she needed to go to the hut of the cheese seller. Her secret way out of the palace came out in the byre where the old woman kept her donkey. Both donkey and woman would be deep asleep by now as should the rest of the village.

As she crept through the shadows of trees and buildings, and finally into the byre – the only sound she heard was an owl hooting.

Maeven knew the tunnels so well now that she no longer needed a light. She emerged in the cellars near the kitchen, moving silently and being careful to avoid places where servants might be awake. No one challenged her and she slipped into the quarters where her mother's women had once lived. They were unused now, had been for years – and nothing remained. Only one other place might have what she wanted – the Queen's chamber. And that was too close to her father's chamber for her liking. Resolutely, she began to creep in that direction.

As she passed her brother's chamber – a slight breeze warned her that the door had opened. She stepped back quickly.

"Inside," a very quiet whisper ordered. Maeven recognised her brother's voice and obeyed. She sensed when the door closed behind her.

"Why did you come back?" Rhovert hissed at her.

"I needed some things," Maeven whispered back.

"What?"

"Hair dye, scissors." She sensed rather than saw her brother nod.

"You should have thought of that," Rhovert chided. "No matter. I can help with those. Wait."

Again Maeven sensed him move. The only light in the chamber came in the half opened shutters. A short while later, she felt a small jar pressed into her hand, followed by something with the shape and feel of scissors.

"Take these too," Rhovert told her. He pressed a knife sheath and something triangular into her free hand. "Your dragon amulet, idiot," he whispered as he felt her trying to see what it was. "Take it! I was going to go into the village tomorrow to give it to you."

"How did you…?"

"Never mind. Father doesn't know about the hut so it should be safe enough for a bit. Whatever you do though, don't come back here."

"Why?"

"Do you really want to marry Tormore?"

"No! But isn't he your friend?"

"Yes and no – anyway – just go. You are better off away from here."

Maeven felt her brother's arms around her for a brief instant. She stiffened.

"I never thought you really liked me."

"Oh, I suppose you are alright for a girl," he said softly. "It's just that I have overheard father saying that he doesn't want any of us molly coddled or we would be useless. And when father remarried and had twins, I didn't know what to do with two infant sisters – plus, I was with my tutors all day. Then when they got big enough to be interesting they were so wrapped up in each other, I gave up. By the time you came along, I had duties that kept me everywhere but here." Impulsively, Maeven returned his gesture. "Thank you for helping me, and not telling father what I am doing." She began to move towards the door.

"One last thing – the amulet – if you feel it get hot it means danger."

"It's cool now…"

"That's because I'm close. It gets cool when another piece comes near."

With a final squeeze of her brother's hand, Maeven slipped away in the darkness.

CHAPTER 5 – THE THIEF

Princess Maeven, now calling herself Ven, crept up to Lord Tormore's town house. She was dressed like a common worker in dark coloured breeches and jerkin. Her once long hair was now very short and darkened by the application of strong black dye.

Maeven waited below the window, where she had been the previous evening, as the Town Guards made their rounds. She had already ascertained that the closed shutters were locked. She listened to the night sounds, tuning out the distant ones and trying to hear if anyone was in the room beyond the window.

When the patrolling guards had gone again for the second time, Maeven felt for the trapped hairs she had left there the previous night. They were no longer trapped, but they were there. She stood up and gently pulled on the hairs, not wanting to snap them. Just as she sensed she was making progress, she heard the sound of feet on gravel. She released the hairs and ducked out of sight. The man who made the sound was just a shadow. He finally moved to the edge of the lamplight. His silhouette was huge, but he was wearing common working clothes, not the uniform of the guards.

Maeven ignored him and returned to her task. Finally the latch inside cleared the slot and the shutter seemed to jump open slightly. At first, she opened it enough so that her slender hand could reach in and lower the latch quietly. With a glance around, she opened the shutter wider, enough for her to jump up and slide in over the sill. After she climbed down from the sill, she turned to pull the shutter closed. That meant that the room was dark, but her memory supplied a picture of the room and she crept inwards without hitting any furniture.

A tingly feeling of excitement suffused her. By now, both Elvira Tormore and Rolliver should be asleep, but she took extreme care anyway. She opened the door leading into the house only a crack and looked out.

The room beyond was a large open area with a minimum of furniture. Just a table and two chairs near the door, which she guessed was the main entry. There were lamp sconces at intervals around the wall, but they supported round, faintly glowing orbs where the lamps should be. It wasn't much light but enough to confirm that the area was deserted.

Moving halfway out of the doorway, Maeven saw a passage going off to the left and two doors across the room. One door was ajar. The floor she needed to cross was of light coloured stone, and in the centre was a dark coloured rug. She moved out fully and began to edge across the floor. She avoided the rug, and kept to the walls of the room, aiming for the partly opened door. When she was close enough to reach out and touch it, her head began to itch.

"Magic," she breathed, looking around and resisting the intense urge to scratch. Down near her feet, an area of floor was glowing faintly. She smiled to herself. She had found the cellar door with its protecting mage lock – now to see if she could open it.

The trick, she knew, was to imagine the thought that the lock was keyed to. For this chance, she had purchased a vial of 'magic', a potion that allowed even common folk to perform simple spells for a short period of time.

Maeven crouched down after swallowing the potion and thought of the numbers that she knew. "1… 2… 3…" Nothing changed.

"A… B… C…" Still no change. She hadn't expected it to be that easy. Tormore was not an uneducated peasant.

On a sudden inspiration, Maeven imagined Elvira Tormore trying to open the door and getting thrown back. For a moment, the glow flickered. She reached out and touched the floor within the glow and pictured the image again. The glow vanished, but the amulet around her neck was becoming warm.

She felt for the amulet and was torn between looking and leaving. It was only warm – not hot… the danger, then, was mild. Just being in Tormore's house was dangerous, so she decided to continue.

Maeven studied the stones in the area where the glow had been. Only one imperfection marred the effect – a fingertip-width hole a small stride out from the wall. She moved to where she could insert a finger and pulled. A square door opened. It was not heavy – being of wood with a thin layer of stone overlaying it.

Steps led down from the opening. Maeven glanced around and began to descend. She had only gone five steps when she stopped. Her amulet had become very hot. She looked down and saw very little – there was no light below. One very faintly glowing orb was set just below the door and on a shelf just below it were a series of ornate boxes – each small enough to fit in her pocket. She reached for one and hid it. As she reached for a second box, she was suffused with a sense of imminent danger. She turned, hastened up the steps and glanced around. She saw no one – but the feeling persisted. She closed the door then touched it and imagined the picture that had locked it before. The glow returned, but the sense of danger intensified.

Not wanting to stay longer, she ran lightly across the rug on the floor to the room where she had entered, making her way to the window. The hair on her head stood up, and sensing a watcher she glanced around. Something hovered near the ceiling. It was like a cloud, glowing faintly red and it began to move towards her.

She scrambled back out of the window, crashing into the bushes and running like demons were chasing her. When she began to heed her surroundings, she was gasping desperately for breath, her heart was pounding and she had absolutely no idea where she was! There were no street lamps, so she was no longer in the elite circle around the palace. The buildings were very close together, and the street smelt of refuse. For a moment, she was distracted by something squishy she had stepped in.

In the moonlight, the realisation of her position hit her like a slap in the face. This wasn't how she had visualised her freedom. That was the cosy little cottage in the village, not this noisome poor quarter where even now shadows were stalking the unwary stranger – her!

Maeven forced herself to keep moving, aware of the shadows following and equally determined that they wouldn't get her. Suddenly two shadows approached at a fast trot. She allowed them to get closer and at the last minute ducked under their clutching hands, continuing to run until something large and unyielding blocked her way.

"Whoa, little man!" a voice boomed. A massive fist lifted her by the collar of her jerkin and held her kicking and wriggling a few inches off the ground.

"Put me down!" Maeven demanded, but the huge man, dressed in leather breeches and a sleeveless short tunic, simply laughed.

"Feisty!" he boomed as he carried her, still kicking and wriggling, to a building that spilled light out onto the street. Above the stone doorway was a hanging wooden sign, painted with a dancing duck.

The lamps were still glowing inside but the innkeeper and his serving wenches were cleaning up. All his patrons had been evicted and the stools were on the tables.

"What have ye there, Marc?" the innkeeper remarked, grinning. "An eel from the river?"

Maeven continued to wriggle and even though she was kicking the man in the shins, he ignored the discomfit.

"A little bit of business," a voice spoke from behind the bulk of Marc. "Lock the door, Binko, and leave us!"

The grin faded from the innkeeper's face and with a grunt to his girls to follow, he left his cleaning implements, locked the front door and went out of the room.

Marc pulled a seat down off a table and pushed Maeven onto it. He remained behind and three men were facing her. Two of the men, thin sallow looking types, had daggers drawn and the implications of trying to escape were perfectly clear.

Maeven recognised the voice of the unarmed and cloaked third man. He was Rolliver, Lord Tormore's lackey. It was obvious that he did not recognise her with her rough-cut black hair and men's clothes.

"Why were you in Lord Tormore's house?" he asked with deceptive politeness.

Maeven remained silent and stared back at him, wondering what sort of magic had betrayed her or if he was only guessing.

"I have no patience for this – Gerrun!"

One of the two swordsmen sheathed his weapon and removed a small phial from his pocket as he approached. Marc grabbed Maeven from behind as she tried to rise and dodge; he held her chin.

"It would be better to talk, boy," he whispered. "Filthy stuff that wizard's brew. You'll babble everything you know and be a mindless hulk for days after!"

"I'll talk!" Maeven agreed, speaking with difficulty. She was trying to hide how scared she was. This was nothing like her illicit trips out of the palace to the village. In her entire life, no one had ever laid hands on her in this rough a manner.

"Answer the question!" Gerrun growled, his finger ready to flick the wax seal off the phial.

Maeven gulped. "I was supposed to mess the place up!" she improvised. "That's all, I swear!" She hoped that they would not try to search her.

"Why?" Rolliver snapped, watching the prisoner closely.

"A girl I know, Maeven, she hated him, wanted to annoy him."

Rolliver's eyes betrayed his interest. "Why didn't this Maeven do it herself?"

Maeven forced herself to laugh.

"Her! She's some rich noble's bastard. Thinks I haven't got her figured! From the way she hates Tormore, I reckon she thinks he's the bastard that sired her – calls him Toadface. She acts tough but I don't think she's got the nerve!"

"Where can I find this Maeven?" Rolliver asked intently.

She struggled, looking around as if trying to find a means of escape. Marc increased his grip on her shoulders and Gerrun flicked the seal of the phial into her face.

"She has her own place in the village near the palace," Maeven said with reluctance and gave directions to her hideout. There was no way she could go back there now.

"Why did she ask you to go? Are you a thief?"

"No!" Maeven denied with passion. "No, I owed her one. She's a friend and she saved me from a thrashing once."

Rolliver looked at Gerrun who shook his head slightly.

"What did you do inside the house?"

"Nothing!" Maeven told him. "I went in and I felt the magic and it made me want to run!" Her captors saw the blush creep up her face as she felt shame at her fears and cowardice. They relaxed, convinced she was telling the truth.

"Keep him here!" Rolliver ordered. "If I have sent no message by morning, let him go."

Rolliver, Gerrun and the third man left the inn and Marc changed his grip to her arm. "Come with me!"

"Why?" Maeven reacted, automatically resisting the command.

"Because you will be a lot safer staying with me than taking your chances out there," Marc said grimly, nodding his head in the direction of the doorway. "The Nob may have gone, but his pals will still be around and I know their type. If they were to decide to keep you in one place, it will be with you tied to a bed and themselves on top of you. Boy or girl – it don't matter to them!"

Maeven felt suddenly nauseous, her mental bubble of invincibility had burst abruptly. There was no way she wanted to go back home, but the alternative had just gone from fun to nightmare. She wasn't safe because she was a princess; she was the worst kind of vulnerable!

"And what do you want from me?" Maeven asked, not sure she really wanted to hear the answer.

"I don't mess with boys!" Marc assured her. "Don't ask questions, neither, less I have to. I like you, boy. You got spunk and smarts, too! You remind me of me, and I can teach you a few tricks that might come in handy for a young lad out on his own."

Maeven did not sense danger from the big man, and her talisman was still cool, so after a few moments' thought and a final glance at the door where the others had gone, she nodded her agreement. Marc released his grip and led the way to a room in the inn's sleeping loft.

True to his word, Marc spent a lot of the night showing Maeven some mercenaries' tricks for self-defence and breaking out of a captor's grip. They were not gentlemanly and definitely not ladylike! He continued to instruct her with means to get out of rope bindings – particularly efficient if she was awake at the time of being bound.

Finally, he said with a deliberate wink, "Now I gotta tie you up!"

Maeven grinned and cooperated, thickening her wrists as she had been shown until the ropes had been tightened. As she lay quietly on the floor, Marc wandered to the window and pushed open the shutters.

"Good night for drying the washing," he said as if to himself. "All the wenches have their skirts hung out with their aprons and stuff." He glanced significantly at Maeven. "Perhaps I should go down to the kitchen and see what the wenches wear to bed!" He did not act on his suggestion, though; instead, he lay down on the rough pallet on the floor and was soon snoring.

Maeven began to free herself and grinned as she succeeded. She forgot her earlier fears as she wondered where she should go. As she untied her feet, she considered Marc's warning about going outside. Where should she hide in case Rolliver came back? Then the nonsense about wenches, their clothes and their sleeping place came to mind and she wanted to laugh.

When Gerrun came in the morning, he raised a big fuss because the mercenary had allowed the boy to escape. He never once looked at the dark haired wench scrubbing the floor only two body-lengths from him.

"You great filthy oaf!" Gerrun screamed at Marc. "Lord Rolliver wants to find Princess Maeven and that boy knows where she is."

The big mercenary glared back at him, unmoved.

The 'Crescent Moon' had an extra worker until the following night. At the close of business, Maeven slipped away to where she had hidden her own clothes and changed back into them. She promised herself that she would never do such drudgework again. When she had amassed enough wealth for herself, she would have servants of her own. She would need a lot more money than she had though, but she knew exactly where to get it.

In the very early morning, Maeven found a wagon string leaving for a distant village. For a fee of a copper coin, she could perch on top of the load as they travelled. Maeven found a comfortable place to wedge herself and made sure her sack of spare clothes and treasure would not fall off if she slept. She should be well gone before the inevitable outcry was raised.

The town of Valeford was four days' travel by cart from the palace and Maeven felt quite safe. She arranged a room at the local inn, one with a sign depicting a fighting dog. The woman who fixed the rooms showed her to a very small one.

"Two copper half bits for a week, in advance," the woman stated. "And don't you go invitin' any o' the girls up here me lad, or ye pay extra."

Maeven spent the next week looking around the town and marking likely targets. The slackness of the town's guards was quickly obvious because they didn't patrol at night. She drank cider in the tavern in the evenings and listened to gossip. On her third night at the inn, she heard a suddenly raised voice from a table nearby.

"… Four nobles' houses were robbed near the palace. The King, may he rot, had his guards searching everywhere and he's got seven of us in his dungeons."

A group of men began muttering angrily at the news. Maeven turned around slightly and saw a short humpbacked man gesturing wildly. She turned back to her drink and smiled into her tankard, congratulating herself for her cleverness.

That night she made a highly successful raid on a merchant's warehouse. The idea had come from a chance-heard remark about a shipment of jewels that were being held there overnight. She hadn't needed any luck; the guard had been sound asleep.

The next night, Maeven slipped quietly into the house belonging to the town's richest inhabitant. The owner called himself Lord Verne, but she knew the names of every lord in Thulor and his wasn't one. So he was rich, and pretending to be noble – he deserved to lose a little of his hoarded wealth.

From the outside the house only looked a little larger than its neighbours and was in no better repair, but inside it was luxurious. Her hand gently moved over the furniture in the entrance hall. It was covered with real leather;

the walls were made of wood that gleamed in the moonlight coming through the clear panel above the front door. She tiptoed around the sleepers on the kitchen floor to investigate the back entrance and returned without rousing anyone.

On the soft mats in the main passage, she moved like a wraith. At each door, she stopped and listened. Finally, she heard snoring. Her eyes were used to the darkness by then and she tip-toed into the room. The small amount of moonlight coming through the barred window showed her a chest at the foot of the bed. It glowed faintly and when she touched it, her head itched fiercely. But oddly, the glow faded. However, it was also locked with some metal contraption but a few minutes' work with a flattened nail was all it took to spring it open.

Listening intently to the rhythm of snores, Maeven's slender hand carefully felt through the contents of the chest. Most of the fabric was silky but there were hard things amongst the folds of the material. Her nimble fingers felt the shape of the first item – some kind of fancy drinking cup. Finally, her fingers encountered a leather pouch with small hard objects within. *Yes.* She withdrew her hand and its contents.

Maeven quietly closed the lid of the chest. The tempo of the sleeper's breathing changed and she froze into a shadow on the floor until the sound became regular again. It was definitely time to leave. The warmth of the talisman around her neck went unnoticed.

Concentrating on stealth as she left the bedroom and crept back along the passage, Maeven was startled by shouts from the behind her. She quickened her steps to the front door. Noises from the kitchen warned her that the servants had woken and would soon be seeking the intruder. She drew her new black cloak around her and ran from the house.

Keeping to the shadows, she made directly to the river that ran beyond the house. The noise of water flowing over the rocky bottom hid the slight sounds of her passage. She left the river at the mill and walked up the cobble-stoned path to the baker's house. Two places beyond that was her destination, the 'Fighting Dog' tavern.

By moving a few boards on the back fence, she entered the tavern's backyard and went directly to a dark corner behind the privy. A large stone hid an excavated hole just big enough for the pouch. Her earlier proceeds were secreted in the inn – under a newly loosened floorboard in her room. One leg of her bed stood on top of the hiding place and tomorrow sometime, the pouch would go there too.

Maeven made use of the privy before returning into the inn. She adjusted her clothes as she walked back to the tavern's rear door.

"Hey, boy!" a voice spoke quietly out of the darkness. Maeven looked around and finally caught the gleam from a pair of eyes above the wooden fence.

"What ya want?" she slurred her voice as if her mind was dulled with sleep.

"Heard any one pass here?"

"Nup" she answered. "Wasn't listening."

The face vanished after having a last look at her in the moonlight.

Maeven continued into the inn and to her room, where she stripped off her outer clothes and slid under her blanket. She lay awake for a long time, reliving the ecstasy of her success.

The next day, the townsfolk were all talking about the daring thief who had robbed the house of Lord Verne. In the inn, near noon, one of the tavern's customers chatted casually to Maeven.

"That's him, Lord Verne himself," the man commented knowingly, watching a tall narrow faced man talking to the innkeeper.

Maeven continued to watch the indicated man from the corner of her eye. His thinning grey hair struggled to reach his collar and it didn't have the strength to move as the man's head shook angrily. All that was audible of the conversation was a furious hissing.

"He's no Lord," Maeven confirmed to herself. *No Lord of Thulor*, she amended, having been in a position to meet all the kingdom's nobles. His face was somewhat familiar though, she just couldn't place from where. Then her amulet began heating up as Lord Verne began scanning the room so she slipped out to the kitchen. There she smiled at the cook and asked for a free feed.

The cook grinned at her impudence. "You bring in enough wood bits to fill yonder box and I'll feed yer!" the cook promised. She thought the boy must be a noble's son if he could afford to lounge around. His hands certainly looked strangers to hard work.

Maeven grinned and went out back to the woodpile, returning with an armful. Hiding in plain view had worked before and collecting wood was less onerous than floor scrubbing. She didn't rush though, for she remembered where she had seen Verne before and that was at the dinner at Tormores house where her father had announced her betrothal. When she returned to the taproom an hour later, the man had gone.

The potboy, Chiv, was serving large tankards of ale to two customers who had the look of swordsmen. When he returned, he was full of gossip that he just had to share.

"Ven, guess what I heard!" he whispered.

"What?" Maeven replied in an equally hushed tone. She had cultivated the pimple faced lad because he always got to hear of the towns doings.

Chiv glanced over his shoulder at the two men. "That thief, the one that pinched stuff from Lord Verne," he began and Maeven nodded for him to go on. "Took 'Chance Stones'. Himself was here talking to Jinkins. Was he ever annoyed! Them two yonder are 'is – I heard 'em talkin'."

"Chance stones. Them things the men play with out back?" Maeven queried.

"Naw, stupid!" Chiv said smugly. "Chance stones – you know, magic things – attract bad luck. Accidents like!"

"Oh!" Maeven said, as she suddenly understood.She had only felt hard stones and thought she had taken jewels. She hadn't dared go back to the hole outside yet, to collect them and look at her loot. "So, like, how many did the thief pinch?"

"A bagful!" Chiv whispered gleefully. "Old Verne paid a wizard heaps of jewels for them and he was due to pass them onto his customers."

"Huh?"

"They reckon people pay him to arrange accidents to their enemies or rivals. He gives them a stone to slip into the person's pocket." Chiv said knowingly. "Didn't yer Ma ever teach you anythin'?"

"What do you mean?"

"Sheese! All us kids were told to be good or Verne'd get us! That thief is as good as dead! He'll be a walking disaster by now!" He spoke with bloodthirsty relish.

"What if he hid them?" Maeven suggested, feeling suddenly ill. She didn't need any bad luck.

"Won't make no difference, them two reckon. They say that once the stones are taken out of the silk stuff, and to be safe they have to be in three layers, they become targeted to the person nearest them."

"So why isn't himself affected?"

"He'd have magical protections a'course."

"What if the thief was protected? Like with a charm off a sorceress?" Maeven asked.

"Still as good as dead!" Chiv said knowingly. "Himself was telling Jinkins to take a message to the Thieves' Guildmaster. He's a bad, bad enemy."

Before Maeven could ask if Chiv was referring to Lord Verne, Jinkins or the Thieves' Guildmaster, a voice summoned the boy back to his duties. She returned to her room.

"No," Maeven muttered to herself. "That can't be what I got. Nothing has happened to me. I mean, I haven't taken them out of their bag…" She thought some more. "I wonder where I can find a charm witch in this town, just in case."

The idea grew in her mind as she thought of a few other charms that might be useful. Then she went in search of somewhere that women congregated. She found a group by the Vale River doing washing but they were not chatting much. A second group was on the benches near the dressmaker's cottage. This lot was gossiping so much that they did not notice her for a long time. An elderly woman caught sight of her and believing she saw a strong young lad demanded help with her bundles. As it gave her a reason to stay around, she agreed. The other women then grew curious about the 'lad' and asked about her. She invented the story that she was on the way to work for an uncle in Thul Run (the furthest town she could think of) but that she wanted to see more of Thulor as she travelled.

A few of the women were married to traders. From them Maeven learnt of several wagon strings due to leave in the next few days. Although it was useful knowledge, it was not what she was looking for.

Maeven's attention wandered, but was drawn back to a discussion of men. She smiled inwardly at a girl's description of her beau. Why the girl was chasing such a yokel she couldn't imagine.

"Roalf's a good man," the girl insisted. "He's just shy."

"Shy!" another woman snorted. "Well I say if you want him that much, try a love potion."

"Where do I get one?"

One of the other women told her where she would find a charm witch.

Maeven helped the old woman with her packages. Fortunately she lived quite close and Maevan was able to watch where the girl went. The girl took her bundles into a house further down the road but then she sneaked out again just as Maeven reached it. It was easy to follow her.

Dusk was deepening and many people were coming into town from the outlying farms, and so the purposeful movement of many men in the opposite direction caught Maeven's attention. She almost lost sight of her quarry at the vital instant when the woman knocked on the witch's door. It was a small cottage on the edge of town.

With the place she wanted located, she sat down to wait for the other girl to leave. Her eyes idly observed the men that had seemed to be leaving the town were situating themselves by the road. They were ignoring anyone entering town but were stopping anyone heading out. A hooded figure was passing a faintly glowing orb, set on a large staff, over each person and wagon before he allowed them to continue on their way.

Maeven continued to watch the witch's house until out of the corner of her eye she saw one of the road watchers coming towards her accompanied by the hooded figure.

"Uh oh," she said quietly, feeling the amulet at her neck grow warm. As she turned to wander off, a massive fist banged into her face, narrowly missing her eye and nose. She stumbled backwards.

"What you do that for?" Maeven demanded, her voice squeaky from the shock of the blow.

"My girl reckons you've been following her," a massive farmer bellowed angrily.

"She ain't your girl," Maeven yelled back. "Or why is she buying a love potion from yonder witch place! I think she looks pretty."

"My girl!" the farmer roared. He wasn't tall but he was strong. He grabbed the front of Maeven's tunic and lifted her.

"She's too pretty and smart for you!" Maeven yelled, intending the men approaching to hear her. A fist hovered in front of her face. It never landed.

"Let the lad go!" a voice of authority spoke quietly.

The farmer growled and released his grip, Maeven dropped several inches.

"Both of you turn out your pockets."

"What for?" the angry farmer bellowed. "I dun nuthin' wrong!"

"Turn them out!" the hooded figure snapped and the farmer began to obey.

Maeven discovered that she too had to obey, but she only had a couple of copper coins. The farmer's pockets contained a number of dirty face cloths and a jewel-studded ring. The hooded figure shook his head and his companion spoke.

"Be on your way, farmer. You, lad, go home, you're over young to be wenching. If I see you on the streets again tonight I'll give you a hiding!"

Maeven grabbed her coins and fled without looking back. When she reached the safety of her room above the 'Fighting Dog' tavern, she had all but forgotten her fright. Instead, she was angry at her own cowardice. But then, suddenly she laughed! If all the guards were watching and checking those leaving town, now would be a good time to visit the last two places she had marked as worth visiting.

The first house was the property of a merchant who had returned from travelling about the time she had arrived in the town. She approached with extra caution. It was as well that she did because she saw a figure watching the house. It was not a large person and it seemed to have a humped back. Maeven backed away quietly, remembering that she had seen a man, who could have made the shadow, in the Fighting Dog. Therefore, she went to the other place and drew closer, very warily indeed.

Feeling edgy, she circled the house and determined that there were no watchers there. Finding an open window at the rear of the house, and seeing candle light coming from the room, she found a safe place to watch and wait until it went out. Occasionally she saw a figure moving about the room; it could have been a man or woman. The plain curtain on the window only showed a dark shape. The person eventually reached arms out through the curtains and pulled the shutters closed, before extinguishing the candle.

Maeven waited a long while before moving to the rear door. It was locked, but with a lock she couldn't trick open. The window she had been watching seemed to be the best alternative even though the shutters were secured from the inside. She moved to the window and used her metal dagger to find and move the wood holding the shutter closed. The way was open and she climbed into the merchant's office and did not have to look far to find the man's stash.

The chest was in the room, in plain view. Her head itched as she got close to it – there were magic protections on it. She touched it gingerly and the itch vanished. The chest was now only locked by a simple catch that took seconds to open. Inside was more wealth than Maeven had seen in one place before. Half of the divided chest held copper and silver coins and the other half held jewels. The latter were quieter to take and more valuable than the coins. She took a pouch from her pocket and filled it, then carefully closed the chest. The little leather sack had a drawstring and could be closed and tied; in this manner, it went into a pocket in her cape. It was time to go.

Back through the window, a few seconds to close the shutter and back into the shadows. Just as the elation of a successful raid began to fill her, someone grabbed her from behind. A rag was shoved in her mouth and she felt herself lifted as a black hood was pulled over her head. She struggled, twisted, and tried every trick the swordsman Marc had taught her, but uselessly. Something hit her head and blackness came over her.

When consciousness returned, she realised that her hands were bound behind her and the rag was still in her mouth, not to mention the hood blocking her vision. The floor was jolting and was, she thought, that of a cart being dragged fast over rough tracks. Instead of struggling further, she began to work at freeing herself from the ropes.

Just as her hands came free and she moved to remove the hood, the cart stopped and a voice said, "Leave the hood on thief! Remove it and you die now!"

Maeven felt a knife prick at her neck and dropped her hands.

"Stand up!"

She obeyed slowly, still dizzy from the blow to the head.

"Walk!"

She was roughly turned around to face what she assumed was the right direction. Feeling her way with her feet, she reached the end of the cart bed but was not given the option of climbing down carefully. The owner of the voice gave her a rough shove that sent her sprawling on the ground into what smelt like hay. She controlled the urge to cry by concentrating on her anger and ignored the murmur of derision. As she stood, her arms were grabbed; warm hands one side, cold on the other.

The hood was removed, the rag as well. Maeven faced a circle of men of all descriptions. Big hulking brutes, small wiry types, slender and handsome, and many who were so common you would never look twice at them. They all had one thing in common – their faces were contorted with anger.

"Ven!" Jinkins, the inn master, recognised her and he stepped forward next to a handsome blond haired man.

"You know the prisoner?" the man asked Jinkins in an educated voice, clearly expecting more information.

"He's guesting at the Fighting Dog, been there for half a score of days."

"Has… he?" the blonde man murmured with a strange emphasis on the last word. "Well, boy, I hope you are prepared to die," he said flatly. "You have caused a great deal of anguish for our Guild. We don't like unaffiliated thieves. We particularly dislike those who directly or indirectly cause harm to our members. Lord Verne has been torturing some of our guild to find out which thief stole something from him. I had to promise to hand that thief over to him. I'm pleased it is not one of my friends."

In the light of flickering torches, Maeven went pale and her talisman was beginning to feel warm. These men were serious. She began to struggle and for her efforts received a blow to her chest. The air was knocked out of her and it hurt trying to get more back in her lungs.

"The Thieves Guild is outlawed anyway," Maeven said imprudently. She was angry at the treatment she was receiving. A second blow landed in her face, bringing tears to her eyes.

"It was outlawed because of greedy and undisciplined thieves like you! Our members are working men, like any other, with families to feed. We are careful whom we rob and we aren't greedy," the blonde man declared. "Now, I need to know where the stones are that you took from Lord Verne's house. Will you tell us, or will I let Alfred and Wakor force it out of you?"

The two so-named stepped forward, bearing the marks of a thorough beating.

Maeven licked her lips that had suddenly gone dry. "Under a rock, behind the privy at the inn," she said in a small voice, but Jinkins and the blonde man heard. The Innkeeper nodded to the other and departed. The sound of the horse's hooves pounding back along the road could be heard from the barn.

"Aren't you worried that he'll be hexed?" Maeven accused the blonde man.

"So, you know what you took. You must have more than the usual arrogance of youth to think you would escape the bad luck. However, in this case, Lord Verne provided him with a protection charm, at my insistence," the blonde man commented. "If my guild had to help find his property – I had to ensure that the guild members were safe. That's my job as Guildmaster. I'm surprised you weren't…"

"Yes, well, look at me now!" Maeven muttered in disgust.

"There's that!" the Guildmaster agreed, narrowing his eyes and studying the prisoner more closely. From his body language, and delicate and clean hands, he was almost certain that this prisoner was not a boy, but as long as the charade was kept up the 'lad' would be treated as one. As a boy, the prisoner could be called 'pretty'– as a girl, those looks could sweeten many a confidence trick. The hands were not rough, so a noble's offspring was a possibility. The prisoner spoke well, had spirit, courage, and certainly was not stupid.

What had really saved the prisoner so far, besides needing to get the stones back, was the delightful notion that Lord Verne had been outwitted by a slip of a girl.

A smile curled his lips. A test! He would set a difficult task for the 'lad'. Assuming the truth had been told, if the 'boy' succeeded and agreed to the guild rules, then the Guildmaster would make him a guild member, and have a means to control him. Success would mean a pacified, Lord Verne, failure, would mean being subject to Lord Verne's punishment. Eitherway would work for the guild.

Maeven wondered what thoughts were passing through the Guildmaster's mind. His expression changed to a smile, but Alfred and Wakor still looked at her as if she were a noxious insect.

It seemed like hours before Jinkins returned. Maeven was tired of standing and almost ready to be sick from worry. She had already decided that dead was better than marrying her father's choice of husband, bu it was the possibilities just short of being dead that she feared. Never in her life had she been hurt as these men had hurt her. She was beginning to fear what they might do if they realised she was a female.

When Jinkins returned, he simply nodded to the Guildmaster.

"Well, it appears that you were telling the truth. A point in your favour!" the Guildmaster announced. That must have been some sort of signal because most of the men walked quietly from the barn. Alfred and Wakor moved back and the two brawny thieves that were holding Maeven went and stood by the door. Jinkins drew from under his cloak the pouch that had been hidden behind his inn.

"This bag is the one from his Lordship?"

"Yes." Maeven glanced at the men by the door.

"Open it!"

Maeven's attention was drawn back to her immediate position – with a spurt of fear.

"Afraid?" the Guildmaster suggested slyly. "You are already under a sentence of death…"

Maeven fumbled for the bag; with shaking hands she eased the drawstring open. Inside was a parcel wrapped in silk; this she pulled out. The unwrapping of the silk revealed a second layer. This, when opened, exposed a dozen tiny silk sachets containing small hard stones. One fell out of its tiny bag.

It looked like an ordinary white river pebble in miniature – dull, white and boring.

"They are meant to glow!" the Guildmaster stated, his eyes betraying anger.

Maeven realised that she did not feel the itch she normally associated with magic.

"I thought they were jewels," Maeven explained hurriedly. "This is the first time I've seen them. When I heard what I'd taken, I didn't dare go near them again."

The Guildmaster's anger simmered. His eyes watched Maeven as he considered his problem. The stones were now worthless. He could not simply hand them back, but…

"You've caused me a major problem, boy," he said, not explaining anything. "I can only see one way out of it. You will put the bag of stones back where you took it from so it looks like they were never gone!"

"NO!" Maeven said, instinctively weighing the risks.

"Or die here and now!" A knife had appeared in the Guildmaster's hand and he looked as if he was serious about using it.

"On second thoughts," Maeven capitulated. "If I solve the problem I caused – where will I stand with you?"

Unexpectedly the Guildmaster laughed. "Boy, if you succeed, you'll live – at least for a while longer!"

"No! If I take them back and that phoney Lord doesn't get me – you'll let me go. I'll leave here and go somewhere else!" Maeven countered.

"You have no bargaining power, boy. You are still a thief, one that doesn't belong to the guild. If you take the stones back and Verne drops his vendetta, you will join the guild and obey our laws."

"And if I won't?"

"You'll be dead."

Maeven could see advantages in joining the Thieves Guild. They would provide her with a place to stay and some protection. The disadvantages would come later when she wanted to go her own way. Thieves joined the guild for life, or so she had heard. Right now, though, she did not have a choice.

"Can I have a ride back to town?" she asked resentfully. She put the rewrapped stones back into the pouch and the pushed it into her pocket.

Alfred, accompanied by Wakor, drove the cart from the barn and back along the narrow tracks. Maeven sat in one corner and recalled the details of the house where she was going. She also watched the backs of the two older thieves. There was no doubt that they were her guards and had a particular interest in seeing she did not run away.

Maeven moved away from her escorts and began to circle the house. She waited at the front this time and her talisman was becoming slowly warmer. If it was warning her of danger, she did not need it. No one with any sense would consider now a good time to revisit this house.

Using the same technique as before, she opened one of the front shutters, listened and then climbed carefully into the room.

It was a small room, like the dressing room in her father's apartments. A single candle was burning there but it gave more than enough light. When she heard sounds from the adjoining chamber, she quickly hid behind a large woven wickerwork chair in the corner of the room. A servant entered and began to light more candles. A second servant started laying out clothes.

Maeven kept in the shadows behind the chair. Lord Verne entered the room and sat down, waiting for his servants to dress him. She could see nothing but her amulet got very hot indeed.

Another servant entered.

"My Lord, two prowlers have been spotted in the rear garden."

"Catch them and bring them to me," Lord Verne ordered.

He meticulously completed his dressing routine before leaving the room.The servants tidied up quickly and followed their master. From their comments, they did not want to miss the excitement.

As soon as the room was empty, Maeven ran to a second door. It was not the one Verne had departed through but one that should lead to the bedroom. The single candle in there was enough to confirm her guess and reveal that the room was deserted. Being concerned less with silence than speed; Maeven opened the chest again and felt the silks within. From her pocket came the pouch and she pushed it to the back of the chest, right down to the bottom as if it fallen there. Quickly closing the chest, she turned and retraced her steps to the dressing room. The candle in there had gone out but there was enough moonlight to illuminate the window.

She had taken only three steps when the room became blindingly bright. A powerful force threw her against the wall and held her pinned there. When her breath returned and her eyes cleared of the sparkling blackness, Maeven recognised the wizard who held the glowing tip of his staff directed at her.

"You should have heeded my warning," he said without emotion.

Maeven did not reply – it was hard enough breathing. A short time later, Lord Verne entered, trailed by Alfred, Wakor and two guards.

"That's him, Lord," Alfred said nodding at Maeven. "That's the thief that's been giving our guild a bad name. There's a death sentence on him and a bounty. My master is furious. We had him and he got away."

Verne pulled two small pouches from his pocket. He threw them in the direction of the two thieves and they clinked as they landed.

"Your reward for services," he told them, his eyes not leaving the prisoner. "Tell your master that this one will bother him no more."

Alfred and Wakor each reached down andgrabbed a pouch then departed as fast as they could.

Lord Verne had blazing hate in his eyes as he eyed the prisoner. "Have you a spell for truth speaking, wizard?" he demanded.

"Yes, master," the robed figure assured him.

"Cast it on this whelp!"

The low-voiced chant muddled Maeven's mind and her talisman burned hotter.

"What is your name?" Verne started to pace.

"Maeven," was the unwilling answer.

Verne stopped pacing. The whelp was a girl!

"Did you enter this house last night?"

"Yes."

"What did you do?"

"I looked for jewels."

"Do you have any of my jewels?"

"No."

Verne turned to his wizard, "She's lying!"

"Did you take any jewels from my bedroom chest?" he tried again.

"Yes."

"Where are they now?"

"I put them back."

"Where?"

"In the chest."

"Why?'

"I felt the magic on them!"

"Are you a witch?"

"No."

"How can you sense magic?"

"I just can. It makes my head itch."

"Why did you come back this night?"

Some of the muddle had left Maeven's mind; she had a little control over her answers.

"The Guildmaster made me." That was true, even if it was not all the truth.

"Why?"

"So you would find the things you lost and to stop him being angry with me."

Verne left the wizard immobilising the girl and walked to the bedroom. Instead of calling for servants, he lit extra candles himself. He carefully began removing all the items and silks in the chest. When he reached the bottom, he saw the black leather pouch. His anger built to fury as he took the pouch and replaced the other items. He felt like a fool and blamed the whelp of a girl. He removed one stone and unwrapped it, knowing he was still protected from its effects. He expected a glow, but there was none. He stalked back to his wizard.

"Your spell, Wizard!" he held the stone under the man's eyes. "It was meant to last ten days."

The wizard lowered his staff; Maeven slumped to the floor, almost unconscious. He examined the stone.

"It has been too close to a counter charm, a powerful one!" he remarked. Then, because he knew his master's mind he added, "Although it was no fault of mine, I will re-enchant them at no extra charge." He valued his life and he wanted to enjoy spending the exorbitant fee that his master had paid for the stones! "What of the whelp, My Lord?"

A gleam appeared in the man's eyes. His mind considered an entire range of painful and degrading options. "Blast it to nothing!" Lord Verne ordered. Cleaning the mess would cost less than keeping it alive.

The wizard chanted and aimed his staff; expecting the thief to turn into a cloud of glowing dust. He was completely unprepared for the magical backlash of the blast. The brilliant ball of incandescent energy flew from the tip of the staff; the recoil as the spell was blocked by Maeven's dragon talisman was almost instantaneous. His protection from the spell's magical rebound was non-existent. The wizard died by his own spell and his master, standing closeby, shared his fate. The room began to burn.

Maeven began to regain her senses. The heat and smoke confused her but something in her mind made her crawl to the window. She pulled herself up even as the sparks ignited her cloak. The fresh air at the window cleared her head and self-preservation took hold. She fell out the window, losing her cloak as it caught on something. She collapsed on the ground and crawled for a few paces before her energy dissipated.

The glow of the fire drew the attention of the people in the villagers. They came with buckets to form a line from the river. The first to arrive were the Guildmaster and his agent Jinkins, who had received a report from Albert. They had come to learn the outcome of the encounter and almost tripped over the unconscious Ven, believing 'him' at first to be dead. Examination proved 'him' to be alive, and so instead of joining the bucket line, they carried 'him' back to the inn.

Maeven wasn't aware that the Guildmaster had also summoned his "inner council" to the inn and proposed that 'Ven' be permitted to join the guild. Once arguments for and against had been aired, the proposal was accepted.

The new member wasn't informed of the decision. A small brazier and iron was brought to the room where Maeven lay. Removing some of the torn and singed clothing to reveal the skin near her left armpit, however, revealed Ven's true gender.

The Guildmaster stilled further discussion. "The decision stands!"

It was too good to be true – and the Guildmaster couldn't wait to further vex Lord Verne. Jinkins branded the new guild member with the thieves' sign – a tiny hand.

"Have your wife attend the girl – the guild will pay all costs."

CHAPTER 7 – THE APPRENTICE

Maeven found the pouch containing the jewels she had stolen sitting beside her low bed. As she considered the implications, she became aware of discomfort near her left armpit. It was easy to infer what that meant. She was now a bonded member of the Thieves Guild. It also meant that they were not going to kill her. Obviously, she had succeeded in putting the stones back, but she could not remember doing it.

The session in the barn was vividly recalled and her face and chest were sore from the attention she had received. She would also have bruises from being pushed from the cart. There was the return cart trip, then what…?

Jinkins the Inn-master came into the room.

"Good, you're awake! Grab your valuables, lad, and come quickly!" he told her. "Leave your clothes, grab everything else. The guards are going to be here very soon!"

Maeven stood up stiffly. She had slept in her clothes and the smoke smell clung to her.

"Help me move the bed," she told Jinkins. He obeyed and asked no questions.

After grabbing the sack from under the loose board, she added the other pouch to it. They moved the bed back again and Jinkins told Maeven to follow him. They went down into the kitchen cellars where Jinkins pulled on a set of shelves and a door was revealed.

"It's as dark as a demon's heart in there, Ven," he warned. "But it's a fairly straight passage. Follow it to the other end. You will be met."

Maeven stepped into the passage and the door shut behind her, leaving her in darkness. She stilled an instinct to panic and wished wholeheartedly that she had enough magic to make a light. Jinkins had not told her how long the tunnel was so she set off slowly, keeping a hand on the wall. After a while, she realised that she could see very faintly the outlines of doors as she walked along but she did not attempt to see where they led. All that was in her mind was getting to the end and the question of whether her father's dungeons were as dark as this.

It was a relief when she walked up to the wall at the far end and felt the rungs going up. She climbed until her head hit a door. It lifted at her insistent push and was opened from above. Hands helped her out.

Maeven saw the Guildmaster and experienced a moment of fear.

"What's happening?" she asked to hide her unease.

"You are hot property, little apprentice!" he remarked. "Lord Verne's wizard tried to blast you and his spell rebounded. The backlash caught both of them."

"Good riddance!" Maeven muttered.

"I'm inclined to agree with you, but Lord Verne had friends in the King's Court and so the town guards, who know you were there, are looking for you. If you are gone, they will have to believe that the spell killed you and there was nothing left."

"Charming!" Maeven sneered.

"So you need to leave town, right now. I suggest you dress as a woman as they are looking for a scruffy boy thief. We can find powder to hide the bruising on your face."

The Guildmaster enjoyed Maeven's discomfiture.

"We will discuss your new status as we travel. Go change – third door on the right."

Maeven went resentfully. She did not like to be ordered around and did not like to be forced to run and hide. More than that, she recognised that this man had the same aura of command as her father and the power to deal with disobedience.

Maeven dressed as a girl of the common, not noble, class. She sat next to the Guildmaster on the front seat of the horse-drawn wagon. She had a kind of bonnet pulled in around her face and was told to keep her eyes down. The guards on the road stopped them, but only briefly.

When they were well away from the town, the Guildmaster told Maeven to pay attention to the rules of the Thieves Guild.

"Rule number one – you obey the Guild Master in all matters concerning the Guild."

Maeven nodded.

"Rule number two – the Guild is your family. We support each other. We don't inform outsiders of Guild matters. We don't rob our fellows, or inform on them or push in on another's territory."

Maeven nodded again.

"Rule number three – if you wish to rob someone or somewhere, you clear it with the Guild Masters first. You tell them of your intent. They will allow it or not. It may be another thief has told of his intent or the Masters have information that may affect your choice. If you state your intention and they agree to it, you have five days to carry out your robbery. Then we withdraw the option to give others a chance. You have to wait at least five days before applying to rob the same place."

Maeven nodded again to refrain from scowling.

"Rule number four – the Guild gets half your take."

"That's robbery!" Maeven retorted.

"That's the rule. But remember, we take care of you if you are injured or sick and unable to work. We hide you if you become too highly wanted. We have people to defend you if the Law servers catch you. We also provide food and lodgings for any member without their own place."

Maeven became thoughtful, deciding that what they did not know would not hurt them.

"The final rule absolutely forbids the use of magic during the times we are actively working! We have no wish to be the target of a vendetta by the League of Sorcery."

"What if you want to retire from the Guild?" Maeven had never wanted to be an official member.

"Once you are bonded, you are in for life," the Guildmaster warned her. "You can retire, stop working, but you can't choose to leave. Break the rules and the Guildmaster will determine your punishment. It could be anything from a loss of privileges or a fine, to death in severe cases. We can choose to kick you out but if there is one thing we hate more than an unaffiliated thief, it is a disassociated thief. You would be as good as dead if you were caught stealing again."

"So why did you put your sign on me?" Maeven asked pointedly.

"The mark identifies you as a bonded thief. You have great potential for one so young and more importantly – you have luck!" the Guildmaster admitted. "Besides, you kept your end of the bargain we made and survived. In getting rid of that lord and his wizard, you saved me a dangerous job. However, don't get me wrong. I may have sponsored you into the Guild, but if you break the rules I won't hesitate to punish or kill you; nor will any other Guildmaster."

Maeven felt chilled right through. She did not doubt the man for a moment and travelled in silence for a long time considering his words in the light of her own intentions.

"Where are we going?" Maeven finally asked.

"To Lorford. The Guildmaster there is a friend of mine, Nayfor. He will train you during the two years of your apprenticeship. He won't take any nonsense from you, so how you fare is up to you!"

CHAPTER 8 – LEARNING

Maeven didn't find being an apprentice thief too onerous. Nayfor was an excellent teacher, even if he never spoke much. He expected her to learn by watching what he did. If she failed to meet his high standards, his comments were terse and cutting.

He thought her to be a boy – and that suited Maeven. She did not want it to be known otherwise. She had an alcove in the thieves' guild house for her own and the privacy was welcome. The other six usual occupants were grown men as varied in description as those she had seen in Valeford. They mostly treated her as a precocious child – ignoring her apparent skill and calling it beginner's luck.

If they had known she was a girl, they would no doubt take more interest in her, and that sort of interest was abhorrent. The older men often bought varied women into their alcoves and the sounds of their sporting made her feel sick.

However, not once did she feel that it was unsafe for her to leave her valuables in the alcove. The other thieves took their guild-oath seriously, yet a sense of discretion kept her from leaving too much money around. She chose instead to keep most of her stash in the guild house safe hole.

Nayfor approved. She was a much better thief than the older men and even with the guild taking half of what she stole – she was amassing wealth at a respectable rate.

Each time she added to her stash, Nayfor added the new amount to the total on the tag of her bundle. No doubt he was also mentally comparing it with the amount she had declared.

For a time Maeven was scrupulous with her reporting, even though she silently resented the hefty tithe. She wasn't yet allowed to do solo work without Nayfor's close supervision. One day that would change, and then…

In his free time, which was rare enough, Nayfor began to teach Maeven various skills. Some of these she could practice using equipment kept at the guild house. Other practice was when she was on a job with him. He told her more than once that nothing that she did on a job with him was to be discussed, neither with him nor with anyone else – for their own safety, he claimed.

Maeven felt that she didn't need to be warned about that. She never discussed her jobs with the others, nor want to know about the jobs the others did. Guild oath or no, it was common sense not to tell anyone who might later sell the information for money, their freedom or their life.

She realised that Nayfor's insistence was an extension of the same principle, with an added dimension. For his jobs were not always robberies. Sometimes he stole or exchanged rolled up documents. Sometimes he made copies of a document, or a sketch of an item in a house. He had been impressed to learn that his apprentice could write and copy neatly. He would set her copying while he searched the rest of the building.

Maeven could read most of the documents that she copied. Mostly they were trade figures or household accounts occasionally a letter or a list. The reason for this was a mystery. However she didn't question what she was told to do, and when Nayfor was pleased wither work, he offered her a choice of coin, jewels or goods for a reward.

At first, she had chosen money and the obligatory half had gone into the guild's stash. After a while, she had thought of something she wanted to do and had asked for the materials that she needed, such as a length of soft leather, some strong twine and some leatherworker's tools. Nayfor had simply nodded and within a week he had the parcel of things for her. She had no idea of the value of her parcel, nor if Nayfor had made a profit from her share. She didn't care.

In the privacy of her alcove, when Nayfor was too busy for her or when it wasn't safe to be thieving, she cut the soft supple leather into squares and made a circle of holes around the edge. The twine was threaded through the holes to make small pouches. The pouches meant that she could divide her stash and if needed remove only a little at a time.

She had thought of another use for the leather that she had come to realise was very expensive. She wanted to put secret pockets into her tunics and trews and jerkins. To do that, however, meant that she needed some things that she didn't want Nayfor to get for her. She would have to wait for the next lot of clan-based travelling traders to visit the town. Unlike the regular traders who merely carted goods from place to place, the clan traders dealt in obscure, hard to get, exotic or rare items. They usually had a range of "fripperies" for women and items much sought after by men.

Maeven had seen the trader clan on a number of occasions, but she had never spoken to them before. Previously she had been more interested in trying to copy the juggling and sleight of hand tricks that some of the clan performed to attract customers. Next time, she would ask them for needles and thread and perhaps about the odd stones she had in her stash – the ones that she had taken from Col Tormore. Stones that even Nayfor didn't recognise.

None of her fellow thieves would have recognised her. She had filched some clothes from one of the inn keeper's daughters and, for the first time since coming to Lorford, she looked like a girl. Her normally short hair was hidden under a bonnet, and she had made the effort to clean herself as thoroughly as possible.

In that guise, she bought her needles and thread, and turned to leave. She had not intended to stay long, but she caught sight of a boy about her age, making coins and other objects appear and disappear in his hands and she knew he wasn't using magic.

The boy saw her watching and sidled closer. He was trying to impress her and Maeven decided to play along and began to flirt shyly with him. In a while, with subtle prompting, he offered to show her how it was done. Maeven tolerated his arms around her as he moved her hands in a slow motion version of his act. She saw enough to know what he did and, from experience, knew that skill would come with practice. After all, that was how Nayfor had been teaching her. Yet the boy had no idea of her thoughts, he just chuckled at her ineptness and cursed mildly when he was called away.

Maeven was relieved and scampered off to where she had hidden her normal clothes. When she was once more looking like a boy, and had stashed the girl's clothes where she could retrieve them later to return to the inn, she sauntered back to the guild house and hid her purchases.

Nayfor was alone there when she returned. All the others had been near the traders' wagons, probably trying to haggle with the traders for tobacco and knives.

Nayfor was writing something when she wandered over to him. He stopped as she approached, and moved a blank sheet of parchment over what he had written. He merely looked at her and waited for her to talk if she was going to.

"Do you remember those matched stones I once showed you?" she said without a greeting.

Nayfor grunted and nodded.

"Do you think the travellers might have seen their like before?'

"Might," Nayfor agreed. "Is it wise?"

"Huh?" Maeven said in surprise. She considered his warning. "Why?"

"A child. Rare baubles. Think you a thief."

"Ye—es," Maeven agreed. "Though I do want to know what they are and their worth so I can sell them."

Nayfor nodded. "Talk to them I will, and ask for you."

Maeven nodded in return. Nayfor could be trusted with them. She had already taken them out from amongst her stash, intending to show the travellers, but she agreed this way was better. She passed the small pouch to Nayfor and watched as he stashed it in his jerkin.

Maeven followed her master when he left the guild house. She kept far enough back so that he was unaware of her, but moved in closer when he began to talk to one of the clan elders. They greeted each other as if they were friends and Maeven saw a roll of parchment pass from Nayfor to the other. Then she saw him draw out her pouch and reveal the contents. She inched nearer, glancing around to be sure no one else was close enough to overhear anything.

"Interesting," the trader said. "Where are they from?"

Nayfor shrugged.

The trader whistled softly and in a while a hooded figure sidled up. The newcomer was shown the stones and lifted one out of the small box.

"Perfect – each of them – all alike. Good for magic."

"What magic?" Nayfor asked.

The second man shrugged. "Anything that requires a link between things or places. Separate them and they will want to be together."

The man could tell them little else – he could not say what a wizard might use them for, nor how.

Maeven inched away when that man left. Shortly after, Nayfor moved away from the trader and walked towards where she was keeping out of sight. As Nayfor walked past, he tossed the bag back to her. She caught it instinctively, and as he continued on without a word, she guessed he had known she was listening. His manner had not suggested he was angry that she had followed him – but how had he known? He must be good, she thought to herself. He had taught her to follow people and stalk them, and had implied that he had never seen anyone who could do it better than her – but it seemed that he was still her master in that, too.

As she walked unobtrusively back to the guild house, she considered what she had heard. That they were used for magic was not an impossibility. Tormore was a wizard of some sort and the stones had been hidden. But the stones themselves were not magicked. They didn't make her head itch. But the Chance Stones that had caused her so much trouble had lost their magic when they had come near her dragon talisman – perhaps these stones had, too. She had no way to know. Nor could she think of any reason why they might have been so close to the trapdoor and so easy to grab.

When she reached the guild house, she put the stones back with her main stash and put the problem out of her mind. The talk of magic reminded her that she had wanted to find a charm witch or find someone who could provide her with an invisibility potion. That had more immediate importance than enigmatic stones.

On her way back out to return to the town, she met Larry the Con, one of the permanent guests at the guild house. He was a handsome young man, with a very glib tongue. She thought to ask him if he knew of a charm witch.

"Never had need of one," he said haughtily. "Unlike many of our fellows here, I can get any woman I fancy."

Maeven controlled her face and didn't smirk. She'd heard many of his women were married to travelling traders.

"Hey, Curly! Know of any charm witches. The lad here is asking."

Curly was a solid thickset man with dark hair and a two day stubble on his cheeks. He was just emerging from his sleeping cubicle, and scratching his head.

"What yer need one of them for? A potion to make your beard grow?" He began laughing at his own wit, and attracted the attention of several other thieves who were still in the house.

Larry countered that with, "Well it sure isn't to get himself a girl. The lad is pretty enough to not need one for that."

"And if he ain't, I can show him how it's done. No need for a charm for that," was the offer from a slender effeminate man, who Maeven knew to be what her brother back in the palace only pretended to be.

"It's not any of your business what I want," Maeven glared at them all as she spoke. "It might just be I don't want to get burnt from the sun again."

That brought out more guffaws of laughter, for she had returned the previous week with face, neck and arms a painful rosy red. They'd believe that reason more readily than any other.

"You're right lad, it's none of our business," one of the others now standing around, agreed. "Anyhow, there's one that travels with the clan. That one has a lot of odd potions she's picked up around the place. Even had one to use on your bitch if she was in heat to stop the dogs getting to her." The speaker glanced at Larry as he said that, and from the renewed guffaws, the others understood the double meaning. "But for common stuff, there's one out the back of Tinklers farm. Has her own little hut there."

Curly leered and said, "I know the one. If you are interested in a tumble in the hay, with your pretty boy looks and courtly ways, you'll likely get lucky."

"Bit of a whore, too, is she?" Maeven asked, playing along with the rude talk.

"More of a nymph if you ask me," Curly chortled. "Men she likes, she gets."

"Good for her," Maeven said dismissively. "I might go see them both. One of them might have something I can take to stop hearing all the snores at night."

She didn't say thanks for the information, just joined the fresh laughter and continued walking out.

She went back to where the travelling trader clan were set up, for they would be moving on soon, and finding their charm witch was easy. The first trader she asked pointed her in the direction of a small travelling van, gaily colouered in green with a row of white daisies around the roof and at floor level. It had the yoke for the horses resting on a large log, since the horses were in a temporary corral beyond the camp. However, steps were down at the back and the door open.

"Hello within?" Maeven called, from a polite position a bit back from the steps. She didn't know what to expect, so she assumed that the old woman in skirts and shawls of brown that appeared was the witch.

"You looking for a charm, dearie?"

"Yes," Maeven admitted.

"Come up, come up."

Maeven did, looking with interest at the inside of the van. Everything was neat and compact. Along one side, was a narrow bed that at that time had a wooden board over it to act as a table. On it was a plate with a half eaten slab of dense dark bread. The other side had a cupboard with doors folded back to reveal a little basin for washing, made from a thin sheet of hammered metal, and wide enough to sit a small charcoal brazier in. Such a brazier sat on the shelf above. The rest of the space held oddments of food, packaged in woven grass. Opposite the bed table, were two chairs, and the old woman gestured her to sit.

"So what kind of charm do you need, dearie?"

Since she was dressed to look like a boy, Maeven decided she wouldn't mention one of her desired charms – something to stop her monthly woman's cycle, but she still wanted the invisibility potion and asked about such a thing.

"Aye, I have such a thing, but I must ask why you want such. If it be for thieving, I 'd be in trouble with the guild."

"I can understand why," Maeven agreed, "But that be not the reason. I just want to make myself proper scarce when me master comes home drunk enough to be wanting to break everything."

"Potions only work for an hour or two," the old woman warned.

"Be enough," Maeven agreed. "Only need it till he falls over asleep."

"Well, we can do business then. Costs a silver half piece per vial."

Maeven considered the small pouch she had with her, recalling the coins with in. "More than I expected," she admitted. "When do ye get back this way next?"

"Oh, not for a month or two," was the considered answer.

"Then, maybe I can make do with six vials till then. Suppose it won't do to be missing every weeks end evening, when he's worst drunk."

"Six it be. Was you wanting anything else?"

"What other potions do you have?" Maeven was interested to know.

"Best ye just ask for what you need, boy," she told her, as she lifted the table, and the bed, to reveal an area filled with vials each racked for safe travelling, and colour coded by spots of dye on the wax sealed tops.

"I'll be thinking then," Maeven agreed readily. Taking and holding the little blown glass bottles as the woman passed them to her. Once the woman's hand touched hers, and the woman gave her a sharp look, but said nothing.

When the silver pieces had disappeared into the woman's pocket, Maeven asked, "How do the potions work?"

"Well, these ones ye just drink – the spell is set in it. Easy for the likes of those with no magic, but me thinks that you do have some…"

Maeven wasn't going to mention her dragon talisman, so she said, thruthfully enough, "Got checked as a little mite, and told I had none, even though some of my kin have the gift. Would have been handy to be able to make a witch light."

"So's lots of folk think, but candles work better," the old woman began to cackle.

"Is there a potion for that? Making witchlight?"

"I call it my fool's gold potion – cost's them who want it a hundred times what a candle's worth and don't last as long."

"But do you have to drink that potion too?"

"That I do different. They just drinks the potion and they's says the words for making light. Not so bad if they want the light to stay with them, I suppose."

"What if they get the words wrong?"

"Won't get light! Might get something as they don't expect. That's why I sets the spell into the potion. Takes real talent to make new spells. Have to know the real power words and we magic folk keep them careful. Don't mean some fool might not speak them by accident."

"Makes sense. I'd rather be sure what I was getting."

"You can be sure enough with my potions, laddie. But sometimes it works less well on a person, when the same batch works perfect for some other."

"So long as the most of me is hidden, I'll be happy enough," Maeven assured her. "So I'll be going and hope to see you again next visit."

"And maybe I might work on a drunken master knock out spell."

Maeven was glad she hadn't yet returned the purloined clothes to the inn, for now she had another use for them. She would need to go as a girl to get the other potion that she knew she wanted, or the fact that a girl was dressing as a boy might just get around. So she went and retrieved them from the hiding place, and changed once again.

As she walked towards her destination, her mind was working. She hadn't been sure how such magic potions worked. She had somehow assumed that something like a love potion would need to be slipped into the target's food or drink, but perhaps it didn't. Unless that type was done diffently again. Maybe she should ask a bit more about that and see if she guessed right. And she would ask this other witch how her potions worked. The trader's witch might very well put the spell in the potion as a reason to charge more – since the witchlight spell potion wasn't made that way. It occurred to Maeven that the same basic potion, might just provide the caster with enough magic to do the spell, and the spell they used, if they knew the right words, could be anything.

If she could get a supply of the basic potion, she only had to steal the spells or trick the witch into telling her the ones she wanted. The idea had possibilities.

It turned out that it wasn't a potion that she needed for her womanly problem. The charm witch who called herself Griselda, kept a blended mixture of herbs for the purpose.

"Take some every day in a cup of hot water," was her directions.

That didn't give Maeven the natural opening for other questions that she wanted to ask, but Griselda somehow discerned her quandary.

"Was there something else you wanted to ask?"

"Um, yes. I don't know if such a thing exists, but is there a magic way to help me clean stuff without extra effort?"

"You don't look like you need it, your hands are too soft."

"Now, they are, but my Da just remarried and she wants me to do all the cleaning for her."

"I make a hand cream that's cheaper, and hard work never hurt a woman."

Maeven was lost for a reply, until one suddenly came to mind – the image with it was strange though, for it seemed like a firelit cavern, not a firelit house she saw.

"It's not doing the work but the time it takes. She's wanting me to remove a hundred years of sooty muck from the walls – rather than just white wash over it."

"A real miserly mistress, is she?"

"Seems so."

"Let me think…"

Griselda went off to get a scroll from a shelf, and returned with it. With it spread open on a table, she ran her finger down its narrow length, and began muttering. Finally she spoke with satisfaction, "That might do it. I'll give it a try."

Her experiment began by getting an old, age blackened pot from her cooking corner. She didn't need to drink a potion to try this spell, and she took a cloth from a bucket of water and began to rub the cooked on soot. Most remained, despite vigourous rubbing, and then she spoke her new spell – the black now came off with ease.

"Oh my," she said in disbelief. "Why did I never think of this before? I can charge what I like for this and the women in town will come with open purses to get it."

With deceptive innocence, Maeven asked, "What was the spell you used?"

Griselda spoke it through, and seemed to be memorising it herself, and then she broke it into parts to explain each bit. Her customer was elated. Once was enough for her to memorise it, and to learn how the witch had joined separate spells to create it.

"Can I try it?" Maeven asked.

"Of course. You'll need a potion, won't you?"

Maeven nodded.

Griselda went off again and returned with a wax stoppered vial. "Before you take it, I want to make sure you have the words right. Repeat after me…"

Maeven deliberately muddled a few words, to hide the fact of her perfect memory, and had to repeat the words until she had it right, Only then did the witch hand over the potion and tell he to speak the spell. Maeven took over the half black and half shiny iron pot and found the black coming off for her too.

With Griselda being so pleased with her new spell, Maeven was able to haggle with her for a hand sized leather sack of the magic potion which she would be able to dole out into tiny vials she bought for herself. Her suggestion that the witch would need all of her current supply for the town wives, had helped the deal. They parted amicably, both feeling they had made an excellent deal.

Lorford was near the border of Thulor, in the north-east of the kingdom and one of the main trade roads passed through it. As a result, many merchants, traders, nobles and others stopped for the night, providing rich pickings.

Maeven was perched on the roof, using the chimney as a backrest. The chimney bricks were warm and pleasant to be near, especially when the night was cold. It was becoming a favourite place of hers, particularly when traders were in. Many of them were in the habit of coming outside to talk and never sensed the invisible ears above their heads. The downside of the position was the smell when the wind blew from the stables or the horse pens. The odour of sour cabbage and rotten food scraps from the rubbish pile or burnt meat from the kitchen was all-pervasive at any time.

Maeven wasn't paying attention to any particular person just then, she was concentrating on palming a flat pebble from hand to hand, and hand to pocket as the invisibility charm she was currently using hid all of her but her hands. She had been practicing for two weeks and was improving, though she didn't think she would ever be good enough to be a pickpocket or to slip things into other people's pockets.

A snippet of conversation caught her attention and her hands stilled.

"… all sorts of chancy creatures. We had to fight two enormous felines. Black as a Demon's heart, they were. They nearly gouged Tod in half. I'll not be taking my wagons back up that way. We heard screams at night, bloodcurdling they were. I don't want to meet the creature that made them…"

The listener leant over to try to hear more clearly.

"… warned us of armed raiders, hiding near Thul Run. So that route's no safer. I'm going to keep heading south. I'll be going as soon as old Thibber coughs up payment for the stuff I've got him."

It was not the first time that Maeven had heard of traders encountering odd creatures. Such stories were being told even before she had left the palace. No one ever said a trader's life was always roses and wine. But brigands at Thul Run – that wasn't far from Lorford, only three days' ride!

Maeven felt her head begin to itch and to sense that she was being watched. She was invisible though; no one should be able to see her up on the roof in the dark. However, most of these "charms" were not perfect, so maybe someone or something could see her. However, rule of thievery, number one, if seen – run!

She scampered up the thatched roof and over to the far side of the inn. A watcher on the ground would have to go right around the inn to try to catch her. It was a matter of moments to reach the roof overhang at the front door of the building and she waited only long enough for two tough looking men to enter before dropping softly to the ground.

Maeven felt the sensation of being watched ease but the itch did not. More ominously, her talisman was becoming very hot. She dragged it by the leather thong out from under her tunic and jerkin.

While still invisible, she entered the inn and was about to slip upstairs to hide for a while when hell itself appeared. Maeven saw rending claws appearing out of the air, heard gnashing teeth, felt intense heat, and smelt sulphurous fumes. Bodiless, hovering eyes seemed to be watching her. The invisibility charm dissipated and from somewhere came the feeling of intense satiated triumph.

The demonic thing began to circle her, so fast she dare not move, but no one else in the room had that problem. They were pushing out through the two doors and diving out the windows. A scream erupted from her as a clawed hand reached for her throat. Then the demon let out a howl of rage, as if it were being denied something it ardently craved. It widened its circle and began rending anything in reach – then, with a sudden snap it was gone, but in her mind was a shrill scream that seemed to go on forever.

Maeven slumped to the floor, saw torn and ripped bodies and brought up everything she had eaten that day.

After a time, she stood unsteadily. The tavern keeper was cautiously raising his head from behind the now blackened and charred half wall of the bar. As he moved, he crunched broken clay pieces. The smell of spilt ale was more pleasant than the sulphur smoke and charred flesh. His eyes surveyed the damage and settled on the only other living creature still in the room.

"You get out! If I ever see you in here again I will set my dogs on you!" he roared, venting his anger. "That thing wanted you! Stay away from here! Do you hear me?"

Maeven heard, vaguely understood his meaning, but was still trying to understand what had happened and why she was not dead. "It didn't get me!" she said, more to herself.

"If it had I would have had one ex-thief. Instead I've got ten of my best customers – dead!"

Maeven took in the fact that most of the crowd that had been in here when she entered were not dead on the floor. She thought, irreverently, that the innkeeper's best customers were the ones too drunk to know they were in danger.

Some of the fleeing patrons had run for the town guard and several others were cautiously peering into the taproom. The first took in the smouldering wood furniture and thatching and called for a water bucket line. There were always buckets kept handy near the rear door, which was nearest the river.

The Guard Leader arrived with his squad and listened to the inn keeper accusing the thief who was leaning on a half burnt table.

"When did you start letting women in here, tapster?" the guard asked him, because although the person was dressed like a man, the torn singed clothes had briefly revealed otherwise.

Thief indeed and definitely female, maybe she could provide some amusement before they notified her guild. Entertainment, and then the guild could pay for her release.The guard dragged the still shocked Maeven over to one wall and tied her wrists to a waist high shelf bracket.

The bucket wielders had saturated everything within the taproom and the water was dripping through the charred areas of the thatch before Maeven regained her sense of self-preservation. Her physical senses were returning. The tortured scream that she had heard with her mind was being replaced by other sensations. Pain from her singed flesh, discomfort from the ropes touching the burnt skin and soreness from her stomach that still wanted to heave. Her eyes felt like they had been boiled dry and her mouth tasted of bile. She was too miserable even to try to escape.

A metal mug of water was placed to her lips and she sipped gratefully. Something moist touched her eyes and they began to focus and she finally recognised the one who was helping her. "Nayfor!" A whisper was all the voice she had.

The local Thieves' Guildmaster was wearing a common guardsman's tunic. "Are you up to helping?" he glanced at the nearest corpses.

Maeven paled even more at the thought.

"If you do, your release fee could be haggled downwards." Nayfor explained. "That means, less money for you to repay the guild."

"None of this is my fault," Maeven argued hoarsely.

"It appears that someone wants you dead. Very, very, dead! Therefore, they will claim it is your fault."

"That's not fair!"

"No, but then thieves are never treated fairly in this kingdom. People think we are no better than brigands. That's why bonded thieves have representation, because even when we have done nothing, we are guilty," Nayfor told her flatly. It was the longest speech that she had ever heard him speak.

"What will I have to do?" she asked reluctantly. If she could have run away, she would have fled rather than agree to help.

A rough voice interrupted the conversation.

"She's a thief, Guardsman Nayfor," Guard Leader Kopje bellowed. "You don't need to coddle it!"

Nayfor glanced sharply at the one he knew as Ven.

"I thought it could help us clean up the mess." Nayfor deliberately referred to Ven neutrally.

The guard leader thought a moment and then a slow smile crossed his face; he nodded. "An excellent idea Nayfor, let's put the wench to work!"

Nayfor cut the rope bindings, but whispered a warning to Maeven. "Watch that one! He sounds like he wants more than work from you."

"I know what to do with his type!" Maeven muttered.

"Come on now, these bodies have to be moved outside for the grave diggers to collect. Most of them have been recognised and most won't be missed." Kopje roared.

Nayfor kept an eye on Maeven as they and other lowly guards moved gory pieces of flesh outside. Soon they were, like the others, covered in blood. Maeven found some amusement in seeing the big bold Kopje looking very green and having to go outside to be sick. She had nothing left in her stomach to lose and could smirk at his discomfort.

"Weak bellied slime crawler," she muttered in his hearing.

The innkeeper passed around a skinful of cheap wine for the guardsmen when they had finished removing the worst of the mess. The men deliberately ignored Maeven, slumped in a corner. She did not mind not having wine, but some water would have been welcome. When all but Nayfor was starting to sound drunk, Maeven saw Nayfor's signal to follow him. No one noticed them leave.

"We are going to see the circuit judge," Nayfor told her. "We'll tell him your story and how you helped. He can see your condition before I take you to a healer. I will promise to bring you if he decides on a hearing, but I am hoping it won't come to that. The circuit judge will be fairer than the local deciders."

The circuit judge did not like being woken in the middle of the night, but once he saw the condition of his guests and realised one was a woman, he went and woke his hosts. When they brought in the refreshments he had requested, he sent the man to fetch a healer. The noble that was hosting the circuit judge looked as if he thought his guests had crawled from the midden. That suited Maeven fine, because Lord Paulus had been at court often enough to recognise her if she hadn't been looking far from regal.

The judge listened to Maeven's suitably edited story. He was impressed by the quality of her speech as it was out of place with her appearance. He verified that she was a bonded thief, which he marked against her, but he did not blame her for being the target of an assassin. Maeven swore she had not stolen anything from the inn or its patrons.

After a period of consideration he decided there was no grounds for a charge against her and he let her leave with the healer.

The healer woman took Maeven back to her own neat cottage. On arrival, she told Nayfor that her patient would be staying until morning. He agreed to return then.

Maeven appreciated the healer's no-nonsense manner; so unlike the tut-tutting old fool who was the physician at the palace. After an herb-infused bath to remove the dried blood and gore from her skin, Maeven dressed in the long sleeved robe that the healer had left for her. In the main room of the cottage, the healer had prepared healing salves and bandages and was ready to treat her patient's burns and scratches.

"You were lucky," the woman commented. "You survived a demon rage!"

"I what…?"

"From the guardsman's description – it appears that the demon killed the other people because it couldn't get to you."

"I don't know why anyone would want to kill me!"

Overall, the burns were no worse than a very bad sunburn and the cuts and scrapes would soon heal. A lot of singed hair had floated off in the bath. She saw herself in a polished metal reflector and realised she looked a mess. The healer obliged her by roughly cutting the unburnt hair as short as the rest.

Nayfor returned in the morning with clothes for her; men's clothes. Her own were not even fit for rags.

"You're alright for a girl," Nayfor commented when they were on their way back to the Guild house, which was an old barn on the fringes of town. Maeven did not comment.

"It's fine by me if you want to remain a boy."

"Yeah, I would," Maeven agreed and Nayfor merely nodded.

"We're moving south," he suddenly told her. "Tonight. There's some trouble I have to sort out. Collin is taking over here."

CHAPTER 10 – THE KING CONFIDES

"Sire, I beg your indulgence for this interruption."

A trembling palace messenger entered the King's private sitting room, appearing pale and clammy as he approached his master.

"You may report." King Westron looked up and assessed the man's behaviour.

"Sire, I went to summon Lord Tormore as you commanded. I found him… dead. Mistress Tormore is also dead. I told the Guard Leader to surround the town house."

"You acted correctly, Messenger Taro," the King commended. He stood up and betrayed nothing of the thoughts passing through his mind.

"Go and find Prince Rhovert and bring him to the town house. If he is not in his apartments, try the tavern in the village."

"Yes, Sire."

The man's trembling eased as his thoughts turned to finding the foppish idler Prince Rhovert, who he could not picture frequenting a tavern with rough merchants and farmers. He then bowed and retreated from the King. When he could not find the prince in the palace, his shivers began again at the thought of having to go to the tavern himself.

Once Rhovert had arrived, the King strode out of his apartment and summoned a servant to assemble the duty unit of his guards. The highly trained King's Own Guards reacted quickly to the summons, leaving dice and card games and scrambling for their weapons. The King expected them to be standing smartly awaiting orders when he arrived at the front chamber. The six men listened to the King's destination and two of them preceded the King out the palace door. Two of the remaining four flanked him and the others followed behind.

It was dark out of the palace and there were not many people walking in the streets. The King was dressed like an ordinary noble in richly adorned tunic and shirt and a fur lined cape, but the presence of the guards indicated his high station.A few people stared as the King walked the short distance to his First Advisor's abode, a surly looking mercenary in tow.

At the town house, the Leader of the Town Guards bowed and began to report.

"Sire, no one has entered and no one has left the house. The physician has been summoned and will be here shortly."

The King nodded and entered the house via the short flight of three steps. The entrance hall was magnificent, panelled with wood from the realm south of Thulor. There was a large animal skin floor rug in the centre of the room. Candle brackets, backed by precious metal were set at frequent intervals around the walls. Instead of bearing candles, they balanced white balls. Except for two that were glowing brightly white, the rest were dull.

King Westron scanned the hall. Everything looked normal there.

"Wait here," he told his guards. "Come only if I call."

He strode forward, one hand on his sword hilt and the other going to the v-shaped talisman hanging from a gold chain about his neck. It was alternating between heat, warning of danger, and the cool of awareness.

He stopped on the threshold of the large entertaining area and studied the scene of horror. For a long moment, his talisman remained cold. Without looking behind him, he spoke, "Rhovert, wait here while I look closer."

Rhovert was dressed as a common mercenary in a knee length-brown leather tunic over a loose fitting linen shirt. His sword hung from a ring that was part of an embroidered belt. His long hide boots, that needed a polish, covered thick, often mended woollen hose. A leather strap kept his light brown hair off his face. He in no way resembled the effeminate he pretended to be in noble company.

"Sire!" was his reply, indicating that he would obey.

The surprise he had felt when the messenger found him at the tavern became irrelevant as his mind took in the blackened walls, the blasted furniture and the fresh red blood everywhere. In this room, a few of the glowing orbs remained intact but they had fallen to the floor.

The King, veteran of many battles, had seen death often, but Elvira Tormore was not a soldier or fighter. She looked as if she had been terrified and fleeing something dreadful before her death. Something had inflicted countless deep slashes all over her body. Her blonde hair was now red. It had not been a quick or merciful death.

The King went further into the room, carefully avoiding the worst of the blood. Over near the far wall there was an open trap door, made of wood backed by a thin layer of stone to hide its presence when closed.

Stone steps led downward into darkness. Rhovert picked up one of the glowing balls and followed his father.

King Westron knew by the coolness of his talisman that his son was behind him. He glanced at his heir, who was clasping a talisman with his free hand, identical to his own except for the glyphs. They both started down the steps and began to feel a tingling as if their hair wanted to stand on end.

"Father, I'm no wizard, but this feels like a place of dark magic."

"Yes," Westron agreed. "Though what was Tormore trying to do?"

Rhovert was shocked. "Are you telling me that your First Advisor was a Dark Wizard?"

"I suspected it," Westron admitted with uncharacteristic frankness. "However he had skills I could use and until now he kept away from the darker magic."

"Well, whatever he was doing seems to have killed him," Rhovert deduced, looking at the headless corpse on the floor. The head was a few feet away but it looked as if the wizard's last thoughts were an ecstasy of triumph.

"I think we will need a wizard or sorceress to interpret what happened here," Rhovert began.

He watched his father suddenly bend down and remove something from the neck of the corpse. The item went quickly into the King's belt pouch.

"We need more light down here," Westron stated. "Bring two more of the orbs from the hall."

Rhovert did not argue or dawdle, and returned in a very short time.

The King took an orb from him, began to shake it and it began to glow.

"Is it safe to bring more magic things in here?" Rhovert queried.

"The wizard balls are not really magic, just substances reacting together. Shake yours and come over to the bench."

The workbench had once contained an array of odd-looking objects, neatly arranged. In spite of the blast, some of the items were undamaged. The King let out an audible hiss of anger. A small object joined the other in the King's pouch.

As the King continued to scan the debris, he said, "Look at his hands, see if he is clutching anything."

Rhovert, curious, did as instructed and managed to pry some brittle burnt stuff out of the rigid hand.

"His hand is rigid. How long has he been dead?" Rhovert asked.

"Not long, I saw him just before sun down. He said he had a lead on your sister's whereabouts and was going to attempt a scrying to see if he could identify her current location. Was there anything in his hand?"

"There is some burnt stuff that may have been hair."

The King nodded. He was examining the remains of the scrying crystal, once a sphere of an amazingly clear crystalline substance. It was now a collection of partly fused fragments. He placed one piece in his belt pouch before gesturing for his son to follow him back up the stairs.

At the front door of the house, King Westron spoke to the guards.

"No one is to enter this house without a letter bearing my personal seal, or unless he is accompanied by me or by Prince Rhovert."

"I can fetch Tormore's associate Rolliver," Rhovert offered, then recalled the man was only a minor wizard. "Though, perhaps it might be better if I got Finora to come."

"This is no place for Finora," Westron stated flatly. "If my calculations are correct, she is still indentured for another two years and I do not want to upset Rolliver at this time."

"I met a young chap a night or two ago, he's a wizard from down south. His name is Roman Golddreamer but he looks more like a farmer."

"Find him and bring him here," Westron commanded.

Rhovert strode down the cobblestone-paved street in the direction of the village where the serfs that farmed the surrounding fields lived. He was certain that something foul was still abroad, just as he had earlier sensed that something bad was going to happen – a sensation so strong that he had left his apartment in the palace and come to a house he maintained in the village to change into his current garb.

The villagers that frequented the tavern had, until that night, been ignorant of his identity. They all knew of him as Berto, a common swordsman. That had changed when the King's Messenger summoned him.

The tavern keeper, Brennan, bowed deeply when he strode back into the taproom. It was now past the hour for serving drinks and the man was cleaning up. His patrons had gone home.

"Brennan, old friend, that is not necessary," Rhovert insisted. "I prefer to be a common swordsman here, if that is possible any more. I must admit, I underestimated my father, I did not realise that he knew I came here."

"A fresh drink, Berto?" Brennan asked reverting to the name with which he was familiar.

Shaking his head, Rhovert declined the offer.

"I'm looking for that southern wizard that came in here two or three nights ago. Where did he say that he was going?"

"My wife suggested Mistress Filmore's lodging house, but the wizard's little red headed wife wanted something better. Try the town! Something about the cousin of a friend of a friend married some Lord or other."

After discerning that Golddreamer was now staying with Lord Jerrin, one of the more influential court nobles, Rhovert continued on to find the wizard. Lord Jerrin looked like a stunned fish with his jaw hanging open when he opened his door to see Rhovert, dressed as a mean looking mercenary, standing there. He had thought that he knew the Prince, but… this was no idling Court dandy!

"Close your mouth, Jerrin!" Rhovert suggested quietly. "You have a visitor from Declanor here, I am told."

"I do, your Highness. A wizard just up from there and his wife. They know a friend of my wife."

"Who is the second woman?"

"The wizard's sister, she claims," Jerrin managed to explain. "Just arrived up from the south."

Rhovert watched the wizard, a solid, well muscled man who was smiling good-naturedly at the bickering between his wife and his sister. The wife, Gisella, was an attractive redhead dressed in clothes that were almost good enough for Court. She was shorter and more intense than Roman's sister Atlantis, who was dressed like the common women in a long leather tunic over an embroidered kirtle; a pair of men's boots was visible below the hem.

"Roman, old man," Rhovert affected his swordsman persona, to the continued amazement of Jerrin. "While the ladies are discussing their differences – may I have a word with you?"

The men withdrew to a different room and because Rhovert did not wish to spread the news of Tormore's death just yet, he made a suggestion to Jerrin.

"Perhaps you could arrange for some refreshments for the ladies?" Rhovert said with a charming smile, startlingly reminiscent of a younger King Westron.

"Certainly, Your Highness," Jerrin agreed. He was very eager to go and tell his wife the juicy news about Prince Rhovert and did not think to wonder why the prince wanted to speak to his guest.

"Your Highness?" Roman Golddreamer asked with a sly grin, highly amused by the scene he had witnessed between the Prince and noble.

Rhovert simply grinned back. He liked this man and the coolness at his neck assured him that the wizard was not dangerous.

"His Majesty, King Westron, requires the help of a wizard in a matter of some confidentiality. If I guess right, he wants someone not associated with his Court. Are you able to come now?"

With a last glance at the door through which the bickering was still audible, Roman nodded. "They will probably be still at it when I return," he commented.

"Your sister is a swordswoman," Rhovert commented as they left the house without a formal leave taking.

"Yes, how did you guess?" Roman asked.

"Well, in spite of the dress, the way she moves and the boots!" Rhovert admitted. "The only other woman I know who insists on wearing men's boots is my sister Leanne, who is also a swordswoman."

"Ah!" Roman exclaimed. "Well, if you listen to my wife, Gisella, she will tell you that Atlantis has absolutely no dress sense. My sister thinks a dress is a dress and one of them will do anywhere. That was the topic of the, um, discussion! Normally she dresses like you or I."

"It seems we are both used to strong minded women," Rhovert said. "We don't have far to go, it is that place with the lighted torches around it."

If Roman Golddreamer was curious about the summons, he hid it well.

The King's Own Guards saluted as Rhovert approached. "His Majesty is still within," the leader reported.

Rhovert nodded and strode up the steps again. In the entrance hall, Roman moved in front of the Prince and drew out his wand from a narrow pocket in his breeches. King Westron emerged from another section of the house.

"Father, this is Roman Golddreamer," Rhovert introduced.

"Wizard Golddreamer, I have need of your skills." King Westron wasted no time on preliminaries.

"I am at your service, Your Majesty." Roman bowed from the waist. "Though, I use the title Wizard Roman when I am being formal."

"Wizard Roman, then. I require you to tell me what you sense and deduce as you move around this house. Rhovert, have a look through there." He nodded his head in the direction from which he had emerged.

Rhovert watched the wizard follow his father before walking into the other part of the house. The first rooms he came to were elaborately furnished guest rooms. There were no signs of damage in any of them. At the end of the passage was a room full of scrolls with a few of the newer written 'books'; pages of parchment bound together at one edge with thread.

The talisman at his neck began to grow warm, so Rhovert studied the labels on the scrolls and books carefully. Several storage holes were empty, and these scrolls were open on the table in the centre of the room. One unrolled scroll displayed writing in a crabbed and spiky script. Rhovert studied the archaic prose style and realised that it was about the Dragon Talisman. The great dragon mage Exconidor created the talismans and gave them to her human apprentice, Frederick, before she died. Rhovert skipped a few paragraphs and saw mention of the attributes each of the talismans developed in its bearer. On the page, shown in careful detail, different runes were drawn, and Rhovert recognised the ones for male, female, magic, logic, intelligence, foresight and stealth but not the rest. However, as interesting as the scroll was, a silver object caught his eye and drew him towards it. The item consisted of two bowl shaped segments that would join to form a sphere.

A door opened, moving a bookshelf with it. "There should be a metal container, Sire," Roman Golddreamer was saying as he appeared.

"Here," Rhovert commented, making no move to touch the object.

Roman looked around. "Yes, that would be the demon receptacle."

"Demon?" Rhovert repeated softly with a shiver of premonition. "A demon did all the damage?"

"Not all of it," Roman corrected. "Two things happened. It appears that the dead wizard had a demon restrained in the receptacle. He freed it under a controlling spell and sent it out at someone he saw in the crystal orb. It also seems, from the damage in the cellar below, that the intended victim had some powerful counter charm and so his spell rebounded and killed him. The spell controlling the demon ended when he died. They are vindictive creatures – it would have returned to kill its master. However, finding that one dead, it killed the next person it saw. The unfortunate lady would have been subjected to a demon squall, or rage, before it killed her."

"So there is a demon loose in the realm!" Rhovert quickly understood. It explained his earlier sensation of something foul abroad. "How do we recapture or banish it?"

"The trick is to find it first," Roman told them. "Then to get close enough to it to draw it back into its receptacle. The attracting spell was reset on the halves so I surmise the wizard was intending to recapture it as soon as it had killed his enemy."

Rhovert met his father's gaze but the King was betraying nothing. Rhovert ceased his questions.

The King withdrew three items from his pouch and placed them on the table. "What do you make of these?"

Roman picked up the talisman and looked closely at it. The raised glyph was complex, as if it consisted of more than one rune, each on top of another. "It is a powerful protective charm. One of the overlapping runes is the symbol for magic; a second is the one for maleness. I cannot read the others. If it is a charm against dark magic then it is no wonder that the man below died when it rebounded on him. It might have saved him from someone else's dark magic but not his own spell returning."

The King's expression became intent as the wizard picked up a clear phial with a wax stopper. Inside was a thick lock of light brown hair and a jewel studded silver ring. Rhovert tried to recall where he had seen the ring before.

"A spell focus for scrying or targeting a spell!" Roman deduced. "The target probably died …" he stopped when he glimpsed the King's face. In the moment before it returned to inscrutable, there had been a look of anguish. He quickly turned his attention to the crystal shard.

"This is part of the scrying orb. The inside surface is fused. I would say he sent the demon through the orb to his intended victim – he probably didn't know the exact location."

"Yes, that is how I read it too," the King said softly. "Wizard Roman, in your opinion, what should be done to make this house safe?"

"There is an outside chance that the demon will try to return. It would be best to keep the place locked up so people cannot get in. The reek of dark magic is very strong. I can perform the protection spells. However if you need to come and go from the house, I will be needed."

"In that case, Wizard Roman, I hereby appoint you as Court Wizard to the Realm of Thulor," King Weston proclaimed.

Rhovert saw the wizard's surprise. He seemed on the verge of refusing, but before he could reply, King Westron strode from the room, taking the three objects with him.

"I can see why you might wish to act so contrarily with respect to your Sire's expectations," Roman said calmly to Rhovert. "Would I have the option of refusing?"

Rhovert smiled. "To keep the argument short – no! However, he is not as obdurate with outsiders as he is with his family. If you were to request the means to set your affairs in order for the period of your absence, I am sure he will agree. You will be expected to take up residence in the palace, as will your wife and sister."

"Of course!" Roman said softly. "My wife will be more than happy at my appointment. As for my sister, well, she has a mind of her own that would be more than a match for His Majesty. My concern is for my farm down south in Declanor. I will need to send a messenger to tell them I will be staying away indefinitely and give my wife's brother more detailed instructions."

"I will be able to help you with that," Rhovert assured him.

"Is that the swordsman speaking – or the confounder of nobles?" Roman queried with a sly grin.

"Neither, it is the effeminate simpleton that Jerrin thought I was, who has the authority to arrange what you need."

Roman laughed. "I have no doubt that he will spread the word of your transformation."

"Unfortunately true, as he is one of the biggest gossips at Court. At the same time, tonight is first time I have considered dropping the charade, as it is the first time that Father has voluntarily shared any of his thoughts with me."

"Is that the reason you choose to try and antagonise him?" Roman probed.

"Yes, mostly, but it hasn't worked. He has never commented about my behaviour. It is as if he knows it is an act and approves of it for his own reasons. It is like nothing surprises him or he has seen ahead in time far enough to arrange things to his satisfaction. My sisters and I have never been close to him, less so since Mother died."

Suddenly, Rhovert added all the evidence he had seen and came up with a frightening picture. The ring had been his mothers – and that meant Col Tormore, who had once been his closest friend, had somehow contrived his mother's death. As for this latest dark magic…

"Would Tormore's victim have been aware of the demon?" Rhovert asked.

"Without doubt," Roman confirmed. "Do you know who …?" he began to ask, but Rhovert had lapsed into a thoughtful silence. At that moment, he looked very like his sire.

The news of Lord Tormore's death soon spread, but the rumours of how he died never approached the truth. Most people assumed an unidentified intruder had killed him.

The person most upset by the death was the new Lord Rolliver. Tormore had no acknowledged heirs, and a letter was found requesting that his estate go to his friend and assistant Rolliver. However, the townhouse and its contents were now the property of the Crown.

Rolliver answered questions posed by King Westron, but pleaded ignorance of Tormore's intentions the night he died, and of anyone who may have been giving his master orders. The matter seemed to rest at that point, but Prince Rhovert saw, on several occasions, a man he knew to be a high-ranking thief speaking confidentially with the King.

His father had mentioned that Tormore was planning to scry for his sister. He himself knew where Leanne and Finora were, and he was sure his father knew that fact. No one knew where Maeven was now, so she was likely Tormore's target. But why did Tormore try to kill her? Was it because she would not marry him or some more sinister reason? And why was his father trying to find her now, when for the past two years he hadn't seemed to care?

Caravans of horses and covered carts were arriving at the Palace hourly. The Lords of the Kingdom of Thulor were arriving for a conclave ordered by the King. The Lords, their wives, children, valued retainers and most prized possessions would occupy every room in the palace. The women would be looking forward to the elaborate entertainments and the formal balls where they could display their newest gowns. The men would be expecting lavish food, free flowing wine and the chance to prove how courageous they were and how skilled at arms and hunting.

Rhovert wondered wryly whom his father had chosen to act as his hostess on this occasion, in the absence of wife or daughters. He also wondered how many of the unattached women would pass through the royal bedchamber. He eyed off some attractive younger ladies and considered their likely reactions to his own attentions. One sure way to sort the fluff heads and those only interested in a future regal role from the ones with intelligence was to see which ones ignored his normal court behaviour. The smart ones were able to see beneath the surface, the rest were not worth worrying about.

Rhovert decided there was an advantage to acting a fool. The Lords would keep on talking as if he was not there. The interesting things he heard became quiet whispers in the ear of the King, who appeared to be ignoring his son. As a result, the King quickly settled some trouble between two neighbouring Lords and he halted a brewing rebellion before it started.

When Rhovert moved amongst the gathering of Lords, Ladies and their grown children, it was with the agility of a dancer. He would catch a snippet of conversation, freeze to hear more and either proceed or greet the speakers with a limp handshake. He would enter the conversation with a thought provoking comment, in a nasal whining voice. They would ignore the words and the rest of the meaningless babble, but later they would recall it and think it was their own thought.

As he spoke, he adopted a left hand on hip pose and his right hand would wave around, spreading a strong smell of perfume from the sachet round his wrist. The ladies loved the scent and admired his clothes, coveting the exquisite velvet material and the rich embroidery. The men were simply sickened.

Prince Rhovert frequently observed himself in the polished surfaces set about the Great Hall. No one considered that he was actually using the mirrors to observe those behind him. In this way, he spotted Lord Jerrin talking to the new Lord of the Western Marches and moved closer. Young Bruthen had met Prince Rhovert, endured his inane chatter and been glad to be away from him.

"What do you mean, Jerrin?" Bruthen demanded. "The Prince is totally useless! With a son like that, the King needs us, his Lords, more than ever. That means more power for us."

Prince Rhovert smiled and moved away. Bruthen had potential; he had taken a casual hint, posed as a disinclination to act and concluded truly that the King needed him. He continued on, charming the ladies with gallant bows, exaggerated flattery and flirting gestures.

King Westron had confided in his son what he required of his nobles. The attacks by a demon on members of his court, could only be at the behest of an inimical enemy, and the realm needed to be ready for a long drawn out war. He had not needed to add that the Lords would resent many of the emergency measures. First, he had to convince them of the extreme nature of the peril and then to get them to fortify their homes, make their villagers store all their produce in the manor cellars and know they had to retreat there if an attack occurred. The Lords had orders to train the villagers to use weapons so that there would be more fighters available.

After the first day of the conclave, the Lords received their chance to prove their fighting prowess. Several of the Lords chose to challenge Prince Rhovert, and each won after a short bout with the seemingly inept Prince. Most Lords began to feel that training a serf would be easier than teaching the Prince!

By the end of the four days, the Lords had agreed to all the King's measures, told him all the little worries that they had in their domains and repledged their loyalty.

Rhovert had found, amongst the beautiful ladies, a woman whose mind was as sharp as his own. He hardly recognised Roman's sister Atlantis Golddreamer – someone had provided her with an exquisite dress, tamed her shoulder length black hair into the latest Court style and convinced her to attend, but they had lost the battle with the boots!

A week after the departure of the Lords, Prince Rhovert entered the Audience Chamber quietly, coming through the private entrance behind the throne. The King was sitting in one of the petitioner's chairs, listening intently to a figure dressed in grey. The figure heard, saw or sensed his approach from behind and covered his head with the hood of his cape.

"…the only suggestion we have heard that may work is using crushed dragon shells, Majesty. Though no one knows where any may be found."

"Instruct your people to continue listening, Barnabas," the King said softly. "What else have your people got to report?"

"Your agent in the North has found something, a black stone, that he believes would interest you. I will send my second to recover it and bring it to you."

"How is that agent?" the King asked, still quietly.

"He has not many days left to him."

The King nodded, looked up and saw his son. He made a gesture and the hooded man stood and walked quickly from the room.

"Sit!" the King told his son when they were alone. Rhovert obeyed and waited for his father to continue.

"I have seen that man before!" Rhovert finally commented. "How long have you been secretly associating with thieves?"

"The better ones serve me so that their Guild will be permitted to exist," the King explained. "That one is my spymaster!"

Rhovert grinned at this deviousness, but sobered quickly when he saw his father's serious expression. King Westron seemed to be staring at nothing.

"What is wrong, Father?" he asked suddenly.

"Send orders to Captain Wyst's sword troop to go to the north border," was the unexpected reply.

"Leanne is in that troop," Rhovert told him in case he did not know. "Finora, too, she is old Ermytrude's assistant."

"Make sure she has a demon receptacle," was all the response he got.

"She started carrying one last month!" Rhovert was surprised into saying. "What have you seen?"

"Nothing that is clear," Westron admitted. "It is like I am looking at a town, a northern one because the rooves are thatched. There is a dark cloud over it. The black stone that Barnabas mentioned is something important. I have read about it or heard something about it, somewhere."

The King finally looked around and saw his son still there.

"I am well! Go and send those orders to Wyst," he insisted. "When you return, bring the wizard with you."

In the absence of his son, King Westron thought hard and was prepared to issue more orders.

"Send a messenger to the King of Declanor requesting permission to send an envoy to discuss a matter of mutual importance," he began, speaking to Rhovert when he returned. "Then send messages to my Council of Advisors. I want them all here in a handful of days. When that is organised, I want you to wander about in your alternate guise and listen to what the commoners are saying about the new measures their Lords are imposing. Find out what will make them more accepting. I have had reports of minor rebellions, so if you can, find out who or what caused them."

Almost as an after thought, the King added, "At the same time, keep alert for news of your youngest sister. Since I haven't heard anything about her these past two years, she is probably not living amongst my nobles. I expect she is making a living for herself in some totally unsuitable manner."

Rhovert kept his face impassive. The tone of his father's voice implied serious trouble for his sister when she was found. He wondered what his father knew about her that caused him to start actively seeking her. His father wouldn't explain though, so he went off to prepare for an extended trip and left the King talking to the wizard.

It was only after he had left the palace that he remembered that he had not asked about the reference to dragon shells.

Maeven was restless. A month of forced idleness was not in her plans. Nayfor and the Guildmaster at Bowry would not approve any of her 'intend to thieve' requests. They insisted that the Bowry Guild healer, a sour little man with a thatch of straw-coloured hair, confirm her recovery.

It was becoming obvious to Maeven that her lack of clearance was related to Nayfor's reason for being there. He was doing something dangerous and they did not want his apprentice accompanying him. That might have been because he now knew her to be a girl.

Feeling back to peak fitness, Maeven made plans of her own. If she was not allowed to rob anyone, then there were some more charms she hoped to find.

She talked to every well-known charm witch in town and quizzed them about the potions they could make. Only one had an invisibility potion, but it was only good for a quarter day at most. It worked for the person that took the potion and anything being carried or touched. That was slightly better than the one she had bought from the trader clan witch, and she was out of those potions now. Then she asked about a spell to help someone sleep, that too, this witch could provide.

Further questioning of that witch led to her being given the name of the woman's teacher, a really old wizard, also living in the town. The old man hadn't brewed any potions for many years, but he had once known how to make the very thing Maeven wanted, a potion that would enable her to magic her belongings into invisibility.

"The potion isn't the thing to matter most," the old man claimed. "Even a weak potion'll power most of yer common spells. It's the cantrip that's matters. O' course most of them little snip witches aren't really int'rested in aught but love potions.

"I got cantrips fer hidin' anything yer want hidden. Pay a bit extra and I'll tell yer the secret to keeping them hidden until yer ready to find 'em agin. Won't work on living things but, very good fer dead things."

Maeven put a silver piece on the old man's table then added several large gems.

"Tell me, good man, how to hide my silver and my gems."

The man nodded, eyeing the items on the table.

"This be the cantrip for hiding yer silver," the man explained. "Ye need to listen careful and repeat the words exact."

Maeven had a good ear for music and could repeat the singsong chant after hearing it twice; the spell was easy. The man was impressed and gave her a potion so that she could try it out.

"Ye did that well, nows I give ye the cantrip for yer joo-els."

Maeven learnt that one just as quickly and made her gems vanish. She didn't need more potion as what she had taken was still giving her enough magic to work the charm.

"Now, good man, the counter charm to recover my wealth." Maeven prompted.

The counter charm was almost like the sound of a drunkards mumbling, but Maeven still had no trouble learning and repeating it.

Maeven carefully repeated the four new cantrips to make sure she would remember them and in doing so noticed a pattern in the wording of the chants.

To test a hunch, Maeven asked, "I want to be able to carry a couple of knives for protection – could you teach me a charm for that?"

The old man spoke that readily; this client had more than enough money to pay him.

Maeven smiled faintly, having just learnt something very useful. In each charm, only about twelve of the words actually mattered – the rest were rubbish words to hide them. Then the old man decided to tell her something that really put a grin on her face. "For two silver bits, how'd yer like to know how to carry yer stuff with out carrying it?"

"You interest me, old man," Maeven said, leaning forward.

"When I was but a very young lad, I met a very old wizard. Did 'im a big favour. He taught me a binding spell. I call it a 'follow me' spell."

Maeven listened as the old man explained how the spell worked, her mouth grinning with eagerness to try it. A second silver bit appeared on the table.

Knowing the way of the other cantrips, she listened very carefully and almost danced with glee when the two silver bits followed her in the same position relative to her hand as they had been when she spoke the spell.

As soon as she had the chant to end the spell she thanked the man, gave both the silver and gems to him and left to return to the thieves' guild house.

The next time Nayfor departed, she was ready to follow him. Most of her money and jewels were hidden both physically and magically in a hole at the guildhouse. Her knives were invisible and ready to her hand thanks to the follow spell, as were several vials of magic potion – leaving her hands free to deal with the donkey's reins and her rolled blanket. She cloaked herself and her donkey with an invisibility charm, then followed a short distance behind her master.

It did not take Nayfor long, however, to realise she was following him. The next morning he had found her sleeping under a bush after her invisibility charm had worn off. The stinging slap he had given her along with the coldly calculated words of reprimand were still vivid in her mind. He allowed her to stay with him, but they rode on in silence.

Nayfor finally stopped on the outskirts of a burnt village. They were on a slight rise and the smouldering ruins were starkly visible.

"Who did this?" Maeven asked Nayfor. She decided that her curiosity was more imperative than her petty determination not to talk to him.

"Brigands," he said flatly. His eyes were carefully noting details of the scene, evaluating it with his highly trained thief's senses. "They appear to have left, probably yesterday. They'll have gone back north. We'll leave the mounts here and go in on foot. Have you any weapons?"

"Two knives," Maeven admitted.

"You should get them out. You might need to use them," he warned, not sure if she would, or could, kill with them. "Note the town's features in case you have to flee."

They were not challenged as they entered the town and Nayfor gave his apprentice a hand signal to separate and search. She obeyed, treating the apparently deserted village as hostile territory. Most structures had been of wood and earth brick. The wood had been torched but it had not all burnt.

Maeven entered every house in the first street. It was the same story in each. Everything of value or use, had been taken. Clothing, cooking pots, eating utensils, plates, mugs – it did not matter what. The two or three rooms of each dwelling had been completely ransacked.

It was worse, so much worse than the mindless demon's slaughter. The brigands must have struck at night, somehow breaching the town's defences, for whole families had been killed as they slept. This was coldly calculated. At least her stomach didn't empty itself, but she wanted to cry, every time she saw a dead baby or child.

In the tenth or eleventh house, she heard a faint wail and followed the sound to a bed in the furthest room. Under it was a dirty child of about four or five.

Maeven spoke softly to the child for a long time, keeping her voice friendly and gentle. Finally, the girl crawled out to her and allowed herself to be lifted and carried out of the house past her dead parents. The girl said nothing as Maeven kept looking into more houses. It was becoming obvious that the brigands had taken young women as prisoners as there were many more male bodies than female. It also seemed that most of the dead children were very young, too young to look after themselves. She didn't like the way things were looking.

Nayfor whistled sharply for her to come to him. Maeven chose to obey without question. This town was too unnerving.

He was standing in the doorway of one of the less damaged dwellings. He saw her coming and made no comment about her companion.

"There are four women inside. Talk to them. They'll have to come back with us! We can't leave them here. I'm looking for more survivors."

Maeven nodded, not sure what she would find.

A sword aimed at her gut wasn't what she expected. The woman wielding it had a tear-streaked face but a look of fierce determination. Her clothes were ragged, filthy and torn in enough places that it was amazing that they didn't fall off.

"I am not going to hurt you," Maeven said in a soft voice. The little girl was still clinging to her desperately. "We came to see what had happened here and we will be going back to Bowry. It would be safer for you to come back with us."

"No! We can't leave our children with those bastards!" the woman announced.

Maeven happened to agree with her sentiments.

"We don't want any men here either!"

"My name is Maeven!"

"Like the Princess?" the woman commented dryly.

"Yeah, like her!" Maeven admitted. "And you are?"

"Roberteuse."

"Well then, how are four of you going to take on the whole brigand rabble?"

"We've got right on our side," the woman declared. "The Gods will help us.”

"Too bad they didn't help you when you needed it before," Maeven pointed out, she had no belief in the powers of mythical deities. "Be better to have might on your side!"

"You and your friend?" the woman sneered.

"No, even two more wouldn't do much. I promise you though; we will get news of your plight to the King. He will act!" Maeven said with sudden confidence.

"Don't make me laugh!" The woman was on the verge of hysterics, but even so, the sword hadn't shifted. "The King won't listen to the likes of you!"

"He'll listen," Maeven promised with discernable passion. "Even if I have to sneak into his bedchamber and stick a knife up his nose!"

The woman lowered her sword.

"You are probably right, though. The four of us aren't much."

Her three companions looked to be still in shock.

"Could you tell me what happened?" Maeven asked. "We'll need to give a report to the King's men."

There was anguish on the woman's face.

"They came at night but I was with old Merlie and had some warning. My friends and I put up a fight but we were knocked down and left for dead. I watched them yesterday, when they thought they were safe. I saw them march north with the children and the women. They had carts for our food and chattels. I won't forget the leader. He was richly dressed, like a lord, but it was a strange style. He was a handsome devil, dark hair and moustache but his smile gave me chills. His horse was the biggest I've ever seen, pure black with a glossy sheen to its coat…"

Maeven listened to all the woman had to say.

"Can you take this child and tend to her, too?" Maeven asked. "I will tell my friend that you will return with us. What happened to Old Merlie?"

"Merlie? They left him. He is almost dead and totally blind. They laughed at him and decided it wasn't worth killing him."

That didn't fit with what Maeven had observed. "May I speak with him?"

"In the back room," the woman nodded as she gently but firmly disengaged the child's hands from around the stranger's neck. The child had found the leather thong that was threaded through her Dragon Talisman. The woman froze when she saw it.

"He used to have something like that a long time ago."

Maeven, free of the child, felt a sudden urgency to see Merlie and pushed past the woman.

"Roberteuse?" a weak voice spoke from the low bed. "I'm thirsty and so cold."

Maeven saw a cup by the bed and gently placed it to Merlie's lips. His hands touched hers and he became still as if divining who she was. One hand began to fumble at her neck. She took out her talisman and let him hold it. Somehow, he seemed to gain strength.

"Finora?" he whispered.

"No, Maeven."

"Why do you have this one?"

"The one I was given made me feel odd. Finora never would wear hers. So I… swapped hers for mine!" She had never admitted that fact to anyone before and had doubted that anyone would know.

Merlie made a strange noise. She realised he was trying to laugh. "The pieces know what they want in a bearer," he told her. "They try to mould them to suit. Finora has the one my sister once had, for magic? Did you wear that one for long?"

"A year or two," Maeven said slowly. "Could it have changed me? They said I had no magic."

"It may have, but this one found you more to its liking."

"Did this talisman make me want to become a thief?"

"Maybe. Were you liking to take things beforehand?"

Maeven wasn't going to admit that she had, instead she recalled something she'd thought just after her mother died. "Once I thought I wanted to find a dragon's egg, hatch it, and have it for a pet that I could love and which would love me."

"That was a dangerous ting to say in the Dragon's realm. Have you ever heard the dragon's voice?"

"Dragons are just a myth. No one has ever seen one." Then Maeven had a revelation, "Father has never spoken about you, Merlie. Are you a thief, too?"

"Yes, but Westron couldn't admit I was a thief, not when he'd outlawed the Thieves' Guild."

"Does he hate you? Before I left the palace, he usually ignored me."

"His father and grandfather were the same. Thought the younger generation had to learn to stand on their own. But Westron and I were playmates once, friends as well as cousins," Merlie paused. "He changed when he received his father's talisman. You should realise that the pieces are all different. I think his shows him the future… a long time before it happens. That's why he does some inexplicable things, and years later… he's proven right. In a strange way, outlawing the Guild has protected us. Perhaps he saw it was necessary to protect you?"

Maeven was silent – she had never thought of things that way. The old man kept talking.

"He knew I was here – he never sent his guards thief-hunting this far north. I was his eyes and ears up here. If I sensed trouble, I'd hold the talisman and think – all the others would sense something. I have been spying for my King, reporting to the Grand Master who has the ear of the King. Tell Barnabas I'm dying…" he dropped the talisman and seemed to fall into a doze.

Maeven retreated, thoughtfully clasping her talisman, thinking of the situation here and Merlie's words. A whistle in the danger cadence cut through her reverie, and she raced to the door.

"That's danger!" Maeven warned Roberteuse, who immediately handed the child to one of the other women and drew her sword again.

Through the partly opened door, Maeven scanned the town, and then sprinted for cover on the opposite side of the street. The whistle came again and Maeven deduced its direction – somewhere near the main town square. She pictured her mental map of the town in her mind and recalled where the structures were more earth brick and substantially intact. She ran in that direction and climbed up to the charred roof beams of the end building at one corner of the square. As she hid amongst the remains of the thatch, she watched two strangers dragging an unconscious Nayfor into the square. They were glancing around as if they sensed they were being watched. The men went back into the building and returned with each carrying a limp child. The children were dropped near Nayfor who had begun to move slightly, as if waking.

Maeven whistled a low carrying tune. The second of the two strangers, the one wearing the richly embroidered over robes, looked around and spotted her. He shouted a command in an unfamiliar language and his companion reappeared and began to run towards the building where she hid.

Maeven reached into her pocket for her last vial of potion so she could activate the invisibility charm. It wasn't there. "Oh no!" she muttered, realising she was in trouble.

On impulse, thinking back to what Merlie had said about her original talisman changing her, she muttered the activation words for the charm anyway. To her surprise and intense relief, her body disappeared except for her hands. That was as good as that charm had ever worked, even with the potion.

Maeven laughed aloud as she moved lightly across the roof beams to the next structure and jumped across. All those tedious dancing lessons, years ago, had honed her balance and taught her how to be light on her feet.

As the infuriated brigands searched the far house for her, Maeven was squatting beside the incapacitated Nayfor. "Nayfor, it's me. What did you find?"

The Guildmaster guessed at once that she was invisible but didn't comment. "In my pocket, a black oval stone. Take it and hide it on you and get out of here. It's more valuable than my life, or the life of any one left in this town. You have to get it away. Go!"

Maeven felt through Nayfor's pockets until she found the object and slipped it into her own. Then seeing the black robed brigand approaching with his knife ready she drew her own, but kept it and her hands under her short cloak. Nayfor was trying to sit up. Maeven drew her second knife and pressed it into his hand.

"Go!" Nayfor hissed urgently as he took the knife. His own was missing.

Maeven backed away, watching the stranger, and almost backed into his master. That one had approached from the other direction and seemed to guess that magic was at work. He was slashing around with his sword, seemingly at random. Maeven fell to the ground and rolled soundlessly away from him. When she was clear, she sprang to her feet. For a moment, she had considered slashing at his legs but her talisman was heating up and she decided to run for the gate instead.

The nearest gate was the east gate and not the one they had entered by. When she reached it, the gate was shut and daubed on the inside was a crude representation of the Kingdom Crest of Thulor overlaid by a black serpent.

Her whole body refused to go closer, her talisman was too hot to hold. She followed the wall to the south gate but that was now shut too and similarly bedaubed.

Maeven continued around to the north gate, which appeared to be open. Nearby, two horses were tethered to a post, a tall glossy black horse and a smaller chestnut animal. Maeven untethered the smaller horse, leapt with effortless ease into its saddle and urged it to run.

There was a blinding concussion of light as Maeven came abreast of the gate pillars. The horse ran faster, frightened by the noise, but Maeven felt like she was being scraped off the animal.

The next thing she was aware of was the dust having got up her nose and making her sneeze, her vision was full of tiny pinpoints of light and her mind was trying to make her crawl forward but something unyielding was in her way. She tried a different direction, which were also blocked. Then she tried to stand but could not even raise herself.

"Damn, I hate wizards!" Maeven thought as her wits returned and her situation became clear. She was in a cage of glowing energy with only enough room to remain curled up.

A high-pitched fluting sound was audible. After a few minutes, the sound of galloping hooves neared. Vaguely discernible through the pinpoints of light was the chestnut horse, now covered in dirt and sweat.

"No harm done, my fine Belior," a foreign sounding voice spoke in gentle soothing tones to the horse. "It's almost a pity …"

"What have you caught, Saradoc?" another voice spoke with a similar accent. This one evoked visions of a slimy greasy floor.

"I'm not sure, my Master," the first admitted. "A pair of hands, it seems. The other thief, I expect. She must have stolen a potion of invisibility – a very low quality one. It will wear off soon. Such potions only last a short time. It will be going nowhere."

"Question it carefully," the oily voice instructed. "The other knows about the Dragon Stone, but so far won't reveal where it is. Have you had any luck locating it?"

"No Master. It is possible that this creature took it and has it hidden somewhere. I cannot sense it. I will check between here and the east gate."

"We haven't much time, Saradoc," the Master warned.

"Yes, Master."

Maeven was aware of the foreigners moving away and thought frantically for a way out of the trap. Her talisman was very hot indeed but she did not need it to tell her she was in a very dangerous predicament. A sudden intuition made her touch the talisman to the wall of the shimmering cage. The shimmer went dark and she could put her arm through it. Removing the talisman brought the glow back.

It was awkward removing the talisman from around her neck in the close confines of the cage but she succeeded and placed it at the outer limit of the spells effect, with the leather thong out side. Now she could and did crawl out of the cage. She pulled her talisman free, and returned it to her neck. Then she muttered her invisibility chant again to reinforce its protection.

She took one last look at the shimmering dome as she stood and stretched before running back to where Nayfor had been. As she ran, she frantically searched all her pockets until she found the remaining phial of the invisibility potion. It was in the secret pocket of her breeches. A smile of malice silently transformed her face.

Nayfor, battered and bleeding, lay where she had last seen him. One of the bandits was dead nearby. Maeven squatted down by her master and felt that he was still breathing. She whispered quietly in his ear.Nayfor opened one eye but said nothing.

"Open your mouth slightly. I am going to pour some liquid in your mouth." Nayfor did as requested and swallowed the liquid. "Repeat after me …" Maeven instructed, and then slowly spoke the chant to activate the potion's effect. Nayfor disappeared except for his hands.

"Let me help you up," Maeven told him, relying on her sense of touch.

Nayfor helped as much as he could. Though he was determined, he could only walk as far as the nearest house where he chose a corner where he would not be casually stepped on. Maeven went back outside and picked up the two children who were still unconscious.

"If you hide them under your cloak, the spell will hide them too," Maeven told Nayfor.

"I told you to go!" Nayfor said hoarsely.

"They've sealed the gates with magic, as I found out the hard way," Maeven reported. "I tried the north gate – it seemed open, but though the horse got through, I didn't. The bastard of a wizard had me caged but I got out. I'm going to go over the wall. That potion should last until the sun is two or three hand spans lower."

Maeven recalled her mental map of the town again and went to a place where a tree grew close to the wall. Tree climbing wasn't new to her. Spoilt, indulged Princess Maeven would not be caught dead getting filthy climbing trees but she was good at hiding and one more servants' brat, climbing trees in the kitchen garden had never been noticed.

Using every bit of caution and stealth she had learned then and since, she scanned around her and ran. She clutched her talisman with one hand and whilst it stayed at body temperature, she knew that neither the wizard nor his master were near. After one last look around, she ran to the tree she sought, shimmied up its trunk and crawled to the overhanging branch. Edging carefully along the branch until she was beyond the wall, she swung down and dropped to the ground. She landed heavily and her feet hurt, but she began to run to the grove where her donkey and Nayfor's horse were. Sore was better than dead, anyday.

Maeven galloped the horse back down the road she had travelled that morning. She felt as if a demon was chasing her. She begrudged even the necessary stops to rest and water the horse or to attend to her own needs. Her mind was full of the urgency to get away and bring help for the captured townsfolk.

The invisibility had long since worn off, but she did not bother to renew it as she kept on riding through the night. Near morning she stopped again to allow the horse to rest but she began to feel like she was being watched and opted to keep moving if only with the horse walking. The slower pace lulled Maeven into a doze. The horse gradually slowed until it was barely moving one hoof after the other. Finally, it stopped as if it were asleep on its feet. Maeven's limbs relaxed their grip on the reins and she slowly fell off.

A man was relieving himself behind a tree when he saw the horse slowly approaching. He whistled a warning even as he adjusted his clothes. Six of his companions approached stealthily and observed the horse stop and the rider fall off. One of the six, an old woman, raised an arm and the group stopped. She alone went forward sensing that the horse and rider were bespelled. The woman whispered a counter spell and the rider groaned. The tired horse began to rear and kick.

"Calm, my friend," she crooned to the horse and it quietened at once.

The sorceress signalled the swordsmen forward. One took the horse and began to lead it back to the camp. Two more carried the rider. The other three scanned the surrounding area for possible dangers.

The healer examined the rider. "Exhaustion," was his conclusion. "Possibly some brain-jarring from the fall."

"We need to talk to him," Captain Wyst told the man. "Can you revive him?"

"Her, Captain," the healer corrected, even then seeking a small vial of smelling salts. The Captain summoned the sorceress and one of the swordswomen of his troop.

Maeven roused and pushed the foul smelling fumes away. With relief, she recognised that these people were from Thulor. The Captain questioned her urgently and Maeven told him all she knew, except of her talk with Merlie. She stressed the magical dangers and the sorceress questioned her about what she had experienced. The questions grew tiring, so Maeven reminded him of the plight of captive townsfolk.

"Warn Finora, Ermytrude," the Captain instructed. "The rest of you, prepare to ride. Now, Ven, you didn't answer my question. What was a young woman, dressed in men's clothing, doing in Thul Run after a bandit attack?"

"I was accompanying my Master," Maeven parried. "He had business there. It was not my place to ask about it."

"Your Master's name and Guild, woman!"

"My Master is Nayfor, and he is a jewel merchant," Maeven temporised.

A tall man had been standing back listening to the conversation; he now approached. "Captain Wyst, I will take charge of this woman!"

Wyst glanced from the man to the woman, his glance one of revulsion. He grabbed Maeven, opening her shirt and jerkin enough to reveal she had the thief's sigil. He made a sound of disgust, then muttered, "Stealing from the dead as like as not," as he pulled the clothing shut again.

"Her horse is beyond further travelling. Bring her with you, Barnabas. We may need her!"

From then on, the Captain totally ignored the woman, making it clear that he detested thieves. Maeven wanted to sleep but the jolting of the galloping horse made that impossible as she needed to maintain her grip on the man in front of her. He did not choose to ask questions and seemed quite used to the punishing pace.

It was well past dark when they reached the town and found the gates open. The scouts from the advance party of the troop were there, alert for trouble. Half the arriving group received directions to camp amongst the trees, the rest entered the town. Maeven was hardly aware of anything as she was half supported, half dragged by Barnabas, who was following Captain Wyst and one of the scouts to a house where they had found women survivors. Maven, forced her eyes to open further, recognised the house where Roberteuse had been tending Merlie, and once inside found a quiet corner and was asleep as soon as she lay down.

"Ven, wake up!" A rough hand was shaking her. Maeven came to instant wakefulness. It was just becoming light and she recognised Nayfor. "Come on."

"What's up?"

"The trackers are moving out. The swordsmen will be following shortly. They want you with them to identify the wizard and his Master. Have you still got the stone?"

"Yes."

"We can give it to Barnabas; he's the Grand Master of the Thieves Guild. He'll get it to the King."

Maeven reached into her pocket feeling for the stone, at the same time she was staring at the man who had shared his horse with her on the ride back. She was trying to recall when she had seen him before.

"Here," she handed the stone to Nayfor, glad to be rid of it. He passed it to Barnabas, who left without a word.

"Get moving," Nayfor reminded her and she went in search of the privy. As she left, Roberteuse saw her and caught her arm.

"Thank you. The swordsmen came just in time; those beasts were burning down the door. When they heard the bugles, they fled. You kept your word."

"They were coming anyway," Maeven admitted. "How's Merlie?"

Roberteuse shook her head. "He died, the night before last. He gave me something for you." She handed Maeven an ordinary-looking key, made of copper, with a hollow shaft, a bow grip at one end and notched bit melded to the other end. "He said you would know how to use it, because you were kin to him. He also said something strange, I'm not sure I remember it right. It sounded like… *'For life, for Thulor, for me.'* Does it make any sense to you?"

A long ago memory surfaced, it was a little jingle she used to sing as she skipped. She repeated it aloud. "Yes, it's a song I knew as a child. I didn't recall now who taught it to me. Thanks for passing this on, but I must get ready. We are going after the prisoners."

Roberteuse suddenly hugged Maeven and whispered, "The Gods will be with you." Then she released her and ran off.

The healer noticed Maeven joining the troop riding out, and caught up to her.

"Have you eaten?" he asked sharply. "You won't be much use if you haven't."

"Roberteuse doesn't have much," Maeven muttered, feeling her stomach contract at the mention of food. All she had on the flight away had been what was left in Nayfor's saddlebag and on the return, a begrudged share of the trail rations. The healer pressed a package into her hands and hurried off.

The main group of swordfighters caught up to the returning trackers who reported that they had found the brigands camp. Maeven had a shock when the two leaders of the raiding party came up to her. Not only was her amulet feeling very cold, but she recognised the two women. She kept her face neutral as they introduced themselves.

"Sergeant Leanne," the swords woman said. "Ride with us."

"Sorceress Finora," the other said. "I'll be cloaking our approach. You need to point out the Master and the wizard."

Maeven nodded, but did not offer her name. If her sisters did not recognise her, that was how she wanted it.

They surrounded the camp and none of the brigands were aware of the danger. The men were unconcernedly going about their morning business. A scout came up to Leanne and reported that six brigand sentries were dead. Maeven spotted the wizard, and she had the strangest feeling that he could sense her.

"Down near the fire, the one in red and orange – that is the wizard. His master is probably in that fancy tent. You won't miss him; he was wearing velvet and silk," Maeven said softly.

Finora began chanting, and Leanne gave the hand signal to move in.

"I'm gone!" Maeven said, turning her donkey to ride away.

Leanne swore softly and Maeven did not care what she thought. If there was going to be bloody work ahead, she knew she had no place in the middle of it.

Out of sight of the attackers, Maeven found a tree to tether her donkey to and spoke the chant for invisibility. While those skilled with weapons were fighting the brigands, those bastards wouldn't be watching the women and children. She might be able to sneak into the camp and bring them out.

She waited for the clash of steel on steel before moving, and then she sidled around the edge of the camp.

Maeven heard sobbing from many of the tents but did not investigate, these sounded like grown women, and they were obviously still okay enough to make such noise. Her first aim was the children and they had to be further into the camp.

A simple holding pen had been constructed near the centre of the camp. The young prisoners were sitting huddled closely within its bounds. She counted twenty or thirty children; all were staring into the distance – too quiet, too calm for it to be a natural state.

Anger burned within her as she approached the pen and climbed in. She could cover two at a time with her hooded robe, but first she needed to wake them so they could help themselves. A gentle shake had the desired effect and the older children quickly accepted the disembodied voice that told them what to do. "Not a sound, we have to avoid the fighting."

The eldest children were about thirteen or fourteen and Maeven took two of these first. Moments later, a ripple of a whisper passed through the group as the first two departed.

She alternated older and younger children so that small groups could keep moving away with the adolescents taking care of the littlest. These younger children could see her.

Maeven did not know if she would have time to take all the children but she had to try. She could take four of the youngest at a time, because they could not walk as fast, and she could carry two. To the small ones this was a game, the older ones knew better.

When they were away from the camp, Maeven told them, "Keep walking. You will come to some of the Kings Swordsmen, in dark blue. They will help you."

The numbers in the pen had dropped by half when the sounds of attack changed and half a dozen brigands ran towards the pen.

"Serpent spare us, half of the little whoresons are missing!" one of the men shouted.

Regardless, each of these brigands grabbed two children who immediately began to kick and bite. Maeven found her knife in her hand and she slashed the legs of the nearest bandit –he collapsed screaming and his two captives ran back to the pen. A second suffered the same fate and two more children raced free. The four remaining brigands had their swords drawn and were still managing to hold two children each. Maeven followed one of those four and dived under his randomly swinging sword and stabbed him in the back. He bellowed and swung around but Maeven had dived low and the children were racing away. Two of the remaining men suddenly froze and the last dumped his burden and ran toward the slender figure of the sorceress. She was calmly switching her spell to the charging brigand. He stopped within inches of her and a blast of energy killed him.

Maeven went to one of the frozen men and pried the children free. They had caught some of the spell and had to be carried. The sorceress was doing the same for the other two and calmly followed the child-sized legs floating in mid air.

The time for stealth was over, Finora directed the older children to take one or two others and run for it. There was no need to tell them to hurry. All the remaining children were following Finora who was, in turn, following the dangling legs.

When a group of Swordswomen peeled off from the fighting to protect the children, Maeven slipped away. Finora was already racing back to the encampment and Maeven felt a similar need and raced after her.

Leanne was fighting with the brigand leader and Maeven did not dare go anywhere near them, but the wizard was watching, ready to act if the woman got too good. Finora was preparing a spell, but the wizard felt it building and aimed a blast of fire at her. The spell was disrupted but she began again.

Maeven decided to provide a distraction. She approached while his attention was on her sister and suddenly spoke from behind him. "Slime worm, son of the midden."

He spun around but Maeven darted behind him and continued to taunt him. He caught sight of her floating hands and growled something vile in his own language. He suddenly recalled that the real danger was not from the invisiblt thief, and began to prepare another blast for the sorceress, but it was too late. Finora had already cast her paralysis spell and he fell helpless.

The second magician was a surprise. Finora must have felt the magic because she was looking around. Maeven, however, could see a woman moving her hands as her sister had done.

"The woman, by the fire, in yellow!" she yelled to her sister.

The style of the magic was more of the level of witch, than sorceress, and Finora spotted the wielder and sent a blast of fire in her direction. Leanne, the target of the witch's spell, ducked suddenly, avoiding its effect. The leader caught the blast instead. He turned rigid mid sword swing.

A wave of such hatred emanated from the witch that Maeven realised this was no witch at all and that the woman form was actually a disguise for something much worse.

"Oh no!" Maeven said involuntarily. She was sure that this was a demon in human form and it had recognised her and was coming after her. Terrified, her only thought was to keep away from people and run and run and run. The witch reverted to demon form, and began to fly after the invisible presence it sensed.

Finora drew from her pocket a silver sphere, something she had carried with her for the past month. She activated the attraction spell and fed more and more power to it. The demon slowed and began to move backwards. Moments later, it hovered above the sphere, became like a cloud of gas and was sucked into the half sphere. Finora snapped the sphere shut and placed a locking spell on it.

The fight went out of the brigands and those that were still alive, surrendered. The swordsmen and women collected their own dead, relatively few, and gathered the dead brigands in a heap to be burnt.

The captured women were liberated, but all were in shock from their treatment since capture. None had escaped being raped and many had been beaten as well. They did however gloat at the fate of their ravishers. Those that could not walk far were allowed to ride the brigand's horses and the swordsmen and women willingly gave rides to the children that they overtook. A small contingent remained at the camp to guard the area until the food and stolen chattels could be carted back to the town. The prisoners were tied together with rope and forced to walk, but the Leader and the wizard were tied both physically and magically, and then strapped over the saddle of two of the horses.

None of the victorious swordsmen were particularly concerned by the curled up, shivering wretch of a thief that they saw cowering a short distance off the road .They all assumed that the creature was a cowardly specimen that had run at the sight of battle. Their crude taunts drove her further from the road.

In fact, only Leanne and Finora would have cared if they saw her, for Finora had come to conclude that the thief had been the one helping the children. None of her guild colleagues had admitted to the act. Leanne believed her sister, but by the time they left the encampment the girl was not in sight.

Nayfor watched for Maeven amongst the returning procession. He had orders from the Grand Master to bring her to him when she had finished here.

Barnabas was impressed by her, was going to do something unprecedented – promote her from apprentice to Master without enforcing a journeyman period. Nayfor had reservations – the girl was young, headstrong and trouble seemed to find her; not to mention the fact that she was using magic – though so far only when she was not actually thieving. Barnabas had not listened to him.

Nayfor finally asked the swordswoman Leanne where the girl was. Her sharp questioning of the troop elicited the information that the thief had been cowering off the road.

Nayfor swore at the Sergeant. "Bitch, Ven is only sixteen! She only had a knife for protection – how much do you expect of her?"

Leanne's expression suggested that he had been corrupting an innocent child.

"Never mind! I'll find her myself." Nayfor stalked off in search of a mount that he could borrow. He was angry at the swordsmen and at his own injuries that had kept him from joining in the raid.It was too bad if his wounds reopened. He was responsible for Ven until she ceased being an apprentice – but if the Grand Master carried out his plan, it would not be for much longer.

When Nayfor found Maeven, she was trudging along the road, traces of tears on her stubbornly-set face.

"So there you are," he stated when she came up to him, but she didn't greet him back. She just walked on, remaining stubbornly silent.

He matched her stride and said, "Tell me about the raid."

"Dragon spit on you! Dragons spit on everyone!"

"I have headrd some of it. I need your view."

Obediently, she reported, but tersely and without mentioning what she had done. From her related observations, Nayfor deduced that she had been in the camp, and not hiding down the track the entire time. He also assumed that she had been using more of the invisibility potion and did not wish him to know. The stuff had saved his life, and he was grateful to her for that, but he sensed that she would use it whenever it suited her.

However, there had to be more to her silence.

Maeven was silent because she did not want to think. Total humiliation summarised her state of mind. It was bad enough that the demon had scared her witless and she had fled – though at least that had been obeying her training, to run and hide from danger.

No, it was that red haired creature she'd encounted along the road; the one she had thought was a woman. It had a soft voice; it looked beaten and ill-treated. She had come out of her own depression to help her. They had walked down to the river and Maeven had offered to tend the woman's wounds with a wash in the river. Then that woman had done something to her.

Maeven found that her conscious will had deserted her and the woman had proved to be an illusion hiding a man. He had completely undressed, and then undressed her. Then he had played with her, rousing feelings that she had never experienced before. She had been unable to do anything, not scream, not beg, not move and not escape his penetration…

All this she could not tell Nayfor, though. She was too ashamed.

They continued on.

They passed through Thul Run on their return, stopping long enough to barter for some food, steal two of the horses liberated from the brigands and fill their water skins.

Nayfor stayed away from the leaders of the swords folk, but managed to overhear a great deal of interesting information. The King was sending a garrison of his Guard up here. They were expected in a hand span of days. It was also being said, in voices of great awe, that the Sorceress Finora, rumoured to be Princess Finora, had captured a demon. There was also talk that the women and children of Thul Run were to be weapons trained to help defend the town in future. All things considered, it would not be a safe town for a thief.

Maeven continued to travel in silence, which suited Nayfor very well. She did what he instructed without delay or comment, which suited him even better.

The flashbacks of what happened kept returning to her.

"My, you were not hard to catch at all!" the man had laughed. "I don't know why my brother had so much trouble. But you are my property now, I own you! You will remember the pleasure I gave you. You will remember wanting to beg for more. You will want me to do this again and again. But anyone else who does this to you will die!"

Then the last of the illusion had vanished and the man could have been the brigand leader's twin, except, that this one was blonde. He had the same type of little pointed beard and the same thin moustache. When he had redressed, his clothes too had lost the illusion of tattered rags and were the equal of any court noble, black, but in that same foereign style as the brigand leader.

He was still laughing when he said, "I must thank you for helping your countrymen to catch my brother and his wizard. I do hope your father hangs them both." He had the same sort of greasy unctuous voice. "It will mean that, in my country, I have so much more power than before."

A long time later, she was still unable to move. One of the lesser brigands, a deserter not a fighter, found her lying naked in the grass. He had used her more roughly, leering all the time, but when he finished he walked five steps and fell down dead.

As soon as the paralysis had worn off, she had redressed in her soiled clothes and begun walking and thinking. Any vague notion she had ever had about returning to the Palace had evaporated. The notion of finding a distant, isolated life grew. She would continue to amass wealth and she would disappear into a distant kingdom where no one would recognise her as a Princess of Thulor.

A disgraced Princess of Thulor!

And the creature had taken her talisman.

CHAPTER 13 – THE CHILD

"Ven! Ven!" the boy from the next shack called quietly.

"What is it Gervain?" Maeven asked politely, straightening up from weeding the vegetable garden.

"The Elders have called a meeting. It's urgent. Everyone must come."

Maeven felt a flicker of alarm, dropped her hoe and began to follow the boy. They walked down the narrow track to what served as a meeting place; a cleared area of the main track near the shack of the oldest resident. The hamlet was almost so tiny that you could blink and miss it. Only this one place was on the main track. The other dozen were reached via goat tracks and were well hidden against the foot of the mountain. Even the vegetables grew in whatever scanty patches of soil existed amongst the rocks and under the trees. The main track was only wide enough for one horse or two skinny goats.

"Everybody be quiet and listen to Phineas!" The speaker was old Adelbart, eldest of the Elders, and even though his voice came out as a wheeze, all conversation ceased.

Phineas was a tall gaunt man who collected wood for the community. He was sweating as if he had been running. "There is an encampment of bandits two hours walk from here. They are setting up near the lip, up yonder."

The women looked scared, the men stunned. Almost every eye glanced up at the scar on the mountain from an ancient landslide. It dominated the skyline.

Maeven remained silent, waiting for someone from the conclave to speak first. She was, after all, the most recent addition to the community, had only been there three months, was only seventeen years old and was five months pregnant.

When the men began to discuss the news, Maeven realised that they were so used to their isolation that they could not conceive of anyone finding them. She'd had enough of bandits and wanted to run and hide.

"I realise that I am new here," Maeven found herself saying politely. "May I speak?"

Everyone looked at her with surprise. They were not stupid folk, just insular.

"You cannot assume they won't find you!" she told them carefully. "After all, I found you. If you were to think of the place Elder Phineas spoke of, there is only one track and if the bandits keep coming they will have to pass here."

Forty faces simply stared at her.

"They haven't come all this way with winter coming on to stay up there! I do not think they are simply going to turn around and go home! If they plan to stay a while, they will eventually find at least one of our homes. They will decide that a shack is better than a tent. To them, we will simply be plunder."

"The girl is right!" Phineas agreed, giving her an approving look.

"What should we do?" a woman called Bertha wailed.

Maeven treated her to a look of disgust.

"You have some ideas to propose," Phineas invited.

"I think Elder Adelbart and his wife should move themselves and their valuables to a safer place. They are the most vulnerable. All of us should take as much of our produce and firewood as we can to the big cave you told me of. If the worst happens, we can all retreat there and hold them off. I know you don't have much in the way of weapons – we can hardly fight them."

"Yes," the old man, Adelbart, wheezed. "The cave is big; it has running water and several ways out. We had best take bedding there as well – and the animals, just in case. We can all pray that they don't find us."

Maeven tolerated the compulsory prayer session, even though she did not believe in such nonsense. After all, these people had agreed to let her join them and had not asked too many questions.

Maeven walked back with Ignetha and Samuel, Gervain's parents, as far as their hut then continued alone.

"Do you need any help?" Gervain called after her.

"Help your folks Gervain, I really don't have much. Thank you for the offer."

Maeven's shack was little better than it had been when she took it over. It had basic furniture such as table, two chairs and bed box. She had made several trips into the trade town with Phineas, two days' travel each way. She now had several rugs, more blankets and the things she would be need when the child she was bearing decided to be born. Her cache of jewels and coins was well hidden in a tiny cave below a rock behind her shack and no brainless bandit would find it. Even one with intelligence would need to know where to look. Her cow was with Gosse's bull, so that come spring she would have a calf and fresh milk. Her donkey, Burro, was tied up behind her shack. The vegetables in her garden were not mature enough to harvest yet so she would have to hope they weren't found.

Inside the shack, she took all of her clay crockery and utensils, except a few, and put them in a corner cupboard. She muttered a brief incantation and the cupboard took on the look of being empty. What else?

The cradle and the swaddling stuff for the baby would not be needed until spring. She bundled the cloths into the wooden cradle and pushed it into an awkward corner of the shack. It was a hollowed niche dug into the mountain itself. Again the disguising chant made the hole look empty. She rolled up the rug covering the rough wood floor and hid it along the wall.

Maeven had very little left to do. She packed her few utensils, plates and all her clothes into Burro's saddlebags, then tied two blankets and her flock stuffed mattress to his back. Then she walked back to her neighbours who had offered to show her the way to the cave. Although not told officially, she knew exactly where the cave was and it had not taken long to find it once she had heard about it. However, she was not about to reveal her extra skills – she knew what they thought of thieves, and it was no better than what they thought of the Royal Family.

The morning was not far off, Maeven pretended to be asleep on her mattress and had the blankets pulled up over her head so no one would know otherwise. The villagers had worked all night to move their valuables, food and essentials into the cave. To her annoyance, she had been put in charge of the youngest children after she had dumped her meagre possessions. Now the men were taking turns at guarding the entrances and everyone else was trying to catch up on sleep. At least the little brats were back with their parents again.

The women would, without doubt, be rising when the sun did. Equally certain, they would comment if she did not! Maeven groaned silently and was glad she did not have a man to answer to. Living by herself meant that she could do as she pleased, rise when she wanted to and organise her own life. The noble pious men of the hamlet believed in hard work from dawn to dusk. They expected their wives to work just as hard and were not averse to enforcing penance when they did not. So far, they had not been too harsh with the poor, young, pregnant girl.

Maeven ground her teeth just thinking about it. Their idea of penance for her unseemly behaviour had been to parade her in front of everybody, tell them all her 'faults' and ask everyone to pray for her and help her learn better.

As if she had wanted to be pregnant in the first place. Grrrr! Generally, however, they were good people.

The older boys like Gervain, who were not quite adult, went out to hide and watch the town. A boring job but they all swaggered like men. Maeven wished she could join them. Being with the staid, straight-laced and regimented group of women was tolerable only in small doses.

About noon on the second day, Gervain returned to say that Elder Adelbart's shack had been found and the six bandits had split up to search further.

The following day, the entire bandit rabble of forty or more rough-looking men had taken over the twelve shacks. It looked like they were settling in for the winter.

A further discussion of tactics ensued but Maeven simply listened to the 'we're safe here until they go away' sentiments with concealed disgust. Alternative solutions occurred to her, but these people would not fight and generally had a strict code of behaviour. They had looked at her with narrowed eyes when her condition had become obvious – as if it had been her own fault. At least they had agreed to hide and not simply wait like sheep to be slaughtered.

Four days passed and Maeven was about to explode with annoyance. Something needed to be done to make the bandits move on so that she could go back to her own place. Just before dark, she slipped out of the cave into the fresh air, claiming nausea. The guard watched her walk into the trees and in a blink, she was gone. Two of the boys, Gervain and his friend Tobi, offered to guard her.

Maeven moved stealthily amongst the trees in the direction of her shack. From a safe distance away, she watched some of the bandits cooking a meal on a fire outside. They were already well on the way to being drunk. She knew, however, that the good folk of the hamlet abstained from alcoholic and brewed drinks. The spirit must have come with the bandits and at the rate they were consuming it would not last long.

Gervain and Tobi crept up to Maeven, making only the slightest of sounds. It was enough, however, to warn her of their approach. She quickly chanted her invisibility charm.

The boys stopped and wondered where she had gone – then from behind them she hissed softly, "Go back."

In the moonlight, both boys could be seen to jump.

"What are you going to do?" Gervain asked, sharing her desire to do something.

"I was wondering if I could divert the stream," Maeven lied. "So it will all flow through the cave and not out here."

The boys liked the idea and offered to explore, going off quietly. They glanced back once but again could not see Maeven.

Near morning, Maeven returned to the big cave carrying a load of weapons. Tobi and Gervain followed her with more, both wearing huge grins at her strategy. The smiles faded into blankness in the face of their fathers' implacable stares. Maeven put her load down, took the bundle from each of the boys and thanked them for their help.

Samuel stood beside Phineas, dark beards almost identically trimmed, and both twitching with controlled rage.

"Why are you bringing weapons here, woman!" Phineas demanded.

"If you intend to argue out here," Maeven stared back at them, "the bandits will find us. I will explain inside."

She maintained her glare until they backed down and allowed her to enter.

"Well, explain the meaning of this!" Phineas repeated.

Maeven marshalled memories of her father in his most diplomatic form.

"I appreciate your unwillingness to use weapons against other people," she began, looking directly at Phineas. He was acting as unofficial leader, as Elder Adelbart was currently too weak to leave his bed. "I am not implying you should use them to kill. You can turn them into plough blades for all I care. What I intended is that they will not be used against us. Without their weapons, the brigands are cowards; they feel undressed. You could approach them now on terms that are more equitable. They may even feel compelled to move on."

"What if they seek out the thief who stole from them? What if they keep looking until they find us?" Samuel growled.

"Let them!" Maeven said flatly. "In a fair fight, I have no doubt who would win!"

"We will have nothing to do with weapons," Samuel said with distaste.

"Fine – I'll take them down to the trade town and sell them! It's no more than those cowards would do with any goods we left in our homes."

"Do you have no shame, woman!" Phineas almost shouted. By now, most of the townsfolk were listening.

Spare me from thick-headed zealots, Maeven thought to herself as the child within her began to kick hard. "I would be ashamed if I let those bastards keep their weapons and go onto the next town and kill every man, woman and innocent child in their sleep," she said. Even the men flinched at her words. "Or let them keep the women alive to amuse themselves, raping them over and over again! Even boys… I have seen what men like those do."

The men were shocked speechless, hearing this from a mere girl.

Welcome to the real world, Maeven thought.

Elder Adelbart had forced himself from his bed to push his way through to talk to Maeven. "It is not our way to steal from our fellow humans," he said gently, as if rebuking a little child. "You will have to recompense them or return their belongings."

I am not hearing this, Maeven thought; then said, "No!"

"It is our way."

"Your way smells like week old garbage!" Maeven said rudely. "I cannot believe what you're saying. You are a group of the most peace-loving people I have ever encountered. That is why I came here. Yet now you are telling me to return weapons to people who would cheerfully kill you all, or to give them means to buy more. No!"

"I do not like to think of you as a thief, child," he said gently, as if he were afraid for her.

"I know what I am, Elder Adelbart," Maeven told him, not backing down. "If your Gods are going to punish me for this, I'll let them. You should ask – who is going to recompense you for the damage they are doing to your homes, for the destruction of things you have all lovingly made with your hands and for the wanton trampling of your wives' gardens. Why don't you men go down tonight and see for yourselves the type of men they are. I doubt that any of them have ever done an honest days work in their lives. Then come back and tell me that I did the wrong thing – stealing their weapons and perhaps forcing them to work to earn money for more. In fact, if you can convince them to do honest labour, I'll give you all the money I have on me to pay them."

Maeven fumbled with a pouch of coins at her waist, money she had stolen from the brigands along with their swords. She threw it down on the ground.

"And don't try to punish Tobi or Gervain – they simply offered to help a pregnant woman carry a heavy load!"

Maeven turned and walked through the crowd of stunned listeners to go to her bed. She lay down fully dressed, hid herself under her blankets and totally ignored any attempts at conversation or the food left for her to eat.

The women were impressed by her convictions, though they bordered on and even crossed the line into heresy. They were concerned for her unborn child if she neglected herself. Little did they know how hard she had wished to be rid of it. Finally, she slept.

It was late, very late. The children had been in bed for hours when the men returned. The women had stayed awake to hear the results of the men's' vigil watching the bandits.

The murmur of male voices was audible, but Maeven did not try to listen. She had said all she intended to say and from now on, they could make all their own decisions. Her resolution was tested when the woman approached, speaking in horrified and appalled tones.

Maeven rolled over in the dark corner and saw two female strangers being tended by the women. There was a girl no older than herself and an old one, possibly her mother. She rolled back and returned to sleep.

Heartbreaking sobs roused Maeven and she knew they were coming from the rescued girl. The cave was dark, the fire only a glow, but Maeven could see clearly enough to walk softly around sleeping people. She sat down next to the sobbing girl and held her gently. It was some time before the girl expressed her fear that her mother was dead. Maeven placed a hand on the woman, felt the cold skin, and moved it to sense any breath. She gave the girl a firmer hug, allowed the tears to continue, and tried not to recall the intense memory of the loss of her own mother.

The men had spent most of the night in a discussion that bordered on argument, and then gone out again, well before dawn. Nearby, one of the younger wives whispered in horrified tones that they were going to make sure these bandits did not continue with their evil ways. The other wives began their own discussion, afraid for their mates, but in agreement that the bandits were bad men. Maeven overhearing this, hoped the villagers fared well, and went back to sleep thinking, *it took them long enough to see sense or did their god get it into their think heads that it was okay to protect their mates.*

In the morning, the women were praising their mates for it seemed that the entire bandit rabble were now prisoners, bound and tied , in one of the caves that had only one entrance.

After breakfast, and some local ritual for random selection, Zeke was selected to ride to the trade town, two days away to report the bandits' presence.

Two days later, he returned with a contingent of the King's Own Guards. Maeven heard the horses trotting up the hill, and kept out of sight, but within earshot. She felt a chill when she heard the voice of the Guard leader and kept well into the main cave. She did not want to be seen by her brother, Prince Rhovert.

During his short stay, Rhovert spoke seriously to the men. In spite of their opinions of the King, they listened to him. Rhovert always did have a way with the commoners.

"The kingdom is grateful for your capture of these rogues," he said approvingly. "We have been looking for this group for some months. There have been whole villages overcome by some form of pestilence. The few survivors all recall a band of scruffians passing through in the days prior to the outbreak. There is enough evidence in the saddlebags of their horses to ensure they are hanged for their deeds. Their mounts we will leave with you in return for your service to Thulor."

The men of the village looked pleased with the outcome. Seems they were not averse to receiving gifts from an official source.

Later, when the Guards had left with the prisoners and the confiscated weapons, Maeven breathed a sigh of relief. She had half feared that they would also want to hand over the thief that had stolen the weapons.

If in the next few months the men preferred to pretend that Maeven did not exist, their wives did not. She had proved her worth, thief or not, and the rapidly recovering Reyna, who had asked to stay in the village, had moved in with her.

As winter set in and life returned to normal, Maeven began to appreciate the other girl's help, company and staunch support.

Maeven was finding it increasingly difficult to find a comfortable position for sleeping. Often she was awake for long periods. This night she was carefully enlarging the waist of a pair of trousers, yet again, to fit over her increasingly large stomach. The other women could not understand her preference for men's clothes but had long since stopped commenting. Perhaps the necessity for wearing the long loose over tunic over the trousers made them happier. Maeven decided she would be relieved to be able to wear her own clothes again.

The sensation of being watched caused her to look up from her sewing. Reyna was asleep across the room, and Maeven would have known if anyone else had entered the shack. It reminded her of a past occasion…

Something flashed past her, a silhouette against the fire's glow. Maeven felt the hairs on her head rise as her head itched. She reached and grabbed, snatching the something as it circled back. Her hand began to burn.

Reyna awoke with a start as the creature, a tiny demonic thing, squealed a high-pitched shrill scream.

"Build the fire up, Reyna," Maeven requested, expecting obedience.

As the glow increased, the creature became more visible. Reyna bit off a cry of alarm.

"What sent you?" Maeven said, staring into the creature's tiny eyes. It squirmed and tried to look away.

"My master," it cried.

"What were you to do to me?" Maeven continued, maintaining eye contact.

"Look! Master said look!" it squealed.

"Look for what?"

"Look only!" it whined. "You aren't what I must look for. You don't sense the same…"

Maeven wanted rid of the creature. "I have caught you. I will kill you!"

"No, mistress, no, please don't kill me. If you let me live, three things I will grant you!"

Maeven thought quickly. "When you leave here, you will tell all of your kind never to come looking for me again, not here, not anywhere," she said carefully.

It nodded. "It will be done, mistress."

"Secondly, you can heal my hand!" She was not sure if it was possible or not.

"Release me and I will obey!" it promised.

"Thirdly – I will retain my third thing until a time of my choosing!"

The creature looked uncomfortable, but nodded.

Maeven released it and it seemed to suck the heat from her flesh before it vanished. She felt shudders racking her body. That had been close, too close.

"Is it… gone?" Reyna asked timidly, starting to crawl across to her friend, but there was no answer. She pulled a blanket with her and simply wrapped it around them both, until the silent weeping stopped.

"What was that?" Reyna asked again.

"A warning," Maeven said very softly. "I can't stay here much longer."

"Won't you tell me what it is about?" Reyna pleaded.

"Someone or something wants me dead," Maeven said after a while. "I don't understand why, but I won't stay here, I won't endanger everyone here. They've been so good to me!"

"Even if the men won't admit you exist?" Reyna said disdainfully.

"They haven't kicked me out!" Maeven defended them.

"Only because they think their God or Gods will punish them if they did!" Reyna retorted, seeing a faint smile come to her friend's face. "And you are good at manipulating their beliefs."

"I've studied manipulation under a master," Maeven said wryly. "I've got to think."

Reyna went to Elder Adelbart the following day and asked for two pieces of parchment and a writing stick. When he heard who required it, he refused the request. Somehow, she knew Maeven would not be surprised.

Her second errand was to ask Lorinda and her husband Zeke to visit. The woman was sufficiently curious to force her husband to come.

Lorinda accepted the second chair at the wooden table. She was extremely curious as to what Maeven was writing on the square piece of linen sheeting. Neither she nor her husband could read or write, and it amazed her that the younger woman could.

"I have a request to ask of you both," Maeven began, speaking to Lorinda because Zeke was staring elsewhere in the room. "I want to ask you to be foster parents to my child."

Lorinda's eyes lit up and her husband's head swivelled around to look at Maeven.

"You will need to discuss it. I am not relinquishing my rights in the child. However, I will not be in a position to raise him or her for some time – maybe several years or more…"

"A thief is hardly a fit person to raise a …" Zeke preached.

"… I will have to recover the child at some future time. I am telling you this now so that you can consider that point, too. If you feel that you will not be able to give the child back, you must say so now and I will have to take the child with me when I go."

"Why are you asking me, Ven?" Lorinda asked, the yearning clearly in her voice.

"Because you and your husband are good people and you would love my child as if it were your own," Maeven told her truthfully. "Go home and talk it over, let me know your decision."

The bemused couple left and Maeven began writing a second copy of her letter.

"I would have minded your child," Reyna said, sounding hurt.

"I know, but, if you are staying here, those parochial Elders would never let you raise it. I am hoping you will be my eyes and ears – a secret guardian – an honorary Aunt. In other words, you can be my insurance that my intentions won't be twisted in my absence."

Reyna straightened up and smiled.

"Let me finish what I am writing. I am stating the terms of the arrangement that I will have with those two. We will each sign both copies. I will have to read it to them or they can bring someone who knows how to read. I'll write something else for you to keep."

After a time, Maeven put down the writing stick. It was a relief; her back was aching with the strain.

"Reyna, when my child is born, I am going to give you a letter to keep safe. It will need to be signed by both of us. It will state that you witnessed the birth of the child and a description of it. I will also include an outline of the arrangements that I have made for its care. If you hear that something has happened to me, or if I stop providing them with means to care for the child, then you must take the letter to the Guards as it will need to go to the King or to Prince Rhovert. They will notify my family, who will be constrained to take over providing for it. Perhaps Lorinda will be able to adopt him or her, though probably not."

A little over two weeks later, Maeven felt the onset of labour. Reyna offered to call the village midwife, but was instead begged to stay.

"You tell even one of those hens, and the whole lot will want to be in here offering their own advice. Who is having this child? Me. I will do it my way, and you are all the help I need."

"I haven't even seen a baby born before," Reyna protested.

"Women have babies all the time, over and over again. How hard can it be?"

"Some of them scream a lot," Reyna offered.

"I don't have a husband to impress, and make feel guilty for putting us through this." Maeven grimaced as a strong contraction rippled across her abdomen. "Besides, I have the feeling that this baby wants out, and isn't going to wait for you to go and rouse Dame Adelbart."

"I guess I should get some water boiling and the baby things ready," Reyna decided. "And build up the fire. Its gong to get very cold tonight."

"Another reason to let the hens sleep. I will never hear the end of it if thay have to come out in a freeze."

Near dawn, the little baby boy finally drew his first independent breath, and gave a lusty cry. Reyna took him to the half barrel that was serving as a bath, and quickly cleaned him and swaddled him. Maeven tried to rise and help, but felt the last contractions, finishing the birth process.

It was full day when Reyna left to herald the news of the village's newest inhabitant. By then, Maeven had cleaned herself and her bedding up, fed her child, and had him sleeping peacefully in his wooden crib. She was going to have to feed him herself for a while, at least until her cow calved, or Lorinda's did. It meant staying longer, and she hoped that whoever sent the little demon, would not try to send anything else looking for her.

Those two months were so precious, and more than enough time for Maeven to regret needing to leave him. She had named him Wystan. He had a crown-shaped birthmark on his leg just like hers, though she had said it looked like part of a cartwheel and everyone now believed that. He was a very strong infant and at the same time very undemanding when he wasn't hungry or wet. For the past two weeks, Lorinda had helped her care for him, and he was coming to know her, but was two months long enough for little Wystan to remember her? Did it matter if he didn't?

It did… deep down.

The child slept peacefully near the fire. Maeven looked at him, memorising his tiny features, trying to convince herself that he looked more like her brother than the bastard who sired him. Tomorrow, Lorinda and Zeke would be taking him. Their cow had calved a week ago and they now had a ready supply of milk for the infant. Until now, there had been no option except for her to feed him herself, since there was no one else in the isolated hamlet with that young a child and no wet nurse was available.

It was still very dark when Maeven left her son with Reyna. In the morning, the girl would pretend she had not heard Ven leave. Everything was ready for Lorinda and Zeke, including a pouch of coins and all the baby's things. Reyna had hidden her letter in a safe place and Ven had taken a copy of the agreement.

Maeven promised Reyna she'd keep in touch, then walked out into the night carrying a small amount of food, a few eating utensils and her spare clothes, rolled up in a blanket. The donkey and the rest of the things in the shack remained for Reyna to use.

Maeven spent a few moments considering her cache of coins and jewels and decided to leave most of it hidden where it was. She would not need it all, and she could collect it when she came back this way.

CHAPTER 14 – THE RETURN

Maeven stopped by the narrow stream. Crouching down, she used her mug to collect some water to drink. As the ripples smoothed again she saw her reflection in the water. The face that stared back at her might as well have been a stranger, though there was still some resemblance to her vivid memory of her mother.

The rumble in her stomach banished the inner reflections. What little food she had taken with her when leaving the high hamlet had been finished the previous day. There would be no more until she reached the trade town.

Maeven straightened up, settled her pack on her shoulder and strode through the tall trees. Even though it was late afternoon, a thick mist was shrouding everything and reducing visibility to about ten strides. The sound of horses was becoming louder so she moved deeper into the trees. With the trail just visible, she watched from cover as the firewood laden beasts plodded past. The rider of the lead horse had the unmistakable profile of Phineas the woodcutter.

As the procession went by, Maeven moved deeper off the track and began to smell wood smoke and the odours of cooking. Hunger urged her to keep moving forward to locate the source of the aroma.

She continued until the sound of a sword being drawn made her spin around. The woman she now faced had actually sheathed the sword. She was short and solid with thick dark hair, trimmed to her shoulders.

"You don't look dangerous," the swordswoman commented.

"I'm not!" Maeven replied without thinking. "I didn't even hear you coming!"

"You weren't meant to! As it was, I only spotted you by chance. I was seeing what the horses were."

Maeven grinned at the swordswoman.

"Why were you hiding from the woodman? Is he dangerous?"

"No, not really. I just didn't want to be seen." Maeven answered.

"So who are you?" the woman asked.

"Ven."

"I'm Atlantis. This is my camp but you are welcome to stay a while."

She led her guest over near the tiny fire where a small pot was simmering.

"This is an odd place for a woman travelling on her own," Atlantis commented as she sat back on the ground near the fire.

"I'm on my way back north. I have matters to see to, personal stuff," Maeven parried, settling onto a fallen trunk close by. "And you?"

Atlantis accepted her answer and did not try to probe further. "I'm heading that way too, sort of. I am actually looking for a place my Great Grand Sire wrote about. I think I am in the right general area but it's not always easy to solve his riddles. You haven't seen any dragons around here have you?"

Maeven looked at her with amusement.

"Dragons? No, I haven't seen any of those. Do they still exist?"

"Maybe, but not many," Atlantis said thoughtfully. "I killed one two years back. She had eggs but when I went back there, I could find no trace of any eggs or shells. It's the shells I want!"

"Atlantis, why do you want dragon shells?" Maeven was curious; the woman was not like anyone she knew.

"It's a long story!" she said.

"Just the important bits then," Maeven suggested, grinning.

"Well, the King, of Thulor that is not Declanor where I'm from, wants them. I think they have healing properties."

"Oh!" was all Maeven could think of to say. Her mind was full of so many questions, most of which Atlantis would not be able to answer. Other questions were decidedly not complimentary. She tried a casual sounding, "You know the King – quite well?"

"I met him a few times when I was staying with my brother," Atlantis claimed. "Roman managed to get himself appointed Court Wizard or something, and he is staying in King Westron's palace."

"I've heard the King is quite a womaniser," Maeven said, keeping her eyes on the fire.

"The servants implied that, though I wasn't there long," Atlantis admitted quite readily. "When the King mentioned he wanted dragon shells, my brother volunteered my services. I think he'd had enough of me arguing with Gisella, his wife. I had certainly had enough of wearing dresses!"

Maeven chuckled; her liking for Atlantis had increased now she knew she had not been one of her father's women.

Atlantis was quite happy to prattle on until mealtime and never seemed to notice Maeven's near silence about herself. She waved aside Ven's concerns about having nothing to contribute to the meal.

"I can catch or find more," she claimed, unconcerned, and began sharing out the meagre meal evenly. "I've been in your place a time or two!"

Maeven sat in the dark by the fire and pulled her cloak and blanket more tightly about her while she waited for Atlantis to return. Between her own excellent night vision and the moonlight, she could see well enough.

Atlantis had been gone quite a while, hunting for food for their breakfast. Maeven had washed their plates and knives in the little trickle of a stream closeby, and had packed hers away in the rough bag with her spare clothes.

To pass the time she thought about her new friend and how different they were. The swordswoman was at home in these remote areas away from people. She actually liked it, preferred it and had learned to look after herself.

Maeven admitted she liked the environment of a town with houses and people. Out here, she felt exposed and vulnerable. Even the sounds of the night animals going about their own business unsettled her.

Atlantis returned with two hoppers and some roots. She was muttering under her breath. The words sounded like some truly awful bardic poetry.

"North of the kingdom of Declanor, Lies the grave of Exconidor. Look up high to the mountain tip; Find the cave before the slip."

"What are you muttering about?" Maeven asked.

"Great Grand Sire's riddle," she answered absently. "I haven't found any other mentions of dragons. There has to be a dragon's lair around here. Have a look at this." She put the rabbits and roots down near the fire and pulled a satchel from under a log further away. Opening it, Atlantis withdrew something wrapped in an oiled cloth. Surprisingly, it was leather bound book. Then Atlantis pulled a ball-like object from her pack and shook it.

She seemed to know exactly where in the book she wanted to look. "Here, look at that!" The ball gave out enough light and Maeven began to read. Atlantis went to start skinning the hoppers.

The script was small, neat and written in purple ink.

"North of…the mountain's lip… slip.

Take the Dragon's Eye with you, where the Guarda hides from view.

Take the tunnel to the west, go quietly through the Dragons nest.

The way is dark and full of dread, keep to the right or you'll be dead.

The prize is worth the hard travail, here lies the legend Frederick's mail.

The gifts he left at his Master's grave are only for the very brave.

If you seek the Serpents Bane - dive down deep and come up again."

There was a faded charcoal sketch showing a mountain skyline. It looked familiar. Atlantis became aware of Maeven's stillness.

"What's wrong?" she asked with concern.

"I think I know where you have to look," Maeven said tonelessly. "You can't see it from down here, but the lip and the slide are visible from that woodcutter's hamlet."

"I wonder if the people there know something," Atlantis sounded excited. "Can you take me there tomorrow?"

Maeven turned pale. "I can take you to the lip, but I won't go to the hamlet. I don't think they will like a swordswoman and, well… they don't like me!"

The morning found them up with the birds, packed and following the track uphill. Late in the afternoon, the woodcutter returned with his string of horses. With plenty of warning of his approach, the women agreed to stay out of sight off the track. They neared the hamlet at dusk two days later and ate a cold snack while waiting.

Maeven insisted on moving past the hamlet after dark and impressed Atlantis with her night vision. It was obvious that she knew the area well.

"I assume that you know somewhere we can stop for the night?" Atlantis whispered

"Yeah."

Ven gave a little laugh when she stopped and showed Atlantis the shallow cave and fire ring.

In the morning, Atlantis was even more impressed by her guide. The lip of the mountain was so close it was breathtaking. The slide, a very old land slippage, was an area of low stumpy trees and bushes. From the top, you could see as far away as Declanor.

The cave entrance was not so easy to find. They scanned the mountain with their eyes and could see no break in the rock. Finally, when the sun rose a bit higher, a long thin shadow appeared at the top of the slide.

"So you never saw dragons when you were living here?" Atlantis mused aloud.

"I never said I…" Maeven began to deny the statement. "No, never a dragon – I told you that."

"Not surprising, I suppose. All dragons have some magic. They could hide themselves," Atlantis continued, as if unaware that her friend had betrayed something of her past. "We'll leave our stuff just inside the cave."

Atlantis rummaged in her pack until she found two of the dull balls and threw one to Maeven. "These things are crudely made wizard balls. You shake them to make them glow. These aren't too bright but they are less fragile that the proper ones," she explained. She strapped her sword to her waist.

"I'll go first."

Maeven followed Atlantis, making no more than a whisper of sound. In the cavern, there was quite a lot of light as part of the cavern roof had collapsed. An opening in the west wall led into a dark passage, as expected, but another led northeast. This was looked at first, but it was a dead end, blocked by the landslip. The dark passage was wide enough for four people to walk comfortably abreast and twice the height of a tall man.

The spurt of flame was as unexpected as it was blinding. It revealed the cavern ahead before the darkness returned deeper than ever. Maeven saw the dragon, then a rumbling voice echoed in her head. *"That human is not welcome here!"*

The women retreated down the passage, away from the source of the flame.

"Well, that makes things awkward!" Atlantis commented, already considering alternatives. "I didn't expect to actually find a dragon here."

"You saw it?" Maeven asked, mostly for confirmation that she had.

"What else would it be? Fire doesn't come out of nowhere."

It didn't seem that Atlantis had actually heard the dragon speak, though.

"Let me sneak back," Maeven offered. The dragon had said nothing about herself being unwelcome.

In the light of the mage light, Atlantis bit her lip and considering. Her new friend betrayed no signs of doubt, so she nodded agreement.

Maeven gave Atlantis her light and walked back into the passage. She muttered the words of the invisibility charm, and began to crawl along the floor. Even in the pitch darkness, she could see a little. Even to herself it seemed funny to see her hands walking in front of her. One day she would find a better invisibility charm!

Crawling slowly around the edge of the big cavern, she began to be aware of something in front of her. In her glimpse of the cavern, the dragon had been on the other side. Looking up then, she saw two green eyes glistening above her. Two more, blue-green this time, joined the first, lower down and to one side.

"Why are you sneaking around like a thief, dragon child?" The mental voice was curious, not hostile like before.

"Because that's what I am!" Maeven stood slowly, watching the eyes and starting to see the two dragon shapes around them. She banished the useless invisibility glamour. "I am no dragon child, though. I would call my father a lot of things, but he is not a dragon."

"He bears a key piece of dragon magic!" the voice came into her mind like a tinkling laugh.

"Have you noticed – I don't?" Maeven responded softly, pointedly.

"You will again – though you must recover yours from the hand of the Serpent."

The vision of a serpent scrawled over the Arms of Thulor came unbidden to her mind.

"Yes, the Serpent is growing bolder," the voice came again. "Thulor is dying and her magic is fading. She cannot maintain the protections much longer."

Suddenly, there was in Maeven's mind knowledge about the nature of the talisman charm she had worn for seven years. It was a sense of something vast, like a huge net hovering like a half sphere over the kingdom. It had eight cardinal points – the pieces of the talisman, and a central hub – part of the old dragon's shell. Then there were side images, people, spread out through the kingdom – connected to the protections but less closely than her father and siblings. More knowledge was peripheral to that, but she had not the words to explain it.

"What must be done?" Maeven asked. *But I only know of six talismans.*

"Talk to Thulor, find her egg and hatch it as Frederick hatched Exconidor's egg!"

"Where is Thulor?"

"In the heart of her Kingdom!"

"And the egg?"

"Once it was here. A long time ago, a wizard came and kept it as a curiosity. A small black oval that looks like a rock. A mage egg."

"I found that. My father should have it now."

"No, it is in peril. The enemy of all the realm has it."

"Then how am I to find it again? I'm not a mage!" Maeven protested.

"You have the Dragon's Eye!"

"What do you mean?"

"You can see things – differently!"

Maeven had no idea what the dragon meant. "Do you mean that I can see in the dark?"

"That, and more. You can see truth, when you look for it."

"We came here to look for dragon shells," Maeven suddenly blurted. *I'm just a thief, not some kind of saviour of the realm.*

"Seek what you need in the crypt of Exconidor."

Maeven saw the tunnel in the wall and could now follow it as it descended into the bowels of the mountain, past deep abysses and other dangers.

"Is that the only way?" Maeven asked quietly.

"It is a way."

"Will you let my friend past you?"

"No!"

It seemed as if the conversation was over. The eyes moved away and a rustling sound accompanied it. The tunnel leading down was almost completely blocked.

"You are welcome here at any time, dragon child."

Maeven walked slowly back to a worriedly pacing Atlantis. "No shells there," she told her friend, who swore softly. "Atlantis, we have to visit the crypt of Exconidor! One way is through there, but it is dangerous and the dragon won't let you through. I think there is another way and I think I know how to get to it but you will need to trust me – I'm good at getting into and out of places."

"So, you're a thief," Atlantis deduced.

"Guilty!" Maeven chuckled. "But I'm good…!"

Maeven insisted that they stay in the cave until dusk so that they would not be near the hamlet in daylight. She knew the men from there often wondered this far.

They travelled by moonlight, following the track at first and then some instinctive shortcut that avoided all the shacks. At the big cave, Maeven warned her friend to follow her carefully. They did not want any light or noise to betray them.

"There may still be stuff in here from when they were hiding from some bandits."

"I wonder if those were the ones Rhovert had to go and collect." Atlantis said in a whisper. "It was about half a year ago."

"Might have been – who is Rhovert?"

"Prince Rhovert," Atlantis said diffidently. "We started off travelling together. He was going as King's Messenger to the King of Declanor. I was riding home to get some stuff and coming back by the cave where I killed a dragon, to look for dragon shells there. We got as far as that town below. I went on; he was going to deal with the bandits."

"What happened to your horse?" Maeven asked curiously.

"Um… I had to sell it!" she admitted sheepishly. "I needed the money to buy stuff."

"On the way out I might just decide to pinch two from out there," Maeven decided.

"Ven!"

"They owe me two!" she hissed back fiercely. "Come on, there's a deep pool through here."

"You are going down there?" Atlantis asked with a shudder as she watched Maeven strip down to a short light under tunic. "Can you swim?"

"Enough."

"I'm coming too. I'll leave a wizard light floating face down so we'll have it to guide us back."

Atlantis divested herself of her outer garments but kept her sword. Then they both waded into the pool until it was above waist deep and floated over to the far wall. Atlantis activated the wizard light and they each took a deep breath, then with a single splash, twisted and dove down deep.

Atlantis was the better swimmer, but Maeven could see where they were going. To her eyes, the water seemed to have a luminescence of its own and she guided them both, down and down, under a rock and up to the surface again. They both gulped air greedily when they broke the surface. It was only when their laboured breathing settled again did they begin to look around.

This cavern was softly illuminated but the light did not seem to be coming from anywhere in particular. The roof was high and the walls were rock but carved smooth. They swam to the rocky lip of the pool and climbed out, dripping, onto the gold-flecked black sand.

"That was too easy!" Atlantis remarked, glancing around as if expecting trouble to spring at them.

"There's magic in here," Maeven warned. Her scalp was itching.

They looked around slowly. Over the far side were the bones and desiccated hide of an ancient dragon. Leaning against it was a suit of shining silver chain mail. Only the wearer's skull could be seen.

"Frederick," Atlantis guessed, recalling her Great Grand Sire's rhyme.

Maeven was finding that her eyesight was strange. The dragon hulk, the dead man in armour and the boxes on the ground near them were all glowing faintly silver, but a reddish glow was intensifying around the edges of the chamber floor.

"Watch out for trouble," Maeven warned again as she crossed the cavern to approach the dragon.

Behind her, Atlantis drew her sword. In Maeven's eyes, one of the wooden caskets was glowing brighter than the rest. Her touch on the wood seemed to snap it open. The contents were not coins or jewels but coarse black and gold sand.

"Seek what you need…" she murmured thoughtfully.

Atlantis screamed a warning. "Ven! Behind you! Snakes!"

Massive serpents, the length of a person and as thick as her leg, were coming from everywhere – from the solid rock near the floor and dropping down from the rock overhead.

Maeven muttered an incantation and the box she was holding disappeared from sight. She sprinted towards the pool, keeping just ahead of the slithering creatures. They were moving faster than she imagined that snakes could.

Atlantis had her sword out and was slashing at the snakes and also moving back towars the pool. Before Maeven reached the water, a snake dropped from the roof between her and Atlantis. Its foresection reared up and in an instant it changed into human shape. It grabbed Maeven and pushed her backwards and a second snake dropped and changed and attacked Atlantis, forcing her to defend herself.

Maeven twisted and writhed in the grip of the first serpent man. She recognised in the olive skin and sharp features a likeness to the Princes of Vatarik. She began to scream as if terrified and trying to call for help.

Atlantis saw the terror in her friend's expression and was aware of whispers, but she could not hear what that other was saying; and her own opponent was whispering to her of defeat to come. She thrust and parried, using all her skill to keep alive. For now, her friend's terror could not be eased – but at least that snake man was not using a sword.

Her mind suddenly recalled the last line of the verse, *"If you seek the Serpents Bane, dive down deep…"*

The creature thought it was making her retreat but Atlantis wanted to go back. As she hopped up onto the rocky edge of the pool, she caught the eye of her friend. She suddenly knew that the shrill screams and contorted face were an act, keeping her captor occupied. He was not looking her way, and not aware of his danger when she reversed her sword and threw it hilt first at the back of his head. The move took her own opponent by surprise for long enough for her to dive down into the water. She hoped he would not follow her. She hoped her instinct was right, for none of the snakes had approached from the pool wall or from where the dragon remains lay.

The unexpected manoeuvre had caught both creatures off guard. The hilt of the sword stunned the first creature, and it fell onto Maeven. She scrambled out from under it, intending to run for the dragon's corner, but the other creature levelled its sword at her in a gesture of warning. The other serpents slithered closer, tongues flicking in and out as if tasting her terror.

"What do you want?" Maeven asked the snakeman.

The answer came from behind her. She had not needed to hear him speak – the wild erotic sensations that coursed through her told her who had come. She screamed deliberately – over and over, getting ever shriller.

"You will cease that noise!"

It was as if her voice had been taken from her. Her mouth opened and closed but no sound came from it. The increased itching of her scalp told her how he had compelled her to obey. She stood still, by choice, not turning to see the speaker. He walked around into her line of sight. Most of her will was intent on ignoring the sensations the man had roused.

"You are still mine," the man said with satisfaction.

"Not in here, slime crawler. Here the dragon is stronger." Now she could speak again.

"Ah, but you lust for me – I can sense it."

"NO! Not that way – not ever."

"Oh, I think you will – one day. Meanwhile, you will deliver a message for me…"

"No!"

"You WILL do what I say." The face above the blonde beard hardened.

"In your nightmares," Maeven told him. She saw Atlantis came up for air and dive again.

"You can only defy me in yours," the blonde man chuckled. "Stubborn you are – but I am stronger. Tell your father to release the Prince of Serpents or a greater darkness will fall on his kingdom."

"Tell him yourself! He won't listen to me!" Maeven said defiantly.

The man with the sword slashed once, so quickly that at first Maeven did not realise her arm had been cut.

"I'm surprised that you want your brother free…"

"There is a power loose in this world that would make you look like a flea. And when he rules Thulor, you will only live if you obey me."

Maeven just stared back at the man. If it were not for her son, she would have dared him to kill her.

"And to whom would I need to be grateful?"

"I am El Haba, Prince of Serpents, Wizard and…"

Maeven interrupted, "Pompous and arrogant. I'll take it as said." She saw Atlantis emerging from the pool. What she held in her hand glowed silver and for some reason, the still slithering snakes were retreating back into the rocks. Then the man snake with the sword turned back into a snake.

"Next time," El Haba threatened. "I'll have you then."

He, too, turned back into snake shape and slithered off into solid rock. The unconscious man had somehow disappeared, too.

Maeven slumped to the ground and hugged her knees, ignoring the cut arm for it did not hurt. She was shivering with reaction and fighting craving for an erotic crescendo, and the desire to race out of the cave and run to her father to give him the message. She would not!

Atlantis trotted over to her, dripping water. "Ven, are you alright? Your arm is bleeding."

"I'm fine," Maeven claimed. "It isn't much. What did you find? The snakes all went."

"The serpent's bane – I think." Atlantis showed it to Maeven and she reached out to take it. It was dish-shaped, about the size of her hand and make of a black substance flecked with gold.

"I wish I knew why those creatures came here when we were here. Do you think they wanted this?" Maeven said aloud.

Atlantis shrugged. "It sent them away – just being close to them. I don't think they could have touched it."

Maeven didn't want to agree. It made sense but it was much too frightening to think they had been looking for her.

A strange thing happened when Maeven closed her hand on the object. It not only went cold in her hand, but it also sent a flush of heat through her right arm; the wound that was oozing blood began to heal. Only later, she realised that the driving compulsion set by El Haba was eased.

"Let's get out of here," Maeven suggested. She wanted to put the whole episode out of her mind. Atlantis did not argue – she recovered her sword and they both returned to the pool and dived.

As they walked out of the pool in the big cave where they had left their belongings, Atlantis remarked, "I didn't see any dragon shells."

Maeven turned her back to her friend, muttered a few words and a wooden casket appeared between her hands. She flipped it open as she turned back.

"Dragon shells," she said, closing it again. "Not as fine as the sand back there."

"Ven, how did you know? And how did you get them up here? You had nothing in your hands."

"As for knowing, I didn't. I just guessed… little bits of information I'd picked up fell into place." Maeven was not going to mention that the dragons had spoken to her. "And, I hid the casket when the snakes came with a hiding spell I pinched."

"You should come back with me. King Westron will probably give you a reward for finding the shells."

"Ah, no. You deserve the reward," Maeven said earnestly as she handed the casket over. "If only for getting rid of those creatures."

"Well, if you are sure – let's get dressed and go. I want to be well away by morning."

They rode down the mountain on the two horses that Maeven had stolen from the hamlet. At first, Atlantis had refused to ride, but she relented once Maeven had explained her reason for believing that she deserved to have them. They stopped for food in the trade town late in the morning but then kept going until they found a clearing near an offshoot of the Guarda River. Here they made camp and slept whilst the horses, loosely tethered, grazed on the fresh grass.

The horses were neither the best nor the worst of the ex-brigands' mounts. Maeven had simply taken one from each of the two shacks that had five horses corralled behind it. The saddles had been in the little lean to sheds nearby.

Atlantis woke late in the day, a small pile of copper and silver coins lay beside her head. Only then did she realise that Maeven and one horse had gone.

CHAPTER 15 – THE BID FOR FREEDOM

Maeven lay awake listening to the quiet breathing of her companion. Atlantis seemed to have no particular worries and liked being out in the wild lands. Perhaps she, herself, shouldn't dislike it, for no one would expect her to be in so isolated a place, but she really didn't like being where there was nowhere to hide.

The desire to flee from the kingdom of Thulor had become almost irresistible. Ever since the little demon had come seeking her, she had known she was not safe. There was no talisman to protect her, and no child of mixed blood to confuse it.

Why she was being looked for she couldn't even guess. She was a thief, not a fighter, or a sorceress, or the heir to the kingdom. Anyone she was around, wasn't safe – look what had happened at Lorford – people had died. That big demon had been foiled, but why had it been after her? Was it simply because she was a member of the royal family? Maybe they thought she was easy prey and any death of a member of the king's family was to their benefit. That would mean an enemy sent them. An enemy like Vatarik.

And those creepy snake men, where else did they come from than Vatarik? They had to have, since the bastard who had raped her had appeared amongst them. He too, had made her want to run. He had roused feelings in her just by his presence, feelings that confused her. He claimed to own her, but she didn't agree. He as good as warned her that he would find her and claim her. All the more reason to get far out of the kingdom of Thulor, in the opposite direction.

He had wanted her to her father with a message. That was the very last place she wanted to go. She was a thief, and if her father had ever even loved her, he would hate her now. And she would not even pretend to claim that she was sorry and whenever had her father needed her to tell him anything?

The dragon though, seeing her had been unexpected, but the beast had seemed to like her, even if her dislike of Atlantis was equally obvious. She had said something about needing to find and retrieve Thulor's mage egg – well she had, or Nayfor had. They'd given it to Barnabas to take to the king. There was nothing more to tell him about that. She had no idea how to hatch it. Surely her father knew, or Finora, since she was the sorceress in the family.

That dragon had said she needed to reclaim her talisman, but how? Thief she might be but to go into the King of Vatarik's palace and take it from his son, by herself, was beyond stupidity.

No, the only thing for her to do was run far, far away.

But there was her son. No one but herself knew he was the King's grandson, and if she wasn't around, her enemies had no way of connecting him with her. He would be well cared for in the village…but dammit, she wanted to look after him. Already, she missed him.

So, how could she? Her supply of money wasn't exactly depleted, but the majority of it was at the other extreme end of the kingdom, at the guild house in Lorford. Most of what she had taken with her when she followed Nayfor to Thul Run was back with Reyna, to dole out to Lori and Zeke for Wystan's care.

Maeven considered her options. Thieving had lost a lot of its excitement, but it was the only way she knew of to get money for herself. The irony was, that when she and Nayfor had met up with Barnabas on the way back from Thul Run, he had promoted her to master thief and she really hadn't cared. Still, that rank had advantages. Master thieves had more freedom than apprentices. Away from towns, for instance, where other thieves were unlikely to be working, she didn't have to state her intention to rob someone. And the guild would not know about her work or expect to get half of the take. Trouble was, she wouldn't rob a poor farmer, or itinerant worker. She had always aimed to take only a reasonably small amount at a time and only steal from the well-off people. Maybe she would find a well off trade caravan, or merchant's pack train.

Her mind began making plans. She would see what she could steal on the way back to a thieves' guild house, and hide that from the Guildmaster. Then she would arrange for her stash to be sent from Lorford…but would that be enough? When she went south, she would collect her son and have him to care for as well. She couldn't be thieving then. She would need to make one or more large heists, and only declare part of it to the guild. Say about the average amount she had made on her heists. Even that much was more than most other thieves contributed.

However, if she was going to go, she needed to leave without Atlantis knowing. She couldn't admit what she was going to do, or why. If her friend got wind of it, she would try to talk her out of it.

Her friend! Atlantis was that, and the only friend she had. What would she think of her if she ran out on her? But then what would she think if she was attacked by a demon who had been looking for her recent companion? No, it was imperative she leave, and try to get a head start.

Her small pack had all her stuff in, the horse was hobbled nearby and she could walk him until it was light enough to see to saddle him properly. But she owed Atlantis something for feeding her.

Lucky that she had discovered that she could still do small spells, without a potion. Maybe the talisman that she'd had first had started to change her into a sorceress, before she'd swapped it with the thief one. Old Merlie had said something like that.

"On the count of four, you will fall into a deep sleep and not wake up until noon tomorrow," Maven spoke softly. "1…2…3…4."

Still moving quietly, Maeven felt in her pack for the last of her coins and took half of them out. These she left beside Atlantis, by way of an apology as well as in thanks. Then she went to get her purloined horse. Her friend never stirred.

As an afterthought, spoke another spell, "Until you wake, no one will come near you."

For the first day, Maeven rode along dirt tracks that led northward, although occasionally she had needed to make a new trail. She tired of this and took to the main trail when she finally came out onto it. Here she passed other slower moving travellers, who called out a greeting to which she replied cheerfully, with a brief pleasantry. Ever since she had joined the main trail, she had kept an illusion of a scruffy young lad on herself. At the end of that first day, she had felt tireder than she had expected to be. First off, she had thought it was because she was unused to riding, but then she recalled something she had been told about the energy it took to do things by magic compared to by mundane means. From then on, she was on the lookout for a way to get clothes that were more suited to a boy than the clothes she had worn from the village.

In the first town that she came to, she bought some black hair dye. She had wanted scissors, but no one had any for sale. Instead, she had to use her knife, freshly sharpened on a smooth rock, to hack her hair short, so that she could if she wished, keep the woven hat off her head. Now she looked more like a boy again, and felt safer.

She didn't stay with the same travellers all the time, and when she left it was well before any of them discovered small valuables missing. Had anyone tried to accuse her, they would find nothing, for the coins or gems were hidden magically.

She arrived at Valeford after two weeks of travelling, having by-passed the palace and the big town around it. Her belt pouch was full, and she had started to form a plan that would give her enough money to finally get away. Until that came to fruition, she needed a place to stay. The thieves' guild house was her intended destination, but she didn't know where it was. However, she knew that Jinkins, the master of the Fighting Dog tavern, worked with the Guild master. She would ask him to send a message for her.

When she entered the bar and ordered a cider, Jinkins himself served her, and seemed to be studying her.

"Day to you, Master Jinkins," she greeted him, making her voice lower than usual.

"Do I know you?"

"You do. And I would appreciate it if you would get a message to Guildmaster Jocelyn for me."

"And who should say is wanting him?"

"Master Ven."

The bushy brows above Jinkins' eyes disappeared into his shaggy hair. "Master is it? You be kind of young for that rank."

"Barnabas himself promoted me. If the Guild master wants to check, he can ask Nayfor."

The names were like passwords, and Jinkins nodded. "I'll have the boy take your message. You can wait here until he is free to come."

Maeven deliberately placed one of her few large silver coins on the counter. "Keep the change. The rest is in thanks for the help you were to me last time I was here."

"It is kind of you, but the guild saw me right," Jinkins gave her change. "Feel free to order a meal or more drinks though."

The idea of a decent meal made her stomach rumble, and she acted on the suggestion, ordering one of the meat pasties that Jinkins' wife was famous for. Eating slowly helped pass the time until the Thieves' Guildmaster appeared.

Jocelyn Chowdry was not alone, and Ven almost quailed when she recognised his companion. It was Nayfor.

"So you finally surfaced again," Nayfor greeted her without friendliness. "What have you been doing?"

"Personal business," Maeven told him bluntly.

"And are you saying that you have not been working in all this time?"

"Working as a common labourer, digging stones out of fields," Maeven told him.

"I can't see that," Nayfor said right away.

"Very well, you are right. I was trying village life, and some brigands moved in. I took all the brigands' weapons so that the benighted pacifist idiots in that village could fight them on even terms."

Jocelyn chuckled. "Down near Declanor was it?"

Maeven nodded warily.

"That wasn't how I heard the story, but I do say, it makes more sense than the god of those religious zealots giving them the weapons."

Nayfor relaxed from his interrogative stance and remarked, "If you want to stay in the Guildhouse here, you will need to pay 100 silver coins for the year, in advance. That is the Master's payment option. Do you have it?"

Maeven shook her head. "Not at the moment. But I can get it once I have access to my stash that was at Lorford."

"Very well, I will arrange that. Then what are your plans?"

"I will need to go back to work…"

"So you will. Just remember then, that Master or not, you still obey the Guildmaster." Nayfor seemed to have no particular friendliness towards her.

Maeven kept her response to a nod, and was relieved when Nayfor stalked out. She still recalled his warning, after they had left Barnabas. *He may have been deluded enough to make you a master, but don't you start thinking that you now know everything.*

That remembered statement, she decided, was a prod to keep her extra-cautious. She had too much to lose now. She would ensure that her preparation was thorough, her requests to thieve aimed at places no other thief would dare to rob.

Her moments of consideration were abruptly interrupted when the Guildmaster suggested, "Perhaps the inn would be a better place for you to stay."

"Why?"

"Everyone else who stays at the guildhouse is male, and likes the company of the opposite sex."

"Are you saying you won't have men there that like men?" Maeven demanded.

"No I am not saying that," he refuted, and then just looked at her.

Maeven turned a shade redder in the face. "Did Nayfor tell you?"

"No, I knew before he found out. I haven't told anyone, although the few who voted for you to join the guild know, and I put a vow of silence on them."

"But you think they might try something?"

"What do you think?"

"I am hardly a pampered high born lady who has to stay a virgin until she is sold off to a husband. I have heard the others at their sport and don't want to share it. But with all that, they shouldn't try, because the first person to try, when he was refused, put a curse on me so that any one that tries…dies."

She had shocked the Guildmaster. "So, I am fine staying at the guild house and would prefer to be there."

"Okay then, I will take you."

Maeven hoped that the word would get passed to the few men in the know that they should not try anything with Master Ven.

The Guildhouse was a mile out of Valeford, in a building that looked like a barn. All comings and goings were able to be discreet, because it backed onto a stand of trees, and was close to the river Vale itself that was in turn, bordered by trees.

Inside, the lower level was used to store hay and grain, but it also had an area that was the privy, divided into several cubicles – all smells magically treated, and stalls for a few horses. Upstairs was divided into sleeping cubicles, an area for eating and lounging around, a small kitchen, and the Guildmaster's private room.

Maeven was given a small cubicle to use, and she was happy with that. The main reason for not wanting something better at the inn, apart from having to pay for it, was so that there was no chance of non-thieves seeing her and potentially recognising her. In this place too, no one would comment on the bitter herbs she bought to put in clay jars around her bed, or the odd rocks with streaks of yellow or red. All of these, she obtained from traders, and were supposed (according to the alchemists of someplace further north even than Vatarik) to protect one from demons.

The guildhouse was also a place where rumours of all kinds were heard. Most were sifted for their potential for thefts, or buying up a commodity that was likely to be in short supply somewhere soon. Maeven listened as intently as all the others, particularly since one vague rumour had mentioned her. Not as Ven the Master thief, but as Maeven Princess of Thulor, an identity none of the thieves, even Nayfor knew. At the time, it had resulted in some crude talk, the mildest of which was, "If I'd been the bitch, I'd have run away too. What with a bastard like the King for a father."

The King's hatred of thieves was well known, and many resented the treatment of guild-bonded thieves, as well as the unbonded ones, when they had been caught and dragged in front of the King's 'justice'.

The rumour had just been a snippet of talk, "There was a man in the inn asking if anyone had seen her."

Intentionally sounding bored, Maeven had added to the talk by asking, "Heard about her years ago, why's they asking now? Does his majesty want to sell her off now?"

It had raised a few moments of raucous laughter and one of the men had added, "Wonder what a Princess is worth if we find her."

The guesses had grown wild until Jocelyn had told them to "forget it!", but it had made Maeven thoughtful and she had gone off to her cubicle to think.

It was a good question. Why did her father, if it was her father and not some agent of Vatarik, want with her? She had no intention of going back to the palace to find out, but could she turn that information to her own use? If she did, she would have to be very careful indeed, and not let a hint of her intentions get back to the guild but she was sure that she could keep the secret to herself.

Starting a rumour was quite easy, and it was amusing to hear how it changed before coming back to her ears. After about two weeks, the whispers had her as a concubine of a brigand leader, which might have been truth if she had not escaped from Thul Run, or a whore for a travelling fair that was currently down south near the Declanor border, or a fortune teller in a town far to the west of the realm. After that, she waited to hear if anyone in particular went enquiring. The result wasn't a clear cut, such and such a person is asking, rather, that the King had sent a squad of the King's own Guards in those directions.

Now that she was reasonably sure it was her father that was after her, she gave thought to how to convince him that she was in desperate enough a plight that he would pay a hefty ransom. That was going to need an intermediary to carry a message, maybe one of the town urchins if she could be sure he would only tell what she wanted him to. For that, she might need to find a witch who had a spell for that, or learn to do a bit of mesmerising.

In the end, she had all she needed. The urchin was grateful to her for getting him out of a beating, and in need of coins to help his mother feed a brood of twelve children. He wouldn't know any more than that he had been given a message to deliver. He had been told that if he had to take a return message that he was to put it in a particular place in the small temple of some obscure god. She could go there invisible and collect it.

Her negotiations began when one of her rumours brought the King's Own guards to Valeford. And once they had received a message, they stayed camped near the Crescent Moon tavern –higher class and more expensive place than its competition, the Fighting Dog tavern.

Maeven went out each day and observed the routine of the guards, got to know their faces and who they spoke to outside their group. She hadn't sent a final agreement yet, she needed to be sure that she would be able to get away once she stole the ransom.

Not only got away from the guards, but kept all knowledge of this piece of work from the guild as well. They would not approve of her scheme in any way, but her next rumours were going to suggest that agents of Vatarik had caught wind of this negotiation and were going to try and snatch the Princess for their own reasons or at least disrupt the agreement.

Finally, all was ready. She had bought enough magic potion to ensure that all her spells would work, even if the King sent a sorceress to assist his messenger. She had oil for the door hinges, and shoes made of soft felt, so her steps would be soundless. Her escape route began as a newly opened up entrance to the sewers under the town. This opening, only known to her, was a mere fifty paces from the front door of the tavern. The route through the noisome tunnels, full of waste matter and left over water from the last storm, was now as familiar to her as the street above, but anyone else would get lost, since she had made a lot of magical illusions to misdirect followers. It came out near a lake to the south of the town, and then it was less than half a mile to the safety of the guild house. She intended to hide the ransom in the tunnels, so her fellow thieves had no idea. In fact, she had gradually taken most of her stash to hide in there, hidden with a 'hide and stay' spell, a variation of the hide and follow spell. Even the run off from a storm wouldn't move it. If need be, she would hide in there.

Once she sent her messenger with the time for the meeting, she was committed. However, she wasn't going to make it easy. She wanted all the advantages, and hedged the time with, the need for the intermediary to feel safe. The King's agent was to come alone, and leave the money in the centre of the temple garden, and retreat. The Princess would get taken there, exchanged for the money, and that would be that. Any attempt to follow the person who brought the Princess would result in the release of a deadly sickness.

The Kings Own guards moved their camp to be nearer the Temple, and Maeven spotted them searching the place for any sign that she was being kept there in the first place. Although, they kept well away after that first visit, so as not to cause a problem.

She easily recognised the King's messenger. Her brother Rhovert was in his mercenary persona, and had now grown a beard that covered all the bottom part of his face. He took a room in the Crescent Moon, arriving a week before the date set.

Maeven dared to enter the tavern on the day after his arrival, and ordered a meal. The man who served her whispered, "This is not a good place to be right now."

"I know, but they can't know me. I have never been caught. I came so I could report back to the master."

The server, a thief, but not one who stayed in the guild house, accepted that and went about his business. Maeven ate slowly, and studied everyone who came in the door. She hid her face in a tankard of cider, when she recognised someone else she knew. Rolliver, the servant of her intended husband, Lord Tormore.

What is he doing here? Did that mean Tormore was here too? She hoped not. He would probably insist on getting married right away if he saw her. Unless he was put off by the rumours that she had been living as a whore. Or was Rolliver working with her brother now? Tormore was supposedly one of her father's close advisors, even if he was some kind of dark wizard and was hiding the fact from her father. As soon as she could, Maeven slipped out via the kitchen and the back door.

The next day, she offered to do cleaning, and the thief, thinking she was still spying for the guild, gave her what she needed and told her what to do.

She had long ago discovered that nobles paid little attention to servants, and her brother was no exception. In the guise of the cleaning servant, she was able to discover which room her brother was in, the fact that two of the King's Own were always lounging in the passage outside his door, and that the chest with the ransom in was in the room with her brother. Not once while she was doing the required bedmaking and clearing the chamber pot, did Rhovert pay her any attention. He just paced the room, deep in thought.

The two rooms on either side of his, each had three of the King's Own sleeping there. The two in the passage took turns about with the others.

On the next three days, she was in and out of the tavern on various errands, looking out for any others who had arrived and stayed a few days. The king might have sent other agents or spies.

The thought of spies made her think of Barnabas, but she had not seen him. That would be a complication. As would Nayfor turning up and deputising for him. But she hadn't seen him since her first day back either, though she knew how good he was at shadowing and watching people.

She wasn't the only thief visiting that tavern, she recognised two who liked to work a con. They would be better not to try anything.

Each day when she left, Maeven practiced her escape route, making sure she had everything in mind. She even had several changes of clothes hidden on the far side of the lake, to change into, so that when she returned to the guild house her clothes and hair would be dry.

Maeven was as sure as she could be that all was going to be done as she had insisted, but she was not going to assume anything. Especially, as she had no intention of going to the temple for the exchange – naturally – since she wanted the money and her freedom. So she was going to wait until that night, and slip into Rhovert's room.

Reminding herself firmly that she was Ven, Master thief, she slipped out from her cubicle using an invisibility spell, and soundlessly left the guildhall. She wasn't meant to use magic during her robberies, but she didn't intend anyone to know what she was doing. The door guard missed the few seconds when she had opened the door wide enough to slip through, and close it again. He had gone out to investigate a sound he had heard – a rock that had fallen from the roof when Ven released a hold spell on it.

Her first stop was to where she had hidden a black hooded cloak that would help hide her without the need for invisibility, should the spell fail. Then she trotted along the grassy edge of the trail, onto the road and along to the tavern. A short distance away from her destination, Ven slipped off the road into a shadow, and looked for watchers. While she did, she added another layer to her disguise, a head covering that made it look like she had shoulder length black hair, instead of clipped short black hair, both so different from her own natural light brown hair. The less she relied on magic, the better. A wizard or sorceress would probably sense magic at work.

She entered the tavern openly, as just another late traveller needing food and drink. Nothing about her actions when arranging for both, and for a place on the floor to sleep, drew more than passing attention. While eating, she made a game of being sleepy, so that it was little surprise to anyone when she finished the food, pushed her wooden trencher aside, and fell asleep at the table.

However, she was very definitely awake and alert, and studying the other guests at the inn, through the dark hair that had fallen over her eyes. She had seen her brother go upstairs, followed by two guards, and wondered how long she would need to wait for him to go to sleep. It would be safest to go up when tavern keeper had sent off the local regulars, and the tables were pushed aside to accommodate the sleepers who would sleep on the floor.

Before then, Ven had noticed two other figures, newcomers that had stayed hooded the whole time they had been in the room. She couldn't tell if they were male or female, but from their movements, going out to and returning from the privy, she decided one was a lady and the other was her guard whilst travelling. What surprised her was that the ladylike one would be sleeping with the guard on the floor, just as she had purported to be planning to do.

When the servers began their routine to close up, Ven slipped out the front door, saying that she needed fresh air. The nearest one warned, "Door's locked in five minutes."

It didn't take her more than a couple of seconds to squirt her magic oil onto the hinges of the door. She returned inside just when innkeeper came to lock the door. By then, the servants were pushing cleared tables towards the walls and she decided to go out towards the privy. There were others waiting, but that hadn't been her destination. She simply needed to be out of sight, to reactivate the invisibility charm.

She needed to be careful going in, for although she was invisible, people would know someone was there if they walked into her. Taking her time, she slipped upstairs after the last of the patrons who had paid for rooms had gone up. There she stopped in a shallow alcove between two rooms at the start of the passage. Except for the two guards outside her brother's room, all was quiet. The only noise came from downstairs where the floor sleepers were getting settled.

Walking silently, she came within touching distance of the nearest guard, stared at them both, and whispered vary softly, "In the space of twenty heartbeats, you will be asleep. Seeing nothing, hearing nothing."

She counted her own heartbeat and when she reached twenty, saw both men stop what little movements they had been making. She smiled, and eased herself between them to listen at the door, before squirting more of her special oil on the hinges and door handle, and returning the vial to her pocket.

Then she turned the handle to open the door just a little, and listened again. She only heard the sound of someone breathing slowly and regularly. Now, she located the bed and the sleeper, stared that way, with an image of her brother in mind and repeated her spell. The breathing remained the same, but the spell should have worked.

The chest had been at the end of the bed, now it was beside it, and Rhovert's hand had fallen down onto it. She moved it aside, and checked the lock. Her hair had not begun to itch, so there was no magic locking it, and that surprised her, but it was all to the good. It only took her a moment to force the mundane lock open, and a few seconds more to remove a leather sack from within. The sack clinked softly, and was quite heavy. Maeven closed the chest again, and positioned it below her brother's hand where it had been, then stood and went to place the sack near the door.

The sack held the coins she had specified, but the gems would be separate, and had not been in the chest. She stopped for a moment to consider, aware she could not stay much longer.

Yes! Of course, that's where.

Her slender white hand reached under the pillow and without disturbing the sleeper's rhythm of snores, felt for and withdrew a soft leather pouch, a hands span wide and nimble fingers felt the small hard objects within the leather. The contents of this little pouch were worth more than all the coins in the other sack. Then, in a moment of introspection Ven let her fingers trace the metallic threads embossed on the leather – the Royal sigil! Recalling the job in hand – the pouch disappeared through a slit in her black, hooded cloak and settled into a secret pocket at the waist of the jerkin below.

Ghost like, Ven backed away from the bed, going towards the door of the room to listen for sounds without before leaning down for the leather sack that had been placed within reach. She had not expected her brother to be so naïve. A novice thief would have found the lock on the chest to be simple

– some sort of magic warding would have been more appropriate! She had been expecting that, and come prepared.

The coins in the sack clanked softly causing her to glance over at the sleeper again, but his breathing did not change. Maeven smiled to herself under the hood of the cloak and as she opened the door a crack to listen before slipping through the soundlessly opening door and into the passage.

The two guards there, clad in formal livery that looked black in the light from a nearby night candle, were still staring vacantly, no more aware of anything than their comrades who were sleeping in in the adjoining rooms.

Ven paused and looked up at the rigid guards. "In the space of forty heart beats you will wake and remember nothing!"

"Oi! Lady, who are you?" a loud childish voice demanded.

Ven pulled her hood further over her face and turned but could not see the speaker. Muttering again the invisibility spell again – she ran back along the passage and lightly down the stairs, followed by the voice now yelling "Thief! Thief!"

Men in the taproom sprang awake, reached for their swords as they rose and looked around. Four sprang for the stairs to go up, blocking her way.

Damn! She needed a dancer's agility to dodge them and they were unaware of her leaping over the stair rail and running lightly over the tables pushed to the side of the room.

Someone bellowed orders for lights to be lit and angry shouts began from the room and passage upstairs.

Only good night-vision and speed enabled Ven to jump down from the tables and weave her way across the room before it became chaos. Now she waited in a corner near the main door but with lights being lit, it was not safe to stay. The spell of invisibility was not perfect. In light, a person still cast a shadow. Not only that – the special oil that had silenced the door hinges would soon lose its efficiency; by dawn there would be no traces left. She needed to be gone long before then.

She glanced around the room, waiting for someone to come over to go out. The two hooded figures she had noticed earlier were the only two standing quite still, but while they seemed to be scanning the room, they hadn't yet looked her way. Those two were making her uneasy.

At last! Ven saw two men about to leave, ordered out to bring the town guard. She moved close in behind them, just as she began to feel the itch of magic at work. Their shadows, and bodies hid her shadow, and as soon as she could slip around them, she was off, running down the road towards her escape route. She didn't pause to glance back, for she was sure that at least one of those two caped figures was a wizard or sorceress.

Had she been able to hear their conversation, before she left the tavern, she would have been even more concerned.

The two tall figures had calmly stepped back onto the raised surround of the fireplace to see over the heads of all the other guests that had roused with the shouts. Then, two sets of green blue eyes had systematically scanned the room, looking for any movement that didn't fit what they saw or heard.

"Something landed on the tables," a deeper voice said, speaking only loud enough for the other to hear. It was worth saying it aloud, for it seemed that this thief was using an invisibility potion. They watched the tables for a time, but saw no other movement there, and returned to scanning the room. They saw the two men going to the door to fetch the town guard, and turned their attention that way, guessing the thief might try to sneak out.

A soft voice from the more slender of the two figures, began to incant a spell.

The other said, "In the corner, by the door. A shadow."

Too late, the shadow slipped out the door. The two hooded figures jumped down and moved between others to go after the invisible thief. Anyone at all sensitive to magic would have felt the tension of the incomplete spell. Once outside, the voice completed the spell, "Reveal thief!"

Night became like day, and a slender cloaked figure could now be seen running down the stone paved street, and disappearing between two grey stone dwellings. The chase was on.

Some of the King's Own from the tavern went after the figure, others were coming from the direction of the encampment, for the sorceress had summoned them the instant the first alarm was raised.

Even when the thief had ducked between houses, the bright ball of witchlight remained above, showing the pursuers where to go.

They blue liveried guards were catching up, and managed to see the thief disappear into a hole in the ground, the witchlight disappearing after her. They knew of no proper entrance to the sewers there, but guessed that was where the thief had gone. The leader of these guards gestured for some to find the nearest proper entrance, he and the rest wriggled awkwardly to get in via the narrow opening the thief had used.

Even that slight delay was enough. There was only the faintest of light down there, and as they moved towards it, even that vanished. The tunnel became as dark as pitch.

"We will only get lost if we try to follow," the leader said. "The bastard probably knows his way down here, and it only would take a few turns to block the light. Let's hope the others see where he goes. Back up and hope we can find the hole again."

"Well?" the voice of the sorceress demanded when the last of the guards had climbed out. "What happened?"

"Mam, when we got in down there the light was fading. Those tunnels twist and turn and would soon block the light."

There was a faint sigh. "It isn't your fault, Guard leader. We expected him to take to the sewers, but we didn't know of this opening."

"I sent some men to the nearest proper entrance…"

The sorceress waved him to silence. "They will no doubt soon lose him too. No, have your men and the town guards spread out around the town – wherever there is an opening to the sewers. That thief knows those tunnels as well as you know the King's highways. Have some of them out near the lake, there is an exit there. If he is smart enough to know how to use the tunnels to block the light, he might know that water will extinguish it."

"I will have to report to His Highness," the guard leader stated, not relishing the idea.

"We will do that," the sorceress offered. "Off you go!"

"That thief is a slippery bastard," the sorceress's companion said when the guard had gone.

"Smarter that Rhovert gave him credit for, but extremely dumb to have used magic. If he is a bonded thief, even his guild will renounce him once I send word to them. If he isn't bonded, he will still have all the guild thieves looking for him. They don't scruple to take a reward for one of their own that breaks their rules."

"What's your next move, Finora?"

"I think, that you and I need to go and talk to that server at the tavern. His wife was a bit tipsy and let it slip that he was a guild bonded thief. I think, though, that you should put the scare into him, Leanne."

"What if he doesn't know the thief we are looking for?"

"I am sure that he does. But if he won't tell us, I'll magic his drink to make him talk. I am sure he knows where the guild house is too. We can send him there to make our complaint."

"Do you want me to talk to that boy again?"

"No, he's been scared enough. I am sure that he does not know any more than he has told us. Anyway, we did see a lad like his description here during the last few days."

"But not tonight," Leanne said, thinking back. "Just that long haired lad in the black cloak. I thought he left just before the servers began cleaning up."

"Leanne, that was about when I started sensing magic, and the light showed the thief was wearing a black cloak."

Leanne growled, "We slipped up there. The exchange wasn't meant to be for two more days. That's where we were expecting trouble. What are we going to tell father?"

"Nothing yet. Let's see what we can learn."

Prince Rhovert, still groggy from being awoken from the bespelled sleep, took a moment to realise what his guards were saying. He nearly fell over, when he turned to check under his pillow. The leather bag of gems had gone too. He cursed.

"Make sure none of the traveller guests leave, but summon the town guards to help us search. If Leanne or Finora are downstairs, I want to see them. And I want everyone who was going to sleep down in the taproom questioned. Who they are, their occupations, reason for being here and what if anything they noticed that might seem odd. All the serving staff too."

His duty guard ran out to yell orders from the top of the stairs, and two of his men who had been posing as travellers, moved towards the door. He saw the two disguised Princesses, going after them. He returned to Prince Rhovert.

"I think the thief slipped out with Havey and Gill. Your sisters went out after him."

"Did you get a glimpse of the thief?"

"No, your Highness. I think he was invisible."

Rhovert refrained from further cursing, but had to pace out his frustration. Sammy, a general hand around the Crescent Moon, breathed easier after the King's Guard had finished questioning him and seemed to accept his answers as truth. Indeed, most of it had been, except the part about knowing the thief. He had his guesses, but he was honour bound not to sell his fellow guild members out to the King's guard, or other officers of the law, just on a guess. He had admitted seeing a lad of the description the guards had given, several times in the past few days, but that was all.

He was relieved to be able to get back to finishing his work, so that when the guards let them leave, he could go back to his pretty wife and tell her of the goings on. More to the point, he needed to tell the Guildmaster of the thief who had stolen from the King's messenger.

He'd finished mopping the floor and racking up the cleaned trenchers to dry, when he sensed he was no longer alone, and turned to see two women behind him. He recognised them as the ones who had kept the hood of their travelling capes up all evening. He had known that one was a sorceress, for he had seen her diamond pendant when the light had caught it. The other, he had been unsure about, but seeing her now he had no doubt that the other was a swordswoman.

Sammy began to feel beads of sweat on his forehead.

"Can I help you?" he tried, glad at least that his voice was steady.

"We just want you to go over what you told Guardsman Tollis," Leanne began.

"I…I don't know anymore."

"Why didn't you tell him that you recognised two of the current guests as thieves?" Leanne demanded.

Sammy glanced left and right looking for a way out.

"My spell revealed them too," Finora told him, "So you needed try to lie. Did you know them?"

Sammy nodded slightly, "But I told them who most of you were and not to try anything,"

"Considerate of you," Leanne said ironically. "They will need to convince the King that they hadn't been in league with the one who escaped. As will you."

"I wasn't, honest," Sammy squealed. "You have to believe me. I've been doing honest work here for nigh on five years. Ever since I got married."

"Yet you still belong to the guild…" Finora said suggestively.

"Lady, honest, if there was a way to get out, I'd have done it, but once you're in, it's for life."

"Well, then, what will your guild do to a thief who stole the ransom for the Kings youngest daughter?" Finora asked, with deceptive sweetness. "And anyone who helps him to get away? This thief used magic too. And I will be reporting to my guild if I don't find that thief."

Sammy had gone pale as well as sweaty. "The Pr…Princess?"

Finora just smiled.

"Th…they might kill him."

"Well, we don't want that, we want to question the thief. Then if he is lucky, he might just spend the rest of his life in the king's dungeon. More likely, for treason, he'll hang."

Sammy's legs turned to jelly and he had to sit down. "He can't do that to me. I've been honest…"

"Maybe you have," Finora said, "For my spell didn't target you, but I want answers. If you make me happy, all will be well."

"But the Guildmaster will have my hide if I tell…"

"He will be too busy finding that thief before his guild is the subject of a full scale purge by the king," Leanne growled.

"All right. But I don't know much more than I said. I saw the lad, slender, like a girl, with short black hair. Hands were not like your high-borns hands, but not work calloused either. I tried to warn him off too, but he implied he was sussing things for the Guildmaster. Never asked his name, nor he mine. I just knew he was one of us because I saw him talking to the Guildmaster one time when I was delivering something to the Fighting Dog. This was a moon or two ago." "Did you see him here tonight?" Leanne demanded.

"No! I swear by the goddess, I never did."

"Very well, do you know where the nearest guild house is?" Finora asked, relaxing her stare down at the sweating servant.

"No. I never went there. I came up from the south and started working here."

"Is that all you know?"

"Yes, I mean, I've heard it is in some old barn, out towards the road to Kettle Gully."

"Before you go home tonight, I want you to take a letter to your Guildmaster," Finora told him. "Will you be able to do that?"

"Yes, Mam," Sammy nodded. "I mean I can take it to Jinkins at the Fighting Dog and he will see it gets there."

"That will do," Finora agreed, giving Leanne a glance and turning to leave. She pretended not to hear Sammy burst into tears and try to smother them on the table.

"Pathetic," Leanne muttered as she went with her sister up the stairs to the room where their brother waited. "The thieves Guild wouldn't kill that thief. But they will, if they are smart, find him and hand him to us."

"If we don't get him first," Finora agreed.

The duty Guards let them in without challenging them.

"Well?" Rhovert demanded when he saw them. "Did you get him?"

"No. He'd made his own opening to the sewers, and lost the Guards that were chasing him. Not that I am surprised, he lost us in there when we tried to follow him," Finora admitted.

"Dragon Shit! I should have had that lad questioned when we first saw him. If only I had known. The damn whelp was even in here acting as a servant! He was right under my nose! If I get my hands on that brat, I will strangle the truth out of him and save father the bother of hanging him."

"Rhovert, calm down. The guards are watching all the openings into the sewers. We have him holed up in there. If he comes out, we'll have him and if he doesn't we can send in searchers with torches," Leanne old him.

"What else has got you so edgy," Finora demanded.

"We have to get Maeven back!"

"I don't know why," Leanne commented. "That spoilt brat was never going to be good for anything."

"That doesn't matter. Father wants her back."

"Why for the dragon's sake? From what you said, he succeeded in getting her to leave the palace. Why has he suddenly changed his mind? I'd say good riddance," Finora added her opinion.

"I don't know why exactly. I think it's something he saw, in a vision. He doesn't even tell me much, but I think that something unspeakable will happen if we don't." Rhovert was serious.

Finora sighed, and Leanne shrugged.

"I'm beginning to think that whoever is claiming to have Maeven, is conning us," Leanne said. "Two of the guests downstairs are thieves who have been thought to have done that sort of thing in the past."

"We can't assume that," Rhovert insisted. "There were those other rumours that agents of Vatarik want to get her too, or disrupt these negotiations."

"Because we have that slimy Prince of theirs?" Finora asked.

"I'd swap Maeven for him if it will get them to stay their side of the border," Leanne declared.

"Will you both ease up? All father has actually said is that he is no longer sure that she is well. He always knew where you two were, and for a while he knew she was fine – mostly. Now he is not. He hasn't had any inkling of her whereabouts for over a year and a half. Now he has seen something that is really worrying him."

"Well, either she fell afoul of someone and is a prisoner, indentured slave or something, and her master is using this as a way to get rich, and will hand her over, or that was never the intention, and they were going to take the money and keep her," Leanne decided. "And it looks like we know which it was. I doubt anyone was going to turn up at the meeting."

"I will still have to go," Rhovert sighed. "And if we can't get another ransom here in time, I will have to try to gain time."

"Are you going to ask to see her? To be sure she is still alive?" Finora proposed.

"Of course. Father insisted on that."

"Very well, we will go out and help the search," Leanne decided.

"The best place to go will be near that lake," Finora considered. "I reckon that thief knows a bit about magic."

Maeven wasted no time once she was in the tunnels. That damn witch light would betray her position and give the guards light to follow her, but not if she left them behind, and around a few corners. But the light was also a boon to her, for she could see her way to run along the paved edges of the sludge filled channels, rather than walk, and would get less of the tell-tale muck on herself.

A river outlet was her first destination but she did not plan to emerge there. To do so would let the witch light illuminate the night sky. Instead, she removed her cloak and wrapped it around the sack of gold coins and the pouch of jewels. A muttered incantation caused the bundle to take on the colour of its surroundings and when pushed into a pile of rocks, snagging a mass of sludge, it became just some more unidentifiable rubbish. A second chant would enable her to find it again, even if this mass of sludge dislodged with the next rain.

Now clad in only trousers and belted jerkin, she made use of the witch light to travel more tunnels to yet another part of town; this time to where the river eddied to form a lake. The opening from the sewers was behind a screen of bushes, and that was all that saved her from being found. The light stayed in the tunnels, hovering just behind and above her – the opening was lower than the tunnel. Little of the light would be visible unless she emerged fully.

Caution was her main concern now. She had the ransom, and just had to get away clean, in spite of the hornets' nest she had stirred. Once back at the guild house, she should be safe.

So it came as a shock to see fires between the trees across and around the lake. It meant that the area was being watched, and her chances of slipping past that many watchers was poor. She would have to wait and watch, and that in turn would make it more complicated to explain her absence from the guild house.

All she could do was keep her ears listening for any little sound and try not to doze off, now that the euphoria of her success was wearing off.

The first tinges of light were colouring the sky when Maeven jerked awake. She could hear voices giving terse commands and the sound of men stirring, animals whickering and the jingle of harnesses being readied. She moved to peer across the pond, and saw that the fires were being doused.

They're leaving! She stood up to get the circulation back in her legs, so she would be ready to leave as soon as they were far enough away that the annoying witch light would not be seen. She wouldn't be vulnerable for long- just until she had dived into the pool and doused it. Then she could sneak ashore where ever she chose. If not to get to her last spare change of clothes, then to where she could run back and dry her clothes that way. The important thing was to get back as soon as she could.

Maeven waited until the last of the sounds of the retreating guards had faded to nothing before deciding it was safe enough to emerge from the tunnel. She ran for the water and dived in. The witch light hovered for a few moments then followed her – only to be extinguished.

With the return of the pre-dawn dimness, Maeven surfaced and swam to the far side of the pool, rinsing the sewer sludge from her clothes and with it the putrid smell. When she had crawled out onto dry land and walked in amongst the tall trees, and through the deserted campsite, she laughed with sheer exhilaration and began to lope back to the Thieves Guild house. She had better think of a good explanation for being out, for she would not be telling them of her night's work.

Finora and Leanne went to the stables and harnessed their horses, ready to ride out. They knew where they wanted to go, and set off at a trot, unaware that they were the object of furtive eyes, looking out through curtained of shuttered windows, as the people wondered at the unusual activity around the Crescent Moon Tavern.

Once they were on the edge of the town, Finora called a halt and spoke a spell over the horses to make their hoof beats become silent. Then they set off again at a fast trot. Shortly, they reached the encampment of guard and slowed the horses to a walk, stopping when the troop leader approached.

"What news?" he asked. "Have they caught the thief then?"

"Not yet," Leanne told him. "But we believe that he will come out this way, if he thinks you all have been recalled. We will be ready to go after him. We need your men to be deployed out of sight along the road – some between here and the Valeford, and the rest between here and Kettle Gully. The Thieves guild house is some old barn that is out this way. Likely the thief will be headed there."

Leanne had enough rank to be able to order the troop leader, but he was already aware that she was acting under orders from the King's Messenger. Her orders were put into action and the men began to break camp and saddle their horses, making no attempt to be quiet, so as to give the impression that they were no longer required there.

Leanne dismounted, and let Finora lead their horses a short distance away from the camp, and lightly tether them near to some fresh grass. They would both be keeping watch on the far side of the lake, to see if their presumption was correct.

"My guess is that he will make a break for the road as soon as all is quiet," Leanne predicted when her sister re-joined her. "We have to get him. If he invokes the protection of his guild, we will never find out if he knows where our sister is."

"I just had a thought, what if the guild itself is involved?"

"Don't be naïve, Finora! The Thieves' Guild is officially outlawed, but I'm sure that they probably pay the local guardsmen to look aside. However, if we heard about the Kings Messenger, you can bet they knew too. In any case, I doubt that the Guildmaster is a total fool – he wouldn't risk the King's anger and no one can bribe the King's Own Guards!"

"How far ahead will the guards be?" Finora changed the subject.

"Where they can watch the main road and the tracks leading off it. I hope to get him before he reaches the first side track, and scare the truth out of him." She went on to outline her plan for an ambush.

Finora was listening, but she was also looking out for her witch light, and interrupted Leanne's planning.

"There!"

The brief moment of light between the thief emerging and diving into the pool was enough to see he was not carrying anything. They watched him swimming across the pool, then disappearing into the trees nearest the road.

Some minutes later, the two horses were again trotting soundlessly along the road, and Finora was preparing an illusion. When she released it, a realistic vision of a horse and rider could be seen and heard, thundering down the road, coming up behind the running thief.

The thief glanced behind and fell into the ditch on the side of the road, and then scrambled into cover. Leanne and Finora spurred their mounts to a faster pace and then stooped just before the place where the thief had gone to hide.

With the day becoming brighter, Leanne could see her quarry crawling back up to the road, and slid from her horse and ran. She was onto her quarry before he could stand. The flat of her blade winded the thief who fell to the road fighting for breath.

Leanne deepened her voice to a semblance of a man's growl. Her almost six foot of height lent credence to the impression. Only her unbearded squarish jaw was visible.

"Where are the jewels and the gold?"

The Maeven made no answer except to struggle as her ambusher began to cut her jerkin with ruthless thoroughness.

"Rigidus!" Finora ordered in a commanding voice. The thief trembled, unable to move, feeling as if a powerful hand held her while wet fabric was torn from her body.

There was enough light for Leanne to see and recognise the tiny thief guild sigil tattooed near her left armpit. She smiled grimly, then exclaimed as she realised that this was no lad, but a girl. Finora came closer, and as Leanne searched through the shredded jerkin, the brightening daylight revealed a crown shaped birthmark on the girl's right side. There was shock on Leanne's face as she met Finora's eyes; they both had identical marks.

"I want the truth, girl!" Leanne spoke, sounding vicious, but Maeven no longer felt terrified. She couldn't speak until Finora relaxed her spell.

"Leanne, you daughter of the beast folk, leave me alone!" Maeven spat at her and to her other sister she said, "Remove your foul spell, Finora!"

"Remove it yourself, little sorceress!" Finora taunted casually. Her delicate triangular face, visible under the hood, betrayed no friendliness.

"You know I can't do magic!"

"No? You did quite well this night past!" Finora told her casually, indirectly informing her younger sister how much they knew.

"I stole the spell!" Maeven claimed, but true to her own code, did not tell the whole truth; unlike other magically ungifted, she did not need a potion to make it work. "And I am not going home, not for you, not for anyone – not even the King himself!" The words were defiant.

"So you planned this little swindle did you, so that you could run off and hide again?" Leanne scowled. "And have everyone in the kingdom looking for you?"

"Get away, yes."

"Maeven, you great fool." Leanne reverted to her own voice and lowered her hood, revealing dark hair cropped very short. "You've got little choice in that. Father wants you back – needs you back, according to Rhovert. That is the only reason he went along with your little swindle. He may be an insane tyrant but he is not stupid. I am sure that he expected something like this. Have some sense come back with us – because in hours the town will be too hot for you!"

"So father sent you to find me," Maeven sneered, "and like obedient little children, you went!"

"No, fool," Finora interrupted. "He wants us back, too, but until our current indenture is up – we're safe enough; thanks to his own convoluted laws! No, we came to give you some advice – go home – before his men find you and drag you back. We won't tell him what you've been up to, and if you go now, you will probably come out of this better than you deserve!"

Maeven swore using a stream of guardroom obscenities; Finora blushed, Leanne did not react.

"Idiot – after three years of disowning you – he wants you back; enough to spend lots of gold trying to find you. If he's that desperate, there will be a means to turn it to your advantage!" Leanne stressed.

"What's it about? I won't go back and marry Lord Toadface! I won't…"

"Lord Tormore had an unfortunate accident!" Leanne interrupted.

Hearing these flat emotionless words made Maeven wonder. "What's it about?" she asked again.

Leanne sighed. "I don't know! I think Rhovert does, but he's not telling."

Maeven spoke dismissively. "It doesn't matter anyway. I've made my own life! I have enough money now to live on for a long time. I have my plans – I won't be found. You two, of all people, can't lecture me!"

"The life of a thief, for the Lady's sake!" Finora protested. "At least the Order of Swords and the League of Sorcery are respectable careers, even for the likes of us."

"I have the protection of my Guild!" Maeven boasted, projecting confidence.

"I wouldn't count on it," Leanne warned. "When details of this morning's raid reach your Guild, do you really think they will want to keep you?" She shook her head with vexation. The rising sun glinted off her silver swordswoman's earring.

"They plan all raids!" Maeven hoped to mislead her sisters.

"Even if they did sanction the raid, which I doubt," Finora added her belief, "they won't like hearing that you used magic. They don't dare risk the wrath of the Sorcery League. We guard our good name!" she absently fingered the diamond studded neck clasp that was the symbol of a sorceress.

Maeven managed to keep her face expressionless.

"Do you even know who you robbed this morning?" Leanne asked casually.

"A rich fool!" Maeven dismissed with equal casualness, even though she had known.

Leanne smiled to herself. Their brother Rhovert, acting as King's Messenger, was neither rich nor a fool in spite of the way he presented himself.

"A word of advice then," said Leanne, changing her line of attack. "The King's Own Guards, who accompanied him, won't turn a blind eye to your guild! If you decide you need our help, we will be staying at the Crescent Moon for a few days. Oh, and don't forget that young children like that whelp at the inn who spotted you, aren't affected by a glamour of invisibility. Even I knew that!"

Maeven struggled again and Finora released her spell, allowing her to pull the tattered jerkin around herself as she stood up. She glared at her sisters and walked off without saying goodbye or looking back.

"Do you think she'll go?" Finora asked aloud, shaking her hood off and allowing her coiled up braids to fall down to her waist.

"If she truly values her skin, she will eventually realise she has no choice!"

Leanne thought aloud. "But she's too full of her own cleverness and if she chooses to ignore the fate of unaffiliated thieves in the kingdom…"

Finora shivered. "Maeven would think it funny, the idea of Father not being able to have her executed for thievery – though from the hints that Rhovert has dropped, Father would probably forgive her if she goes back."

"A year ago he would not have forgiven her, and I don't think the Thieves' Guild will now either." Leanne suppressed a shudder. "I am torn between not caring what happens to that selfish brat and what unspeakable thing will happen if she doesn't go home. Maeven has never done us any favours and I don't think she really cares what it's all about. I wonder why we bothered. If it wasn't for Rhovert's insistence…"

"It must be important for him to side with Father …" Finora interrupted.

"Let's go back to the inn. We'll tell Rhovert we found nothing; I'll give Maeven that much chance to go by herself."

Maeven reached her partitioned off corner in the Thieves' Guild house without seeing anyone. She quickly changed into a dry pair of trousers and an undamaged jerkin. Then she searched her pack for a vial of a thick liquid and poured some onto her palm and rubbed it into her short black hair. Grabbing a rough piece of towelling, she rubbed her head with that. The towel became black and her hair returned to a shade that was only a little darker than her usual light brown.

When she emerged, intending to make herself some breakfast, she found Nayfor waiting for her. His short, solid form blocked her way.

"You were at the Crescent Moon!" he greeted her stonily.

Maeven said nothing, neither admitting nor denying his accusation and trying to decide whether he was out to trap her or if he really knew. His next words decided her.

"The King's Own Guards are searching house to house; they have your description. Where is the take?"

"Hidden in the tunnels," Maeven finally admitted. Nayfor nodded thoughtfully.

"Downstairs with you then, bring all your things! They will be here before the sun is a handspan higher."

Nayfor waited whilst Maeven gathered all she owned including the part of her horde of gems and coins that she still had in her cubicle and then walked off. He did not wait to see if she followed, so he did not see her turn pale. She had not really believed her sisters' warning and only now decided that she really did want to know what was going on. What could make her sisters act for her father?

Her sisters had predicted this raid. Surely they had not told the guards… no, there hadn't been time. Who then? That dratted child who should have been seen and not heard? Did Rhovert guess?

Nayfor led her downstairs and showed her the bolthole constructed for emergencies such as this. It was no more that an excavated dirt hole, roughly shored up. There were no windows and only a long tube, a handspan wide, to provided ventilation. A log too heavy for her to lift barred the far door – but escaping now would be foolish. The door she had entered through clicked shut behind her; it had locks and bolts on both sides.

Maeven checked her pocket; yes, she had transferred the special key to it. It looked like any old key but by using a certain incantation, it would mould itself to open any lock; some added insurance.

While the day progressed outside, Maeven made plans but not one of them included going home. She had enough wealth to live the kind of life she wanted now – wealth stolen in part without the knowledge of the guild and not reduced by their usual levy of half. The thought made her smile.

The door opened finally – Maeven scuttled out to find herself facing a semi circle of her fellow thieves. Nafor was at the front, with Guildmaster Jocelyn a half step back from his right shoulder.

"You're out, Ven!" Nayfor told her coldly. "No Guild house in the Kingdom of Thulor will shelter you henceforth!"

Maeven looked around at the ring of implacable faces.

"Why?" she asked Nayfor.

"Are you a witless fool, girl?" he asked without emotion. "Many of us are in the King's dungeons now and you have endangered all of us by disregarding our rules. Not only did you rob a King's Messenger who was carrying the Princess' ransom, but you also used magic! You've been a good provider in the past, Ven, but we can't let you stay and imperil us any further. We've hidden you from the search and you can stay until tonight, but you must be gone by morning. Do you accept this?"

Maeven slumped visibly. "I accept," she murmured.

Nayfor nodded and all but Jocelyn, and his second, a man named Gilbert left. These two moved and gripped Maeven by the arms as Nayfor unlaced her jerkin enough to reveal the Thieves' Sign. She stiffened, realising what was to come. Nayfor took a tiny long handled iron from the fire in a small brazier that was burning on a side table. The red-hot end formed a cross and it was touched over the Thieves' Sign. He was not a cruel man, so his action lasted no longer than necessary and was over quickly, but the pain remained. Maeven managed not to scream and, when released, was allowed to re-lace her jerkin.

Only Nayfor remained in the room when she finished. He stared at her with expressionless features. She straightened under his penetrating gaze.

"You planned all this," he accused, raising the cooling iron to emphasise his point. "Why?"

"You said it yourself, Nayfor!" Maeven told him, her whole manner full of satisfaction. "He was carrying the Princess's ransom. I just bought my freedom!"

Nayfor stared, his face betraying nothing, but the tension in his stance told her that he hadn't known who she really was. Without a further word, he turned his back and walked away.

CHAPTER 16 – THE HOME COMING

A laugh wanted to bubble up from inside Maeven as she walked boldly past the watching Guardsmen. They could not see her of course – she had made herself invisible again. No doubt, they assumed that as she was a thief, she did not use magic. They would be less alert now, too. It had been three days since she robbed the King's Messenger. The past two days she had watched the guards beating the bushes and grasslands – uselessly. She assumed that her sisters had reported that the thief had emerged and run off, and they had lost her. Neither the Town Guards nor the King's Own Guards had even begun to search in the sewers where she had been hiding.

That morning, when she had checked, there was no such activity and she had felt it safe to emerge. She had even dared to wash herself properly in the lake, so none of the strong smell clung to her.If she was going to have to dodge their watching posts along the roads, she didn't want them to smell her. This quartet of guards was the third one she had passed and these were the King's Own Guards too, the best in the realm. Life was good.

Her planned route did not involve going all the way from Valeford to Palacetown and taking the main highway but she had needed to come this way a while before cutting south through the open farmland and royal forest.

Maeven walked across old Hedwig's fields. He grew cabbages and maintained neat weed free furrows between the rows. She strode along the rows, which led uphill, until his field met those of Farmer Osbert. He had wheat planted now but there were tracks through his field too if you knew where to go. On the far side of the land that Osbert farmed for Lord Falloner was an open area, and beyond that was forest. The King owned the wild land but the peasants could collect nuts, mushrooms and firewood and Lord Falloner authorised hunting parties in there. The trails through the forest shortened the way south by many miles.

Maeven skirted Hedwig's field until she came to the opening in the waist-high grain. It was growing well, though being early summer it was not ready for harvesting. Her path continued up the hill and the breeze was rippling the grain stalks and hiding any movement caused by her passage.

The laugh finally escaped her – she was free! Free of the Thieves Guild. Free of her father and free to head out of the Kingdom, to collect her son and live the life she wanted.

Along with her meagre pack of possessions, carried openly on her shoulder, she had with her all the wealth she had accumulated since leaving the southern hills. This was magically hidden and was obeying the "follow" spell. That piece of magic was her most useful find of all, especially as she had discovered how to modify it each time she added to her hoard. When she wanted a particular part of it, she simply had to incant the relevant counter charm and the item would be in her hand. No bandit would think her worth robbing. Assuming they could see her of course! She laughed again.

A low growl became audible from a little way ahead. Maeven had never heard anything like it. It didn't sound like a dog. Her pace became cautious and her eyes darted everywhere, then an enormous black feline sprang suddenly onto the path. It was turning its head this way and that trying to find her scent.

Oh, no! Maeven thought, bringing her knives into her hand. The traders in the north encountered these beasts in the wild stretches between towns, but they should not be this far into the realm. It was only a day's travel to the King's Palace.

She backed slowly away, but the breeze was still coming from behind her. She edged sideways into the wheat stalks. The feline saw the movement and ran forward, still confused by being unable to see the prey it smelt. It growled, almost howled, in frustration.

The instinct to flee took over. Maeven crashed through the wheat plants, flattening them as she passed. Some sprang back up, enough to slow the bounding pace of the cat. Her path zigzagged to the south.

The fierce growls and the mysteriously moving grain attracted the attention of the guards down the slope. Four guardsmen went to investigate. They mounted their horses, drew swords or nocked arrows into bows and galloped towards the activity on the hill.

Maeven did not want to run towards the guardsmen, although that would have been the smartest move. Instead, she stopped suddenly and crouched into a ball. The cat kept coming; it was not yet aware of the approaching horses.

The cat changed its tone from a hunting snarl to a confused growl. It had lost the scent of its prey. A louder growl of defiance indicated to Maeven when it became aware of the approaching men and horses. Would it attack or flee?

The cat chose to run; two guardsmen archers and one of the swordsmen rode in pursuit. The fourth guard watched the field from the back of his mount. This man knew the cat had been chasing something. He wanted to know what. It may have been a dog but the disturbance as the prey had run suggested a bigger creature, an animal on two legs. Someone who should have been visible – but was not.

Maeven waited until the sound of pounding hooves and growling quietened into the distance. The sounds of the creatures hidden in the wheat returned to normal. She uncurled slowly, moving the grass as little as possible. Her heart was still pounding in her chest but her breathing was slowly quietening.

The horseman approached silently. The first hint that she was not alone came when she sensed something flying through the air. She turned around. Too late, she registered the rope noose falling around her. It was a lucky shot for she was still not visible. She dropped into a crouch and pulled the rope off before it tightened, but she had betrayed her presence. The man knew where to aim his sword. His thrust was rewarded with a stifled cry of pain.

"Reveal yourself!" he ordered, confident of his superior position. He was not instantly obeyed, so he pushed the sword a little harder. This time he heard a soft mutter, the words being spoken with difficulty.

"Well, well, well!" he said more to himself. "That creature did our work for us!" He studied the writhing figure dispassionately. He made a mental comparison between this vagabond and the one they were seeking. Short in stature, slight in build, close cropped darkish brown hair and dressed as a man. The details matched well enough.

"Get up!" the guard ordered.

"I can't!" Maeven gasped. Her hands were trying futilely to stop the sword gash in her leg from bleeding.

The man dismounted warily. The wound was a bad one and the woman was wanted alive. He did not intend to risk himself so he recovered his rope, slipped the noose around the woman's neck and tied the other end to his saddle. Maeven was not stupid, she stopped moving and lay still. The guard tore strips of fabric from the bottom of her tunic to bind the wound.

"Thank you," she said quietly.

"Don't thank me, thief!" he said unsmiling. "Robbing a King's Messenger is treason. The King has traitors hung. Get up!"

There was no pity in his voice, nor expression, as Maeven pulled herself up. She was dizzy with the pain and clung to the horse's bridle to stay upright.

The animal was well trained and stood rock steady. After a moment, the guard gave it the command to walk. The prisoner had to keep up or be dragged. Traitors deserved no consideration.

As she stumbled along, using one hand to hold on to the bridle, Maeven slipped the other into her pocket. She whispered the revoking chant on the piece of dragon shell she'd taken from the cavern in the south. Touching the shell sent a flush of heat through her and the dizziness vanished. A prickling feeling intensified about the wound and the leg felt stronger, moment by moment. When they were about to enter the town she hid the shell again.

Four others joined the guard, and the procession continued back to the Crescent Moon tavern. The first maintained hold of the neck rope and two others pushed the prisoner's hands behind her back and bound them with the other end of the rope.

"Summon Prince Rhovert!" Maeven's captor ordered the innkeeper. He watched his prisoner warily and wondered if she had banged her head and was not aware of the seriousness of her position. All other thieves he had caught fought desperately when told they were likely to hang.

Maeven steeled herself to face her brother. She did not fear him, and did not believe that her father would actually hang her. Minute by minute her strength was returning and the opportunity to escape would come.

It was not Prince Rhovert, though, who descended from the sleeping loft. Maeven recognised Lord Rolliver, the former servant of the unfortunately dead Lord Tormore. She quickly turned her head away and the guard felt the fluttering of panic in his prisoner.

"Prince Rhovert was summoned by the King on a matter of some urgency," Rolliver suavely informed the guard. "I am in charge of the search in his absence. Is this the thief we are seeking?"

"The description matches, Lord."

Rolliver grabbed the prisoner's face and forced it around. Recognition was instantaneous and the noble's face took on a feral look. The prisoner tensed.

"Where are the coins and jewels you stole from the King's Messenger?" he asked in a voice oozing malice. When the prisoner did not answer, he tried again. "Where is Princess Maeven?" This time silence was met by a stinging slap. It brought tears to the prisoner's eyes and a look of anger. The reaction pleased Rolliver but after ten minutes of questions and slaps, the prisoner still refused to talk.

The King's Own Guards were getting restless. It was their duty to take the prisoner to the King and his representative was approaching the point of unnecessary behaviour towards the prisoner.

"There are two rings set into the hearth. Procure some chain and secure the prisoner there. Then go and supervise the town guards – instruct them to search the sewers, starting with the opening to the back pool. This thief must have the ransom hidden in there."

At times during the rest of the day, Rolliver repeated his attempts to get answers. His failure brought about a shortening of the securing chain. At first, she had been able to sit in reasonable comfort but by evening, she had been forced to stand at an awkward angle. She was getting desperate for a drink and had an urgent need to use the privy. Her arms and legs were aching.

The guards returned at dusk and the troop leader eased the chain on the prisoner so that the fire could be lit in the hearth. The regular patrons of the tavern were turned away.

Just before the Guard leader turned in for the night, he allowed the prisoner to use the privy and gave her a small drink of water.

Maeven slept fitfully, waiting for the guardsmen lying around her to be asleep. She tested the metal cuffs on her wrist and tried to slide her hands free – failure. Ideas for escape twirled in her mind. Finally, her foggy brain remembered she had a key. Hope cleared her mind as she moved her hands to feel about in her pocket. *Yes, it was still there.*

She had the lock holding the chains in one hand, the key in the other and very softly chanted a song that she had known since childhood. The key changed shape in her hand and flowed into the lock, opened it and flowed out into its original shape. Before moving further she put the key back in her pocket and hid it. Movement caught her eye and she feigned sleep.

The taproom was oddly dark when she opened her eyes again. The same numbers of candles were lit but they seemed to cast less light. She heard whispering, recognised the tone of Rolliver's voice. Slowly, she moved her head to try to see who the other whisperer was. By the fire, opposite Rolliver, was a dark shadow. It seemed to have no substance but that might have been illusion. She moved to hear more clearly.

"…In its dormant sstate, it will passs through magical sshields. Activate it insside; it will make everyone in your viscinity asleep. Get the talissmanss and free the Prins," the shadow spoke in a hissing whisper.

"The King and Prince Rhovert are away, Master," Rolliver murmured, just audibly. "I arranged for the uprisings in the east to worsen. I will have to enter the King's apartments. While he is away, the Royal Seal is in a locked safe hole. He used it to activate the mage locks on the cells. This time he didn't take the Queen's talisman. I also sent the two Princesses back to the palace on the King's orders."

"You know what to do! I will not acsept failure. Bring me all the talissmanss and releasse my Prins. If he iss not free by ssummer ssolstisce, releasse the blight in the palasce – but enssure you are protected."

"Your will, Master."

The shadow began to fade and the candles began to emit their normal light. Rolliver stood up and walked to his sleeping prisoner. Though he checked the chains, he did not notice that the lock was no longer secure. Then he went quietly to the door and slipped outside.

Maeven quickly finished freeing herself, muttered the invisibility chant and followed. When she reached the door and peeked out, Rolliver was leading a saddled horse out from the stables. A short way down the road, he mounted and urged the horse to a gallop.

The stable was behind the inn. Maeven ran there and looked inside. The stable lad lay crumpled on the floor, dead. She found a rope, saddle and bridle then chose and prepared the nearest mount. She was glad the King's stable master had made her learn to tend a horse in the dark. Moments later, she too was galloping down the road.

Part way to the palace her mind asked her why she simply did not turn south where she wanted to go, but the desire to thwart Rolliver was too strong to make her change direction. It certainly was not out of concern for her sisters.

Near the palace, Maeven slowed and approached the cheese maker's cottage. In the woman's backyard, which backed onto the castle wall was a trapdoor. It led to a tunnel that ran to the palace keep, to the cellar below the kitchens. She led the horse into a lean-to next to the cheese maker's donkey.

Maeven went directly to the trapdoor and entered the tunnel. She knew it well enough to run along it and this time she could see a faint glow – it was not total darkness.

Coming out into the kitchen was a necessary step, but a short distance away was the entrance to some hidden ways that Rolliver would not know. Again, there was a faint glow, easing the darkness as she ran to the steps that led to the sleeping level. In the secret passage, she counted doors until she came to her father's apartment. She was feeling the itch of magic and entered her father's dressing room quietly. There was no sign of Rolliver, so Maeven went to the location of the locked safe hole. This was the secret place where her father kept his valuables and the Royal Seal. It was no challenge to open because Maeven had practiced on it before leaving home. She reached inside and felt a round orb. The demon receptacle went into one pocket; the Royal Seal went into another, along with her mother's talisman. She reached in again and felt around – there was nothing left. A moment was wasted wondering about the black oval stone – the dragon's mage egg. It should have been there!

A noise at the door of the lock being forced reminded Maeven of her position. She relocked the secret place and hid behind the wall drapes.

The piece of dragon shell in her pocket, even though hidden by magic, grew cold then flashed hot. Maeven peeked out and, in the light of a single mage light, saw that the holder of the light. Rolliver, had two talismans around his neck. One was on a green silk ribbon and the other on a leather strap.

The air seemed to grow thick as Rolliver neared the safe hole. He fiddled for five minutes, and muttered some spell before the lock opened for him. He growled his annoyance when he found the hole empty.

Then he seemed to sense a presence and looked around. With an angry swish, he dragged the wall hangings aside to reveal the one who had preceded him. A knife came into his hand and his eyes blazed with hate. There was no veneer of civility, no sense of fair play, just the fierce desire to kill. He did not like this thief, who had somehow managed to get free and beat him to the palace, and did not want her to reveal what she knew.

Maeven concentrated on defending herself – bouncing, shuffling, ducking and continually moving in random ways. A knife came into her hand, by magic. Occasionally she attacked to good effect. Rolliver's tunic was slit in many places. Her sisters' amulets were on the floor, cut from around his neck.

Maeven did not hear the door open but Rolliver saw a chance to turn the fight in his favour. In the moment that he yelled, Maeven stabbed him in the gut. "Blast her!" he yelled and suddenly realised his injury.

The result was instantaneous. Maeven fell to the floor, stunned – as Roman Golddreamer went to Lord Rolliver, who was trying to speak.

"She robbed the King's safe and the ransom from the Prince. Put her in the dungeon with water only. No one is to approach her. She's dangerous. Tell the King she was going to free the prisoners."

Roman drew his wand and incanted a healing spell, but it was too late. Rolliver was dead.

Roman switched his attention to the thief, placing magical restraints before she woke. His next action was to search her pockets. He withdrew the demon orb carefully, then checked the locking spell was still functional. There was nothing else in that pocket. The other contained the Queen's amulet, the Royal Seal and he felt something that was as cold as metal. The cold object stayed stubbornly in the pocket, even with the pocket pulled out. The object could not be moved and it was invisible. Roman chanted a revealing spell and touched the item he could only feel. What he revealed was concave, gold lined and black on its outer surface. *A piece of dragon shell.* He tried several chants before the item came free.

Everything but the black and gold shell went back into the safe hole and he placed mage locks on the door to it.

He recovered the two amulets from the floor. His own, the one the King had given him, was cold.

He hurried to the chamber shared by the Princesses Finora and Leanne. The air here was thick, the two women barely breathing. He placed the amulets on them, remembering that the green silk-laced one was Finora's. There was no improvement.

He reached for his wand and thought of how to deal with thick air. A breeze spell actually made the air thicker. He thought of the shell he had found in the thief's pocket and drew it out. He caught a glimpse of a fine gold etching on the black shell. He recognised the Arms of the Kingdom of Thulor. The air began to move.

Finora stirred first, sensing the flow of magic. She sat up suddenly, already incanting a focussing spell. Her eyes settled on Roman and she realised that her talisman was in her lap.

"All is well now, My Lady. Tend to your sister."

Roman went briefly to his own chamber but everything was as it should be. It was unusual, though, that no servant or guard had been alerted to his walking around. He gave a bellow for guards. After a full minute, though, the castle was still silent. He ran back to the King's apartments, recalling belatedly that even in the monarch's absence, the chamber was guarded – but he had not seen the guards.

He used his wand and a simple spell to illuminate the passage. The air seemed normal but the bodies of the two guards lay in alcoves away from the King's door. Someone had stabbed each of them, and they were both dead.

He returned to the King's apartment. The thief lay there, still unconscious and controlled. Using magic, he lit some candles. The thief had a young face but he had no compassion as he hefted the unconscious body and carried it easily down to the dungeons.

The dungeon guards challenged him but he was immediately recognised. They opened one of the darker cells for the prisoner and heard what had occurred upstairs.

He placed his burden on the dirt floor and let the guards search her for hidden weapons. Then they efficiently secured the prisoner with chains set into the wall. When the cell was closed, Roman placed a mage lock on the door. He left one guard there and the other went to rouse his fellows, agreeing with the need for more guards in the dungeon and the Royal Apartments.

The guard returned, calm in spite of his news. "I cannot rouse any of them."

"Stay here," Roman commanded as he ran for the guardroom.

The air was as thick there as it had been in the Princesses' chamber. Roman pulled out the etched shell again. Now he was feeling its magic operating and the air thinned towards normal. The guards still did not rouse. Roman walked to the nearest one and felt for a heartbeat. The man was alive and began to wake at the wizard's touch. Each guard had to be touched in turn and Roman realised that the black and gold object helped to restore them.

The first guards to wake soon sensed something abnormal and challenged the wizard.

Roman tersely explained the situation he had found. He mentioned what he had done and what he thought should be done. As he continued to revive guards, the temporary Captain of the Guards issued orders. Although they did not normally take instructions from the wizard, his suggestions were sound. More guards went to important positions and others went to search the castle for more pockets of the mysterious malady. A guard messenger departed with a report for the King.

Within half a candle mark, the castle was secure. Roman had moved to the servants' quarters and was working to revive all he could. So far, seven of the less robust servers were dead.

He looked up finally and saw Princess Leanne. There was a stubborn, angry look on her face.

"The thief you caught did all this?" she almost snarled.

"Apparently so," he agreed, seeing the anger rising.

"Where is the thief now?"

"The thief is a prisoner in the dungeons," Roman said calmly. "There is to be no contact with her until the King returns. Lord Rolliver, two guards and seven servants are dead."

Some other emotion suddenly dampened part of the anger.

"What did the thief look like?" she asked intently.

"Short cropped darkish hair, young and female," Roman wondered what her interest was.

"Was she searched?"

"Yes, she had items from the safe hole in the King's apartment. Her knife remains in her victim. There was nothing else."

Some of the tension left the Princess but not the determination. Roman moved to the next unconscious servant.

The King's Physician, an elderly man, was only now stumbling down the stairs into the servants' dormitory. Leanne saw him and stalked off before he decided to examine her.

Roman merely shook his head and kept working. It was not hard to deduce the reason for the Princess's anger. The thief had bettered her, could have killed her and she resented being so helpless.

Princess Finora was talking to Gisella Golddreamer when the wizard returned to his own apartment. He walked unsteadily across the chamber and collapsed into a chair. He was confident that the King's Own Guards had everything under control.

"Thank you Wizard Roman," Princes Finora said softly. "What was the nature of the spell we suffered?"

In a tired voice, he described what he observed. He commented that the effects had been strongest in areas where the greatest opposition to the thief's presence would likely come from.

"Lord Rolliver tried to stop the thief. He managed to tell me he thought she was going to try to release the prisoners. She also had the demon receptacle and your mother's amulet."

"As she took ours. Why were you spared?"

"The thief may not be aware that I had a talisman," Roman said immediately. "I am surprised that yours didn't warn you of trouble. I felt the dark magic and came to locate it, though I have employed other protections as well."

"I feel traces of dark magic still," Finora admitted. "How did it penetrate your shields on the castle? I checked and could find no flaw in them."

"I will test them later," Roman pledged.

"I will add more protective spells around myself and my sister," Finora said thoughtfully. "I believe it was you who suggested to Rhovert that we wear anti-scrying charms?"

"Yes, My Lady," Roman confirmed.

"It is well we do! The spell has protected us a number of times."

"Prince Rhovert was concerned about your youngest sister," Roman mentioned casually. He saw Finora's face begin to scowl.

"He needn't bother. I doubt if the devil himself would want her!" Finora stood and nodded a parting.

Gisella was still in bed but when Finora had gone, she berated her husband for walking into danger.

"I'm not a child, wife!" he said placidly, getting up to give her a kiss.

"Atlantis, you may as well return to bed. The danger is past."

His sister, who had just emerged from another room in the suite, was fully dressed in her swordswoman outfit, complete with sword.

"You aren't going to walk around like that!" Gisella reproached her sister-in-law.

"Princess Leanne does and the King is not here!" Atlantis said flatly.

"What about Prince Rhovert?" Gisella snickered.

"He doesn't object!" Atlantis glared at Gisella, who had been teasing her since she had returned from her last trip. It had not been hard to deduce that she, along with Prince Rhovert, were the latest topic of the Court gossipmongers. Just because they had departed together…

"Oh, well," Gisella appeared to back down. "You know what they say about him…"

"They are wrong!" Roman stated flatly, surprising both women. They expected him to say more but he only said, "I'm for sleep!"

Late in the afternoon, Atlantis roused her brother.

"There is a messenger waiting with a missive from Prince Rhovert," she told him before returning to the outer chamber so he could dress.

Roman had not fully undressed before collapsing into bed. It was the work of moments to don his shirt and breeches. Gisella often chided him for continuing to look like a farmer but he simply told her that Court Wizards did not have to follow Court dress customs.

"Where is Gisella?" he asked Atlantis as he emerged.

"Oh, around!" was her too casual reply. She laughed and continued, "She is soaking up Court gossip like a dish cloth soaks up water."

Roman's face creased into a grin at his wife's expense. He sobered quickly when he saw the begrimed messenger.

"Lord Wizard, I have a letter from Prince Rhovert," he handed over a leather satchel.

Roman withdrew a scroll and broke the green wax seal imprinted with Rhovert's sigil. He read in silence, aware that Atlantis was reading it around his shoulder.

"Maintain utmost vigilance of all prisoners," Rhovert had scribbled hurriedly. "No one is to approach them until the King returns. I will be there as soon as I have reports from all parties about the capture of the thief and her escape from the Crescent Moon. It is interesting to note that no guards were aware of Rolliver's departure. A stable boy was found dead this morning. If you have not done so already, place a preserving spell on all victims. Show this letter to the King's Guards."

Roman went to obey the Prince's command and showed the letter to the guard at the King's apartment. He was granted access and placed a preserving spell on Rolliver's body. Nothing had been touched in there since he left. He repeated his spell on the dead guards.

The dead servants had been laid out in a hastily cleaned chamber on the domestic level.

"The King commands that any rituals be delayed until his return," the guard informed the steward. "The wizard is placing a preserving spell on the dead. Further visits to these unfortunates must wait. The room is to be sealed."

Roman took the hint and sealed the chamber. He knew it would upset grieving friends and relatives, but they must obey their King.

CHAPTER 17 – THE PRISONER

This had not been an auspicious homecoming for the Princesses. Their unplanned and unexpected return three days ago had caused a stir in the castle. Gisella had heard rumours of dire things likely to occur. Now the servants were saying they were right and the latest rumours were wild and ominous.

Thanks to Prince Rhovert, the Princesses were well informed of all the events that had occurred in the castle in their years away. In fact, the first thing they had done after changing from their travelling clothes had been to seek out wizard Roman. They knew that he had received a talisman and could be trusted.

Now that the palace was quiet again after the magic attack, attempted theft and murders, they were still not able to return to sleep. They were very uneasy in their minds. Wondering if they had made a deadly mistake letting their sister go. But they didn't want to say anything yet, for the thief the guards had caught, may not have been Maeven. Their sister might have been working with another girl thief.

They had tried on several occasions to go down to the dungeon to see if the prisoner was their sister, but the guards had refuse to let them by. All they could do was wait for their brother or father to return.

Shortly before midnight, Prince Rhovert did arrive. He was dressed in dusty travelling clothes and his face was begrimed and strained. He went to see his sisters and found them in the suite chosen for them, talking to the wizard and his wife.

"I am glad to see that you arrived here safely," he greeted his sisters.

"When we would have preferred to stay with our troop," Leanne countered. "I didn't believe that yes-man Rolliver when he told us we had to come here. Captain Wyst confirmed it or we wouldn't be here."

"Now can you tell us what this is about?" Finora demanded, even before he had a chance to pull up a chair.

"Not just yet. I can tell you that Father bought out your indenture. He wanted you here!"

"And Maeven?" Finora asked with deceptive sweetness.

"In good time!" Rhovert tried to hide his frustration with his failure to find his youngest sister.

Roman saw the twins exchange a glance.

"We gave the Guards a description of the person we saw coming from the sewer exit," Leanne reminded her brother. "It was a girl, but is there any indication that the thief who stole from you was male or female?"

"A short, dark haired wench was caught," Rhovert answered warily.

"Is it the same one that came here?" Leanne asked.

Rhovert glanced at the wizard, to which Roman answered, "It appears so."

"What concerns you, Leanne?" Rhovert asked.

He had the unexpected sight of seeing both his sisters turning white faced. His watched them with concern, waiting for an explanation.

Finora gave in first. "We told you we didn't catch the thief that came out of the sewers…"

Leanne continued. "But we did. It was Maeven herself, we saw her birthmark."

"We told her to go home," Finora told him. "We said it would be advantageous for her…"

Rhovert controlled himself with an obvious effort.

"Why didn't you simply bring her back?" he glared at Leanne.

"Why didn't you at least tell me?" he demanded of Finora.

"A lot of people are dead…" he stopped short of voicing the thought in his mind that his youngest sister was an unprincipled murderer. Neither Leanne nor Finora wished to voice that thought either.

"Do you wish to ascertain the prisoner's identity?" Roman offered calmly.

"No! No one is to go near the prisoner until Father's return," Rhovert said harshly. "And this matter is not to be mentioned outside this chamber." His eyes met those of Gisella.

"No, My Lord," she promised.

"I have more than a few questions, but they can wait until morning." Rhovert rubbed his hand through his hair. He strode out and headed for his own chambers.

Roman and Gisella made their own departure.

Gisella was finding it hard to contain the juicy gossip she had heard the previous night. However, she was mindful of Prince Rhovert's command. She liked being the wife of the Court Wizard. It would not serve her position if she disobeyed his request for silence.

In the bathing room later that morning, Atlantis asked Gisella how her evening had been. Fortunately they were alone, because Gisella was soon telling her sister-in-law what she had heard about the thief. Atlantis saw Gisella's horrified look as she shoved her fist into her mouth.

"Oh! I was told not to say anything."

Grinning, Atlantis commented, "I won't tell anyone what you told me! It's a relief to know that my brother has efficiently solved the thief problem – whoever she is. Mind you, I've never heard anything nice spoken about the younger Princess!"

"No, I haven't either," Gisella, agreed. "Most of the servants sounded glad to see the back of her. There was a rumour that she was to be married to Lord Tormore – the one that died just before we came here!"

Atlantis shuddered. She had heard some nasty things about that man. If she was betrothed to him, she would have run away, too!

"Drop it, Gis," Atlantis suggested. "His Majesty will sort it out when he returns."

Prince Rhovert strode into the Queen's Apartment on the following day "and found his father soaking in a full-length bath.

"How long have you been back?" he demanded rudely.

Even in the bath, the King was still The King.

"When I have recovered from the rigours of my trip, it will be time enough to hear your inquisitor's report. Or are you so anxious for me to preside at a hanging that you can't wait?"

Rhovert recoiled at the thought.

"It is the question of the prisoner's identity that I wish to resolve," Rhovert attempted to sound non-committal. "You said no one was to go near the prisoner until your return."

"The thief who robbed you was caught?" the King asked pointedly.

"We believe so, but…"

"The thief is now in the dungeon?"

"Yes…"

"Then the question of identity can wait a few hours longer," the King said urbanely as if he was on his throne not in the bath. "A few days in the dungeons makes prisoners more cooperative. As it is, I do not intend to welcome my daughters home looking like the stable sweep. That, I feel, is more important than the comfort of a mere thief and murderer."

Rhovert ground his teeth in annoyance.

The King continued, "Have my daughters attend me in half a candle mark and when you return, bring my wizard with you. I would like to behold the condition of my apartments."

At the appointed time, Leanne and Finora arrived at the apartment that had been their mother's. Leanne wore a new leather tunic and trousers. Her sword gleamed and her boots shone. Even her hair was tamed into a neat plait. Finora had chosen a crimson silk gown and her hair was braided and coiled about her ears. Each looked every inch a professional of her chosen career.

The King was standing in the alcove containing a large window when his daughters were announced. As they entered, he turned and smiled at them.

Each managed to say, "Hello Father." They didn't know what else to say.

The King studied them intently for a long time, making them uneasy.

"You have both fulfilled my expectations," he commended them.

"Do you mean, you wanted us to go off and do what we did?" Leanne blurted.

"Indeed. Neither of you would have become so skilled had you remained here."

"But Mother would never let us -" Finora began to protest.

"Your mother was a lady from a rich merchant family," Westron cut her off. "They expect different things of their daughters. I knew I needed you to be strong, self-suffient and skilled."

Both women visibly relaxed, accepting that he was not angered by their furtive departure of six years ago and were happy to sit when invited to do so. The spread of refreshments began to look inviting.

"When are you going to tell us what is going on?" Finora asked after a period of polite talk.

"In good time," the King assured her. "Have another pastry."

"Why did you buy out our indenture?" Leanne asked instead. "I object to being bartered with like a slave."

"An apprentice is little better than a slave to his master," the King remarked casually. "As I have been aware of your progress, I took advantage of a loophole in the laws I created. I needed to be able to call on your services when I needed them."

At that point, Prince Rhovert entered before the guard could announce him. Wizard Roman, who was dressed in his finest farmer's outfit, followed him. It was a marked contrast to Rhovert's over fancy Court finery. They sat in the two empty seats.

"Now, Rhovert, I would like to hear your inquisitor's report," the King invited. He gave his son his full attention.

"No one contacted me at the Crescent Moon," Robert began. "That is if you don't count the thief that robbed me. I went to the agreed rendezvous at the agreed day and time, and saw no one there. Either they were never going to be there or they had heard about the robbery and stayed away. We couldn't get any more information out of the child who was acting as messenger, except for a description of the one who gave him the work. If I had known that sooner, I might had caught the damn thief. He was in and out of the Cresent Moon every day between my arrival and the robbery."

Rhovert continued to report all his findings except for the part where his sisters had identified Maeven and let her go.

"So, have you come to any conclusions about whether this was a ruse of my youngest daughter, or a ransom proposal?" King Westron asked his son.

"Why do you think it might have been a ransom demand?" Leanne asked, interrupting.

The King looked thoughtfully at her and decided to answer.

"I occasionally experience 'flashes' from the other talismans. Not as clearly as your Mother did, but enough for me to be sure the wearer was well. For the past year I have been receiving some very odd impressions and I stopped being sure of your younger sister's wellbeing."

"I thought you didn't know where she was," Rhovert accused.

"I didn't," Westron admitted. "I simply knew she was well. Do you have an answer to my question?"

Leanne answered, "Maeven was behind the ransom demand."

The King's eyebrows lifted as if in surprise.

"Finora and I followed the thief that came out of the sewers and cornered her. It was definitely Maeven — we saw her birthmark! We told her to come home."

"That was very civil of you," his Majesty commented mildly. "So who was the thief that was caught?"

"That's what I want to find out. I think it is Maeven!" Rhovert told him.

The King looked thoughtful. "Are you saying that she was responsible for all the magic and malice that occurred here yesterday? It is my understanding that Rolliver had the thief a prisoner in Valeford, mere hours before events began here."

"The thief escaped during the night," Rhovert admitted.

"It is unlikely to suppose that the thief, if she escaped, would choose to come here."

Leanne and Finora glanced at each other, sharing a consideration of that likihood and both decided that Maeven had admitted no such intention, rather the opposite – to flee out of the kingdom.

"The description matches," Rhovert attested, looking at Roman for confirmation.

"There could be many young women that fit that description, and I have never met the youngest Princess," Roman said calmly.

"Perhaps, Wizard Goldreamer, you would give me an account of the events here as you experienced them."

After Roman finished speaking, the King stood and said, "Well, if I am to accuse my daughter or any other of theft and murder, I should examine the evidence for myself. Wizard Roman, would you unseal my apartments? We shall proceed there. Leanne, Finora you may wish to wait here."

"No, Father, we will come," Finora decided, ignoring the tacit command and challenging him to object.

"Very well!"

He led the way to the adjoining rooms. The guard stationed there saluted and stood aside.

The king prowled his desecrated private chamber, keeping his thoughts to himself. There was no doubt that the thief's knife had killed his noble. Rolliver was still clasping his own bloody knife.

"There were two talismans on the floor?" the King repeated when Roman had finished.

"Yes, Majesty," Roman confirmed.

"The spell you encountered – would you consider it Dark Magic?"

"It was used for a dark purpose," Roman considered. "The spell itself was not, in essence, evil."

"Repeat what you found on the thief?"

Roman itemised the objects once again.

"Interesting! Where are the items now?" the King asked.

"I returned the demon receptacle, the Royal Seal and your wife's talisman to your safe hole, Majesty," Roman told him. "I have the other object with me. I believe it is a piece of dragon shell. It was invisible in the thief's pocket.

It appears to have healing properties and it helped clear the thick air when magic made it worse."

Roman took the item out of his pocket and handed it to the King.

"If it was in the thief's pocket, why make this invisible and not the rest?" Westron mused.

"I had wondered that myself. That was why I kept it apart. Initially I assumed that it had been in your safe hole too, but my sister claims to have seen it before."

"Have a servant summon your sister to the Queen's chamber. I would like to learn more of this. I have never seen it before but you are right, it is a piece of ancient dragon shell." He thought on this for a second, then continued. "I have one last question, Wizard. Did the thief have any wounds? I recall Rhovert said the guard had injured his prisoner."

"I saw dried blood on the thief's breeches and her clothes had been slashed, possibly as Rolliver fought with her."

The King ushered them all back to the Queen's Chamber. He made no comments on what he had seen.

Atlantis was escorted in. She dropped an awkward curtsey and sat stiffly on one of the stools.

"My Court Wizard tells me you recognise this…" King Westron said as he held up the etched dragon shell.

"Yes, your Majesty," Atlantis replied. "I recovered that at the same place that I found the casket of dragon shells. My Great Grand Sire referred to it as the Serpent's Bane. It was at the bottom of a very deep pool. When I recovered it, the serpents that had appeared began to slither away. The two men threatening Ven transformed back to snakes and disappeared."

"Ven?" the King asked softly. "Please tell me of your adventure from the beginning."

Atlantis obeyed, strating from when Ven walked into her camp.

"You saw a dragon?" Rhovert interrupted at that point.

"No, it was too dark, but the flame had to come from somewhere."

"Let her continue," the King directed, but he was interrupting her moments later. "You believe she was speaking to a dragon?"

"She came back and told me where we had to go, and said the dragon wouldn't let me go through the lair but that she knew of another way to the crypt."

The King's expression was unreadable, but Atlantis thought the mentopn of dragons held some impotance for him.

"Go, tell me what happened next."

At the end of her telling of events, King Westron asked, "What did this 'Ven' look like?"

"She was wearing dusty coloured breeches and a similar coloured tunic over a short cream under tunic. Her shoes were of soft leather with wood nailed to the bottom. She had shoulder length, light brown hair, braided and coiled under a short hooded cloak. There was a leather pouch on her belt."

The King looked at his twin daughters and noticed that they were visibly uncomfortable. "That description means something to you?"

"When we caught her, Maeven didn't look like that," Leanne said, because her twin was at that moment in shock from something she remembered. *Could Maeven have been the thief at Thul Run who had helped save the children and distract the demon?*

When their father turned his attention from them, Leanne whispered, "I doubt it, she was never interested in anyone but herself." She had sensed her sister's thought.

Finora wasn't convinced, but she turned her attention to what their father was saying.

"Normally, I'd have the wretch sent up to me. However, considering how dangerous and slippery she is – we will proceed to the lower levels."

The servants who saw thw procession of royals heading for the dungeon quickly deduced that the King was going to question the thief and murderer. Some were already looking forward to the spectacle of the inevitable hanging.

In the dungeon were a number of hollowed out rock caves of various sizes. Some had light entering through angled shafts and a barred wall; others were completely dark with only a tiny barred window in a solid oak door. The more dangerous prisoners were kept in the latter and of these, one door glowed faintly. The King dismissed the dungeon guards, who saluted and went to join the King's bodyguards up in the kitchen.

"Wizard!"

Roman obeyed the implied command and removed the mage seal on the door. The faint glow disappeared. "I have mage bonds on the prisoner. They restrict movement, your Majesty," he explained quietly.

The King entered first, followed by his wizard who magically lit the candles set on high wall brackets. Revealed in the light was a slight figure lying on the dirt floor near the far wall. Near her head was a bucket of water, refilled from the passage via a u-shaped channel. The bucket was full and had overflown. An empty cup was near the bucket.

The figure didn't move or seem aware of the presence of other people. Rhovert entered, followed by Leanne. Atlantis stayed in the passage with Finora until she heard Leanne speak.

The Princess hadn't waited; she walked around the prisoner so she could see the face.

"My, how the mighty have fallen!" she sneered, recognising her sister in spite of the circumstances. The prisoner's eyes opened and they glared at her tormentor. She tried to speak but no voice came out; tried to moisten her lips but her tongue seemed as dry as her mouth and it was a useless gesture. The cup to get water from the bucket was just out of her reach. The chains securing her wrists had enough length to reach it but the additional mage bonds made that much movement impossible.

Atlantis peeked into the cell and then forced her way in. She strode to where Leanne stood looking down. Pity filled her eyes and she squatted next to the prisoner and reached for a mug of water. Whilst the others simply watched, Atlantis supported the girl at a slight angle and placed the cup to her lips. The sound of gulping water was loud in the stone-walled chamber.

"Go away, Leanne," Maeven said hoarsely. "You're a beast!"

"Drink more, slowly this time, Ven," Atlantis cautioned and she saw tiny tears form in Ven's eyes. Her own sight was blurring when her friend managed a weak smile.

Atlantis was angry at the way her friend had been treated. It was not that she hadn't deserved to be in the dungeon, but the way her own family were making no move to even greet her. That was not to mention that she had been placed so she couldn't even reach water or the privy hole. Atlantis cradled Ven's head and felt her tremble when the King spoke, even though he wasn't talking to her.

"Leanne, go and order a bath to be filled in the Queen's chamber," he spoke mildly, but it was a rebuke and Leanne knew it. She scowled and stalked off. "Finora, go to the kitchen and arrange for some light soup to be prepared and sent up there too." Finora went without protest. Her initial pleasure at seeing her sister's situation had been destroyed by Atlantis calling her Ven. Now she knew that her sister had been at Thul Run, and had helped save her life and that of her twin.

"Rhovert, please go to your apartment and select one of your less suitable court costumes – one of your older ones."

Rhovert grinned slightly at the clever pointed barb at his usual mode of dress.

"Wizard, remove your magic restraints. We will adjourn to more friendly surroundings."

Atlantis glared at her brother.

"Roman, she won't be able to walk! I remember what Todd's bull was like after you had it tied up that way!"

Roman simply nodded, walked to the prisoner and lifted her with great gentleness. Even the strong smell about her didn't affect him. He quietly spoke a healing chant, one he often used on animals.

"Maybe I won't hate you, Wizard."

"My apologies, Princess," he said softly as he followed the King along unfamiliar and dark passageways. Atlantis kept close to him and was surprised to step out into a small dressing room.

The King turned. "One moment," he said softly, hearing servants in the bathing chamber beyond the door. His eyes met those of the woman Roman carried. He let his recognition of her show but said nothing.

Maeven did not greet him and she had no strength to pretend that she did not care about the state she was in. The King turned away when he saw the start of tears in his daughter's eyes. He acted as if he had not noticed.

When the bath was filled with warm water and fragrant soap and oils, and the servants had left, Roman carried his burden into the bathing chamber and placed her on her feet. Atlantis steadied her and glared at her brother and the King until they retreated.

"It is good to see you, Atlantis," Maeven told her friend.

"No wonder you didn't want to speak about your family," Atlantis said venomously. "They don't like you, do they?"

She refused to let Maeven undress herself, aware of how weak she was. In the better light of the bathing room, bruises and half-healed grazes were vivid against the pale skin of her face. Other scrapes showed around her wrists and ankles, and a recently healed wound on her leg looked to have been deep.

Atlantis bit back the questions she wanted to ask. Instead, she concentrated on helping Ven into the bath and gently washing her.

"You aren't my slave," Maeven protested. "You shouldn't have to do this."

"I'm your friend and it is my privilege," Atlantis assured her gently. "And I don't think even a King should be allowed to treat his daughter this way." She meant having her in the dungeon under such harsh conditions.

"I didn't exactly come here as Princess Maeven." Ven tried to smile. "And, although you may not agree, he is actually being quite considerate."

Atlantis snorted in disbelief.

"He knows that I would never let my sisters help me, so he let you help me instead. He figured out that I don't prefer women's garb, so he sent Rhovert off to get some of his…"

"Effeminate costumes?" Atlantis suggested. "A compromise and they will probably look better on you than him."

"He also rebuked my sisters by sending them off on servants' errands and he is not allowing the servants to see me like this!"

"But he hasn't even greeted you!"

"I doubt that he will," Maeven said uncomfortably. "You have to remember – I am a thief. He must know that and I did kill that bastard Rolliver. He's executed thieves for less than I've done."

"But…"

"I may be his daughter, but I am not above the law. I know that! I intended to spite him when I became a thief and he knows it. He won't act like I'm his daughter, any more than he has, until he is sure he won't have to repudiate me."

"Hang you, you mean!" Atlantis said, thoughtlessly blunt.

"Yes," Maeven admitted, covering her face with soapy hands.

"I'm sorry," Atlantis apologised.

"No, you are right. He is giving me some benefit of doubt and granting me some consideration as an offender of rank. That is all! I do not deserve your pity. Save it for the poor serfs who are hung because they stole food for their starving families. I chose my life!"

"Does the King do that? Hang starving serfs?"

"Some of the Lords do."

"If he decides to… are you going to tamely accept it?"

"It's not going to come to that!" Maeven said, but she did not sound certain.

CHAPTER 18 – THE INQUISITION

Atlantis privately thought that Maeven looked the very essence of a Princess. She walked proudly and no sign of her fears showed on her face. Wearing her brother's over fancy outfits, with the short hair trimmed and brushed, she looked the height of Court fashion. Only the bruises on her face belied the picture.

Roman Golddreamer stood solid and calm to one side of the King. Westron himself occupied one of the comfortable chairs as if it was his throne. Prince Rhovert stood to his father's other side, slight and visibly unsettled. The twin Princesses perched on a long couch and seemed to share their brother's unease.

"Sit down," the King instructed quietly, looking at his youngest child.

Maeven perched on a stool facing them all. Atlantis stood back, hoping she could stay.

"I have been told about your ransom trickery. Tell me what happened after one of my guards caught you."

The King was watching his daughter intently. He did not miss the slight tremble that belied her proud posture.

Maeven spoke to her audience dispassionately as if the events had happened to someone else. She stopped when she reached the point in her narrative where the wizard stunned her. The thoughts that had filled her mind as she lay in the dungeon were no one's business but her own.

The King gestured to the wizard and Roman muttered a low chant. Maeven knew it was aimed at her but until the questions began, she did not realise that he had put a truth spell on her. The realisation brought her almost to the point of panic. There were things she did not want to reveal.

Prince Rhovert, knowing more of the recent events than his father questioned his sister more gently than he would have a stranger. The only additional detail she now revealed, was the way she had been treated. She had glossed over that initially. The three other women paled, glad it had not been them.

The King mentioned the other deaths in the palace, other than the Lord Rolliver. There was no doubt in any of the listeners' minds that she knew nothing of them. He nodded, for she had entered his chamber from the secret passage, and Rollivers knife had blood on it – more than could be accounted for by the scratched he had given her. He switched his questions to the brigand raid at Thul Run.

"You were at Thul Run," he stated.

Maeven wanted to deny it but could not. "Yes."

"You were to identify the leader and his wizard?"

"Yes."

"Where did you first encounter them?"

Maeven's trembling increased, as if she were fighting the truth spell. The words tumbled out of her mouth, describing scenes she vividly recalled. She even told them of her talk with Merlie and the admission that she had swapped amulets six years ago. She told of the leader and his actions to her and to Nayfor.

"You helped free the children!" Finora finally admitted aloud. "You distracted that wizard and the demon!"

"And I ran and ran and ran …" Maeven was crying now, so afraid that one more question would reveal her shame.

"Where did you lose your talisman?" King Westron asked as if he knew the answer.

Maeven collapsed on the floor.

Atlantis sat in a chair by the pallet where Maeven lay either unconscious or sleeping, finding some amusement in seeing Princess Leanne making a bed and Princess Finora finding the things a guest would need.

The King had stated that no servant was to be allowed in the Queen's Chamber. It was obvious that he did not want his daughter's presence advertised. Atlantis wished she could see into the King's peat bog of a mind and find out why he was putting Maeven through such a trial.

Prince Rhovert returned quietly, startling Atlantis who scrambled to her feet to curtsey. He waved aside the ritual greeting. She waited for him to speak but he simply collapsed into a second chair and stared at his sisters. Leanne and Finora finished their tasks and left the room.

"What is going on, Rhovert?" Atlantis asked softly, knowing she could neglect his title in private.

"I don't know everything. I am not sure Father does, but it is always hard to know what is on his mind. It is many things, nothing major in itself but unsettling. Incidents of pestilence, crop blight, epidemics, odd beasts appearing in populated areas rather than just the wild lands, raiders, rebellions, weird weather and demons – we seem to be reacting to one crisis after another."

"So why do you have to be so horrid to Ven?" Atlantis asked bluntly.

"Father believes that she is the key to what's happening."

"That she is causing it?"

"He didn't go that far! He said he would have to make sure of her loyalty. I do not question that, but I cannot believe she is a dark agent. If she were, my talisman would grow hot, not cold like it always does near another bearer."

"That should settle it!" Atlantis said firmly.

"In theory, but he has to be sure. If Maeven was telling the truth, then Rolliver was a dark agent and we never suspected him. If it comes to that, I never guessed Col Tormore was one either, and he had a seventh talisman we never knew about!" Rhovert stated aloud. "When your brother put the truth spell on her, she was fighting it. Something happened, after she was at Thul Run and before you met her, that she doesn't want us to know!"

"Maybe she doesn't want everyone to know all her secrets!" Atlantis chided. "A girl has to have a few!"

"And she hasn't got her talisman any more!" Rhovert finished.

"So what? What is so important about them?" Atlantis asked impatiently.

"The Dragon Talismans make up a powerful protective charm," Rhovert explained. "It has protected the Kingdom of Thulor for a Dragon age. Some dark force is trying to steal the parts and weaken the protection."

"Why?" Atlantis asked. "Do they want to invade the Kingdom?"

"It looks that way …" Rhovert began and then he took on the unsettled look she had noticed earlier. "I feel like something really bad is going to happen and we are running out of time to stop it. Father is convinced that Maeven knows something that she won't tell us."

"Maybe you are not asking the right question!" Atlantis said as if stating the obvious.

"What do you suggest may be the right question?" Rhovert asked with a hint of sarcasm.

"I haven't known her long, but perhaps you should ask her what the dragon said to her and what the serpent man said," was her sensible suggestion. Then she seemed thoughtful for a moment. "Perhaps you should ask her why she was afraid of the serpent man. It seemed odd to me. It was more than just surprise and out of character, considering that she had fearlessly re-entered a hostile dragon's lair!"

"You are a breath of sanity around here, lady," Rhovert praised, starting to feel hopeful.

"Perhaps I should blow through the King's ears and air a few of his thoughts?" Atlantis snapped disrespectfully.

Rhovert looked startled and then smiled. "I wouldn't suggest that! He may take a liking to you and that is something that I will not permit. I will make it my duty to teach you respect for the King of Thulor!"

Atlantis turned to hide a blush and asked instead, "What is your father doing now?"

"He is instructing the steward to have his apartment redecorated!" Rhovert sounded disgusted.

"Where is he planning to sleep? In here?"

"I know better than to ask that question," Rhovert said carefully. "Or who with … However, there is one thing we do agree on – this needs to be worn."

He drew out an object that looked to be a piece of bone carved into a triangle with a cameo design on it. Atlantis took it tentatively and saw the design was not a head but overlapping runes. A gold chain was threaded through a small hole.

"The King thinks the talisman will accept you as a bearer," Rhovert said intently. "Put it on; wear it next to the skin."

"This used to belong to your mother, didn't it?" Atlantis asked holding it. Rhovert nodded.

"This isn't some kind of proposal is it?" Atlantis asked carefully.

"No," Rhovert sighed deeply. "I know your opinion of marrying in general, and marrying Princes in particular. Traditionally, though, it is worn by the Queen and passed down to the heir's wife when the King dies or the new king marries. Father finally decided that it was I, and not he, who should find the next bearer. However, in the interim – it needs to be worn. If you keep it hidden, there won't be any more rumours about you and me!"

"And there will be one less reason for Father to sample women!" a snide voice from the bed beside them said tiredly.

Atlantis put the chain around her neck cautiously, expecting to feel different, but she did not.

"Have you eaten yet, sister?" Rhovert asked casually.

"No, and I am not hungry!" Maeven told him.

"There is soup waiting on the hearth," Atlantis mentioned.

"See that she eats some, will you, Atlantis?"

"Is that a Royal Edict?" Maeven asked snidely.

"As it happens, yes!" Rhovert glared at her. "You have had nothing to eat for four days."

Rhovert endured Maeven's smirk. "Father does not wish you to starve yourself to death."

"Is that so that he can hang me?"

The smirk had gone.

"Keep this attitude and I will enjoy watching!" Rhovert told her sharply. "Do you really want him to?"

Maeven turned her head away and did not answer.

"You're an idiot, Ven!" Atlantis said, when she returned from seeing Rhovert out.

"I know!" Maeven admitted, sitting up "I don't want to stay here and I just can't help irritating my family."

"You had better not try it on His Majesty, or I will be without my very best friend," Atlantis warned soberly. "You are in deep trouble, Ven. Princess or not, please don't disobey your father."

"Run away, yes, disobey…" Maeven broke off as His Majesty entered the room unannounced.

"Would you bring my daughter some soup, Lady Atlantis?" King Westron requested quietly.

The unexpectedly ennobled Lady obeyed in a daze. She did not deem it wise to say anything as she brought the wooden tray, soup and spoon to Maeven and positioned cushions to support it.

The King stood watching and when Atlantis glanced at him, she decided his neutral expression was her cue to leave.

At the door, she heard the King ask, "Did my daughter have her talisman when you met her, Lady Atlantis?"

"No, Sire," she told him.

The King waved one hand in a gesture of dismissal. He sat himself in the comfortable chair with armrests and stared across the room.

Maeven began to eat the soup slowly, finding that the tasty broth was making her appetite return. She kept glancing sideways at her father as she ate. His presence was unnerving but at least he was not staring at her. When she pushed the tray away, his eyes met hers.

"You have exceeded my expectations," he said carefully.

"Is that because I am both a thief and murderer?" Maeven said bitterly.

The King seemed to ignore the comment.

"When you escaped from my guards, why did you come here?" he asked instead, not looking at her.

"I wanted to spit in Rolliver's face by getting here first and taking what he wanted."

"What were you going to do then?" the King probed.

"I hadn't really thought about that!" Maeven admitted.

"Why did Lord Rolliver dislike you? I was not aware that you had anything to do with him."

"I didn't," Maeven agreed. "The night after I left, I decided to visit Tormore's house. I knew he was going off on a trip for you. I went in, had a look around and was on my way back out when I had a really strong sense of needing to run."

Maeven pretended she was describing something that happened to someone else. A faint smile briefly showed on the King's face.

"So he disliked the thief and could not recognise the person he wanted when you were right under his nose." He sounded thoughtful.

The King stood and walked to the door. He opened it and spoke to the guards outside; one returned with him.

With a start, Maeven recognised Nayfor.

"Spymaster, are you acquainted with this thief?"

Spymaster? Maeven looked up.

"Ex-thief, Majesty." Nayfor was not one to waste words.

The King raised his eyebrows in surprise.

"What is your evaluation of her ability as a thief?"

"She was highly skilled. However, she was young, headstrong and disregarded too many rules. She did not think far enough ahead and endangered our members. Although she has luck, trouble finds her," Nayfor answered his King. "I disagreed with Barnabas over her promotion to master thief."

"Tell me what you know of her," the King requested.

Nayfor ignored Maeven and gave a concise account of her activities as the girl thief, Ven. His accurate and cutting words made Maeven squirm. When she wanted to speak, the King silenced her.

"Thank you, Spymaster," King Westron said at the end of the report. "That is all for now."

Nayfor departed quietly. The King looked at Maeven and considered what he had heard.

The longer he looked the less comfortable Maeven felt. Knowing how he hated thieves, the recital of her activities was damning.

"Do you know why you survived the Demon rage?"

"The talisman?"

"Yes, but you were lucky. That attack should have killed you. The person had knowledge of the talisman pieces and had deduced a means to negate yours."

Maeven remembered the incident clearly.

"Who tried to kill me?" Maeven asked intently.

"Col Tormore." The King saw the loathing on his daughter's face. "It seems he did not realise that you swapped pieces with Finora. The spell he sent through the scrying crystal, the one controlling the demon, back lashed onto him."

"Good riddance!" Maeven was pleased by the manner of his demise. "How long do you think I would have lasted if I had gone with him?"

"I knew you would not," King Westron said calmly.

Maeven glared venomously at him, angry that he had so successfully manipulated her.

"I knew what you thought of him. I also knew you always avoided him where possible and that it was because he had thrashed you when you were nine…"

"You knew about that?" Maeven accused, still angry with him.

The King waved her grievance aside.

"We also discovered in his house, evidence that he murdered your mother."

Maeven's anger died, replaced by the remembered anguish of her Mother's death.

"What did the Dragon say to you?" Westron said after a moment.

Maeven was caught off guard and told him what she had not intended to say.

"She called me dragon-child. She told me you wore a piece of dragon magic and my piece must be recovered from the hand of the Serpent." Maeven paused but decided that she might as well continue. "The dragon said that Thulor was dying, her magic was fading and she could not maintain the protections much longer."

"Go on," King Westron urged quietly.

"She also said that we have to talk to Thulor, find her egg and hatch it; like Frederick hatched Exconidor's egg." She was as tense as a spooked horse. "Do you have the egg?"

"No."

"Nayfor had it at Thul Run. He gave it to Barnabas, to bring to you!" Maeven mentally urged him to say 'yes'. "It is a small oval shaped rock."

"I have heard nothing from Barnabas since he left for Thul Run," King Westron told her emotionlessly.

"I saw him near there when I got back from the bandit's camp," Maeven insisted. "That's when he graduated me from apprentice… he was your spymaster, wasn't he?"

"He gave me nothing!" The King was silent for a time. Maeven felt the stirrings of panic.

"Tell me about the serpents in the crypt of Exconidor," the King asked.

Maeven described the appearance of the serpents from the red glow, then how first one and then a second had transformed into men. She told of being unable to move to escape, but not the humiliating helplessness.

"What did they say to you?" Westron insisted.

Maeven wilted under his gaze.

"I was to tell you to release the Prince of Serpents or a greater darkness would fall on your kingdom."

"You waited almost a season to tell me this," Westron accused softly.

"I wasn't going to come back – not ever!" his daughter said defiantly. She looked away and wished she could walk away, but a single mage bond still kept her from walking very far from the bed.

King Westron still knew there was something Maeven was hiding from him, and knew it would not be easy to get her to reveal it. He could see her trembling with barely controlled panic. Earlier she had fought the wizard's truth spell to avoid telling him. He had to know the reason why she no longer had her talisman. He had deduced that the incident she was avoiding had happened before she had returned from the raid on the bandit camp and before she had disappeared for over a year. Nayfor had mentioned her odd behaviour, how on the return trip she had not been cocky and arrogant but angry and obedient, too obedient. It seemed as if something vital had been taken from her.

"What happened when you ran away from Thul Run?" he asked gently enough, but with an implacable look on his face.

Maeven hid her face in her hands, but her father gently pulled them away and forced her to look at him.

The words would not come.

"No one else will know," he said quietly, "but I must know. An envoy from the Realm of Vatarik will be here in two days to negotiate for the release of the brigand leader and his wizard. If one of theirs did something to you …"

Between tears of remembered humiliation, Maeven finally told her father what she had endured. She repeated what her ravisher had told her and of the second brigand, the one that had died. She stopped before she mentioned the child.

King Westron stilled his arms from the instinct to hold her. He had known, long before they were born, that he could not be soft with his children. They could not have the option to give up and run home to safety. They had to be strong, independent, and skilled at what they needed to be. For the good of the kingdom.

When Maeven hid her face again, the King stood and walked to the door. Outside he sent one guard with a message to the Lady Atlantis, asking her to return. The woman and her wizard brother were proving their worth as members of his Court.

Atlantis was still hugging a softly weeping Maeven when her brother, Roman, entered some time later.

"His Majesty has asked for a promise from you," Roman spoke to Maeven. "He has said that you will be free to roam about these apartments if you do not go beyond them. If you do, his guards will, without hesitation, return you to the dungeon."

Maeven sniffed and mumbled, "Tell him that I will stay, for now, in my luxurious dungeon."

A brief muttered counter spell removed the last mage bond on her. Roman Golddreamer left the room. There was no need to tell her that he had spelled the outer extremities of the rooms to give alarm if she tried to go past them. He believed, however, that her safety depended on her remaining out of sight. He doubted that Rolliver was the only dark agent in the palace.

Wizard Roman answered the King's summons and was surprised to find him sitting in the dark in his apartments.

"Have a seat, Wizard," King Westron invited.

Roman walked in further, his heavy boots causing echoes off the wood floor. The woollen carpet had been removed, along with the drapes. Some moonlight came through the expensive glazed windows. He found a seat opposite the King and waited for him to speak.

"I have seen visions of the future, Wizard," King Westron said after a long while. His voice sounded old and tired.

"What have you seen, Sire?" Roman asked, keeping his voice calm.

"I have seen the darkness that will fall – slavery, misery, hunger and hopelessness. If I fail, here, there will be no one to stop the blight spreading to other realms."

"What must you do, Sire?" Roman prompted when the King stopped talking.

"I have to fight the Serpent – whoever and whatever he is. Then the visions come like a shattered piece of glazing, with each piece reflecting a different possibility."

"What do you see?"

"A kingdom at peace, my daughter at the head of a vast invading army, the castle here collapsing, storms where serpents rain down, pestilence and people dying, blights on crops and people starving, a dragon breathing fire, my entire army strung on stakes, my daughter holding a key, my daughter holding a dragon and a demon…"

The King stopped after a while and said, "Maeven is the key. Through her actions, the Kingdom will fall or the Kingdom will endure. If I can trust her to obey me, I can see a way through the hardship to peace – but if she won't, the Kingdom is doomed."

"Princess Maeven is loyal, Sire," Roman said.

"She acts in the interest of the Kingdom when it fits in with her will!" the King stated. "She came here to get revenge, not to bring me important information that she received a season ago!"

"You need to give her a compelling reason to obey you," Roman suggested.

"What if the safety of the Kingdom is not reason enough?" the King countered. "The dragons spoke to her. For the first time in centuries, the dragons spoke to man! They confirmed what I already knew – the protections are failing. That is why I drew my children back here. They are so longer safer away from here. The problems have arisen because Thulor, the daughter of the dragon-mage Exconidor, is dying. She left an egg, a mage egg, her successor. Maeven told me that we have to talk to Thulor, find her egg and hatch it. I had a message that it was in Thul Run. Barnabas, my spymaster, sent Nayfor to recover it. The Serpent sent brigands to get it first. Nayfor found it, passed it to Barnabas to bring to me – it never arrived. The egg will reveal the way to Thulor's chamber. Merlie gave Maeven the key to the chamber and she has the dragon sight – dragons cannot hide from her. That is why I must be sure of her obedience!"

"Tell her what you expect of her, Sire," Roman suggested. "Give her the chance to choose freely. She did agree to remain in the Queen's Chambers …"

"Did she promise?" Westron asked pointedly.

"No Sire, not formally! However, she has not attempted to leave. I will know if she does."

"If she swears obedience – I will trust her. I will risk everything," the King said. "If not…"

"I could imprison her, like those below," Roman proposed.

"What if you were killed, or a more powerful wizard came here?"

Roman's silence was answer enough.

"If she gets into the hands of the enemy… I promised not to talk of something, but I think I must. The brother of the prisoner below encountered my daughter…" King Westron spoke of what Maeven had not wanted to reveal.

"A controlling spell, Majesty," Roman identified. "It is simple for the wizard that set it to remove, but dangerous for the victim if others try. Such spells deeply wound the spirit. It is worse for those with more pride. The touch of a demon has a similar effect."

"I can see no other option then. If she won't promise obedience – I will not be able to risk her alive."

"It is a difficult choice to make, Sire," Roman said gently.

"I will speak with her again; give her until sunrise the day after tomorrow to consider the options. This must be resolved before then."

Wizard Roman knew that the envoy from Vatarik was due that day, here in the palace, close to their controlled one.

"It would be a powerful statement to your enemy," Roman stated evenly, but his thoughts were far from calm. "A dangerous path indeed, Majesty."

"It would not be a decision made without regret. Do you have a better idea, Wizard?"

The silence was echoing.

Finally, "No, Sire, but I will give it some thought. If you will tell me what it is that you will need your daughter to do if she swears the oath."

CHAPTER 19 – THE CHOICE

"I require several things from you, daughter."

King Westron sat back in the chair near the fire. Maeven sat opposite. Her tears had dried and she was calm again.

"I need to know your degree of commitment to my kingdom."

It was not so much father to daughter as King to Subject.

Maeven said uncertainly, "I wouldn't do anything to endanger the kingdom."

"How far would you go in fighting an army that is attacking the realm?" the King persisted.

"I'm not a swordswoman or a sorceress," Maeven pointed out the obvious.

"You have other skills," her father reminded her. "Stealth, sneakiness, thieving, dragon sight…"

"You're the one that forced me to become a thief!" Maeven interrupted rudely.

"No, that was your choice, based no doubt on my publicly known dislike for them."

"You didn't dislike Merlie, he told me so."

"Indeed," the King agreed mildly. "However, we are talking about you. You were of no use before then, just an infuriating, spoilt and pampered brat; someone with no scruples about taking things from other people, who disobeyed orders to stay in the palace, someone who lied and demanded her own way!"

"Bastard!" Maeven said to his face, as she could not help her face going red at his words.

"I order servants whipped for showing disrespect for me!" he reminded her, his voice hard.

Maeven felt her stomach do a flip, and reminded herself that her father was the most powerful person in Thulor. He may never have taken a hand to her but he had plenty of servants who would obey without question.

"I am sorry, Father. You are right; I wasn't a very nice person. I should never have said what I just did either," she apologised with great meekness.

"Personal feelings aside, in the short time you have been away, you have developed the skills I need."

"To be a spy and assassin?" Maeven countered, seeing a reaction in the faint hardening around her father's mouth.

"I will not ask you to be an assassin," he said neutrally, "unless you have developed a liking for murder."

Maeven privately admitted that her father had accurately returned her jibe.

"No I haven't," she assured him sourly. "I don't see myself as a spy either."

"What does a spy do?" he asked her and watched for her reaction.

After a moment's thought, she said, "I see your point, but why me?"

"I have seen you listen to what is said and you seem to know what has not been voiced. From what you hear, you make astonishingly accurate deductions. You have skill at thieving – entering places, finding things, retrieving things and escaping. It seems you have a well developed sense for saving your skin. Luck, perhaps, or intuition and an ability to manipulate…"

"I learnt that from you!" Maeven interrupted.

"You are also the only person in centuries that the dragons have spoken with. Dragon magic empowers the protections on the Kingdom – those protections are failing. Do you remember what the dragon told you?"

Maeven did not want to remember.

"Someone else can find the talisman and the egg," she insisted. "As Nayfor told you, trouble finds me."

"A useful side effect, to always be at the centre of the action, the pivotal point where the future can be altered," the King said softly. "It is a position of power!" He paused to give Maeven a chance to consider the idea before he continued. "You also have the dragon sight, and can see things with eyes and mind that other people cannot."

Maeven recoiled "I do not *ever* want to go near that creature again! Ask someone else! I just want to go away, be left alone!"

The King knew to whom her forceful statement referred, and continued carefully. He knew that what he was seeing was a 'run and hide' instinct; part of what made her such an accomplished thief. Without doubt, she too was sensing the still formless danger to the Kingdom. This was her natural instinct.

"Yes, I could ask someone else," the King admitted. "I have servants who would walk into extreme peril at my command. The mage egg will be well hidden and difficult to find. I prefer to send the person with the most chance of success and survival. Dragon sight works best in the presence of Dragon Magic. The dragon egg is a powerful object of Dragon Magic. You will be able to 'see' its hiding place quickly, others won't."

"If I go, what's in it for me? If I get the things, will you let me go – leave me alone?"

"I won't let you go until the kingdom is safe," the King's voice was definite. "If the Serpent wins, nowhere in the world will be safe. If it is wealth you want – I will pay you well. Initial services will be paid from what you stole from me when you robbed my messenger!"

"I will not go near that creature!" Maeven insisted, and then forgot again that she was talking to the King. "I'd rather be dead!"

"That can be arranged," her father said without smiling.

Maeven shivered.

"Will you swear the Oath of Obedience?"

"Why must I?"

"If you do, I will be sure of the strength of your commitment," the King told her forcibly. "If you won't, I will not permit you to endanger my kingdom."

His words echoed ominously in Maeven's ears and she did not answer. A vision of her son sprung into her mind along with the thought of not being able to go to him. She felt a longing to see him again, to protect him from the still formless dangers her father had hinted at.

"You have until dawn, the day after tomorrow, to decide."

King Westron rose quietly and left the room.

Atlantis gave up in disgust. Trying to talk to her brother was impossible. She had left all of their Great Grand Sire's journals with him. He could mutter and read them to his heart's content.

Gisella was little better off. Her husband had acknowledged her presence and then impatiently quizzed her until she had betrayed her total knowledge of magic. Then he had ignored her.

"I think I told him about every charm I can make, every potion I can brew and their side effects," Gisella complained. "He won't even tell me what it is all about!"

"He won't talk to me either," Atlantis sympathised, in accord with her sister-in-law for once. "Even worse, he has had Rhovert in there with him since evening."

It was now almost midnight.

The personages of their complaints emerged. Roman had a scroll of parchment and Rhovert carried a small square of vellum.

"Gisella, we need these potions," Roman said seriously. "Rhovert says you should be able to find the ingredients in the still room off the infirmary, or in the Queen's Garden."

Gisella took the scroll and glanced at the list of potions and ingredients. Three were variations on common ones, the fourth completely new to her. She handed the list to Atlantis to read.

"How soon do you need them?" Gisella asked.

"Before the envoys from Vatarik arrive."

"Is this ethical? Using magic to help with your negotiations?" Gisella quizzed.

"Or do you think all is fair in preventing a war?" Atlantis queried the alternative.

"Father desires a certain outcome, for the good of this kingdom," Rhovert said cryptically.

"And what is that?" Atlantis insisted.

"You don't need to know the details. It is all aimed at getting an agent into Vatarik without them thinking that the person could possibly be an agent."

"You are starting to sound just as cryptic as your father," Atlantis accused him.

"Show this to the guards," Prince Rhovert instructed, passing the square of vellum to her, intending to end the conversation. "It will tell them you are on the King's business. Lady Atlantis, please assist Lady Gisella."

Atlantis bowed slightly and wondered if Rhovert knew just how like his father he looked just then.

Gisella held her tongue at her husband's unusual brusqueness. Even she could see that Prince Rhovert was the one in charge.

When the men had left she said, "That last potion, is a strange one. I wish I dared ask what they expect it to do."

"I doubt asking would be any use. I have the sneaking suspicion that whatever those two are up to, they don't expect us to like it," was Atlantis's opinion. "It might help if we knew who they were trying to get into Vatarik."

"We'd better get busy. Two of these potions take a while to prepare and brew."

The two women each took a candle and left to begin their task.

Maeven had spent a sleepless night, arranging her arguments logically in her mind. Reasons why she couldn't go to Vatarik, why someone else, anyone else, would be more appropriate. Near morning, she dropped into an uneasy sleep, knowing her father would come at dawn for her answer.

The sound of the outer door to the suite opening brought her instantly awake and throwing on the first garment to hand – a brown under tunic.

The King did not have to ask permission to enter any room in his own palace and the coming interview would not proceed well if she were still in her sleeping shift.

King Westron entered the sleeping room as she was brushing her hair. He was dressed in the richest of his formal day wear outfits.

"I have come for your answer," he said without greeting her. "Will you swear obedience to me and promise to retrieve your talisman and the mage egg?"

Maeven put her brush down and assembled her rehearsed speech and plunged ahead. "I am sorry Father; I cannot swear an oath that I may not be able to keep. I have important business that I must attend to down south…"

She glanced at her father when she finally finished her speech. He appeared unmoved.

"Sometimes we have to make difficult choices," he told her, his voice controlled. "So far in your life you have pleased only yourself. Explain to me why it is so imperative that you go south."

In the face of the King's controlled expression, her reasons sounded tame. She did not intend to mention her major concern – her child.

"Your reasons are unacceptable. Will you swear obedience?"

"No."

"Is that your final word?" the King asked quietly.

"Yes!"

"Then I have no choice…" the King said almost sadly.

Maeven was glad when he left. She felt relieved that she had finally stood up to him.

A short half candle mark later, when Atlantis had joined Maeven for breakfast, and before they had a chance to say much to each other, four of the King's Own Guards walked in unannounced.

Two marched around behind Maeven and held her, and another stood behind Atlantis. The fourth guard unrolled a scroll.

"It is the decision of the King's Council that the thief known as Ven be returned to the dungeons to await the sentence for crimes committed."

"What sentence?" Atlantis asked, starting to rise from her chair. The guard pushed her firmly back down.

"The Council has passed the Death Sentence," the guard said with no emotion. "It will be carried out at noon today."

Maeven was stunned speechless, unable to think past the announcement. The guards dragged her unprotesting out into the passage where she finally regained her wits and began to struggle fiercely.

Atlantis struggled to go after her friend, convinced it was a dreadful mistake. She screamed and yelled to no avail. The guard held her in her chair until the screaming in the passage had died to nothing. Her eyes brimmed with tear. *This was wrong!*

Strong, gentle hands touched a cup to her lips, held her head still, and urged her to drink. Tears were blinding her eyes so that she did not see who else was with her. It was not until she had been violently ill and had dried her mouth and eyes that she saw her brother leaving.

Gisella came and hugged her.

CHAPTER 20 – CONSEQUENCES

On their arrival, quite early in the morning, King Malokin had demanded to see the prisoners. His host had agreed. The prisoners were awake, no longer in a magic induced coma and had been fed, bathed and allowed to stay conscious but were still restrained.

The procession of dignitaries from the two countries walked down into the dungeons, past a barred cell with a struggling prisoner, restrained by chains and cursing loudly. She was dressed in a coarse brown tunic and was barefoot.

King Westron ignored her. One of his ministers hissed an explanation to Prince El Haba that the wench, both a thief and a murderer, would hang that day. The Prince of Vatarik dropped back from the main group to study the woman. He caught the sick expression on his Thulan counterpart's face and asked with a casual taunt, "Are you squeamish about hanging wenches, Prince? I find it quite… exciting."

The sick expression intensified. Rhovert could sense that El Haba was using magic, see that he was having an effect on Maeven and felt the kind of sensations they were. It was obvious that there was mutual recognition between his sister and the visiting prince. His father had been right. Would the man also try to get her free?

"Not squeamish, El Haba," Rhovert said. "I find it personally humiliating that my sister is a thief, traitor and murderer." He said no more, simply returned to his father's side. He watched his foreign prince from the corner of his eyes. As they returned from the dungeon after the tour, Rhovert could see Prince El Haba and his Father King Malokin whispering urgently.

They all went to the small council room, where King Westron with his four ministers, sat down around a table with the King of Vatarik and his ministers to begin negotiations for the release of Malokin's eldest son and his wizard companion.

The Vatarins began by demanding the unconditional release of the two men. King Westron in turn demanded compensation for the victims of the destruction and massacre at Thul Run. He also insisted that the King of Vatarik be responsible for preventing further incursions across Thulor's border with his country. Neither side seemed prepared to back down from their initial demands.

During the morning while the two Kings were continuing their sometimes heated exchanges, El Haba wandered about the room, most often stopping to watch the scaffold as it neared completion. He had Prince Rhovert shadowing him, and took malicious delight in talking about the prisoner.

"You want her dead, why not give her to me for a wife?"

"A thief and a traitor? Someone who murdered a noble, so she could get away?"

"I am sure I can make her behave."

"No. My father will not agree. In our kingdom, murderers of nobles have but one sentence."

"Well then, I will just have to enjoy the spectacle. I hope I will be permitted to watch?"

"Do as you please," Rhovert told him, turning to walk quickly from the room.

Roman Golddreamer watched the scaffold being built and examined each part, ostensibly for magic or mundane tampering. He found none. He tested the rope – it was supple and the noose moved freely. He gestured to the guards to surround it. As he walked around the small courtyard, he identified the places where an observer could hide. On the second level of the palace was the small council room with its balcony. The King was meeting with the envoys from Vatarik in there. The scaffold was in position to give an observer on the balcony a good view.

It was a little more than half a handspan short of noon now. Roman motioned to a guard, passed a message, and retreated into the shadows to watch.

Just before noon, a messenger came to tell the King that all was prepared for the execution.

King Westron summoned a maid to distribute refreshments for his guests. The woman wore the white linen over tunic of a senior servant, and went from guest to guest, and then the King and his ministers until everyone in the room had a drink.

"Rhovert," King Westron summoned his son, who had returned and had been avoiding El Haba. He continued in a quiet voice, to which El Haba listened intently. "Supervise the sentence and advise me when the prisoner is dead."

Rhovert merely nodded, looking pale and ill. He left the room with El

Haba following him, but no one objected. They walked out into the sunlight. The prisoner had not yet come from the dungeons. There was, however, a woman dressed as a senior maid tied to a pole near the scaffold.

El Haba commented, "Who is that wench?"

"That is an ally of my sister," Rhovert explained. "In fact she looks a lot like her. The two of them often changed places to provide each other with an alibi. Our wizard has mage bonds on her so that no trickery will occur today."

El Haba looked thoughtful and asked to look closer. As he walked around the pole, seeing how the woman was restrained, he enjoyed the discomfort of the effeminate Prince of Thulor; the man disgusted him.

Rhovert saw the King staring at him from the second floor balcony and gave the command to the guard squad leader to bring the prisoner out. That guard saluted and passed on the order.

The wench was still struggling, swearing and trying to break free, even though wearing chains. The guards dragged her to a point beneath the balcony and pushed her onto her knees.

Rhovert approached her unsteadily and unrolled a scroll. He could not face his sister.

"You have been found guilty of theft of goods from a King's Messenger and the murder of Lord Rolliver. Do you have anything you wish to say to His Majesty?"

Maeven stopped struggling and straightened, looked towards the balcony, and met her father's gaze. She repeated the ancient Oath of Fealty.

"I pledge my life, my service, my will for the good of the Kingdom of Thulor… I renounce all loyalties and bindings to any other person, country or cause. I place myself at the mercy of the Monarch of Thulor."

Westron did not move and kept his face impassive.

"Father!" the prisoner screamed, trying again to break free. "Please don't do this to me. You can't do this …."

Two guards dragged the screaming and struggling prisoner to the scaffold.

Atlantis stood beside her brother, eyes reddened with weeping. The sedative that the King had insisted that she have had done little as she had been violently sick moments later. She ignored the orders to stay in her chamber, but it was too late to do anything. Until this moment she had believed that the King would not go this far, that he was only trying to get

Maeven to promise to obey him.

"He can't do this!" she yelled at her brother, who was watching impassively.

"Silence, woman!" he ordered in an uncharacteristically fierce manner. "The King has commanded. I must obey!"

"He's wrong! You can't let him do this!"

He turned and grabbed his sister tightly, insisting, "Be silent, Atlantis. There is more going on here than meets the eye. What is being done is for the safety of the Kingdom."

Maeven seemed to have fainted. One guard held her and others continued to remove the chains and bind her hands behind her. When they covered her head with a black hood, and the rope around her neck, Atlantis broke free from her brother and began to run.

Time seemed to stand still.

Roman Golddreamer stood still, watching the scene before him. Prince El Haba was the only person moving. Everyone else in his line of view was frozen in mid-action. He sensed the foreign wizard's power; holding more than a dozen people static was no party trick.

He had ascended the scaffold and took the the rigid Maeven from the guard who was holding her. He loosened the noose then lowered her none too gently to the ground near to the serving wench tied to the pole, then jumped down.

The serving wench was untied and stripped of her over tunic. The white garment went onto the liberated prisoner. The hood covered the head of the serving wench who replaced the original prisoner in the noose. Maeven, rigid under the man's spell, replaced the maid tied to the pole. The man stood back, surveyed the scene and walked out of sight.

Time resumed its normal pace.

Atlantis tried to fight her way past the guards but they held her tightly. She caught sight of the dangling figure and fainted for the first time in her life.

The sun lowered by a finger span. The King of Thulor had returned to his meeting but Prince El Haba had stayed outside and was still watched the dangling figure and the tied wench with ill-concealed enjoyment.

Rhovert felt sickened but still had a duty to perform. He ascended the scaffold, attended by the guard's physician. Prince El Haba was watching him with disgust, thinking him weak and no threat.

"The prisoner is dead, Prince Rhovert," the elderly physician pronounced.

Rhovert turned to the guard. "It is the King's will that the body remain here until dusk when it will be cremated in the knacker's paddock. The other prisoner is to remain until the King pronounces sentence."

Rhovert strode down the steps, crossed to an ornamental garden and was messily ill. The guards were snickering.

Roman Golddreamer approached the pole with the serving wench and felt for a pulse. It was weak but steady. He dropped his hand and moved away.

The physician ignored the Prince and went instead to crouch over the unconscious but stirring Atlantis. He forced some liquid into her mouth and she swallowed it.

"Take the lady to her chamber, good Sir," the physician instructed Roman Golddreamer, who looked like a servant in his farmer's outfit. "I have given her a sleeping draught, to help her overcome the shock. This was no place for any woman to be."

Roman hefted his sister easily and followed Prince Rhovert inside, but turned off before the meeting room to walk to his suite where Atlantis was staying. The medicine would keep her asleep until well into the night.

Smirking, Prince El Haba returned to the meeting, exchanged looks with his father and stood staring out the window. He listened as Prince Rhovert reported to the King of Thulor and heard him ask for permission to leave the meeting. His father, with a resigned look, told him to stay and the pale and sweaing Prince took up a position well away from the window.

El Haba sidled up to Rhovert. "What is to be the fate of the other wench?" he asked slyly.

"Its crimes are minor," Rhovert said, unsuccessfully feigning boredom. "Father may decide to dismiss it, or give it a week in the dungeons first then send it away."

To King Westron's ministers, it seemed that the spectacle of the hanging had made a deep impression on the foreginers. They stopped demanding fewer concessions from King Westron and agreed to his demands – compensation for the survivors of the massacre at Thul Run, and a promise to help prevent incursions of bandits from Vatarik into Thulor.

Westron had originally proposed that when the agreed amount of the compensation was received that the prisoners would be released and escorted to the border. Malokin had surprised him by providing the amount in gold ingots, that he had, apparently, brought with him.

When Malokin professed the desire to leave immediately, rather than accept the invitation of hospitality for the night, King Westron had generously given him a gift of a horse and cart to transport the two newly liberated prisoners, his son, El Rasho and the wizard Saradoc.

When the cart finally trundled out of the castle gate, a third figure had joined the liberated prisoners. The serving wench, dismissed casually by King Westron as being of no importance, was now on her way to serve the foreign king. The only condition he had stipulated was for compensation to be given to the Lord of his Realm who had given him the woman's service as part of his tithe. The visitors had considered that a minor consideration and paid the small fee, such was their desirc to leave.

King Westron was as anxious for his guests to leave as they were to depart. He had achieved more from the negotiations than he had hoped, more than his departing guests realised. He had bought time for his Kingdom.

He was certain that the forces of the Serpent had a base in Vatarik. He was also convinced that Prince El Haba and his brother Prince El Rasho were servants of the Serpent. He was not as sure about King Malokin.

However, Westron wondered if his daughter would ever forgive him for this. That she had finally given him her Oath was like a promise of salvation. The scheme his son and the wizard had come up with had been complex, but it made use of all the knowledge they had, and in the end had played out as intended. Maeven was on her way to Vatarik, would have no trouble entering the country, and would be in position to find the dragon's egg. He could now trust that she would react for the benefit of Thulor. He retreated to his chamber and ordered his personal servant to light the fire.

The floor was still of bare wood, but there were new drapes hanging about the walls. Fragrant candles floated in bowls of water, providing soothing aromas. He sat back in his favourite chair and relaxed until his son and wizard joined him.

Prince Rhovert had changed from his fancy Court costume into something his father found more acceptable. He looked much better now that he had taken the antidote to the brew that Lady Gisella Golddreamer had concocted to make him queasy.

"A highly successful day," King Westron commented. "Now, I would like to know the outcome of your clandestine activities."

"After thoroughly disgusting your guests with his normal at Court behaviour," Roman began, grinning at Prince Rhovert.

"I let slip to El Haba that the prisoner who was due to be executed was my sister," Rhovert continued. "When we had refreshments at noon, the wine contained a potion to make everyone more susceptible to suggestions. I only had to think about being sick… Anyway, we had a convenient decoy available and Roman fixed the noose so that it would only tighten so far."

The wizard continued, "El Haba is a strong wizard. He froze more than a dozen people while he switched Maeven from the noose to the pole. The decoy was one of the dead servants. We explained the aura of magic about her by claiming to have mage bonds on her."

"What if my daughter had not come to her senses?" the King asked, stilling the mirth generated by the successful ploy.

"Then the tablet Nayfor slipped her would have been a fast acting poison," Roman said soberly, "as per your wishes, not simply a sedative containing a voice potion with a side effect of neck rigidity."

"What about the controlling spell?"

"There is a good chance that it has been broken, Sire," Roman said. "Now that she has chosen life, the shock of what we put her through should have had the desired effect. He won't catch her unawares again."

"I hope you are correct, Wizard," King Westron said, waving a hand to dismiss them.

"Let's toss a chance stick to see who deals with Atlantis and tells her of her next errand," Rhovert suggested as they walked back to their own chambers.

"My sister is less than impressed with me right now," Roman admitted. "She is less likely to run you through with her sword than me. I'll trade and deal with your sisters. They will be out for blood when they hear about this on their return."

"True, but I am not sure whether it will be because they were sent away on an errand or because we found a way for Maeven to survive," Rhovert said seriously.

At first, it was as if she had just been born. There was the sudden realisation that she existed.

Her eyes opened and she saw – but what she saw meant nothing to her.

A black robed and hooded figure fed her and gave her drinks, washed and dressed her.

A man dressed in lavish and colourful fabrics often brought his face close to hers and his mouth made meaningless sounds. Sometimes he would slap her and she would cry at the sudden hurt. He would retreat, his handsome face contorted into a scowl.

The anonymous figure in black would come and hug her, whispering soothing sounds until she slept again.

The colourful clothes delighted her eyes. The view beyond was so dull; sandstone yellow, unchanging.

"You are mine! Do you remember that?"

The words came from a red mouth, with a thin line of blonde hair above and a triangular beard below. The eyes were deep, dark and penetrating. Familiar?

"Your father ordered you hung! Do you remember? He thinks you are dead! I saved you! I put that little maid of yours in your place. I saved you and you are mine!"

She remembered a tall man with steel grey hair, standing impassively, ignoring her pleading. She remembered that moment – when she realised she was going to die! She didn,'t remember dying.

The black-robed woman hugged her again. The colours had gone.

"Maeven, Maeven." The whispering seemed to mean something. "He didn't kill you, but it had to look that way! My friend, do you understand me?"

"I won't forgive him!" A very faint whisper.

The hug tightened.

"I don't think I will either, but it got you here! They don't suspect you of being a spy for your father."

"Atlantis?" Maeven whispered as more memories flooded back into her mind. Another hug.

"I won't forgive that blonde bastard either!" Maeven vowed, still in a faint whisper.

"We think the controlling spell is broken," Atlantis advised.

"I can't move much," Maeven said helplessly, crying again.

"Hush, he's back." Atlantis lay her friend down again, then retreated.

The colourful man returned with another in an all red, hooded robe. The newcomer looked at her eyes, felt her neck and prodded her all over. Maeven could feel his touch very faintly.

"Some response, My Lord," the voice was high pitched. "You have told me that she had a severe shock, what kind?"

"She was going to be hung!" the colourful man drawled suggestively.

"Ah, yes," the man in red squeaked nervously, and his hands felt his patient's neck again.

"I don't believe the neck is broken," he almost giggled. "A massage with some of my special oils may help. I'll send some to you!"

The red-clad man tip toed from the room. The tall, blonde man in the colourful clothes stared at his captive with a long, intent, considering look. He gestured to the black robed bedchamber servant.

"Prepare a hot bath," he snapped.

The robed figure moved immediately to obey. It was the best way to be anonymous in the enemy's stronghold.

The bath was a huge, sunken octagon with a low ledge around it and big enough for four or five people, and the servants had devised an ingenious method of heating that much water. Somewhere nearby was a large metal cauldron, kept full of water and constantly simmering over a fire. The water drained into a funnel and went via a pipe to the bath. Servants poured in buckets of fresh water to refill the cauldron.

To fill the bath, Atlantis only had to take out the block which stopped the water pouring from the pipe. Nearby, the man she knew to be Prince El Haba poured fragrant oils onto the water. When the water reached the Prince's preferred level, she replaced the block and received instructions to prepare his 'wife' for a bath.

She was aware of Maeven's look of panic but said nothing as she removed the flimsy fabric from her friend. Silence was expected of servants in the presence of their Master. Speaking without permission brought immediate punishment, particularly from this Prince and his elder brother.

El Haba had stripped to the waist. He came and lifted his foreign Princess, taking her to the bath and placing her in a sitting position. Then, without self-consciousness, he undressed completely, stepped down into the bath and began to massage his 'wife'.

Atlantis was glad that her robe hid her blush. There was nothing wrong with El Haba's physique and he was confident of his perfection. She wondered at his reason for flaunting Maeven's talisman, still on a leather strap around his neck. She also wondered how he could stand to wear it. Countless women had tried on her own talisman over the years. Until she had received it, no one had been able to keep it on more than a day.

Atlantis watched the actions of Prince El Haba without being obvious. She did not underestimate his potential for evil, but he was, at the moment, prepared to be patient with his new wife.

When the discarded clothes had been collected and fresh ones placed ready, and towels laid out on the rock ledge near the fire to warm, Atlantis stepped back by the wall in the accepted manner to be invisible.

She had time to ponder what she was observing.

Prince El Haba had let no one except that quack healer into his bedchamber since his return five days ago. He had coupled with none of the other women who were also his wives. He was treating Maeven like a prized possession. It seemed merely having her gave him more power in the eyes of his family. He probably hoped to use her against the King of Thulor.

Atlantis smiled nastily in the depths of her hood. She recalled her slight experience in the art of lovemaking, or more correctly lust creating, which had taught her the signs of arousal. The Prince was aroused, but Maeven was staring ahead as if he was not there or touching her. He would want Maeven to fear his advances or at least react.

After a time he grew tired of the lack of response and lifted her out of the water and sat her on the stones by the fire. He summoned the servant without moving to cover himself. He was still aroused and had intended to use the servant to ease his need but something about this one subtly repelled him.

"Bring Delilia here," he ordered.

Atlantis obeyed at once, returning a few moments later with the named wife. The woman was wearing a flimsy flowing gown of an almost sheer substance. None of her voluptuous curves were hidden. She was a match for the Prince, physically beautiful and aware of her power as a woman.

The green eyes of the dark haired woman glittered with spite as she saw that her husband had another woman present – an inexperienced child at that.

Delilia strode around as if she owned the Prince and surpassed her usual responses as if to emphasise her worth and belittle the newcomer. She had no way of knowing that Maeven, her rival, was completely glad that the Prince was turning his attentions elsewhere, especially when the Prince chose to take the woman on the hard stone floor.

While the Prince was totally involved in slaking his lust, Atlantis dried and dressed Maeven and put her back into the Prince's wide bed. Some more movement had indeed returned because Maeven could sit unaided.

"Thirsty," Maeven said quietly.

Atlantis poured some water into an ornately carved, short stemmed drinking cup.

"Put this pellet in your mouth," Atlantis directed quietly, placing something hard against Maeven's lips.

Maeven opened her lips slightly, took a huge gulp of water from the cup and swallowed the pellet.

"It was made from dragon shells; we hope it will heal you. The drug Nayfor gave you sometimes has this effect on people."

Maeven managed a slight smile, feeling waves of heat and cold flushing through her body.

"Can you remember two simple spell chants?"

Maeven nodded and Atlantis whispered first one and then the other.

"The first is a spell to raise lust, in case you want to use it. I would not try it just yet; he is lusting enough for you now. The second is a controlling spell; Roman thinks you have enough magic to use it."

"Do you have a knife?" Maeven asked. Atlantis nodded even though she knew that in this citadel a servant found carrying a weapon received severe punishment.

"I want my talisman!"

Atlantis nodded again and helped her friend lie down.

Delilia was dismissed and escorted by the servant back to the chamber she shared with the other wives. When Atlantis returned, El Haba was deep in the sleep of the satiated. He did not feel the gentle hands hold and deftly cut the leather strap around his neck. The talisman slipped off the strap and Atlantis threaded a scrap of ribbon removed from the skimpy gown, through the hole and tied it around Maeven's neck. Simply having it on had a positive effect.

Maeven slept after a while and Atlantis took the opportunity to eat her portion of the food that was sitting unnoticed on the little table by the door. Then she sat close by her friend and dozed, ready to spring up at the least noise.

The Prince awoke near morning and rolled over to examine his bed companion. He ran his hands over her and felt a reaction. He sat up. In the dim morning light, he saw the woman's eyes were bright and alert and she was wearing her talisman.

Anger, fierce and raging, roused in the Prince and he reached out and grabbed the talisman, intending to tear it from the slender neck, but his hand burned when he touched it. His eyes took in the black robed servant, staring at him from next to the wall. He rose from the bed and walked around to where the servant stood, not in the least worried about being naked.

"You took it!" he accused the servant in a voice full of menace. The robed figure stood still, not dropping her head in a sign of guilt or fear. "I will have you whipped!" he promised and had the satisfaction of seeing a faint shudder move the servant's robes.

He sensed movement on the bed behind him and turned quickly. He saw blazing hate in Maeven's eyes. His instinct was to gloat. He had her, he controlled her and soon he would teach her to be a wife to him.

Maeven began the chant that Atlantis had told her as soon as she had eye contact with El Haba. When he understood what she was doing he laughed, but the laugh died as he realised, too late, that he was trapped.

As a wizard, he knew the weaknesses of the spell and he dived onto the bed before Maeven could specify the terms and tell him what he must or must not do. His hands went to her throat and began to squeeze until he felt something cold, metallic and sharp touching his groin.

His sword was in the steady hands of the black robed servant. The message was clear and without betraying any emotion, he withdrew his hands. The sword remained, unwavering in the same position.

"You will not do harm to me or to this servant," Maeven began, her voice sounding hoarse as her neck pained her. "You will do all in your power to protect me from those who would control, harm or kill me. You will obey the commands that I give you. When I ask, you will tell me your thoughts.

When I ask, you will answer my questions truthfully and as completely as possible. You will treat me with the utmost respect from now on. If you or any other tries to break this spell without my consent you will end up no better than a eunuch."

The flash of hatred in his dark eyes betrayed his thoughts.

"Will you be trying to break the spell?" Maeven asked as evenly as she could and hiding her enjoyment of controlling him.

"No!" he snapped. Whatever he had intended to say after that was, judging by his facial contortions, thoroughly disrespectful.

"My lady," he finally elucidated.

Maeven indicated that Atlantis could remove the sword.

"Do you still claim to own me?"

"Yes," he tried to snarl. "By our laws, the King and Princes of Vatarik can take any woman they choose within the borders of Vatarik. When I first had you, you were within our borders!"

"What if the woman is unwilling to be taken by you?" Maeven continued, trying to maintain an even voice.

"The woman does not have the right to refuse!"

"Do you always have to bespell your women to entrap them?" Maeven was taunting him now.

"No, only those that deserve to be humiliated," he told her truthfully. "The dangerous ones."

Maeven considered the idea of her being dangerous to this normally arrogant, self-assured wizard.

"You may continue to enjoy the memory of humiliating me, at least for now!" Maeven watched his face change to mirror the ecstasy of the memory. She prepared to say the words that would forever ruin it.

"I carried your bastard for a few months," Maeven said, seeing El Haba's expression change to rapt attention. "Then as soon as I found someone who would help me, I got rid of it. I didn't care, but it would have been a boy!"

The reaction was more than Maeven hoped to receive. It repaid him in kind for every minute of humiliation she had felt because of him.

"What are you thinking now?" she asked when the expression left his face.

"I hate you Lady," he said in a dead voice. "I would willingly give half of what I have to the woman who could give me a son."

"I don't want half of anything the Serpent has touched!" Maeven spat. "I don't want you except as a key to something I must have. Give me the black oval stone that is the dragon's egg and I will go out of your life! Where is it?"

"The egg is in the Serpent's temple," El Haba told her.

"What are the dangers?" Maeven demanded, her thief senses already warning her.

"The Serpent doesn't like the children of the Dragon," El Haba said truthfully but with a nasty smile. "However, there will be no danger if I accompany you."

"I don't like the Serpent!" Maeven stated. "Take me there!"

The smile grew bigger and Maeven wondered what El Haba was thinking.

"What are you thinking?" she asked suspiciously.

"The Serpent is more powerful than I am," he told her truthfully. "It is possible that he could overcome your commands."

"If he tries it, you will have no chance of fatherhood! If that possibility concerns you, you should hope he does not try!"

"Am I permitted to dress myself?" El Haba said politely, changing the subject. His mind was testing the amount of control this woman-child had.

"I am not controlling all of your actions," Maeven told him. "You are free to act within the constraints I have spoken."

He dressed in all black, in a loose shirt gathered at wrists and having a plunging v-shaped neckline and loose trousers gathered at waist and ankles. He complemented the clothing with a wide black leather sword belt and matching ankle boots.

Maeven had little choice in the matter of clothes. The only clothes available were the filmy garments that El Haba had supplied. It would draw attention if she sent him off for a slave's robe. The thought of borrowing some of El Haba's clothes crossed her mind but he was so much taller than she was and the very idea was abhorrent. Footwear was considered unnecessary for Royal Wives, and servants too for that matter, so she acted as if barefoot was normal.

Maeven walked slightly behind El Haba through corridors made of the same sandstone as the rooms they had left. Richly woven rugs covered the floors, and niches in the walls displayed valuable looking items of sculpture, pottery or jewelled weapons. Every chamber they passed had either a closed wooden door or a drawn curtain, and if any slaves were normally in this passage, they must have had warning to vanish. The small group of three, for Atlantis was following, saw no one. They left the citadel via a small door into an ornamental garden.

"The Garden of the Wives!" Atlantis murmured quietly to Maeven.

The private garden was enclosed by sandstone walls, twice the height of El Haba and too smooth for any one to climb them.

It was a large area with trees, fountains, stone benches and paths between potted plants and flowerbeds. They followed a paved path away from the building and in the direction of what looked to be a lake.

Maeven glanced briefly over her shoulder and saw the minarets on the corners of the citadel's flat roof and the guards within, watching them.

The sky was a cloudless azure blue, deeper in colour than Maeven was used to further south. The sun, though, did not seem to be as bright as it ought to be.

In front of them, still some distance away but within the protecting walls was a small building. It seemed round and had windows at regular intervals. Beyond the building was an arm of the lake they had seen from the citadel. On the far side of the lake was the sandstone wall. The round structure seemed to be their destination and it too was constructed of the same yellowish stone.

El Haba had shortened his normal stride to match that of the woman who controlled him. He resented that control, but was not obviously fighting it. It would be beneath his dignity to reveal that a mere woman-child had bettered him.

He knew a great deal about controlling spells, more than this woman did. There were still ways by which he could circumvent her commands. He could still relish the idea that the Serpent and the power behind it would be more than a match for her slight magic ability.

There was no door to this building, just an archway in one of the seven sides. Inside the building was black and the light coming in the windows cast reddish shadows on Maeven's light coloured clothes. The other two were difficult to see.

"I am permitted to pass freely," El Haba explained in response to a question Maeven posed. "I have never been bothered by any of the Serpent's creatures. The Serpent is most eager to meet a child of the Dragon that has been given the death sentence."

The statement was true, even if it bordered on being disrespectful.

"Why do you serve the Serpent?" Maeven asked as they began to descend a flight of sandstone steps.

"He gives me power," El Haba admitted with a passion that gave both Maeven and Atlantis shivers.

From a ledge by the start of the tunnel, El Haba took a woven rush torch and lit it magically. After a short way, when they had descended about a man's height, the steps gave way to rock. Maeven reached for Atlantis's hand and wished she dared ask if her friend felt they were calmly walking into deadly danger. Atlantis returned he grip.

CHAPTER 22 – THE SERPENT'S LAIR

The flickering torchlight revealed passages leading off left and right and El Haba seemed to be taking turns at random. It was quickly apparent that this was a labyrinth where strangers would quickly become lost. This idea made Maeven shiver. She did not feel confident of the strength of the control she had on El Haba and she was not naïve enough to think that a stronger wizard would not be able to overcome her spell. If that happened, she and Atlantis would have to fight their way out.

Maeven forced herself to appreciate her father's strategy. She had come this far without a fight – getting out would not be so easy, even with the compelled El Haba helping them. She was finding that the unsteady light interfered with her strange ability to see in the dark, so she concentrated on memorising the route she was travelling.

The path led through to a huge cavern where crystal spires grew down from the roof. Occasional drips of water fell on them as they passed beneath them. Many tunnels led off this area, but El Haba still proceeded with confidence. Finally he stopped in a large cavern that had torches lit at intervals around it. A huge black throne dominated the far side. The empty seat was illuminated by four torches.To the left of the throne was a table made from the same black stone as the throne. On it was a lumpy pile covered in black cloth that wriggled fitfully. To the right was a raised area reached by two carved stone steps. In this area, a small fire was burning.

Atlantis moved back into an area of shadow as Maeven slowly walked forward – impressing the scene in her memory. As she moved, Maeven caught the silhouette of a single spire rising from the cavern floor. It was directly in front of the throne and it was perfectly formed, unlike the spires in the earlier cavern. Her head began to itch fiercely as she drew closer to it. Suddenly, an oval object, no bigger than her hand, began to glow a pure blue. It seemed to be suspended in the air – a hand span above the spire. It drew her closer.

Maeven inched towards it – knowing instinctively that this was the dragon's egg. Reaching out, she touched an invisible wall around the spire and a sensation like stinging nettles raced along her arm, El Haba grabbed her wrist and drew it back.

"Lady, if you wish to touch that egg, you must follow the runes in the right order. If you cross the lines, you will experience agony beyond your imagining." El Haba's face had an unpleasant smile. It was the exact truth, and he had been forced to warn her about it, but he could hope she would befoolish enough to try.

On the floor at her feet, where El Haba had glanced, were faintly glowing runes. The light faded as she backed off. The itch in her head subsided too.

"Do you know the correct sequence?" Maeven demanded.

"I've never been interested," El Haba drawled.

"Well, I want that thing. How do you think we can get it?"

"We wait. You should greet your host first!"

"Bastard! You are meant to help me get the egg – not to help yourself get free. That's what you are hoping for – isn't it?"

"The thought had crossed my mind," El Haba admitted, seemingly without the compulsion forcing him.

"Well, I would prefer not to meet your snaky former master," Maeven said tartly. "And I don't like it down here."

"Like it or not – he is the key to the puzzle."

Maeven made a rude noise and began to move around the cavern, stopping and staring into the darkness between the torch lights.

El Haba simply watched her for a time. He did not comment as he saw her shade her eyes from the flickering light. Finally he spoke.

"The Serpent is coming and you should not assume that your puny attempt at control will remain."

"You'd better hope he doesn't break it," Maeven turned around trying to discern the direction the creature referred to as the Serpent would come. The name suggested something that would crawl. She saw El Haba watching the fire on the raised area and looked there too, starting in surprise as the flames went from yellowy-orange to green.

The odd fire held her attention, but she kept watching El Haba from the corner of her eye. Then she heard the sound of a stone dropping onto rock and saw a small glowing green pebble rolling off the raised rock and coming to land near her feet. She picked it up and it burned her hand but she didn't relinquish it.

"Lady, your host – the Serpent - comes."

Even though she hated all El Haba stood for, Maeven edged nearer to him as a shadow hovered above the fire and grew in size. Once again her head began to itch.

The creature that stepped from the fire was enormous. In silhouette it was man-shaped, and it towered over her and El Haba. Ignoring them, it walked to the black throne and sat there, filling the huge seat comfortably.

The green fire faded back to yellow-orange and the lamps around the throne grew brighter. The creature's face was now lit and clearly visible. It should have been a handsome face, but the glowing orange eyes made it terrifying. It stared at the two creatures who stood in front of the throne.

"Approach!"

El Haba nudged Maeven forward. Every instinct she possessed was insisting that she run and run and run. She forced herself to resist the urge, and to refrain from looking to see where Atlantis was.

Two black caped and hooded figures had appeared from the darkness and they now flanked the throne occupied by the orange eyed creature. Servants waiting to do their master's bidding.

Those weird orange eyes drew Maeven forward as if they had control of her will. Her skin began to prickle – like something foul had touched her.

"Dragon sspawn," the creature hissed. Its tongue flicked out as if it looked on something tasty.

Now she couldn't run. Her feet seemed stuck to the floor.

"Dragons be damned!" Maeven retorted in instinctive garrulousness. "They don't exist. And my father is a bastard, not a dragon."

The creature laughed. The hair on her head tried to stand on end, but the creature had broken eye contact with her. She sighed quietly. She would not let those eyes affect her again.

"Who Prinsce, iss thiss that has captured you?" the creature demanded of El Haba.

"The youngest whelp of the King of Thulor, your Magnificence," El Haba drawled, ignoring the hint of censure. "I saved it from Westron's death sentence. It seems it killed one of the Thulan court nobles. Perhaps he would have spared her if he had known that the creature she killed was one of ours. One who had started to be too independent?"

"How deliciouss, to have tricked my enemy into doing uss a favour."

With the orange eyes off her, Maeven studied the huge figure in the flickering torchlight. His upper torso was bare – covered only with a round pectoral disk. His skin seemed to be etched with glowing purple splotches. They seemed to have no other significance. Her eyes returned to the disc. She guessed it was made of copper, judging from its colour in the fire light.

There was a design etched around the edge and in the centre a huge black serpent was etched and outlined in gold.

The creature stood up. The chest muscles, visible either side of the disc, rippled with controlled power. Maeven swallowed hard, barely controlling her terror. She forced herself to look and remember. From the waist down, he was wearing tight black leggings. The sheen from the fabric suggested it was made from fur – perhaps from one of the sleek black felines that had once hunted her. His wrists and ankles were adorned with gold bands. The overall effect was of a physical perfection that made El Haba look like a gawky adolescent.

The creature walked closer to her, she tried to ignore him and study the pectoral disc. Her talisman began to feel so hot it should have been glowing.

"Have you come to sserve me?"

"Who are you?" Maeven demanded, looking up at the man creature that El Haba had called the Serpent, but not meeting its eyes.

The creature smiled and it was frightening. "I am Ciabolo." It sounded like SSSiabolo.

"So?"

"I am darkness. I am the Serpent. I am the nemesis of all who follow the dragons."

"Really? So you take man shape so that you can walk around rather than slithering on the floor?" Maeven asked, casually taunting. She widened her eyes to appear innocent while she watched for his reaction, gauging how far she could push him.

Atlantis, standing unnoticed by the wall, hoped Maeven knew what she was doing. It wasn't wise to provoke powerful enemies.

"I have many formss!" Ciabolo said calmly, still amused by the presence of his enemy's child. "Have you come to sserve me?"

"No!" Maeven told him bluntly.

"Why are you here?" Ciabolo asked.

"I came to get that bit of rock!" Maeven pointed to the dragon egg and her tone implied that Ciabolo was mentally lacking. "I heard my bastard of a father saying he wanted it. I came to get it and take it to the edge of the world and drop it off!"

"Why doess he want it?" Ciabolo asked intently.

"I don't know!" Maeven snapped, stamping her foot on the stone floor. "He wants it! That is all the reason I need!"

"That iss a powerfully magical object!" Ciabolo told her, watching her closely.

"That? No way!"

"It iss a dragon'ss egg!" Ciabolo sounded amused.

Maeven laughed in his face.

"Dragons' eggs would be at least ten times that size!" she snorted realistically. "If that is a dragon's egg, it must have been laid by the first dragon and it has shrunk over time. What do you expect to do with it? Hatch it?"

Ciabolo waved his hand as if dismissing the question. Maeven did not observe any reaction to her suggestion.

"It iss no matter. You may not have it."

Maeven forced a nonchalant shrug. "I guess I will have to settle for making sure he won't get it."

"Yess. Sso it sseems." Ciabolo agreed, staring at Maeven who was keeping her eyes away from him.

"I'll just be going then," Maeven said calmly. She turned to find two more black-clad servants behind her, blocking her way.

"Why russh?" Ciabolo coaxed. "You and I have a common enemy."

Maeven turned back to face him. "Who?"

"Why, your ssire of course," Ciabolo stated. His eyes were glowing bright again. "Perhapss we can work together to kill him."

"I have no intention of ever going near him again!" Maeven said with utter conviction. "So unless you intend to go there yourself…?"

Ciabolo waved her to silence. With faint movement of his left hand, he spoke, "A drink for the Prince and his guest." The servant on that side moved off immediately, and soundlessly.

"That is not necessary, your magnificence," El Haba demurred, but Maeven felt him shudder by the touch of his clothes on her bare arm.

Maeven glanced at him: she felt he was trying to warn her of something, but his face was inscrutable.

Seeing Ciabolo's intent gaze, as the blood red drink in a shiny silver goblet was pressed into her hand, gave Maeven shivers. She was certain that she did not want that drink. However, she pretended to sip and taste it. El Haba made no move to drink from a similar cup in his hand.

"If I agree to work with you – what's in it for me?" she pretended to be thoughtful.

She saw the evil smile on Ciabolo's face. "I can give you what ever you want…" was his suggestive answer.

Except the dragon's egg, Maeven thought to herself. Ciabolo seemed to be waiting for her to answer.

"Gold, jewels?" she suggested.

Ciabolo nodded.

"Tapestries and treasures? Power, knowledge?"

"Of coursse. I can give you fabulouss foodss, the richesst of winess, ecsstasy and blisss."

"So how do I know that you have all that? I can get riches for myself – I'm not interested in being a rutting bitch, and I don't eat much – what's left?"

Ciabolo spoke words in a language that Maeven didn't know. Around the main cavern, previously hidden side caverns opened to view – their contents illuminated by a steady reddish light.

Without moving, Maeven could see piles of gold, silver and copper in one cavern; piles of colour sorted gems in another. She moved a few paces and saw the vision of a feast in a third cavern. She was not allowed to move far enough to see what was in the cavern that had opened up behind the throne.

"Impressive. How many kingdoms did you rob to get all that?" Maeven pretended to have another sip of the red drink. "What kind of knowledge and power?"

"Knowledge of magic, of other worldss, of alchemy and the power of control, the power to perform magic without potionss and poorly crafted sspells."

"I will have to think on those things. What would you want from me? I'm no fighter or sorceress or wizard."

"Your obediencse. Your knowledge of Thulor and thosse who are royal. Your knowledge of dragonss."

"And if I don't do what you want – or can't, even if I want to …"

"I'm ssure that someone who hatess King Wesstron of Thulor won't fail me."

Maeven pretended to have a third sip and muttered in her head, "*Rend me limb from limb, suspend me in agony, turn me into a snake…*" Her tartness countered the seductiveness of Ciabolo's words.

"Have you ever seen jewels like these?" Ciabolo held up a glittering gem which was threaded upon a silver chain. In the torch light, the gem showed flashes of red, blue and green as it twisted in front of her eyes.

"No," Maeven admitted, without thought. Her attention was thoroughly caught by the rainbow stone.

The previously motionless El Haba moved at the same instant as something clattered near the furthest store cavern. Maeven was distracted by the sound, as was Ciabolo, who cast a spell to have the caverns hidden again.

In that moment, El Haba whispered. "Lady, in his hands, the rainbow stones steal the minds of men."

Ciabolo returned his attention to his guests. "Your answer, dragon-sspawn?"

"This is an important decision. Can I think on it?"

"I am ssure we can have a productive relationsship." Ciabolo scoffed the rest of his drink.

Maeven pretended to take a mouthful. "This drink is unlike anything I have ever tasted before."

"It's goats' blood – curdled with spices from distant lands," El Haba told her.

Maeven dropped the metal goblet.

"You Thulans are so squeamish." El Haba made the observation sound like a taunt.

Ciabolo stared at Maeven. She stared back, focussing on a point on his forehead.

"Sserve me and I will put you in your father'ss place. You will be able to indulge every whim; have abssolute control over all in Thulor."

Maeven had no doubt that her absolute control over Thulor would be subject to his absolute control over her. For once she kept quiet.

"All I want from you iss to know where the dragon iss."

"You are obsessed with dragons," Maeven retorted. "Legend has it that one protects Thulor but its nonsense!"

"You wear a dragon amulet. You ssurvived the wrath of my sservant. You caught it at Thul Run."

"My sister caught it!" Maeven said quickly, intent on belittling her role. "As for the rest – the amulet is worthless. Mother's didn't protect her. Mine didn't save me from the attentions of your prince. As for that maniac demon – it couldn't get me when I was hiding in the rain water barrel."

Ciabolo's attention jerked away from her. He seemed to be listening. A tiny demon flew to Ciabolo. He hissed a command and sent it off.

"I am losing patience, Dragon sspawn. I will have your answer before you leave here."

He turned and strode away from her towards the table and its wriggling contents.

Maeven sidled away, backing off towards the wall. She saw Ciabolo wrench something off the table. There was a single screech of agony, then silence. In the flickering light, Ciabolo seemed to be munching on a haunch of meat. After a while, he threw the remains against the wall and tore off another haunch.

Something sinuous and barely visible brushed past Maeven. The ghostly shape stopped to lick up the spilt drink. Another such shape brushed past and soon she heard bones crunching.

Maeven was like a shadow as she moved around. "He's not going to let me go, is he?' she asked El Haba, who had obediently followed her.

"No lady. He will make you serve him – unwillingly if not willingly. You are a child of the dragon – you are too precious, too useful to be allowed to leave. Soon he will stop playing with you. What greed doesn't achieve – pain will."

Maeven was looking for Atlantis, but was glad she was no longer where she had last seen her for Ciabolo let out a bellowing roar. He stalked over to her and with his left arm straight out and not touching her – he made her rise half her height from the ground.

He shook her so hard that her neck hurt. "What are they doing?"

"Who?" was the only answer she was able to voice.

"Your Ssire'ss man-daughterss. They are up above ground."

"How would I know? They hate me too. If they know I'm still alive – they are probably trying to finish the job."

"I wouldn't trust that wench, Master Ciabolo."

Maeven knew that greasy voice, even if she couldn't turn her head – El Haba's brother, Prince El Rasho. Ciabolo knew it too. He didn't turn to face the speaker. "Why are you here when there iss trouble above?"

"The guards are handling it. The dragon bitches are making the lesser slaves riot. They cannot enter the palace," El Rasho was silkily assured. "This one, though, is a slippery one, and inside your defences. She could be more trouble than her bitch sisters."

"Is that why you came down here to hide?" Maeven said to the faceless voice. "You couldn't get the better of me – and you are afraid my sisters will better you, too?"

El Rasho moved around into Maeven's sight. He made no secret of staring at her body through the scanty fabric. "I intend to have you."

"The whelp is mine," Ciabolo stated. "It will learn to obey me. As you do, Prinsce."

For a moment, Maeven thought El Rasho shuddered. He began to back off as if a little afraid to defy the Serpent.

"Anyway, greaseball," Maeven said. "Your bastard of a brother got me first. And I am sure he'd like you to try something now – he made sure that anyone else who tried to rape me would die."

El Rasho looked at his younger brother as if noticing him for the first time. El Haba was smirking.

"I saw her first!"

"And you wasted the chance," El Haba taunted. "I had her first in Vatarik."

"Is she as barren as the rest of your women?" El Rasho snarled the insult.

"I do not believe you are a father yet, brother."

Maeven saw the chance to inflame the hatred between the brothers. Ciabolo seemed content to listen to them snipe at each other. "I'm not barren," she proclaimed. "However, I decided not to bring your brother's bastard son to birth."

The look on El Rasho's face was of fear until he understood what Maeven had said. "Nor are you a father, brother."

"Ssilence!" Ciabolo ordered. He did not have to be loud, but both men obeyed. "Prinsce – go up and bring the bitchess to me. I will have three dragon whelpss for you to try and get with child."

El Rasho smiled as he walked away. He disappeared into a different tunnel from that through which El Haba had brought her.

Ciabolo dropped Maeven. She landed heavily but on her feet. Two black servants appeared from nowhere and grabbed her and then she began to feel scaly bodies twisting about her legs so she could not lift them. She looked at El Haba, about to hiss an insult at him since he was meant to protect her, but he was rigid, his sword arm held tight to his side by a snake. With a chill, she realised that he was even more constrained than she was.

"Foolissh child!" Ciabolo hissed, bringing his face close enough for her to smell his foul breath. "You may have a ssmall amount of control over my sservant, but I own him! I will make him do my will; even if he cannot do it by hiss own choisce. And I will deal with him when I am finished with you."

"I don't care what you do to him!" Maeven told the Serpent. "I hate him, anyway!"

"Do you care what I do to you?" Ciabolo hissed, implying dire things. He forced her to look in his direction by simply moving his hand.

"Go away!" Maeven said defiantly.

Ciabolo laughed in her face. "You will give me the glowing sstone that you sstole from me."

Maeven tried to keep her hand closed, but saw to her dismay that it was opening. Her arm was stretching out to Ciabolo. He plucked the no longer glowing stone from her palm without touching her. He held it at the level of his eyes – between two fingers. It now looked like a clear amber coloured teardrop. That soon changed as the stone began to glow green once more.

"You will sserve me, Princesss of Thulor," Ciabolo promised before striding off towards the fire next to the throne. He dropped the green stone into the fire and when the fire flared green, he stepped into it.

"He's gone," Maeven sighed with relief. El Haba did not answer her comment. "And I've seen stones like that one before."

"I doubt it," El Haba told her flatly. He had stopped trying to free himself. In spite of bringing King Westron's daughter to him, Ciabolo would punish him for his stupidity in allowing this woman child to get the better of him. He would consider, that while she was controlling him, that he was a traitor.

"I have, though," Maeven insisted.

"They are demon stones. Who in that weak kingdom of yours lacks the squeamishness to deal with demons?"

"Lord Toadface. He tied to kill me with one. I found the stones at his place."

"Impossible. They can only be activated and used by demons. Major demons."

"I don't know that he used them – but he had them. He was a traitor."

"He was a fool."

"That too. Ciabolo used the stones – so he can use demon magic?"

El Haba sighed with exasperation. "Have you not realised what it is that you are trying to antagonise?"

Ah… She hadn't.

"Can humans use them?"

"No. Demons are creatures of fire; humans are of the earth."

"Dragons?"

"No, they are creatures of the air. Dragon magic is not compatible with demon magic."

"So do the stones summon demons?"

"No – they are simply a means to travel between places. There is always a fire here and another in my… in the palace. It is a permanent portal. A stone anchors each end – the one you saw is the portal key, which opens the way."

"What if you had two stones? One to open the portal and another."

"If you could make the demon walk into the fire – he has only one way to come back out."

"Oh."

"And just throwing the stone into the fire won't activate it. Nor, if it was activated, could you touch it. The dragon magic in you would neutralise it. Like it did to that stone you picked up. Ciabolo had to reactivate it."

Maeven had to admit the truth of that – at least to herself. She recalled the chance stones that had led to her joining the thieves' guild. Forget that problem for now.

"What would have happened if he'd thrown the activated stone into the fire but not followed it right away? Would the portal stay open?"

"While the fire still burns, or until it is deactivated – yes. Though when it has been open and activated for a while, some force begins to act to draw the demon into the fire."

"What do you mean?"

"The force I noticed does not seem to be magic. Its more like an irresistible elemental force."

Maeven looked blankly at El Haba.

"It is a bit like the effect of the rainbow stones on a human. They attract demons on an unconscious level."

That made a kind of sense – but she could see no use for it in her current predicament. Especially when what she hoped were portal keys were hidden in a small cave a whole kingdom away.

"So why did toadface Tormore have them, kept in such an accessible place, if he couldn't use them? How did he get them?" Maeven wondered aloud.

"If he had a means to activate them, or could use demon magic stored in some artefact he may have felt they would protect him or give him power over some demons."

"How?"

"To trap a demon, he would need to have a portal stone in a fire somewhere – perhaps near where a demon might come. Then he would need to have a demon receptacle – ideally with a fire in it too. When the demon is compelled through the fire – the trap is sprung."

"Sounds dangerous – anything else?"

"If he wanted to banish a demon – he'd still need a fire elsewhere with a stone but he would have to trick the demon into accepting a second stone and make him go through the fire. Then the nearest fire would need to be doused."

It would be good if she could douse the fire here but she couldn't move. She looked down and saw the snake like thing immobilising her feet. This was like the ones that had come into Exconidor's crypt, except these were not emerging fully from the solid rock. They were magic in some way because her head was itching.

Maeven reached for her talisman, intending to remove it from her neck and swing the talisman down to touch the snakes.

El Haba watched impassively, but seemed forced to say, "More of his servants are coming – you would not get far. And the snakes can leech magic from that amulet. They are humans, changed so they can move through rock. If they taste the dragon magic, they will be changed back."

Maeven pictured men stuck in solid rock and straightened. She had no more time, because she heard the sound of footsteps approaching. She tried to see what was coming but the firelight countered her dragon sight.

Human-seeming hands put chains on her wrists and ankles, the snakes were now winding around her waist. From the corner of her eye, she was aware that dark robed shapes were doing the same to El Haba. Slaves with newly-lit rush torches urged them to walk into one of the passages. The snakes had moved to allow her to walk as directed. They finally came to a smaller chamber with a gigantic red crystal set in the roof. Loose lengths of chain dragged behind them but when they were told to stop, the end of the chain seemed to fuse into the rock. The snakes twisted back down to the ground.

Maeven sat down on the rocky floor and waited for the torches to recede from view. Her father was right, her dragon sight, if that is what it was, had improved. In her mind, she could see and trace the passages back to the throne chamber. The mage egg seemed like a bright glow in the darkness.

She sought for the passage out and followed ways to dead ends, traps or the lairs of creatures. Then she began to free herself. Her bonds were purely physical, or her amulet had neutralised any mage spells on them. And she had a magical lock pick, or that is what she now guessed Merlie's gift of a key actualy was.

Maeven closed her eyes, imagined she was wearing her normal style of men's clothes. She put her hand where it would be if it were in the secret pocket of her breeches. A smile formed on her face as she muttered the revealing chant; the key was warm in her hand. She applied the key to the locks on the chains and they fell off her.

El Haba watched her as she re-hid the key. He did not ask for release and he had too much pride to beg.

"You are such a good servant of the snake," Maeven assured him. "He'll let you go when I am gone!"

The look he gave her was poisonous. "Whilst your spell is still on me, he will not trust me. Why else do I find myself as trapped as you were?"

Maeven ran quickly back to the throne chamber, already considering ways to reach the dragon egg levitating above the rock spire. She found Atlantis half way through the puzzle.

"I'm in trouble," Atlantis said quietly. "It's getting harder to remember what comes next. The sequence follows the runes on Ciabolo's chest plate – west, south, east and north. I've only gone six steps …"

Maeven recalled the metal disc she had studied; the runes come quickly into her mind and she focussed on the seventh and touched her talisman. She told Atlantis to hold her own.

Atlantis moved a step forward, choosing her next step to match the one that came into her mind. While she still clutching her talisman, the eighth rune sprang into her mind and she moved ahead another step. Eight more steps brought her to the narrow clear space around the spire and she reached for the egg. It was so cold it almost burnt her hands.

"Throw it!" Maeven hissed. Atlantis obeyed and the egg seemed to fly directly into her friend's hand, but disappeared a second later.

Atlantis was about to take the first step back when she looked and saw that the runes had changed. "They are all different," she whispered. "I've never seen any of these before!" Her voice betrayed her fear but she was not about to panic; she had been alone in tight spots before.

"Did Father choose you for Mother's talisman?" Maeven asked, surprising Atlantis with what seemed to be a trivial question.

"Rhovert did!" she amended, her mind busy trying to find a way out. "But your father agreed."

Maeven nodded, also thinking hard and aware that creatures of some kind were approaching.

"How did you figure to use the runes on the chest plate?"

"It just suddenly occurred to me," she admitted. "West first, because the creature is of the dark and that is the way the sun sets. We are underground, so I went to the south next. They want to destroy the creatures of the light, so east and then north."

Maeven took a deep breath. "Atlantis, I don't know the way out, but I think you will know. Hold the talisman, clear your mind of all thoughts, and then turn around slowly. When you feel the need to step – trust the instinct."

Maeven almost wished she believed in praying. She was not completely sure her suggestion would work, but it felt right – or as if some sage had whispered wisdom to her. Such feelings had given her quick or easier solutions to problems before. In addition, the talisman that Atlantis wore was prone to give its bearer visions.

Whatever was approaching was very close and Maeven silently urged Atlantis to hurry. Unlike her friend, she had absolutely no skill with a sword and her survival instincts were urging her to run.

The instant that Atlantis had both feet out of the spelled circle, Maeven grabbed her friend and dragged her behind the huge throne as she muttered the words of the latest invisibility spell that she had stolen.

Normally it would hide her and anything she was carrying. She had never tried it whilst holding another human being.

"Stay still," Maeven whispered. They were standing with their backs to the stone of the throne.

The creatures were in a pack. In the dark, they were difficult to see. In the torch light, the narrow tailless bodies had spindly legs, tall pointed ears with red glowing eyes and sharp white teeth.

"Cave hounds," Atlantis identified very quietly.

"What do you do with them?" Maeven asked in an equally low voice. The animals were snuffling and growling around the front of the throne but so far had not come behind it.

"Give them something big to eat or keep a fire between you and them," Atlantis said, having encountered the beasts once before.

"Did my brilliant father have any ideas about getting out of here?"

Maeven asked sarcastically.

"Your sisters are creating trouble upstairs, causing the servants to revolt. They said they knew how to cause a diversion!" Atlantis revealed. "Well, they have got the Serpent away from here!"

"I guess so!" Maeven admitted. "Anyway, I know ways out of here, but I don't want to walk between those things. Some of them might decide to snap at something and it might be me! They aren't the only problems either!"

"The hounds aren't coming right up to us," Atlantis commented. "My brother put a repelling spell on me. I think it kept those black clad servants from sensing me and it seems to be working on the creatures too. We could try edging around the wall."

"Let's go!" Maeven urged.

The slow inching around the wall of the cavern only had a slight effect on the hounds. They could still smell what to them was food, but they were unable to find it.

There was now growling coming from the grotto with the red crystal in the roof. Occasional bursts of light, reflected dully along the tunnel.

"Maybe they have found dinner!" Maeven said casually.

Atlantis quietly shuddered; she had seen hounds like these tearing a troll apart. It was not a pleasant sight. The hounds around them left to join their fellows. "I wouldn't wish that fate on anyone…except maybe Ciabolo. That Prince has obeyed you well enough."

"Only because of that spell, I'm sure."

Maeven dragged Atlantis into the third tunnel they came to. For now, the tunnel was empty. They continued on to another small grotto, one with four more tunnels leading off it. At that point, she unerringly chose the one leading east.

As they progressed along this passage, the air began to grow foul. The two women needed to use a fold of Atlantis's cape to breathe through. The smell of fumes began to have a burning, choking effect.

Atlantis pulled Maeven down to the dust floor; there was a layer of fresher air down there.

"Is there any other way?" Atlantis asked.

"Yes, but this is the quickest," Maeven admitted. "Somehow, I think we will be in trouble whichever way we go. There are a lot of traps and creatures, I doubt if I have seen them all. This place reeks of magic."

"Then we will have to crawl," Atlantis said in agreement. She was better off than Maeven for this because under the black slave's robe she was wearing her leather breeches and a heavy linen shirt.

When they were almost at the cavern with the hanging spires, Maeven cautiously lifted her head. The foul smelling smoke had gone but her eyes looked up legs, loosely covered in torn black fabric, black covered chest and into eyes that glittered with hate.

Her invisibility had gone.

Only after a moment did her mind register that the elegant clothes were torn and the hands that helped her up were scratched and bitten. El Haba chose to say nothing, simply turning his back on her and blocking the way to the grotto where a crowd of black-robed figures were walking silently into the space under the spires. Maeven shivered – something was not right with those people.

"What is wrong with them?" she asked El Haba.

"The Serpent has their souls and their obedience," he said flatly. "They chose to serve him."

"Can they be freed?" Atlantis asked, but she was ignored. Maeven repeated the question.

"Only by death!"

A voice rang out in the grotto. It spoke a language with strange cadences. The black robed figures fell to their knees and the Serpent appeared.

Left standing in the midst of the kneeling crowd were two figures Maeven recognised. She tried to push past El Haba but he grabbed her and held her tightly. "They are bait for you!"

"What!"

"The Serpent wants you! Fortunately, he thinks you are long gone with the egg. He can no longer sense it."

"Why does he want me? I'm not dangerous!" Maeven asked softly.

"Aren't you? He hasn't been able to kill you."

"When did he try?"

"Several times. He deals with demons. As for today, you recovered that egg. No one else could have done that."

Maeven did not wish to draw attention to Atlantis by admitting she had been the one to take the egg. She also decided that she would not admit that she had been lucky – or her luck just might run out.

Maeven shook herself free of El Haba's grip. His brother El Rasho had arrived and his eyes glittered with spite as he beheld the two female captives that had caused so much trouble above ground.

Leanne recognised him and began struggling, Finora began to chant a spell; their efforts had no effect.

Maeven asked Atlantis for her black robe and received it without question.

El Rasho could not help taunting the prisoners. They could not move their arms or legs because the snakes were twining around them. It was easy for their tormentor to reach over and remove their talismans.

"You are my captives now!" he was saying. "I intend to keep you helpless but alive, awake and begging for release. I intend to humiliate you as your King humiliated me!"

The Serpent was watching the scene impassively. His eyes constantly scanned the area, watching for something. More snakes were weaving amongst the people on the floor.

"Too bad we can't make a hole in the roof," Atlantis commented. "Drain the lake! Those snakes don't like water do they?"

Maeven told El Haba to go and start an argument with his brother.

"What will you be doing?" he challenged suspiciously, his mind telling him that she was planning something dangerous and he was commanded to protect her as well as obey her.

"I'll be following like an obedient slave!"

El Haba strode out into his brother's sight. There was no mutual respect between them. It gave the Serpent something else to watch.

"Are we under the lake?" Maeven asked Atlantis.

"Yes, the water dripping through cracks causes the spires."

"How can we make the cracks bigger?"

"Ground tremors?" Atlantis suggested, and seeing a thoughtful expression on her friend's face asked, "What are you planning to do?"

"What I'm really good at; being sneaky and getting people really angry at me!" was the oblique reply. "And pushing my luck!"

Maeven chanted her invisibility spell and checked with Atlantis that it had worked properly. Being sure she was not able to be seen, she carefully walked around the motionless slaves and the slithering snakes. Part of her attention stayed on Ciabolo. If his eyes did not fix on her position, she was probably still safe.

Finora was closest to her and therefore her first target. As she approached, the snake seemed to slither back down to the floor. Maeven examined the rope bindings that were cutting into her sister's delicate flesh. She recalled one of her knives from the follow spell and carefully cut the tight bindings. Finora must have sensed she was there but she gave no sign. The snake tried to start crawling around Maeven's legs but she stabbed it with the knife.

"Cup your hand, Finora," Maeven whispered.

The order was obeyed. Finora kept her eyes on the brothers who were taunting each other and ignoring the prisoners. Maeven took out the dragon's egg and dropped it into her sister's palm. The sorceress would be aware of its power.

Maeven moved the few steps to Leanne and used the knife again on her bonds. This time she pressed the knife into the now free hands.

Her next target was El Rasho, who still had the two talismans dangling from his hand. Maeven reached and carefully clutched them. She spoke the spell that would hide them and make them follow her. When she moved away, the talismans pulled out of El Rasho's hand. He guessed at once that she was around. He bellowed angrily and then heard a disembodied laugh.

"That's twice, you slimy fool," she whispered close to his ear.

El Rasho grabbed, hoping to catch her. He reached for his sword and that was gone, too.

A blast of magic energy passed very close to Maeven, killing one of the slaves. It was time to move.

"Not close enough, snake!" she yelled then, her voice echoing around the chamber.

A second blast felled more slaves, near to where she had been.

Leanne moved to the disarmed El Rasho and began to lunge at him with the knife. Finora was chanting spells and firing energy blasts of her own at Ciabolo. El Haba was trying to find Maeven, but stopped before using his own spells to reveal her.

Ciabolo was returning Finora's blasts, but they did not hit her. She was drawing on the power of the dragon egg. He was also sending blasts in the direction of the taunting voice of the human woman-child; the one he saw as his nemesis.

Maeven moved to where the roof above her was thinnest. With all her strength, she tossed El Rasho's sword upwards. It clanged on the spires and broke some off. Ciabolo, reacting to the noise, sent a blast at the roof. More spires fell, many hitting and killing slaves.

With each death, Ciabolo seemed less substantial.

"Tricked you!" Maeven yelled. "Keep that up and you will bring the roof down on yourself! Ha! Ha! Ha!"

She did not distract her sisters, but then they were used to ignoring her!

Coming back near El Rasho, Maeven whispered one of the chants that Atlantis had told her. He immediately looked at Leanne and began to feel lustful. Maeven had no doubt about her sister's ability to handle him in that condition. He was trying to drag Leanne into one of the side tunnels. Atlantis started to follow Leanne. Maeven quickly recovered the sword from the ground and yelled for Atlantis to catch it. It was as well that she did not because Ciabolo sent a blast in the direction of the now visible sword. Atlantis ducked and recovered the weapon before the Serpent aimed again.

Unfortunately, Maeven stayed in position a moment too long. Ciabolo's next blast knocked her to the ground, stunning her and causing the invisibility to dissipate. He readied his next mage bolt, but his aim was spoilt by a well timed blast from Finora. Before the Serpent could send another bolt at his helpless victim, El Haba came and stood in front of her. Ciabolo glared at him.

"Move asside, Prinss," he ordered, but Prince El Haba stood still, his body compelled to protect the woman-child.

The Serpent's eyes glittered dangerously. He sought to punish those who defied him.

His snakes began to writhe over Maeven, pinning her to the ground. They slithered around El Haba and drew tight. He resisted the desire to cry out, and then he couldn't as the very breath he needed was squeezed out of him.

Ciabolo smiled an utterly evil smile, as he sent blast after blast at the roof of the grotto. Broken spires and pieces of rock fell, killing more slaves, but missing his immediate targets. Maeven sensed that El Haba, was still barely conscious and using his own powers to deflect the rubble while he could.

Finora moved to the edge of the grotto when the Serpent's attention was off her. The occasional drips were becoming like rain off the edge of a roof. The snakes were retreating a little. More rocks were falling from the roof, more slaves were dying and Ciabolo was no longer a solid figure. As the slaves died, Ciabolo lost control of their souls and part of his power. Finora trotted off after her sister.

The snakes retreated further, no longer stopping Maeven from crawling away. Ciabolo had no power to spare to control them. They hated water – the floor was very wet now and the trickle a torrent.

Suddenly, Ciabolo realised what he had been tricked into doing. He aimed one last blast through the water at Maeven, uttered a shaprp incantation and turned to flee before he became too weak to defend himself.

The still alive slaves began to rise from their kneeling position and come at Maeven, ignoring the commands El Haba tried to give to them to halt. Then without warning, the slaves transformed into the growling, snapping cave hounds. Two went for Maeven, still on the ground, digging their teeth into leg and arm.

A blast of power from El Haba, now released him from the coils of the snake, felled the rest of the creatures. Their dying screams drowning out those Maeven could not help uttering. He turned to kick the two hounds biting her, and when they turned on him, he blasted them into pieces of purplish flesh. El Haba lifted Maeven out of the ankle-deep water and carried her towards the tunnel where his brother had gone.

The tunnel was the one leading upward, the water flowing into the grotto from the roof, was flowing downward to the lower levels. Part of the roof collapsed behind them and sunlight lit the cavern.

"Put me down!" Maeven insisted. Her leg was on fire but it supported her weight. She looked back at the mess that was behind her, the rubble and water, and then further, trying to find where Ciabolo had fled. She did not think that he was dead.

She found no trace of Ciabolo, and strangely, most of the creatures she had sensed before were gone too. This time she found a faint spark of life in a rock bubble off the red crystal grotto. Who ever was imprisoned there deserved to go free, too. She could not leave the person to die there when all Ciabolo's slaves were probably dead.

El Rasho was not dead, but for now he was subdued, he was controlled, as his brother was, but by Finora.

Leanne took charge and ordered them upwards, and only smirked as Maeven pushed past her and seemed to want to lead the way. She did not care that Maeven kept getting further ahead.

Maeven, however, had a purpose for getting well ahead of the others. If she tried to return to the red crystal grotto, she knew that they would all try to stop her, particularly El Haba. She was not ready to free him of her commands yet. So she waited until she was ahead around a bend in the tunnel, made herself invisible again, pressed herself into a shallow cavity in the wall and waited until the others had passed. Then she ran quickly back along the passages to the grotto.

In the cavern where the roof had collapsed, she walked carefully through the knee-deep water, trying to avoid the worst of the rubble. Her bare feet, normally hardened to walking without shoes, were water softened. The water came to mid thigh when she finally reached the red crystal cave. Bodies of dead cave hounds floated around her. She walked to where her dragon sight showed her the imprisoned man. He was barely keeping his head above water. With her normal sight, she could only see rock between her and the prisoner. She closed her eyes and felt the rock under her fingers.

The sense of something behind her made her turn. A shadowy shape was forming in the light coming through the red crystal. It was tall…

"Ciabolo," Maeven breathed. The insubstantial form was vaguely demonic in shape, a man's shape but with wings and a tail. She felt a strong urge to run but it was between her and her only route to escape.

A solid feeling hand grabbed her arm, the bitten arm, and sent waves of intense burning agony through her whole body. "You really can't kill me, can you?" Maeven taunted weakly.

Ciabolo shook her in frustration. "Why?"

"Look at yourself!" she forced herself to say. "Weak, puny and stupid."

Ciabolo shook her again and the pain intensified further.

"Stupid! I'm merely a decoy," she said, it was almost a whimper. "You waste time and energy chasing me when the others are doing what needs to be done. I'm no swordswoman; I'm no wizard – all I can do are a few simple stolen spells. I don't have the skill to create any…"

"You are lying!"

"No, if I was the only thing that could stop you – do you think that my father would kill me? He has always been infuriating but never wrong! If I was all that would save his precious kingdom, he'd forgive me for whatever I'd done."

"My demons can't touch you."

He finally eased his grip, interested in her words.

Maeven caught her breath as the pain eased slightly.

"Your weak, useless agent Tormore, good riddance to him, had his spell rebound on him. It killed him before the demon killed me. So of course, the demon was dragged back. That other little brainless thing didn't recognise me. I was pregnant, hadn't got rid of El Haba's bastard then!"

"How did you get the egg?"

"I didn't, one of the others did. He was dressed as a servant and you never paid any attention to him. He's probably well on his way back to Thulor by now!"

Ciabolo accepted the mixture of truth and lies.

"I can sense the dragon's magic on you!"

Maeven managed a weak laugh. "I pinched my sisters' talismans back from your idiotic servant El Rasho, and I have my own. I'm a thief Ciabolo, that's all I am. Killing me will simply please my family and weaken you further. Your enemy wins either way."

Ciabolo fell silent; his concentration seemed to be elsewhere. Maeven risked trying to sense where the others were by following the tunnels. The passageways were empty.

"Where are they? I had them trapped!"

"Did have. You fell for the decoy again!" Maeven laughed faintly. "Let the prisoner out."

"Why?"

"He was a dangerous man. It will anger my father if he goes free," Maeven lied. "If I can make him better, he'll be grateful to me. I can make him kill my father."

Ciabolo looked intently at the woman. "Do you hate your father that much?"

"All my life," Maeven said, allowing all the emotion she had walled off infude her voice, "all I ever wanted was for my father to hug me. He never has. Not even once. If he had told me, even once, that he loved me – I would cheerfully have died for him. He cares nothing for me."

Maeven looked back as steadily as she could. The creature had to believe her when she said, "He had me hung!" There was no mistaking the pain of that final rejection by her family.

The rock wall vanished and the man became slightly more animated. He was able to stumble unsteadily to his feet. Maeven went to support him, afraid that the Serpent might change his mind, but before he had a chance to do more, the red crystal exploded into a mass of shards. The shards missed Maeven where she stood in the rock bubble but many passed through the ghostly Ciabolo.

The sudden brilliance of sunlight blinded Maeven, but Ciabolo shrieked in agony. Whatever was left of his essence fled, able to bear the sun only when its energy was filtered through the red crystal or he wore the body of a human.

Maeven helped the man to walk into the sunlight. He was dirty, his clothes merely rags, his hair long and knotted with filth. She was not sure if his mind would recover, but thief or not, she did not think Barnabas deserved to suffer any more.

"Maeven, you stupid little bitch," Leanne's voice called down to her. "We are dropping a rope, can you climb up?"

"There's someone else that needs to come out first," she called back.

"I'm free?" Barnabas said in a voice hoarse from disuse.

"Soon," Maeven promised, tying the rope under his arms. He was little more than a thin layer of flesh between skin and bone.

Leanne had seen what her sister was doing and lifted the man gently with help from her twin and Atlantis. El Haba simply stood watching.

"Help my sisters, El Haba!" she ordered.

He smiled a smile of bitter mockery.

Barnabas was soon above ground. The rope still looped fell down again. Maeven tested its strength and began to climb. Part way up she had to stop. The rope was cutting into her water softened feet, her leg and arm where the cave hounds had bitten were throbbing.

Whilst she dangled, she did not realise that El Haba was pulling her up. The ground when she felt it was very welcoming.

"Typical," Leanne commented. "Passing out and expecting to be carried home."

"Go away, Leanne," Maeven muttered. "I don't want to go home."

"The cave hound bites will need to be tended," El Haba volunteered.

Maeven stared at him, wondering why he had volunteered the information. He stared back at her, betraying nothing.

"I don't want that red robed charlatan near me!" Maeven growled at him.

"I don't need him. The bites have a magic poison. Only magic can negate it before it dissolves the flesh," El Haba told her.

Maeven glanced at Finora.

"I have had no experience of those creatures," she admitted.

"Why do you care?" Maeven scowled, turning back to El Haba. "Don't think I don't realise you are gloating at me right now, when you probably fixed your own wounds first."

El Haba smirked, and said, mockingly, "You commanded me, Lady, to protect you from those that would harm you – even if that person is yourself. To do that, I need to be well."

Maeven scowled, really wanting to tell him to take a long walk. "Treat the damn bites then!"

"Stubborn," he whispered quietly, as if talking to himself. He placed his hand over the bite on her arm and recited a spell. The pain in the arm noticeably eased. He repeated the procedure with the bite on her leg. Then without a word, he rose, walked to Barnabas and spoke a few words. The man gained colour in his ashen face.

"You placed the mage bonds!" Finora commented as she became aware of their removal.

He shrugged, admitting nothing.

"We need to leave!" Leanne reminded the company. "Finora, what are we doing with that creep?" She was looking at El Rasho.

"He can stay here!" she said. "He will behave better than he used to."

"Maeven?" Leanne nodded at El Haba.

"He can stay here, too!" Maeven said, not wanting to endure more of his company.

"I am compelled to protect you Lady," El Haba reminded her again, this time without mockery.

Maeven forced herself to speak calmly. "I do not require you to protect me any more. I command you to work with your father to help repair the damage the Serpent did to your country."

There was an unreadable expression on El Haba's face, and Maeven didn't demand to know what he was thinking. She no longer cared. She had no further need of him. He turned to stare at his brother. El Rasho, controlled by Finora's spell, was angry and visibly fighting its effect. He looked like he wanted to kill everyone in the group, including his brother, but without his pet wizard, he wouldn't get free and he was helpless to engage in vengeance. He'd keep.

"My father is not here at the moment," El Haba said neutrally. "I will accompany you to our border."

Maeven rode with Atlantis, several horse lengths behind her sisters, who were taking it in turns to lead Barnabas' mount. El Haba was riding level with the older women, but not talking to them. After a while, he dropped back.

"You don't like your brother," Maeven commented to him.

"No."

"Why?" Maeven asked, thinking now that such contention might be a useful weak spot for the armies of Thulor to breach. "I would like to know what you are thinking."

El Haba felt the tug of the controlling spell but hid his resentment. "In my father's absence he, as eldest son, is in control. While he was in your father's prison, that power was mine."

Maeven shivered, reminded of her first meeting with this man. Her control spell seemed to have muted his arrogance.

"I still hate you!"

"You are still my wife!"

"I do not consider myself as such!" Maeven insisted. "Besides, you have six other wives, you won't miss me."

El Haba did not answer that. It was a statement, not a question, and he was no longer thinking of her as just a useful conquest, and had no wish to volunteer those thoughts. He simply stared ahead.

"If you dislike your brother so much, why don't you kill him?" Maeven asked, deciding that perhaps she did like El Haba slightly better than she liked his brother, and maybe it was another way to incite internal trouble in Vatarik.

"It is not that simple," was the oddly quiet answer. "I cannot kill him and he cannot kill me. Our father made sure of that. Where do you think I learnt about controlling spells? I have one advantage over my brother, though. I am a wizard, and he is not. Saradoc, the wizard that was imprisoned with him, has been mindless since his return and so far, my brother has not found another compatible wizard."

"Surely that makes you more useful to the Serpent?"Maeven suggested.

"There is only one way that I might become pre-eminent. If I am the first to sire a son, who lives, I will usurp my brother's position and become my father's heir."

"What does your father say about you being a servant of the Serpent?"

"He sold his soul a long time ago!"

"Are you glad that the Serpent has lost his power?" Maeven was not sure why she asked that question.

El Haba stared into the distance. "He will be back. As strong as he was. I cannot see a way to be rid of him. I chose to serve him. I chose to have power and not be a mindless slave. I enjoy the power he gives me."

Maeven sensed that he was being honest, but could it be that there was a trace of regret? There had been a change in him since the Serpent had fled. She recalled that he had been gentle when tending the bites on her arm and leg. That memory caused confusion in her mind.

She knew he still resented her control, but he was not testing her limits any more and the arrogance had lessened, the taunting mockery was gone. Was he trying to manipulate her?

It did not matter. When the Serpent returned, and she was sure it would, El Haba would willingly become the bastard he had been. He had admitted as much and she had still not forgiven him.

"What will happen to you when you go home?" El Haba asked carefully. "Your father thinks you are dead."

"I'm not going home!" Maeven told him, and spurred her horse until she was abreast of Barnabas. It was a subject she did not want to think about.

Atlantis gave up trying to make conversation with Maeven who insisted on riding in stubborn silence. Barnabas was too weak to talk and neither Leanne nor Finora were interested in paying attention to their sister. Even though she had helped them escape, Atlantis doubted they would even say thanks.

Maeven's mood did not improve even when El Haba stopped at the border, watched them cross and abruptly turned his horse back down the road. Atlantis finally settled for simply riding beside her friend as they took their turn at leading Barnabas' horse.

When they camped at night, roughly, on the ground with only a blanket for cover, Maeven kept herself apart but always made sure Barnabas was comfortable. She ensured that he ate and drank, but ate little herself.

"You're scared," Atlantis accused Maeven on the last morning of their journey home. They would be at the palace by nightfall.

Maeven did not deny it; but she could not just run away either, not until she had help for Barnabas.

"I have an idea," Atlantis thought aloud. "I'll suggest to Leanne that we send a messenger ahead and have someone meet us with some more suitable clothing. We all look like vagabonds now, but if we arrive looking like well-dressed ladies, no one will associate you with the dead thief. Everyone will be so surprised at Princess Maeven's return."

"Finora will be the only one overjoyed with your idea," Maeven finally spoke. "The rest of us have discovered that you can't ride horses properly when you are dressed as Court Ladies!"

"And order a carriage," Atlantis added hastily, glad to have had a response from her friend.

"You are right," Maeven said. "My bastard of a father…"

"He's not really…" Atlantis interrupted.

"My father was careful to refer to me as Ven, the thief, wasn't he? He did not let the servants near me and he does not usually use the Queen's Garden for hangings! Go on, you suggest we stop at an inn, I have to send a message, too."

Maeven's message was answered before the one sent to the palace. The innkeeper's youngest son handed her a much-creased piece of parchment with only the name of another tavern on it. She recognised it as being in the same town as the place they were waiting and recalled it was close enough to walk. Atlantis joined her as she led Barnabas out the back door.

"I'm not sure you will be welcome where I'm going," Maeven warned, but Atlantis only shrugged.

"Do I look like a delicate Court flower?" she retorted.

"You are as crazy as I am," Maeven replied in kind.

Atlantis grinned. She was not about to mention her instructions from Leanne to ensure that Maeven returned to the inn after delivering Barnabas to the care of the Thieves Guild.

"You've got a nerve coming here!" the innkeeper of the "Fattened Goose" told Maeven with a sneer. He was a swarthy man with thick, hairy arms and Maeven had met him before.

"Please advise Nayfor that Ven is here and needs to talk to him," she asked politely.

"Nayfor has better things to do with his time than talk to you!" He made no move to deliver the message. "Didn't I hear that the King had you hung?"

"Do I look like a ghost?" Maeven said intently, making her knife appear in her hand. "Did you also hear that I killed one of the King's nobles?"

Maeven's calmness as she spoke and the way she examined the edge of her knife made the innkeeper decide to call for help and report to Nayfor.

Four large, muscled men appeared in the room where Maeven waited. They all recognised her. Two had just recently been released from the King's dungeon and the other two had narrowly escaped the same fate when the King's Own Guards were searching for her.

Maeven stood her ground and stared back at the hostile thieves facing her. She had hidden her knife again because she had not intended to use it. It was just as well because it would be taken as a challenge by these four brutes and she had no chance against them.

Nayfor finally appeared, assessed the scene and dismissed the four thieves. He said nothing and his expression was neutral. He waited for Maeven to speak.

"I have recovered something that belongs to the guild," she said guardedly. "Will I have my friend bring in what I found?"

Nayfor nodded and Maeven went to the door of the tavern, beckoning Atlantis.

For the first time since she had first met Nayfor, he betrayed surprise. It was obvious that he recognised Barnabas.

"He was a prisoner, near where I have been recently." Maeven knew that as her father's spymaster, Nayfor would be aware of recent events. "He will need a lot of care," she added.

"We will tend to him," Nayfor promised.

Maeven did not expect anything else. She glanced at Atlantis and they both turned to leave. As they reached the door, Nayfor spoke. "You may ask for me again."

Maeven gave him a considering glance and nodded, then left the tavern.

"What did he mean?" Atlantis asked as they walked back to the other inn.

"I'm no longer a member of the Thieves Guild," Maeven admitted. "Generally that means they don't intend to have anything more to do with me. Nayfor has simply left one line of contact open. If I need to, I can ask to see him and he will not refuse."

"Did you intend to leave the Guild?" Atlantis asked suspiciously.

"You may say that!" Maeven was smiling smugly. "I wasn't intending to come back. Staying a member of the Guild was becoming restrictive."

"Do you always set out to annoy people?" Atlantis asked after a while. She decided that preaching to her friend would have no effect.

"It usually just happens. It depends whom I am talking to and how they treat me! I'm glad that I met you; you are the only one that seems to ignore my faults or at least doesn't try to change me! Maybe you met me in a moment of weakness."

"No, I think it was because you were the first person I'd ever met who accepted the presence of a lone female in the back of nowhere without questions," Atlantis admitted. "It didn't hurt that you needed help and wouldn't ask for it."

"I had got used to looking after myself," Maeven muttered, not choosing to dwell on less than pleasant memories.

"So have I," Atlantis agreed. "I'm not sure I want to give up that independence."

The two women continued to walk in a comfortable silence.

The innkeeper and his wife were in a state of excitement when Maeven and Atlantis returned. The reason soon became obvious. Prince Rhovert had arrived in the Royal Carriage and they had never had Royalty stay at their inn before. When they had discovered that two of the earlier arrivals were Princess Leanne and Princess Finora, they had still assumed that the other two women were servants.

Rhovert was organising a meal for them all when he glanced up and saw his sister and her friend.

"Sister, Lady Atlantis," he greeted them with every appearance of pleasure.

Maeven smiled back, more because of the reactions of their host and hostess than anything else.

"The suitable attire that you requested is ready for you upstairs," Rhovert told them both.

"Thank you, your Highness," Atlantis said with a slight bow.

Maeven's smile became thoughtful as she wondered what "suitable" would prove to be. Then her smile broadened when she heard the innkeeper's wife whisper loudly. "That must be the other one, Princess Maeven!"

Prince Rhovert followed his sister up to the sleeping loft.

"We don't need help dressing," Maeven commented snidely.

Rhovert ignored the comment. "I came to warn you that when you arrive there will be an official reception." He grinned at the look of disgust on his sister's face. "So I borrowed some Court dresses for you both! Just for tonight! By morning there should be something more acceptable ready for you. But you used to like having lots of fancy dresses!"

Rhovert's comment made Maeven thoughtful as he had intended. Appearances were important. Not one of the Court nobles or their wives would imagine that Princess Maeven was a thief. No one that she knew as a thief, except for Nayfor, would imagine that Ven was Princess Maeven. She would be hiding in plain view again. She had always been careful to keep her two identities separate. Maybe it would be nice to be pampered again for a time, have the servants cook, clean and do her washing for her.

Rhovert seemed satisfied with her lack of scathing comments. "There are also some useful rumours circulating amongst the nobles, so of course the servants know, too, that you have been down in Declanor for the past year or two," Rhovert said innocently as he passed a cloth wrapped bundle to Maeven and another to Atlantis.

"A convenient piece of misdirection," was the dry comment from Atlantis. "They will assume I met Maeven there and that you met me as a result."

Rhovert chuckled. "There will be a light meal ready in the little room downstairs by the time you are dressed."

He went back downstairs to wait with his other sisters.

Atlantis removed the material that was protecting one set of clothes as Maeven was doing the same to the other. She unfolded the dress that she had been wearing when Rhovert had first noticed her and she flushed with pleasure. She kept her head down as she changed into the dress so that her red face was not noticeable. When she finally looked up, Maeven had a strange expression on her face and she was wearing an exquisite light blue gown.

Maeven became aware of Atlantis, looking at her with concern.

"It looks like it was made for you," Atlantis commented.

"It used to be my mother's," Maeven said with a catch in her voice. "I didn't know that Father kept them."

"I wonder if your father knows you will be wearing it." Atlantis echoed what Maeven was thinking.

Maeven asked her brother when she saw him downstairs.

Rhovert grinned. "He does! I asked him if I could borrow one for you and he agreed. In fact, he suggested that one was your favourite."

Maeven nodded, relieved.

It was a gift, a token of apology perhaps, but it told her that her father was not angry with her, that he would be welcoming, not critical. Going back home might be bearable. It did not mean that she had forgiven him yet, but maybe they could make it a new start.

CHAPTER 24 – THE SERPENT SUPREME

The occasion was the King's traditional and lavish Summer Solstice Ball and not one of the three princesses of Thulor were in the habit of remembering when these grand gatherings occurred.

Even though it was a very long time since they had attended a Royal Ball, they all knew how to behave at one. The correct etiquette had been absorbed from childhood and reinforced at every opportunity. That did not mean that any of the three yearned to attend. If Maeven were to agree with her sisters on anything, it would be that. All of them would have voted to delay their return if they had remembered what day it was. However, it was too late now. King Westron had decided to use the occasion to officially welcome his daughters back home.

The Royal carriage arrived well after the festivities had begun so the newest arrivals were able to retire discretely to their assigned quarters to freshen up.

Rhovert took Maeven to the rooms that had been prepared for her and left her with the maid that had been assigned to her.

Maeven recognised the woman at once. Jilli was the maid that had served her before she had left home. Back then, they had achieved a hostile truce, now there was a guarded expression on the woman's face as if she was trying to discern how things stood now. Maeven was in a mood to be gracious; tomorrow she would remind the maid of the rules.

"Jilli, I just need to wash my face and fix my hair. I don't have anything with me – we weren't expecting a formal occasion the minute we arrived."

The maid acted on her request but still seemed to watch the Princess as if mistrusting the new demeanour.

Maeven forced a smile on her face as she joined her sisters in a small room off the Grand Gathering Room. King Westron waited for them there, and bestowed an approving smile on them all before he ushered them out into the assemblage of nobles.

His steward, acting as herald for the occasion, announced the Princesses. The crowd hushed immediately. Most of the guests already knew that Leanne and Finora had returned. Maeven's presence was a total surprise, all eyes turned to look at her. It took all her nerve to stay.

The King put a casual arm around his youngest daughter as he spoke the words of welcome. Maeven did not glance at him but his touch made her feel safe, welcomed, forgiven, loved. He had never hugged her before; she wanted to stay in that moment. It was a haven of safety amongst the multitude of eyes.

When an entertainment was announced, the King's arm tightened a moment before he moved away.

Maeven continued to feel the target of many eyes but she thought it was probably just simple curiosity. Her talisman was cold from being near her father and siblings, and was returning to normal body temperature. It would warn her of danger. Her mind was still reliving the warmth of her father's greeting.

"May I get you some refreshment, Princess?" a voice asked from beside her in formal court tones.

Maeven turned around to face the speaker, automatically trying to identify him. The man was young, about her age, so he was probably new at Court. His face did seem familiar.

"Thom Chevron," the young man supplied his name. "You may have met my father, Neve Chevron."

"Oh, yes," Maeven agreed. "Yes, a drink of fruit juice would be most welcome, thank you."

Maeven watched as Thom walked to the table set at one side of the room. His attention was both surprising and flattering. As Thom returned, two of his friends, also younger sons of Court nobles, joined him, these were Nichol and Stevan. They were all trying to impress her.

A fourth man came up, looking annoyed. His friends teased him because the girl he was interested in did not want his attention.

"I had a gold bracelet made for her," the young man, Jasen, said sadly. Then his eyes brightened. "It would be a shame to have no use for it. Would you accept it as a welcome back gift? Nothing more than that. Well, maybe, could I visit with you sometime?"

Maeven saw through his feigned innocence but when she glimpsed the gold item, something in her wanted it. It was truly beautiful, made from braided gold with tiny coloured jewels embedded in it. She accepted it shyly and agreed to let Jasen and the others to visit with her sometime.

Unexpectedly, in the moment she put it on, her amulet began to grow hot and an entirely new set of instincts came to the fore.

Not sure of where the danger was in this opulent setting, she carefully scanned the gathering area. Most people were watching the juggling and tumbling performers. Servants were moving amongst the guests with refreshments and guardsmen were unobtrusively watching from around the walls. Several guards were near the prepared fire in the central fireplace. They were there to discourager revellers from lighting it before midnight.

The first thing she noticed was that her sisters both had three or four young men around them. She looked for her brother and found him with a number of men who were each dressed in clothes that were fancier than the normal male Court attire, though not as fancy the outfit Rhovert wore. The second thing she noticed was that all the men around her siblings were, like those around her, wearing black cloaks and black coloured shirts with loose necks that flopped over the front of the varicoloured round necked tunics.

Maeven thought that, odd as it seemed, it might just be the latest court fashion for the male courtiers. In fact, the men her father was talking to wore the same type of clothing. Then her careful thief trained eyes, scanned the general crowd and saw no other men wearing such costumes.

Her appraisal had only taken moments and her sense of danger intensified. It was time to act. With a sudden smile of pretend mischief, Maeven grabbed Jasen's hand and began to drag him with her.

"Come on, I want to be introduced to more of your friends. I may not have another opportunity for years!"

The four lads were happy enough to comply and that was good; they were not ready to act yet.

Maeven had spotted Nayfor, again in the guise of one of the watching King's Own Guards. The spymaster must have left to come here soon after she saw him at the inn.

There was a large group of young adults nearby

Maeven began whistling as if enjoying herself, but her tune included the thieves' "danger here" sequence. She did not look at the spymaster but in her side vision, she saw him stiffen and begin to scan the room as she had done. When she risked a glance over her shoulder, Nayfor had moved in the direction of King Westron.

Just as Maeven reached the group that was apparently her target, she heard a voice address her from behind. Atlantis stood there, and she curtseyed to the correct degree for greeting a Royal Princess.

"Princess Maeven, I have been asked to bring you to Lady Arrabella," she said politely.

Maeven glanced at the group ahead wistfully. "Do I have to go and talk to that gaggle of old geese?" she pouted.

"Your father expects it!" Atlantis said firmly.

"Just when I start having fun!" she grumbled but excused herself, politely, from the young men. They began to follow her so she teased them.

"You don't really want to entertain those old dames, do you?" she asked with a wicked chuckle. "Could you wait for me near the drinks table? I don't intend to stay long."

The four young men fidgeted, torn between keeping her in sight and avoiding the old women. They waited where she suggested but watched the door of the small side chamber avidly.

"The guard will remove those four," Atlantis whispered. "Nayfor said to wait in here. What's going on?"

"I am not at all sure. My amulet is hot, warning me of danger and all of my family have three or four oddly dressed people around them. Those ones, like the ones waiting for me, are the only ones wearing that type of outfit. The loose neck of the shirt can be pulled up over mouth and nose. There is something I heard that I need to remember, someone I heard talking mentioned the summer solstice…"

Maeven clutched her friend's arm. "Rolliver! Before I snuck back here, whilst I was still tied up at the 'Crescent Moon', I woke and heard Rolliver talking to some dark shadowy figure. I remember hearing, 'If my Prince is not free by summer solstice, release the blight in the palace – but ensure you are protected.'"

"But the Prince is gone and Rolliver is dead!" Atlantis reminded her.

"I assumed that it was referring to something that he had just been given, and I know Rolliver would not have had enough time to do anything before I saw him. What if the blight was already in place, waiting for someone to release it?"

"You weakened Ciabolo, surely he can't be strong enough yet to be able to strike here, now?"

"Its mid-summer's eve," Maeven suggested. "What sort of legends did you have in Declanor about tonight?"

"We have bonfires and people come together to keep evil spirits away," Atlantis said, growing more alarmed. "I'll go and get your sisters, but I wish

I had my sword!"

Moments after Atlantis had left, King Westron entered the room with Rhovert and Roman Golddreamer. As Maeven explained her fears to her father, she began to feel an urge to be somewhere else. It was as if someone was calling her.

Maeven did not realise that she had stopped speaking to listen to the mind voice. The King gripped her gently and seemed to hear the voice also.

"Can you see the way to the dragon?" King Westron asked urgently.

That was it! It was a dragon's voice!

Maeven stared around with eyes unfocussed. She was not seeing the room she was in, but beyond it to where a strange glow attracted her attention. She traced the tunnel from the dragon's chamber.

"We have to go to the dungeons, to the cell where you had El Rasho and Saradoc."

King Westron spoke to his son, "Wait for your sisters and Lady Atlantis, then you and the wizard bring them down after us."

He opened a secret wall panel and allowed Maeven to precede him into the hidden way that led down to the dungeon level. The dungeons were currently unoccupied. The last of the prisoners had received an unexpected Royal Pardon the previous week, so there were no guards down here either.

Maeven unerringly led the way to the cell where El Rasho had been imprisoned. She shivered involuntarily as she passed the cell where she had been after killing Rolliver.

Atlantis moved around the edge of the dancing couples to where Princess Leanne was talking animatedly to some young men her age who were boasting about their sword skills. She approached close enough to quietly interrupt the conversation. Leanne knew that Atlantis had a talisman and that made her like one of the family. Over the past few weeks, they had come to like each other and find they had many things in common.

Leanne did not betray her alarm at what Atlantis whispered in her ear. She just gripped Atlantis by her arm, excused herself from the boring group of braggarts and moved towards her twin. She, too, wished that Court dresses allowed for sword belts.

Finora had caught the surge of alarm from her twin at the same time that she felt the heat of her talisman. She began to move towards Leanne, but one of her companions stepped in front of her.

"No further, Princess!" The man changed form in front of her, from a familiar childhood companion to a stranger. He placed his left hand on her right shoulder and she felt something prick her neck. Then the awareness she had of the magic inherent in all things began to fade. Her eyes widened with alarm, but when she tried to move, her body would not obey her. People were dancing past and no one sensed anything was wrong.

Leanne felt her twin's alarm and began to walk faster to reach her. The one who had touched Finora turned with a pleasant smile on his face and bowed with the correct degree of respect. He held out his hand as if presenting her with a gift and a puff of vapour wafted into her face. She stopped moving in mid stride, her eyes the only part betraying her anger and a degree of panic.

Atlantis stopped when Leanne did, knowing something was wrong. Men in the odd court robes surrounded Leanne and one grabbed her arm and told her to keep walking. It was so smoothly done that no one was aware that anything was wrong.

Atlantis slipped back into the dancing crowd, and spotted her sister in law. With a grace that she usually lacked, she reached Gisella without barging into anyone. They exchanged glances and Gisella immediately bowed to her partner and followed Atlantis. In very few words, Atlantis told Gisella what Maeven feared and warned her to hide away and have something to cover her face. That was all she had time for as she saw more of the oddly garbed men coming towards her.

"Go," she hissed at Gisella, and then began to barge through the dancers at an angle to take her away from them. Something tripped her, she opened her mouth to ask for help but felt something sliding around her neck and was suddenly very afraid.

Reality seemed to be fading, the music seemed to die away and the people dancing around her became like wraiths. The men around her were very real and they were pulling her to her feet and at the same time pulling up their loose shirtfronts to cover nose and mouth. Somewhere in her mind, she heard a voice say, *Maeven was right*. She could not remember about what or who Maeven was.

Finora had no control over her body but she fought to keep her mind clear by mentally chanting a sequence of focussing spells. They had no magic effect but such chants were more a form of meditation than magic anyway.

Leanne concentrated on her anger at the traitorous members of her father's Court and that something like was happening in her father's palace. Her anger blazed hotter in her mind when another figure suddenly appeared in front of her.

El Rasho, dressed in finery the equal of any around him, was smiling an evil smile and gloating with sensual satisfaction at having in his power the two who had bested him twice.

"The power of the Serpent is supreme," he sneered at Leanne.

He turned to Finora and said brutally, "The Serpent broke your puny spell in a second and used its peculiarities to track you and focus his arrival spell once you were back here."

Finora's mind froze, realising what he meant. Every time a wizard or sorceress cast a spell, they put a part of themselves into it. What he had done was not much different to the way he used the souls of his slaves and the notion scared her to her very core. She wished she had a way to call to her father's wizard or to warn her father and brother.

A maid entered the side chamber where Rhovert waited. She brought in a tray with a ceramic bottle and several copper goblets and balanced it skilfully as she curtseyed before the prince. The man beyond the prince, dressed worse than the palace serfs, was totally ignored. The maid placed the tray on a small table by the door and smiled provocatively at Rhovert as she pushed the door closed.

Roman Golddreamer watched, amazed at the woman's brazen behaviour. She moved close to the Prince and put one arm around his neck and the other reached into the front of his breeches.

Rhovert was not in the habit of treating women roughly, but he recognised this maid and knew of her reputation. He gripped both her wrists, and firmly dragged her right hand out of his breeches and the other from around his neck.

"I am not interested in what you are offering, woman!" Rhovert said coldly. "Try that on me again and I will see that you are whipped!"

The maid's eyes brightened and her breathing became faster as if the idea excited her. "Are you man enough to do it yourself?" she breathed, pushing her body towards him.

"Father's hunting bitches are more selective in their mating habits than you are, woman!" Rhovert continued to hold the woman off; as he did so, the door opened.

Rhovert saw something bright flash past his eyes and heard Roman grunt with surprise.

The door opened wider and a stranger walked into the room.

"You are losing your touch, Jillicen," the man remarked casually.

"He's not man enough for me!" she sneered. Rhovert suddenly released her and drew his sword.

"Go find your Mistress," the stranger told the maid. "The Master wants that one, too. On your way, send in those servants who failed to watch her and the King."

The man did not seem worried by the threat from the sword. Rhovert lunged at him as soon as the maid was out the door. The stranger dodged easily but betrayed surprise at the skill of the thrust.

"Lucky stoke, Prince, but I think you are not good enough."

Rhovert lunged again, but fell awkwardly as something bit him in the groin and something slimy wrapped itself around his neck. The sword was removed from his grasp as his body went weak.

"I knew you would be no trouble." The stranger might have well been talking to himself. His victim was writhing on the floor, stoically refusing to scream. "I am surprised, Prince. You limp-wristed types usually scream most satisfyingly."

The black robed slaves glided into the room, eight of them with their collars pulled over their noses and mouths. These were the ones who had lost sight of the King and Maeven.

"Find out from this weakling Prince where his accursed father has gone. There is no need to be gentle. It is time he learnt how to behave as a man. If you can, find out where the things are that his sister stole from Vatarik and where the dragon is," the stranger instructed. "If you succeed, the Master will continue to let you serve him, if not, he will feed on your souls and leave you mindless husks."

All of the eight men trembled. They had chosen to serve the Master, who had promised them great power when he overthrew the Royalty of Thulor. They all craved that power but they had learnt to fear the Master and now the wizard, Misk, had told them the price of failure.

Maeven scanned the walls and floor; she sensed rather than saw where the door must be. A trap door, made of wood but covered with layers of filth, existed in one corner of the cell with a tunnel leading down from it. She knelt down, oblivious to the dirt that now stained her borrowed dress. Her hands found the ring to pull it up but it would not lift.

"You need the key Merlie gave you," King Westron said quietly.

Maeven recalled the position where she had last 'hidden' the key. The flimsy dress had not even had pockets! She muttered and the key appeared in her hand. After more scratching around in the filth, she found a blocked up keyhole. She muttered to recall her knife from its magical hiding place and cleared as much of the dirt away as she could. Now she could put the special key into the strangely shaped keyhole, speak the words to work the key spell and watch it flow into the hole, unlock it and flow back out.

King Westron lifted the heavy wood door, whilst his daughter re-hid the key and knife. He let Maeven precede him into the tunnel and pulled the trapdoor shut behind him. He needed to stoop, but he continued to follow her along the completely lightless passage, keeping one hand lightly on her shoulder and knowing that she could see where to go.

Maeven liked the feel of that hand on her but it did not distract her from her purpose. The dragon voice calling her was becoming more imperative, more urgent. She was at home in the dark passage and glad now that she had never grown as tall as her sisters. Her father had to duck to walk the low passage.

The tunnel finally opened into the dragon's chamber. There was a low but visible glow illuminating the large cavern. The King walked over to the huge dark hulk of the dragon. Her scales were a dull grey, quite different to the glowing silver of the dragon's youth.

Maeven studied the cavern as her father bowed and greeted the dying dragon. In one corner was a pile of animal bones, near to that a trickle of water flowed down one wall and disappeared into a crack in the ground. There was only one tunnel opening off the cavern. How did the dragon get here and how did the animals she fed on get there? The puzzle teased Maeven's mind.

"Welcome, Dragon Son," Thulor, the dragon mage, greeted the king of her realm, in the ancient form of the language.

"My greetings to you, Thulor, first amongst dragons," Westron spoke in the same tongue.

"My time grows short, Dragon Son, and the Serpent draws closer. I will not survive this night and my successor is yet to be born."

"What must we do, Dragon mage?" Westron asked quietly.

"Bring down the eight pieces of the Talisman my mother created and the shard of my birth shell. The presence of the shard will enable the pieces to join when they are in the right order. This will provide the protection that my daughter will need for her birth."

"I have knowledge of only seven pieces," Westron murmured.

Maeven turned from her study of the cavern to listen closely to the voice she heard clearly in her mind.

"The one with the runes for healing and anti-magic is missing," Westron commented, recalling what he had learnt from an ancient scroll.

"Anti-magic?" Maeven thought to herself, but it seemed that the dragon heard.

"There is a touch of anti-magic in all the pieces, dragon child," Thulor told her patiently. "It is the ability to select which magic you wish to neutralise. Perhaps you have noticed its effects?"

Maeven though of the times when she had touched chests with magic locks and the spell had gone. "Yes," she admitted in her mind.

"The rune of healing is important," the dragon spoke again to Westron. "The ring of protection cannot form if a piece is missing. The magic can't flow if the circle is incomplete."

"What are the pieces made of?" Maeven asked the ancient dragon.

"Stone formed from the ground up shards of dragon shells, pressed hard together deep in the earth," was the dragon's reply.

"We have the shell shards that my daughter helped to recover from your mother's crypt," Westron suggested. "I understand that they have healing powers."

"They do indeed, Dragon Son," Thulor agreed. "My daughter, Mortmellor, recovered from grievous wounds inflicted by a human barbarian by eating the shells of her clutch."

Maeven felt the urge to giggle.

"It was Mortmellor I spoke to then? No wonder she didn't like Atlantis!"

She sobered quickly, aware of her father's stern look, even in the faint light. An idea suddenly occurred to her.

"If I can press crushed shell shards into a substance that dries hard, like wax, and shaped it to fit, would that work?" she asked the Dragon.

"If the stone piece is not available, you must try it, but the ring of protection will not be as strong, so all must be wary. The Serpent will not wish my successor to live."

"What else must we do?" Westron prompted.

"The egg must be heated so that it can expand to the size of a normal egg. Do not allow the egg to grow cold once you start, until the egg has hatched. My daughter will be very hungry when she is born. First, she must devour her shell; that will give her all the knowledge that I have. Then she must eat a demon, as that will stimulate her dormant mage powers. Finally, she must be protected until she is fully grown, only then will she reach her full power. Until then, Dragon Son, my realm will be vulnerable to the attacks of the Serpent."

"Yes, I have seen that," King Westron said thoughtfully. "Is there more we must do?"

"Stay with me, Dragon Son," Thulor asked. "I am tired. All of my energy is with those who help me protect my realm. I have none to spare for myself."

The King bowed deeply and drew his sword. At least the protocol for formal Court occasions permitted the King and his Heir to bear their swords, though no one else had that privilege.

"The dragon child will bring what is required."

Maeven received from the ancient dragon a sense of warmth, approval and love. She had moved closer to her father as the dragon had spoken. She met her father's gaze and saw the same things mirrored there. He reached out and hugged her warmly.

"Be careful, I do not want to lose you. While you live, your mother is not gone. You are the one most like her."

In that instant, she felt willing to die for the sake of the Kingdom. A moment later, she finally realised the lesson that he had needed to teach her. Anyone could die for the Kingdom – she had to live to serve it.

When Prince Rhovert began to take notice of his surroundings again, the first thing he saw was Roman Golddreamer lying very still on the floor. Only the intent stare from the brown eyes assured the Prince that the wizard was alive.

When Roman saw the Prince looking at him, he said calmly, "I have been caught by a tangling net spell. If I fight the spell, the net will tighten. You need to remain calm too, and not make any sudden moves. The wizard has two trained vipers on you. At the neck, a bite will weaken you, and lower down the effect is painful."

Rhovert moved and tried to sit up. He saw Atlantis tied up and staring at the ceiling. His eyesight was too fuzzy to see if she was breathing or not. As he stood, he saw his twin sisters standing very still a little way from Atlantis.

The brightness of their emotions blazed from their eyes. They appeared to be controlled, but otherwise unhurt.

The black-robed slaves began to fire questions at him.

"Where is the King?"

"Where is the dragon?"

"Where are the things your sister stole from Vatarik?"

"Where is your younger sister?"

At first, he refused to answer, and this made the slaves more fearful and therefore angrier. They took turns to hit him for each refusal. Rhovert felt his lip split and several teeth become loose. Later two savage blows landed in his right eye and he could no longer see from it. A fist with a ring opened a gash on his left cheek. He knew he had to hold on until his father or sister or the spymaster realised what was happening and could act. His greatest fear was that the Serpent's slaves would begin to treat the women this way. He began to scream false answers at his tormentors, a different lie every time they repeated a question. More than anything else, he wanted to sink into the oblivion of unconsciousness, but he must not. To distract himself, he wondered what had happened outside of the room. Everything had gone quiet. He kept away from the thought of how easily the enemy had overcome him.

El Rasho sat on the throne of the King of Thulor and contemplated the power he would have if he ruled two kingdoms. Misk, his new wizard companion, left the room with the prisoners. His action of pulling up the neck of his shirt to cover his mouth and nose, reminded El Rasho that he needed to protect himself too. If he did not, he would be worse off than his brother was now. He unclasped his cloak and covered himself and the exciting woman next to him.

The blight, planted by the maid Jilli many years before, would pervade the whole palace. It was a fine cloud of particles, which if breathed in would make the victim mindless and a creature of the wizard.

El Rasho peeked as the wizard, Misk, cast the spell to release the blight. Pockets of the tiny spores exploded into the air at the same time, turning everyone in the vicinity into a mindless statue. In air, the blight lived only a short time but inside a victim, it thrived.

The music stopped, the people all stopped in mid-action. They were now no more than fodder for the Serpent.

The Serpent had used the life energies of his slaves to send El Rasho to

Thulor and he would use the life energies of his remaining slaves in Vatarik to get here himself. Once here, he would feed off the life energies of the blighted ones to maintain his power.

El Rasho hoped that the Serpent would also drain his brother. It would serve El Haba right for allowing that bitch of a child thief to control him.

When the wizard Misk lowered the fabric from his mouth, El Rasho did the same.

"See if the King or his youngest bitch daughter are amongst the crowd," El Rasho ordered the black-robed slaves who were unaffected by the blight.

As the slaves moved slowly about the room, Misk departed the gathering room to seek the enemy elsewhere.

CHAPTER 25 – THE NEW DRAGON MAGE

A sense of urgency gripped Maeven and she ran back along the dark passages to the trap door. The special key again opened the lock that had snapped closed when the trapdoor had been lowered. The heavy door was difficult to push open, but the feeling of urgency gave her strength. She allowed it to close again before she left the cell to return along the secret way.

The feeling of urgency developed into a powerful sense of something wrong. It increased in intensity as she neared the main part of the palace.

At the secret door from the room off the gathering area, Maeven stopped and searched for the spy hole that would enable her to see if it was safe to leave the passage there. Her dragon sight worked best seeing into the dark.

Through the small hole, she saw a ring of the black robed slaves of the Serpent. Where had they come from? One of the figures moved and his hood fell back a little. Maeven recognised Thom, the young man she had met earlier. He looked and sounded angry, and then the subject of his ill humour stumbled into view. Maeven spared a moment of sympathy for her battered-looking brother. She gripped her talisman and thought at him that she would get help when she could.

First, she had to get to her father's safe hole. She raced for the hidden stairway leading up to the upper level of the palace. The view through the spy hole here and her own instincts told her the dressing room was empty. When she emerged from the passage, she could see that someone had already searched the room. Clothing and toiletry items were strewn around the floor, the furniture was upended and the cushions ripped.

Maeven went directly to the safe hole and although she could not see the little door, her fingers could feel it. There was an aura of magic around it, courtesy of her father's wizard no doubt. Her touch did not make the magic go away, nor did the direct touch of the talisman.

Anti-magic indeed, Maeven thought, but realised that the talisman may not affect magic akin to its own. The wizard! She needed to find him!

Maeven whispered her spell for invisibility and ran down the servants' stairs towards the gathering area. She met no one, not even servants, and her feeling of wrongness increased further. In the doorway to the dancing area, she saw in the flickering candlelight, a multitude of motionless people. They were standing and silent, like trees in a forest. Then she saw some movement.

A black-robed slave was walking between the rigid people, looking at each as if searching for someone. Across the room, occupying the grand throne was El Rasho. He was gloating and beside him was Jilli, looking like his queen.

Maeven spared only a moment to wonder how El Rasho had got there, when only days ago he was a controlled wreck. No doubt, he had arrived in the same mysterious way that his brother had appeared in the dragon's crypt. There was no mystery in her mind as to why Jilli was attracted to El Rasho.

Using every trick of stealth that she knew, Maeven moved through the motionless crowd. At the door to the small room where she had seen her brother, she stood on a wooden bench that was next to the wall so she could look over the heads of the black-robed slaves.

She could not see Rhovert. In her line of sight was a pale-looking Finora and an obviously angry Leanne; both women were immobilised by enormous snakes. There was no sign of Atlantis or her wizard brother.

Still invisible, Maeven turned to face the large room and gave a piercing whistle. She saw El Rasho stand up and look in her direction. He now knew someone was around and not afflicted. A second whistle sounded from further around the room – Nayfor! Two more whistles answered hers.

El Rasho looked – not confused, but wary.

Black-robed slaves pushed out of the little chamber and more appeared from amongst the crowd. Maeven could now look into the room and saw that Atlantis and her wizard brother were both immobilised by the snakes too.

El Rasho called loudly to the slaves. "The bitch is probably invisible. Ignore her, she is not important. I can find her when I need to. We must find the King. Go back to the prisoners. If the Prince won't talk, start on the women!"

One of the figures in black was scanning the room more carefully than the rest were. Maeven moved to touch the leaves of a nearby potted plant. It was the slightest of movements but the figure moved casually nearer and stopped with his back to her. A hand moved into Maeven's view and briefly formed into the thieves' secret sign of recognition.

Maeven leant forward and whispered quietly. "Nayfor?"

A very slight nod was the only response.

"I need the wizard. Can you get to him and release him?"

A faint shake of negation.

"He put mage locks on the safe hold! I can't get through them and I must!"

"I." A faint return whisper.

"You can?" Maeven whispered hopefully.

A slight nod.

"Father's dressing room! Do you know it?"

Another nod.

"I'll meet you there."

Maeven moved away from the small room and closer to El Rasho. From within the crowd of rigid courtiers, she gave a loud laugh. The Prince of Vatarik rose from his seat again.

"Yellow bellied slime crawler!" Maeven taunted, moving as she spoke. "Too cowardly to do your own dirty work, are you?" she continued. "I see you are too afraid to go near Princess Finora. Does she still control you? Are you afraid she will make you into a eunuch this time?"

"The Serpent will kill you this time, bitch!" El Rasho promised.

"My, my! The big bully runs home to Daddy! I bet you couldn't even take their talismans this time!"

El Rasho did not choose to confirm her guess.

"Oh, I do want to thank you for keeping my siblings out of the way. I'm going to go down into the dungeons; I plan to save the kingdom single-handed. There is a secret tunnel that goes from the cell you were in!"

El Rasho laughed. "You'll keep, bitch! I know what you are trying to do. I will not fall for your tricks this time! I will not go down there to be captured!"

"Too bad!" Maeven laughed from the doorway nearest the main stairs. She turned and ran to the stairs and upwards.

Nayfor was opening the safe hold when she arrived and made herself visible.

"How did you do that?" Maeven could not resist asking.

"Just because Barnabas made you a master, don't assume you learnt everything about thieving," Nayfor told her bluntly. "I did not agree with having your apprenticeship cut short!"

He stepped aside to let Maeven take what she needed.

"The dragon shells are not here!" Maeven said, as she pulled the mage egg, the demon receptacle and the Serpent's Bane from the hole.

"They will be in the little room off the infirmary," Nayfor told her.

Maeven gave the Serpent's Bane to Nayfor and hid the other two items.

"My siblings, the wizard and Atlantis are in the little room where I was before. There are snakes controlling them. The snakes don't like water or bright light. They also move away from the Serpent's Bane," she hurriedly explained to the spy-master. "Take it back to where my siblings are and give it to the wizard. I think it is powerful enough to free them. Tell them I will meet them in the dungeon where the brigand was kept."

Nayfor pocketed the shell shard and left.

Maeven became invisible again and raced through deserted corridors to the stairs and down to the infirmary. The few patients in the beds were staring at the roof and the infirmary assistant was staring at nothing, frozen in the middle of taking a step. Maeven walked around him and went to the little herb room.

The casket of dragon shells was neatly stowed on one of the shelves. Maeven lifted it down and checked the contents. After placing the casket on a bench, she went hunting for a candle, a small dish, a knife, a flint and some tinder to light the brazier.

With her ears alert for unexpected arrivals, Maeven lit the brazier and began to pare flakes of wax off the candle, collecting them in the small dish that was heating over the little flame. Into the molten wax, she added pinches of the ground up dragon shell. She continued to add wax and shell until she had enough of the mixture for her purpose, then she moved the dish with a wad of rag and doused the flame. As she waited for the wax to cool and harden, she looked through the cupboards in the room to see if she could find anything of use.

She smiled when she found a supply of spare clothes. It only took her moments to change from the blue court dress into a shirt and breeches. She pushed the gown into the cupboard and made it invisible.

Using the knife, she scraped the cooling wax out of the dish and used her fingers to mould it into a roughly triangular shape. It hardened quickly and went into her pocket.

Maeven grabbed the selection of sharp knives that she had found and made them follow her invisibly.

The guards' room was close by and Maeven detoured there, collecting three swords from rigid guards. She hid the swords with the knives.

Seven-foot tall Ciabolo, seven-foot tall, towered over the rigid people as he entered the Great Hall. Seeing him approaching, El Rasho stood up hurriedly from the throne, hoping Ciabolo would not guess at his moments of fantasy as he sat there.

Ciabolo sat down in the carved throne as if it were his by right. El Haba stood close to Ciabolo's side tied to the Serpent by a glowing magical tether.

El Rasho gloated. His brother, his arrogant wizard brother, was under so many controlling spells that he was no better off than the forest of silent people in front of the throne.

"Misk tells me that the King and his youngest whelp have escaped," Ciabolo said directly to El Rasho. "He also told me that the little worm came through here and you ignored the chance to catch her."

"I'm no wizard, Master. The bitch was invisible and she has been tagged. Knowing her tricky ways I was not going to believe what she said!"

"I do not accept excuses!" Ciabolo snarled. "I want that worm. I want to slice it up and turn it inside out. That deceitful slime crawler is the most dangerous of them all."

Misk whispered to Ciabolo.

Ciabolo glared at El Rasho and included the woman, Jilli, in his glance.

"Go find that worm and bring her to me!"

To Misk, he said, "Bring the Prince to me! If he has not revealed the truth to my slaves, he will not refuse to tell me!"

The nearest entrance to the secret ways was the gathering room and beyond there, the kitchens, but a row of black figures blocked her way. The stairway was still clear, so she ran back up to the King's apartment.

The door to the King's bedchamber was open. In an automatic gesture, she glanced in. Two figures were writhing together on the King's bed. Maeven recognised El Rasho and Jilli, the maid. She spoke without thought.

"That diseased bitch will make a woman of you, snake scum."

El Rasho looked up and moved away from the woman who was moaning with unsatisfied lust.

"She makes mindless slaves of whoever she couples with. You will be no better than those black robed creatures with no mind of your own!"

Maeven was only guessing but there must have been a germ of truth in her words. He grabbed the woman's clothes and threw them at her. Jilli was livid as El Rasho stalked toward the door.

Jilli was yelling, "Show yourself, bitch!"

Maeven had not waited any longer. She regretted her outburst, recalled her purpose and ran for the dressing room and the secret door.

The door shut behind her and she heard pounding on it, but did not wait to see if El Rasho broke through. She fled to the dungeons.

Five figures stood warily in the cell as Maeven appeared. She wasted no time in greetings or insults but went directly to the trap door and once again unlocked it. Roman Golddreamer helped her lift the door.

"Go down, quickly," Maeven urged. The sound of running feet was getting rapidly louder.

Maeven waited to enter last, to ensure that the trap door resealed. As the door closed above her, she felt something slimy wrap around her neck. The rest of the thing was stopping the door from closing properly.

Whilst Maeven kept her hands between the slimy thing and her neck, Rhovert and Roman were pulling down on the inside ring of the door, stopping whoever was above from lifting it. Finora aimed a spell at the slimy rope and Maeven fell down, gasping for breath.

By the light of a glowing ball that hovered above Finora's palm, the slimy thing looked like the tail end of a snake. It continued to writhe, even though it as no longer joined to its head. Roman looked at the obscene creature and burnt it to ashes with a flame from his wand.

"Let's go!" Rhovert urged.

"Mind your heads!" Maeven said hoarsely.

Jilli ran back to the presence of Ciabolo.

"El Rasho has discovered a secret way and is chasing the bitch, Maeven," she reported, out of breath.

Ciabolo made a gesture, Jilli's eyes took on an unfocussed look and she smiled ecstatically for a time before slumping to the floor. The Serpent then waited for El Rasho to return, using the time to draw more power from the rigid people in front of him.

Misk returned, alone, trembling in fear. "Master, I plead your forgiveness. The prisoners have escaped, your servants are unconscious and the snakes have fled."

Ciabolo closed his eyes. Misk stood rigid, all control of his body taken from him. Pain, acute and agonising, suffused him as Ciabolo stole his life, his essence and his soul. The body that was once a wizard was now simply an animated husk. Jerkily it walked to the unlit fire and climbed onto the pile of wood. A brief flare of power lit the wood and the flames devoured the wizard's remains.

By the light shining above Finora's palm, the six people walked quickly along the passage. Maeven kept up with the others, even though her neck was sore and she was panting for breath.

They all stopped suddenly as they reached the now torch-lit chamber. Only Maeven had known what to expect.

"Do you have what we need, dragon child?" Thulor spoke so all heard her. She sent a wash of healing magic over them all.

"I hope so; I am definitely not popular up there!" Maeven admitted.

She brought the mage egg and the demon orb into her hand and walked to her father. He accepted them from her but passed the demon receptacle to Finora.

Roman Golddreamer pulled out the Serpent's Bane as King Westron pulled off his talisman and explained what they had to do.

"Hurry!" the dragon urged. "The Serpent is close!"

Everyone gave their talisman to the King who was squatting on the floor; his v-shaped talisman was resting in the curve of the dragon shell.

Maeven withdrew three swords from their invisibility spell and Rhovert smiled in spite of his battered face. Leanne grabbed one with an exclamation of anticipation and smiled vindictively. Atlantis reached for the third, but Maeven kept it.

"Help my father. Putting the pieces together is a puzzle."

Nothing more needed to be said. Atlantis turned and squatted beside the King.

The five other humans in the cavern stood looking outwards, watching.

Maeven felt useless holding the sword. It was heavy and needed two hands to lift; she had never used a sword in her life.

"The red glow near the floor – watch out for snakes!"

El Rasho returned and reported to Ciablo. "The prisoners have escaped through a tunnel in the dungeons. The entrance is protected by magic."

Ciabolo's flash of anger was felt by El Rasho as a moment of intense pain, which he endured. The Serpent smiled at him, pleased in spite of the set back.

"They are all together; the children of the dragon and my enemy who is weak and dying. The fools have not yet hatched the egg and if Thulor dies first, there will be nothing to stop me from ruling this entire world. Those that have served me faithfully will have the rewards they deserve."

Ciabolo smiled at El Rasho but ignored El Haba beside him.

"Messenger!" Ciabolo called suddenly.

Moments later, a small demon alit on his huge forearm.

"Find the one tagged with my golden serpents," Ciabolo ordered, flinging the creature into the air where it promptly disappeared. He followed its progress and saw in his mind the tunnel leading to the dragon's lair.

El Rasho dared to ask a question. "Why is that piece of excrement, the thief, so dangerous? She is neither skilled with sword nor magic."

Ciabolo answered almost absently. "She is full of draconic deceitfulness. She skulks around, hiding and watching. When she faces us, she mixes truth and lies to mislead us. She has little magic but Thulor powers her spells for her and protects her more than the others. I have seen her in my sleep visions and I know she could destroy me."

El Rasho glanced thoughtfully at his brother, who was a powerful wizard. Perhaps that was why he could not break free of the worm's spell. Too bad though, Ciabolo believed what he had been told. El Rasho had claimed that his brother had not wanted to break free of the spell, had wanted to defy the Serpent and wanted an excuse to disobey his master.

It had been delicious, watching his brother grovel before the Serpent, pleading for another chance to serve, agreeing to the humiliation of his current position, simply to keep his life! El Haba was only alive because he was a Prince of Vatarik. If he was simply another wizard, he would be no more than Misk was now! Nothing but absolute obedience would protect him from that fate in the future. Well, maybe he had been given the chance to prove himself for another reason. He had managed to make that soon-to-die dragon worm pregnant, even if the worm had obliged by aborting it.

Unfortunately, that was more than El Rasho himself had been able to do with any of the women he had taken. Maybe, El Rasho thought, he would be permitted to keep the other two women alive and controlled…

It was not a snake that arrived first but something that whizzed around the chamber circling closer and closer. Maeven looked at the blur, dropped one hand off the sword, reached up, chose the moment and grabbed. Her hand began to burn and something began to shriek. She recognised the creature.

"Mistress, mistress, please don't kill me!" the little demon pleaded.

"You broke your promise." Maeven let it see her anger. "I told you never to come looking for me again!"

"Didn't, didn't," it shrilled. "Looking for gold thing."

The demon touched the bracelet she had accepted from Jasen. It began to grow hot.

Maeven began to feel sick. She dropped the sword and tried to remove the bracelet but she could not do it. Then, the three strands of the braided metal began to writhe and she saw with loathing that they were little golden snakes.

"Ven," Atlantis interrupted her panic. "The other piece, we need it!"

Maeven stopped trying to remove the bracelet and felt in her pocket for the wax piece. She threw it to Atlantis without losing her grip of the demon.

"It won't fit!" Atlantis wailed desperately. She was aware of snakes slithering into the cavern from out of the red glow.

Maeven made the sharp knives visible again and let them drop to the floor. Atlantis grabbed the nearest one and began to pare wax from the edges of the makeshift triangle.

King Westron suddenly moved, slashing at a snake that was heading for the dragon. Atlantis kept her attention on her task, hoping that the others would keep the snakes from her.

Rhovert and Leanne had begun to slash at snakes, but for every one they killed, two more took their place. Finora and Roman were using magic to blast the snakes, but more came at them faster than they could draw energy for another attack.

A serpent transformed in front of Maeven and a sword was suddenly at her throat.

"Let the little demon go!" El Haba ordered her. There was no hint of compromise in his eyes.

"No!" Maeven screamed at him. "Leave me alone!"

"You cannot order me anymore! Release the demon and stand aside."

"No!" Maeven repeated, defiant. Her terror was apparent to El Haba as he moved his sword to touch her skin enough to draw blood.

"If you do not move aside, I must kill you!"

"Will I kill him, Mistress?" the demon offered, keen to be free of the third command promised to this woman.

"No, demon, you have another task," Maeven told it without looking away from El Haba. She was wondering why he had not killed her already.

"Kill her, Prinss!" a hissing voice sounded in the cavern!

"Step back, dragon child," a mind voice came at the same time.

Maeven moved and twisted but she did not avoid the blade completely. El Haba had moved with her, injuring her in the side with a deep stab and slash.

As Maeven fell, feeling pain shoot through her, she saw a shimmering barrier come into being in the centre of the cavern. It was dome shaped and Ciabolo was the only being outside of it.

El Haba turned suddenly and realised the barrier had trapped him. Rhovert and Leanne continued to kill snakes but now no more were appearing. They spotted El Haba standing over Maeven and approached him with swords drawn. Roman came over to the fallen Princess and incanted a healing spell, enough to stop the bleeding and dull the pain, the demon was struggling to be free but Maeven kept holding it.

"Don't kill him," Maeven said weakly. "Ciabolo is in control of him."

"Kill me and Ciabolo will enter in here," El Haba said with difficulty. He was feeling the pull of the compulsions that Ciabolo had put on him. He was feeling the Serpent's anger at his failure to kill the Princess. He had a strong urge to throw himself on his sword and let the Serpent enter, but with the barrier interfering with the full strength of the compulsion, he could fight it. He threw his sword away across the floor.

"I have failed him twice. The Serpent does not forgive." El Haba slumped to the dirt floor, visibly trembling. He knew what he had chosen to do. If the Serpent entered the dome, it would be his death.

Maeven had no energy to spare worrying about El Haba. In her mind, Thulor was telling her to get up and bring the little demon closer. She forced herself to stand, her whole body stiff.

"Father, I need the egg!" she said hoarsely, but her father was already reaching into his pocket for it.

Maeven took it; the egg feeling cold. "Demon, this is my third command. Hold this egg in your hands and warm it, do not let go of it until I tell you. My command to you will not end until I tell you it is complete."

"This is a dragon's egg," the demon shrilled, trying to ignore the command and escape Maeven's grip. "Dragons hate demons."

"Die then!" she said calmly, reaching for the knife Atlantis was holding out to her.

The demon took the egg.

Frantic flashes of mage energy were striking the barrier as Ciabolo saw what was about to start. The energy was deflected by the protective shield as sparks of light.

Everyone but King Westron and his youngest daughter turned to look in the direction of the attacks.

"Wizard, Sorceress, you must be ready to control the big demon when my daughter hatches," Thulor ordered, and now they all heard her mental voice.

King Westron joined Rhovert, Leanne and Atlantis with his sword drawn, ready in case the protective field was breached.

Maeven stayed stubbornly upright, watching the black egg slowly expand. She forced the threatening blackness away from her mind. Something was trying to draw her energy away from her, but she must not lose control of the little demon.

Her legs grew very weak but strong arms were around her, supporting her. She felt safe, until she realised that it was El Haba who held her. Her body stiffened.

A voice spoke in her ear, "Give me a reason to fight him." The voice was full of pleading. "I no longer want to kill you!"

King Westron, hearing the plea, moved to his daughter's side, raised his sword and spoke with the full authority of his position.

"Do you wish to be free of the Serpent?" he asked touching the sharp edge of his sword to the side of El Haba's neck.

"Yes!" was the unforced answer. "Yes," he repeated and his soul seemed to be in his voice.

"Repeat after me…" the King instructed. "I pledge my life, my service, my will…"

"I pledge my life, my service, my will…," El Haba echoed.

"For the good of the Kingdom of Thulor…" the King continued.

El Haba repeated the words of the pledge as he watched the increasingly powerful magic blasts stressing the protective barrier. He knew that breaking free of the Serpent would not be easy.

"I renounce all loyalties and bindings to any other person, country or cause. I place myself at the mercy of the Monarch of Thulor," he finished the pledge.

Roman collected El Haba's sword and at a nod from the King, returned it to Thulor's newest subject.

Maeven felt El Haba trembling, and tears falling on her head. He had made his choice and it was the one most fraught with danger.

"Give me a reason to fight him," he had whispered.

Maeven was moved by his decision to walk away from the Serpent, from his position of power, from the chance of becoming king in his country, from his family and to live in fear of the Serpent's reprisal.

"Our son lives!" Maeven said in a very soft whisper. "I can show you proof of his birth."

El Haba's trembling eased and his arms felt stronger.

"He is in the care of good people, in the safest part of my father's kingdom," Maeven added, suddenly becoming aware that the now large egg in the demon's grip was jerking.

The dragon, Thulor, was crooning gently and had turned her head to watch the egg hatching, her daughter's birth.

"Place the egg on the ground, dragon-child," Thulor said quietly and Maeven eased herself down, out of El Haba's grip, until the demon held the egg as it rested on the ground.

The shell suddenly cracked, and a black miniature dragon poked its head out of the small hole in the shell. It began chewing the shell to make the hole bigger. It continued to eat the shell as it gained knowledge and learnt why it must do so. When all but the circle on which it sat was devoured, the baby dragon caught sight of the big demon, newly liberated from the receptacle but controlled by two magicians so it could not avoid its fate. A high-pitched shriek erupted as it felt the little dragon begin to feed on it. The shrieking continued until nothing remained of the demon.

As the dragon devoured the evil creature, it had been growing and was now twice its birth size. The black scales had become clear, and were now glowing silver.

At that moment, the blasts from Ciabolo finally penetrated the protection.

Maeven grabbed the baby dragon and released the little messenger demon. Instinct was driving her to act, even as Thulor's fading voice said, "Protect my daughter, dragon-mother."

She made herself invisible, grabbed two of the knives from the ground, hid them and ran for the passage out. Behind her was chaos, with Finora and Roman fending off mage bolts, but taking some hits. The King, Prince Rhovert, Leanne and Atlantis were again fighting the snakes that crawled with greater frequency into the cavern.

El Haba was waging a war of his own, using his mage powers to send the snakes back to where they originated. While it seemed that the Serpent was ignoring him that was not the case. In the absence of the dragon's protection, the Serpent's controlling spells met no resistance. El Haba felt himself responding to the demands of the Serpent and he yelled out a denial. A voice in his head told him to raise a shield about himself and he obeyed it. Something hard hit him on the head and he collapsed into a heap on the dirt. He was stunned for a brief moment, but upon regaining consciousness he realised he was secured with mage bonds, unable to act – but also unable to escape the blast of energy that the Serpent aimed at him.

Maeven ran for the trapdoor into the dungeon, but before opening it sensed danger beyond. She could think of no place to hide and be safe. Her life did not matter; but the little dragon's life did; the little mage was the future of the Kingdom of Thulor.

Heavy thumps were landing on the far side of the trapdoor. Someone or something was determined to break through it.

"Dragon shards! I can't go that way, I can't go back and there is nowhere to hide."

Maeven backed away, her mind grappling with the question of how the dragon had got into the cavern and how the small animals that sustained her had come in. There had to be another way out. She scanned the darkness but could not see beyond the cavern where the mage battle was continuing. She was petrified of going back there and into Ciabolo's reach. Just as panic began to sneak up on her, a new young voice came into her mind.

"I know where we must go. I am Petulor, trust me!"

Maeven had the sensation of being a ball kicked into the air, as the baby dragon propelled them through rock and darkness. She felt about as safe as if her infant son had said, "Trust me, I can drive a cart!"

Finally, when she knew she could bear no more of the strange mode of travel, she heard another voice, gentle, warm and welcoming. "You are safe now, dragon-mother."

A very deep darkness overcame her.

CHAPTER 26 – AFTERMATH

Thulor, dragon-mage, prepared her final spell.

The wizard and the sorceress were blocking what they could of the evil one's mage bolts. Some were hitting her, but she had known it was her time to die. Four of the other five were protecting her from the bites of the snakes, but they were mere annoyances at worst.

Thulor targeted her enemy. She had to kill him or at least damage him so that he would be weak until her daughter was strong enough to face him.

Ciabolo came into the centre of the cavern, towering over everyone. Tall, solid, frighteningly barbaric with skin etchings glowing purple and the orange eyes flashing with evil determination, he stared at King Westron, who stood between him and his enemy. The Serpent had stopped blasting the dragon, and seemed unaffected by the bolts being sent by her puny defenders. It was almost as if he was absorbing the energy. Finora and Roman slowed and stopped their attack, ready to start again in an instant.

"Weakling," Ciabolo sneered at the man facing him. "I could blasst you where you sstand!"

Westron continued to stare at the Serpent. "Why haven't you?" he challenged in a deadly serious tone.

It was a bluff, but Westron did not betray the fear in his mind that the dying dragon could no longer protect him. Ciabolo had tried to kill him before and failed each time. Would he waste his energies trying again, or hoard them for a final attack on the dragon?

"Move asside, dragon sspawn!"

"Move aside, dragon-son."

Ciabolo gloated as he finally faced his oldest enemy but even as he prepared to blast the dying dragon, Thulor released her spell.

The cavern was lit by a brilliant light, blinding everyone within but affecting Ciabolo most. He screamed, and seemed to become two creatures instead of one. A man-shaped creature fell to the ground as Ciabolo lost the power to maintain the unholy union. King Westron ran his sword into the man's heart without a qualm. The second creature was indescribably ugly and no longer human in appearance. It screamed again in angry impotence as mage bolts blasted it and forced it to twist in the air. It flew around the cavern, revealing wings that had been hidden by the human body it had worn. Whilst aiming mage bolts of its own at its attackers, it was also grabbing the lighted torches from the wall brackets and throwing them into a pile on the floor.

As it flew it shrieked defiantly, "If thiss iss the besst you can do – your kingdom iss doomed, Dragon-sspawn. The dragon iss dead! I live! And I will return when you leasst expect me and kill you all – sslowly, painfully extracting every tiny trasse of magic power you have ass I ssuck the flessh from your boness."

Westron stood calmly. "Really? Thulor's time had come – but her mage daughter lives."

"A baby dragon?" Ciabolo laughed and the sound raised the hackles on all who heard it. "No doubt sstolen already by your whelp. Believe in a baby and a traitor if you will. It will make my victory ssweeter when I feed on your whelp and have dragon for desssert."

The flames from the piled torches turned green after a gesture from Ciabolo. It dived into the flames and vanished.

"Douse the flames!" Atlantis yelled. "Before it returns."

Finora reacted fastest and smothered the flames with a blast of power. The cavern became absolutely dark until Finora and Roman formed balls of magic light.

Leanne looked around. "Where are Maeven and the baby dragon?"

Everyone except El Haba looked around the cavern. Rhovert gestured for Finora to bring her light into the shadowed area of Thulor's cavern. When they returned to the dungeon from checking the passage, she shook her head at her Father's glance of inquiry.

"Something is still trying to get in through the dungeon – she can't have gone that way."

Atlantis glanced at her brother. He shook his head. He had not spirited them away.

Leanne stated bluntly, "There is no other way out."

"Rabbits and water come in," Atlantis said. "Have you noticed that the water has stopped flowing?"

"What do you mean?" Leanne demanded, turning towards her.

King Westron was staring at the dead hulk of Thulor as he answered. "Thulor was a dragon mage. She could have brought food in here by magic – just as she hid her presence here from us for untold years."

"Did she send them away?" Finora asked.

"No, all her strength went into distracting the demon so they could get away."

"But how?" Leanne persisted.

"They are gone," Westron said calmly. "That is what matters."

Rhovert suddenly laughed. "I salute her! Our little thief took the dragon away from under the Serpent's nose."

"Ciabolo will seek her," Atlantis warned. "I want to look for her."

"You will not, my Lady," Westron ordered gently. "Thulor ordered her to go. I believe that her daughter-mage knew how and where to go. If you follow her, you may in turn be followed."

"But…"

"He's right, Atlantis," Roman spoke softly. "The baby dragon has power – although only a fraction of her potential. If Maeven stays near her she will be safe – Ciabolo's messenger demons won't find her."

"One found her here – and Thulor was alive," Atlantis insisted.

King Westron answered. "Perhaps Thulor planned it to draw her enemy here. We needed the little demon, as well as the larger. Apart from that, Thulor was hoarding her remaining power to confront that demon. The power for the talisman shield had been stored in the pieces."

"But what if Ciabolo does find her?" Atlantis persisted.

"She has proved, in the past, to be resourceful," Westron said. "I trust her to have a strong sense of self preservation."

Atlantis turned to El Haba. "What if he does that jump out of the fire trick – right in front of her? He isn't dead. He may have lost a lot of power, but he only has to go upstairs to pull it from those traitors with the black cowls."

Westron moved to Atlantis. "What have you seen? Have you seen him come through fire?"

Atlantis nodded. "He did it in Vatarik, but this time I saw it like a waking dream. I felt I was Ven. He wants her. He left as soon as he realised she had gone."

Westron squeezed Atlantis's shoulder gently. "What can you tell us, Prince of Vatarik and Thulor?"

Freed and healed by Roman, El Haba looked up from where he crouched beside his father's dead body. "Now that he exists in the true demon form, as a winged serpent, he is more vulnerable. When he merged with my father, he gained protection from the burning light of the sun. He also added my father's powers to his own. Atlantis is right; he will go to the nearest source of power – his converts and those affected by the blight he released. He won't stay here – he will most likely return to Vatarik using a demon portal."

"What is a demon portal?" Finora demanded.

"Demons are creatures of fire. Demon portals are fires that are keyed to each other – so demons, usually only major demons, can move from place to place. We always had a fire burning in father's suite. Ciabolo had permanent portal keys between there and the caverns."

"What are the portal keys like?" Atlantis asked, feeling on the verge of a revelation.

"They are sets of matched stones," El Haba told them. "Odd looking stones. A permanent portal needs a set of three – two to anchor the portal fires and the third to allow passage between the fires."

"Maeven had two odd stones…" Atlantis said slowly. "She described them to me soon after we met. Then, in the cavern in Vatarik, there was a glowing green stone that she grabbed just before Ciabolo appeared…"

El Haba shook his head. "As I told the princess, if there are only two Ciabolo can bounce back out of the fire if he chooses – or go to the nearest other fire. But your friend will not be able to activate them. It needs the touch of demon magic."

"So what can we do?" Atlantis demanded.

"For now – nothing," Westron commanded. "We have more immediate concerns. Whilst that major demon is fruitlessly seeking Thulor's successor, we need to regain control of my palace."

"I should have reset the attraction spell on the demon receptacle," Finora berated herself.

"And I should have expected a major demon," Roman Golddreamer said calmly.

"At least we know what we are up against," Leanne growled.

"All that is unimportant," Westron told them. "Rhovert, Leanne – clear the way out of here. Wizard Roman, Finora – I want this cavern sealed. Lady Atlantis, I ask you to help protect El Haba until matters upstairs have been settled."

Westron watched Rhovert and Leanne begin to move, and then walked to El Haba, still kneeling beside Malokin's dead body.

"Do you wish him returned to Vatarik?"

El Haba took the cold hand of his father. "No. My brother would not care and I doubt that the people there will mourn him. To me, he has been dead for twenty years, ever since he made the pact with Ciabolo."

"Then I will inter him with honour in Thulor," Westron offered.

"Honour, Sire? I do not understand."

"Once he was a king."

"An ambitious, greedy unscrupulous murderer… even before he became a despicable tyrant." El Haba admitted softly.

"Perhaps. Yet it is a gesture to the people of Vatarik that I do not hate them."

"My brother will think you weak and foolish," El Haba warned. "And the people will wonder if you are another king of the same ilk."

"Let them," Westron invited with a faint smile. "Being underestimated by one's enemy is useful, and if the Vatarins fear me, they will be less likely to support a push to steal my kingdom."

King Westron leant down and picked up the Serpen'ts Bane, the talismans and the shard of the new dragon's shell. He pressed the new shard into the hollow of the Serpent's Bane, as Thulor had told him that he must. When Thulor's mage daughter came into her full power, the protection would return and be even stronger. Until then, his realm was vulnerable; his children needed to be careful.

He returned talismans to Atlantis, Roman and Finora. When he held Maeven's in his hand, a clear vision came into his mind and he stared thoughtfully at El Haba. The man was nothing like the creature that had visited his palace a month ago.

"The pieces know what they will accept in a bearer," King Westron spoke, catching El Haba's gaze. "It seems that this one saw something of value in you, and my daughter has lived without it before."

El Haba accepted the talisman and bowed deeply to the King.

"I am yours to command."

King Westron nodded in acknowledgement.

"Who will take over in Vatarik?" he asked.

"My brother! He will be aware if Ciabolo has gone and will probably ride for home as fast as he can. I would not like to be a serf in my homeland now, nor would it be wise for me to return. Now that our father is dead and no longer controlling us, my brother will not permit me to live."

"I will deal with your brother in time," King Westron promised. "However, we should all return upstairs to my guests. I must see if my spymaster lives and discover if I still have a kingdom to rule."

"I hope Gisella is all right," Atlantis said quietly to her brother. "I managed to tell her to hide in a cupboard and have cloth to breathe through. We will need her to make up more of the dragon shell pellets to help those affected by the blight."

"Not the traitors," Rhovert qualified, coming back into the cavern. He had no sympathy for them. Westron handed him his talisman.

"It is not totally their fault," El Haba said quietly. "When my father visited here some years ago, he met a woman who had a lust for men. He put a spell on her so that whomever she later coupled with would become an agent of the Serpent. They were all infected by a craving for power, and agreed to do anything to receive it. I was no different, but I grew up knowing power. If I had not agreed to serve the Serpent, I would not have survived. I did not want my brother to have it all."

Westron nodded his understanding, and glanced at Rhovert.

"The way up is clear," he told his father.

Leanne waited in the dungeon. The metal grille was locked. She shook it in annoyance. Soon after the sound finished echoing along the stone passage, she heard footsteps that sounded to be hurrying. She slipped back into an area of shadow between the torches.

She recognised the man jiggling anxiously at the door. He tried to open the door and failed.

Leanne stepped forward.

"Princess! Thank the dragon!" the man exclaimed.

"Can you open the door, Jays?" Leanne asked the young man.

He looked startled then stammered, "Oh, of course."

"Why are you down here?"

"Oh! His Majesty is needed upstairs. Almost everyone up there looks dead, or like a statue. I returned from visiting my parents and that red-headed witch grabbed me and told me to find His Majesty. There is a strange guard officer up there and he told me you were down here. What has happened?"

"Too much to explain. Was the midsummer fire lit?" Leanne demanded.

"Yes, but it was almost out."

Leanne swore. "Stay here, my father will be up soon. Did you see anyone else beside the witch and the guard moving around up there?"

Jays shook his head.

"Tell my father I am searching the palace for the traitors."

Jays had no chance to ask further questions. Leanne raced off, her boot-steps echoing loudly off the stone walls.

Rhovert surveyed the scene in the Great Hall. He noticed the changes from his first look several hours ago. The statues were now lying in neat rows all over the floor. Atlantis, El Haba and Gisella were moving along the rows. Those that had been lying down before were no longer in sight, but a row of covered bodies lay near one wall. He saw his father talking to a hooded man and waited until the king finished talking to his spymaster.

"What have you found?" Westron asked his son.

"There are eight dead traitors in the side room," Rhovert began. "The rest of the traitors are missing, as is the wench, Jilli. El Rasho has gone. Leanne and I believe we have found everybody affected by that blight."

Westron nodded. "My spymaster was warned, so he and two of his men were not afflicted. He saw the giant that was Malokin and the demon. When that creature left – to go to the cavern below – El Rasho took over my throne and was gloating over the fate of my nobles and guests. He proclaimed to the captive audience that he was now king of Thulor. When he saw a portion of the guests slump to the floor – he grabbed the maid and began racing for the door. Moments later the demon form materialised from the fire, roared a curse and vanished back into it."

Rhovert saw El Haba stand up from beside a prone figure and approach.

"Sire, there is little I can do to help these people. I have tried all I can but I have never seen this blight before. Lady Gisella's pellets are helping. They have brought movement back to those people that were still alive. I believe that all should recover if they are able to be given nourishment – they have all been drained of life force and energy."

Atlantis stood and stretched. "We have managed to get some to drink water but it takes time." She looked at El Haba and asked, "Are you sure they are not like those black-robed ones in Ciabolo's cavern?"

"These were unsuspecting and unwilling pawns. Those others swore their lives to him." El Haba explained.

"Which sort is El Rasho?" Atlantis asked. "Since he raced out in such a hurry."

"He is sworn to serve Ciabolo," El Haba said thoughtfully. "I don't know if he had any way to know that Malokin was dead or that Ciabolo had failed. I think that he was spooked and is racing back to Vatarik. He had better hope that his other wizard friends can protect him because I believe that Ciabolo will wish to merge with him now that our father is dead. I do know that my brother has no wish for such a union."

"As much as I detest your brother – I don't think I would wish that on anyone," Atlantis commented. "Your Majesty, we really need more people to nurse your guests. Giz told me that some of the older nobles, who looked most likely to die, have begun to wake up."

"You may tell Lady Gisella that when the help I have summoned arrives, she may order as many people as she needs to help her."

CHAPTER 27– THE SERPENT IS BANISHED

Maeven awoke, head pounding with an enormous ache, and not helped by the hard nose nudging her face. A voice in her mind was very insistent.

"Dragon-mother?" Petulor asked plaintively. "I'm hungry."

A small brightly glowing dragon shape pushed itself into her face again. Maeven tried to push it away. Beyond the hatchling, wherever she was was quite dark.

"I guess you are, Petulor," Maeven said aloud, and groaned when she tried to sit up and felt a hot stiffness in her side. She felt like she had just been pushed through a narrow hole in a very wide mountain. "But I have no idea what you need to eat or where to get it."

Maeven then heard a deeper toned rumble in her mind and something large and faintly glowing rose from the stone floor and moved further away.

"I can help you, Dragon-mother," the voice promised. "I am Mortmellor, Thulor's youmgest daughter. I have had young of my own, and I can help you raise my sister."

"Your help would be appreciated," Maeven admitted to the old dragon.

There was a rustle of membranous wings and a stirring of dust and the glow vanished.

Surprisingly soon, she heard scrabbling of talons on stone, the rustle of wings folding and the faint glow, huge in size, that was Mortmellor, approached. A moment later, Petulor was crunching on something that might have been a whole rabbit.

"I don't know what to feed you, Dragon-mother." Mortmellor's voice was apologetic.

"I've eaten rabbit," Maeven admitted. "Preferably cooked – but I am hopeless at catching them. I might be able to find edible roots, but right now my stomach feels full of the mountain that I was dragged through by Petulor."

Mortmellor's voice rumbled. "She will learn that humans are more delicate that dragons."

"I can't think why Thulor thought I could raise Petulor alone."

"You are not alone," Mortmellor corrected.

Maeven sighed. "No, I suppose not."

Would the dragon understand how her current thoughts mocked her? Probably not. Dragons seemed to be pretty literal. Mortmellor would probably think as little of her as she had of Atlantis, who had tried to kill her, if she said how she had wanted to find and hatch a dragon, so she could own it, make people pay attention to her and show everyone… well, she couldn't remember what she had wanted to show everyone back then, only wanting to be away from the palace, from people who were always telling her how to behave, away from her grief and her father's unfair restrictions.

Well, here she was. Where that was exactly, though, she didn't know – so presumably her family didn't either. Hopefully, her noble sisters were honourably defending the dying Thulor from the Serpent, preferably killing him. They hadn't noticed her departure.

Trouble was – when she had finally left the palace, she had intended to amass lots of wealth, and retire to the farthest reaches of Thulor and live in a grand manor house with lots of servants.

Petulor snuffled at her legs, "I'm still very hungry."

The large silver glow of Mortmellor vanished out the cave entrance once again. "You'll get more soon, Petulor."

Maeven sighed again. When she had decided to be a rich thief, she had forgotten about her dream to find a dragon, and fly away on it. At the moment, her later desire still wasn't impossible – it had just been delayed, until Petulor wasn't so helpless.

Memories of the last moments in the palace dungeon returned to her. She chuckled now in relief. The Serpent, Ciabolo, would be livid now – that is, if her family hadn't finished him off. He'd told her she couldn't have the mage egg. She'd got it. He wasn't going to let her go – but she'd escaped. He didn't want the egg to hatch. It had and she had escaped with the new dragon mage without him noticing. He had not been able to touch the hatchling. The thrill of contemplating those successful deeds energised her and she forced herself to her feet.

It was dark where she was. Her eyes only saw the silver glow of the baby dragon. Yet she had 'dragon-sight', a skill that allowed her to see in the dark. The cavern she was in was quite large. It was high enough for Mortmellor to stand up to her full height. It would probably be at least as large as a minor lord's keep.

"Stay here, Petulor," Maeven said, finding the young dragon's head and patting the soft scales. "I'm just going to feel my way around in here."

Well, she had seen what Atlantis had done…

"I can do this," Maeven told herself, holding her knife awkwardly and trying to decide where to start. Another cramping spasm of hunger motivated her to begin.

The skin of the creature was tougher than she had expected, so her best effort was very rough indeed. When she fastidiously used the knife to pull and scrape the rabbits innards out, Mortmellor snapped up the gory mess with a sound of satisfaction. Maeven shuddered. She was going to have to get used to dragon ways.

Since she had nothing to use as a spit, nor any skill at skinning the little beast, she decided to cook it in its fur and poked it into the ashes were they were glowing reddest.

Something to use as bedding was her next thought. She had not found anything in the cave to use – so while the rabbit cooked, she ventured outside.

In her head, she heard Mortmellor warning her to stay close. Since she didn't want to get lost, she decided to heed the advice.

At the cave entrance, Maeven looked around. The night was almost as dark as the cave. There should have been a full moon, but perhaps it was later than she thought and the midsummer moon had already set. There didn't seem to be any stars either, which was odd. The evening had been fine and clear when she had arrived back at her father's palace. Even now, there was no smell of rain to suggest that clouds were covering the sky. In fact what she did smell, very faintly, was the taint of rotten flesh.

There was nothing to rouse her sense of danger. So she adjusted her eyes to see better in the dark and looked for leafy bushes. Fortunately, she found something that would do that was fairly close by and began breaking off branches.

It took her several trips before she decided she had prepared a soft enough bed. By then, she was too hungry to wait any longer to eat. She was almost asleep by the time she had eaten enough. It had been a very long day.

Her last thought was of satisfaction – she had got away from everyone.

Sometime during her sleep, Petulor crawled next to her, producing a warm presence and a soothing rumble.

The morning sun was reaching into the cavern through an open section of the cavern roof when Maeven was woken by a starving baby dragon. The place seemed familiar.

A shadow blocked the cavern entrance for a moment. Maeven watched with interest as the shadow became Mortmellor. The dragon tossed a rabbit to Petulor, who wasted no time eating it.

Maeven wandered to the cave entrance and looked out. Now that it was daylight, she recognised the features of the scene she saw. She was in the cave she had visited with Atlantis, above the village where she had stayed until Wystan's birth. She couldn't stay here! If Ciabolo hadn't died, although surely the rest of her family had killed him, he'd come after her, looking for Petulor.

"Is there somewhere else we can go, that's not here? Do you know of other caves where we can stay, that Petulor can take me?"

The old dragon snorted. "Petulor just hatched. She can't take you anywhere."

"She got me here…"

"That magic was Thulor's – and we are safe here. The little one can draw on the magic from below – from where our dam was hatched."

"You don't understand! If my family haven't killed that bastard, Ciabolo, then he'll come looking for me and Petulor."

"We are safer here," Mortmellor insisted. Then she twisted her long neck and touched her nose to Maeven's right sleeve. "Perhaps you should take that thing off you that reeks of vermin."

Maeven looked at the gold snake bracelet around her wrist and shuddered. She had forgotten about that… it was Ciabolo's mark. It seemed to be loose on her wrist, but the moment she tried to remove it, it tightened. She would have to ignore it. Her clothes, however, also reeked of something like rotten eggs, dragon ichor, and putrid meat.

"I need to wash my clothes," she said aloud, more to herself.

"There is a river down below," Mortmellor told Maeven. "You can wash there."

Maeven turned with surprise, "I thought you said there are traps all the way down."

"The traps won't hurt you – the magic recognises you."

"I am not all that fond of being deep in the ground," said Maeven. She remembered how the snakes had found her down below. She had nothing to scare them off with now, and no Atlantis to protect her. "I could go down past the village to where the river comes out."

She had the thought that she could sneak back past the village, stopping near her old hut, now being used by her friend, Reyna, and get some of the stuff she had stashed away before leaving.

However, that thought was cut short by Mortmellor's offer. "I'll get my whelp Darknor to take you there. He can hide you. Those humans in the place below are little better than those who stay here at times."

"Okay," Maeven accepted the offer. "The villagers don't like me, and I don't want them to see me anyway." Inwardly she chuckled at the dragon's description of the villagers, but to be fair, they were nowhere near as bad as the brigands had been. Probably smelt cleaner, too.

A short time later, a smaller dark coloured dragon flew to the cave entrance, perched there briefly while Maeven moved out of its way. Then it furled its wings, sniffed her, and scrambled in.

"This is Darknor, my most recent whelp. He will take you to the river, but you are in danger every moment that you are away from Petulor."

"I don't intend to take long."

A faint snort, then, "You reek of demon. Why didn't you kill it?"

"The rest of my family were dealing with Ciabolo."

"Well, those vermin are hard to kill. So if it was his smell on you…"

"I'll be fast," she promised, her gut clenching at the thought of him finding her by the smell. All the more imperative that she get clean. And better to do it now, when she can watch for dangers and when Ciabolo could not tolerate the bright daylight.

Darknor allowed her to climb onto his shoulders once they were again outside the cave. Then his nose nudged her into the best position, and told her to hold onto his neck. She felt pressed down onto him when he gave a strong down thrust and sprung into the sky. When the pressure eased, she made the mistake of looking down. She immediately began to feel giddy and sick. She closed her eyes and concentrated on hanging on.

She felt the air turning from warm to chilly, although the sun seemed hot on her back. After a few minutes of flight, Darknor began to spiral down. He landed with only a minor thump, in a small cleared area by the water. Maeven slid gladly from his back, not sure she wanted to repeat the experience.

"Can people see you?"

A low rumble was the immediate response. Then in her mind, Maeven heard, "We can hide ourselves from humans. We have had to, to survive."

"I'm going to wash," she said, "but I want to go back past the village and get some stuff I stashed there a while ago. Why don't you go and hunt? I will get my stuff and go back to the cave. When I get there I will light a fire to dry off."

Darknor moved uneasily, and didn't do as she said.

"Are there any humans nearby?" Maeven asked him.

He moved his head this way and that and smelled the air. "No."

Seeing that he was going to stay, Maeven quickly pulled off her outer clothes, just leaving on the silky things that she'd had under her ball dress – had it only been yesterday? She carried the clothes with her into the river, which at this time of the year was merely cool.

Her mind stayed alert as she tried to scrub her arms and face with her hands. When she began to try to freshen her clothes, her mind began to scan the area around her. Down here, even allowing for the trees shading her from the sun, the light still seemed duller than it had been high up on Darknor's back. Was it her imagination? The night just past had also seemed unnaturally dark.

She began to feel a sensation like the hairs on her head wanting to stand up – even though they were soaked. Darknor also seemed to sense something, and he was looking around. He stopped still, head looking up into the sky through a gap in the trees. Maeven emerged from the water, and followed his gaze. Up in the dull sky were what looked at first glance like a flock of birds… only they were not moving like birds.

As quick as she could, Maeven pulled on her now-soaking tunic and trews, but draped the wet jerkin around her neck. The flying creatures were not birds, but tiny messenger demons such as she had seen before.

"Darknor, get back up to the cave. Tell Mortmellor to get down to the crypt – I assume she can – and take Petulor there. I will come up as soon as I get some stuff I need."

The young dragon didn't want to go without her.

"Go! I have some ideas to deal with these little demons before they find Petulor – and they are using me to find her, so it is better I am not with her."

Darknor took no further urging, and launched himself into the air. aeven whispered the words of her invisibility spell and hoped she still had enough of Thulor's magic about her for it to work. Then she began to run along a familiar path that went around the village.

She had to help guard the baby dragon mage, but she couldn't help thinking of her son when the sound of a baby's cry carried from up the hill from her. She had a sudden intense desire to hold him again, to see how his newborn face had changed, and to take him with her. Then her sense of survival took hold. She couldn't look after him, not yet. Not when the safety of the kingdom depended on a baby dragon, and she had to live with the dragons in a cave. It was no place for a child. And what if a pack of brigands came by the cave, or Ciabolo? She'd have to hide – certainly she couldn't fight them.

At least, in the village, her son would be protected, even if those parochial peace lovers wouldn't fight. She hoped that they were no longer as naïvely trusting as they had been.

Maeven felt her eyes grow hot, warm drips mingled with the cold rain. She didn't want to leave her son again. This wasn't the way she had planned to have her life. Once she only thought of herself, and did as she pleased. Now she had a son and responsibilities to him. She wanted to be a better mother to him than her father had been to her. She stifled the thought of how she was hiding him from his royal grandfather.

It wasn't the time to think of her father, either. She was still ambivalent about him. He had never seemed to care about her, had used her, but for that one brief moment when she had arrived at the ball, he had hugged her and she had known that he loved her and was proud of her… even if she was a thief.

Forcing herself to move quietly, Maeven walked up a narrow path and went to the tiny cave in the rock upthrust near her former hut. Before she had left, she had put a lot of her spare things in the cave and covered them with rocks, as well as magic. Well, the latter wasn't as effective now, and she banished the spell and began to drag out what she wanted. First was a blanket, and she used this to bundle everything else.

Part of her mind was alert for anyone approaching, and she had just tied the corners of the blanket when she heard twigs snapping. She spun around, ready to run.

"Who's there?" a female voice called.

Maeven began to edge sideways, towards the nearest trees. She didn't answer. No one should be able to see her…

Reyna emerged. "Ven?"

Looking down and able to see a vague outline of herself, Maven answered. "Yes." She whispered the counter spell to become visible.

Reyna ran to her, hugged her. "What are you doing here?"

"Just getting some of my spare stuff. I can't stay."

"Come and get dry…"

"No. I have to go."

"Where?"

"Best you don't know." Maeven wriggled free. "I'll be going far away from here. Don't mention I was here."

"Who is after you?"

Maeven just shook her head. She wasn't going to mention all she had just been through, or the new dragon mage. Who would believe her? She didn't even want to think about Ciabolo, actively looking for her. As for her father, if El Haba told him of their child, he would hunt high and low for her.

"I just have to keep moving," Maeven said, her eyes begging her friend to let her go.

"May the gods of the villagers keep you safe," Reyna adopted the pious tone of the village elders, even as she twisted the formal words.

A grin forced its way onto Maeven's face. Neither she, nor her friend, believed in the villagers' god. However, some instinct caused her to say, "If weird things start happening around here, suggest that they petition their god to protect them."

Reyna looked perplexed as she watched Maeven run back to the trail up to the cave.

The run kept Maeven from feeling chilled, but even though the circling flock of demons seemed to have lost her, she wouldn't be able to avoid them forever. Somewhere, Ciabolo was directing them – he had to be – and he would find her. She had no desire to face him again, had been content to let her siblings have the glory of saving the realm. She wanted to hide.

The cavern was empty. She hoped the dragons were all down in Exconidor's crypt and would stay there until it was safe to come up. Somehow, if Ciabolo turned up, she was going to have to convince him that Petulor was nowhere near. Rather, she wanted him dead, but if her family hadn't killed him, there was no chance that she could, being neither warrior nor sorceress.

She only had her wits to protect her, and Ciabolo might not be tricked again. And this time, she didn't even have Thulor's protective amulet. She was truly on her own, and she had to keep alive to protect Petulor – at least until the baby dragon mage was old enough to protect herself and the realm of Thulor.

Since coming into the cave, she had begun to shiver, and tried to tell herself it was from her wet clothes, and not from fear at having to face Ciabolo. She wanted to run…

Near the fire ring and its barely glowing embers, she dropped her wet jerkin and the blanket bundle of her things. Her first idea was to change into dry clothes, but wet ones might be a minor protection from Ciabolo – he hated water. What other weapons did she have? Two knives that she still had following her invisibly – they were very sharp, but she rather not be close enough to the demon to be able to use them. What else?

Iron bucket and cook pot, iron eating utensils, and an iron trivet… did demons fear iron? She made a line of the iron things between her and the fire, and pulled the soaking jerkin closer. If nothing else, she could throw them at Ciabolo.

Light! She needed more light – she didn't want to face Ciabolo in the dark. There was still some of the dry stuff Mortmellor had collected for the fire, and some of her bedding stuff should be dry enough to burn.Once the fire was alight again, she felt better and went back to sorting through the spare clothes, trying to find the two small pouches – one of coins, one of gems – that she had grabbed. The former went directly into a pocket hidden in her trews, but her hand stopped before pocketing the gem pouch. Inside the soft leather, some of the gems seemed to have stuck together. In the firelight, she tried to study the leather. The bag wasn't one she had made, but her mind recalled the glinting embossed sigil. These had come from the house of Lord Tormore on the night she had run away from the palace to become a thief. The clumped demon portal stones gave her an idea. If only she could pull it off.

Suddenly she could hear noise like distant screams, and she ran towards the cave entrance. Then a sense of another presence came over her, sending more chills down her back. She spun around. The fire interfered with her dragon sight, but she heard no sound of movement. She stared into the darkness, her hands fiddling with the gem pouch to bring out a set of the clumped stones and hide the rest. She separated the two stones and hid them in separate pockets in her tunic.

The flames of the fire grew larger as if the greener wood of her bedding was now burning – but the light was not getting brighter.

She had seen that effect before, and now atavistic shivers were crowding up her spine. Instinctively, she muttered a counter spell and the two knives she had brought from the palace, under the invisible follow spell, appeared – one in each hand. Her eyes watched the fire as she slowly edged her way to the cave entrance. Her head began to itch, as it did in the presence of magic, and now an even deeper shadow was hovering over the fire – still partly in it.

The memory came flooding back. Rolliver! The night when she was a prisoner, the hissing voice she now knew the owner of. To confirm it – the bracelet on her wrist began to writhe.

"Oh, no!" she heard herself moan, and turned to flee, only to find that her legs seemed to be filled with rocks and the dozen steps she needed to reach the entrance seemed like a hundred.

Before she was half way to the entrance, something shoved her in the back with such force that she fell forward onto the rocky floor. As she rolled to get back to her feet, she sensed something dark and deadly fly over her. She scrambled to her feet, the fear acting to numb her throbbing face and arms. She had fallen awkwardly, so as not to lose the knives in her hands.

The darkness solidified in front of her, blocking her way out, and it was only due to her dragon sight that she saw the vaguely human shape about the glowing orange eyes. The shape moved, allowing her to see the silhouette of half furled wings behind it.

"Going somewhere, Prinssess?"

Maeven felt her whole body freeze – not into immobility, because she could feel every muscle trembling with the desire to flee – but like a trapped animal.

"Ciabolo," she said aloud, letting her mouth say what it would while her mind sought for a way to escape. "It's the old snake himself – almost didn't recognise you without your human suit. What happened to it?"

"It doess not matter," Ciabolo growled. "Where iss the dragon?"

"Quite frankly, old snake," Maeven heard herself say while her body was prepared to jump sideways if he tried to grab her, "I don't know and I don't care either."

She stared at a point just above the demon's eyes. No way was she going to let him mesmerise her as he had tried once before.

"I don't believe you, dragonsspawn." Ciabolo leant forward, bending over her. "The royal line of Thulor existss only to sserve the dragon mage vermin."

"Not me!" Maeven declared and she brought one of the knives up and slashed at the demon's face. Ciabolo drew his head back quickly, but otherwise ignored the knife. "I've had enough! It's taken me until now to realise that Thulor has been pushing me around like the lowest serf, for years! I'm getting away from here – far, far away! I only stopped here to get some stuff I left here."

Ciabolo's hissing laugh made her skin crawl all over. He lunged forward as if to grab her, and she swiped again with the knife, or tried to. Some force wrenched it from her hand and sent it flying into the far rock wall.

"Puny human! I will enjoy ssucking the flesh from your bones."

"How do you know I'm not poisonous?" The smart retort distracted Maeven from the feeling of needing to visit the privy. "Anyway, I'm surprised you are still alive. I thought Thulor would finish you."

"Dragon magess overrate themsselves. The vermin iss dead."

Risking a grab from Ciabolo, Maeven eased herself back to her feet. "You've met other dragon mages then?" She was talking just for the sake of it, and began to wave the other knife in front of the demon's face, recalling from somewhere that demons did not like the touch of iron, and seeing that he was keeping some of his attention on it. She danced sideways and lunged, hoping to seem more dangerous to him than she felt.

Ciabolo leapt away from the knife, issuing a contemptuous hiss. Maeven dived for the narrow gap between Ciabolo and the cave entrance. The reaction was immediate – a sizzling bolt of magic brushed her side, melting the metal of the knife and making the skin on her face and right arm burn.

Maeven yelped with the pain and Ciabolo laughed as he lifted her, using a single pointing finger, from the entrance to the back of the cave.

"You are inssignificant. Lower than vermin." Ciabolo's eyes glowed brighter and now a trace of the purple tattoos was showing on his skin. "If dragon magess cannot kill me, what makess you think you can? Iss your tongue a ssword?"

"That is an interesting idea, snake."

Maeven was breathing quickly, trying to ignore the pain in her arm and face. Her mouth was the only weapon she still had. Well, that and her brain – used to finding weakness to exploit – in people's security, and concentration.

And Ciabolo hadn't tried to kill her yet. Did he still think that he couldn't? Or did he have some purpose he wanted her for? Just to find Petulor?

No, there had been that idea of making her and her sisters into breeding machines for Prince El Rasho. Why did he want a Vatarin/Thulan hybrid anyway? Stop thinking of that. Her son, just down the hill, was one, and she had to keep this bastard away from the village – better to keep thinking she had indeed aborted El Haba's bastard. Wystan's existence was an exquisite secret, provided that El Haba in his new allegiance didn't mention him.

Maeven began to see the walls of the cavern start to glow faintly silver to her dragon sight, and a memory stirred an idea for escape.

In a deliberately high pitched, whiny tone, Maeven let her tongue take over again. "I really don't know where Petulor is."

"The new dragon mage named hersself to you?" Ciabolo pounced on that piece of information and half leapt, half flew closer to her.

"So what if she did? Thulor threw me and that barrel-sized eating machine through what felt like a whole mountain, into a rank cave where there was an ancient crone of a dragon, who positively hates humans… probably as much as she hates demons, which she said she could smell on me. I am surprised I woke up alive. I had a pounding headache, and Petulor demanding food."

The whining tone seemed to be annoying the demon as much as it had her nurse of years back. It seemed though, that Ciabolo believed her half-truths.

"Where iss the dragon whelp?"

Maeven increased the pitch of her voice to a screech. "I told you, I don't know!"

She grinned faintly as she saw Ciabolo's face contort.

"I managed to make a deal with the old dragon. I promised to give her some gold if she took over feeding Petulor five rabbits everytime she was hungry and she brought me here."

"Then when sshe returns…"

Maeven shook her head. "She dropped me from her talons and muttered 'good riddance', then hovered until I went and got the gold I had stashed around here. Soon as she had the gold, poof! She was gone."

"Did you ssee the way you came from?"

Maeven saw the demon watching her avidly, and she stared back at his forehead. "Are you joking? I was being dangled from so high up, I didn't dare look. I had my eyes closed."

"Puny humans."

In her mind, Maeven thought, "underrate me at your own peril, snake!" She made her shoulders slump as if in defeat, and turned to walk towards a dark passage. Her idea was dangerous, and with an uncertain chance of success.

"How did you find me anyway?" she asked.

"I have marked you."

"Oh, you mean the snakey bracelet?" Maeven wished she had her talisman. The dragon magic in it – if any was left in it – might have negated the demon magic. Too bad, she didn't, and anyway, the amulet hadn't done anything when she was first wearing the thing.

"So you came through the fire to see me," Maeven went on. "I'm touched that you care. Don't you need a portal key to do that trick? And make the fire go impressively green?"

"What do you know of portal keyss?" Cibaolo pounced after her.

"Oh, I had one once, but I was told that you need two or three of them to make them work."

"What creature gave it to you?" Ciabolo growled dangerously.

Maeven spared a glance over her shoulder. "I pinched it from your Thulan traitor, Tormore."

"He isss dead, my creature killed him!"

"Yeah, he outsmarted himself – no great loss though."

"I will have it!"

"Nuh, uh! Only if you let me out of here so I can go far away."

"No!"

"What possible use am I to you?"

"Dragon bait!"

"By the time that Petulor can fly, she will have forgotten me and that old-hag dragon will have poisoned her mind against me."

"I will have it!"

Maeven felt the pull he was trying to exert on her mind. She fingered the stone in her pocket that was smooth on one side and rough on the other, and closed her fingers onto it.

She was right beside a passage that smelt faintly of cinnamon. Taking the stone out, she flung it with all her strength into that passage, and said, "Find it then…"

Whispering her spell for invisibility, Meaven leapt sideways, out of the way of the furious demon who had dived after the stone. As soon as he had disappeared into that passage, she took the other – the one leading down to Exconidor's crypt.

She didn't go far, just to where the rough walls of the passage had a deression she could press herself into.

"Hide me," she thought to whaever power dwelled there. Then she turned her dragon sight towards the passage where Ciabolo had gone.

Hearing a bellow from the Serpent and his talons scrabbling on stone gave her some amusement. She'd flung the stone into the dragons' privy – although, she had only just realised it. The contents of that deep hole, glowed brightly silver.

She stayed perfectly still, and a short while later, something covered in silvery dust moved rapidly past her position, displacing air that now smelt pungently of cinnamon. As it passed, she heard loud sniffing noises, and the words, "You won't esscape dragonsspawn."

"But will you?" Maeven murmured, hoping that the nasty traps further into the passage would seriously hurt him. He was angry enough that he might be careless.

When all seemed quiet, Maeven crept back to the main cavern – hoping that Ciabolo had found the stone. Now to plant the other.

The paired stone was in her pocket and she now drew it out. As El Haba had explained, it needed to be activated by demon magic.

An itch around her wrist gave her reason to smile. She rubbed the stone against the bracelet, and it began to glow green, and grow warmer. She closed her hand around the stone and crouched into a small heap behind the fire. The iron objects were all close to her and her unmelted knife was in her free hand. She waited to see if Ciabolo survived the nasty traps.

A loud pop heralded the return of a furious demon, which whizzed around the cavern bellowing, "I can ssmell you dragonsspawn."

Maeven remained quiet, and after a time, Ciabolo slowed, landed on his feet and furled his wings. He paced around the cavern, sniffing the air, and moving closer and closer to the fire.

In a moment when his head was facing away, Maeven tossed the glowing stone into the fire. The flames went abruptly from orange to bright green.

"No! It iss not possible!" Ciabolo bellowed, seeing Maeven who had risen from her crouch. "You are human, you cannot use demon magic."

"Can't I?" Maeven asked maliciously? "I am good at stealing magic – human, demon, dragon..." She shrugged.

"No!"

"Okay, if you prefer… I lied. Who else might have opened the portal?"

Ciabolo made to leap over the fire to reach her, but as he reached the apex of his leap, above the weird green flames, he was sucked down, bellowing a denial.

Maeven quickly tossed all the iron objects onto the fire, and then her still wet jerkin – smothering the flames. When she was finished, her heart was pounding.

A quiet chuckle made her jump and twist in mid air. A silvery figure was forming, along with a cool, soothing breeze that caressed her still smarting face and arm. With relief, she recognised the touch of dragon magic.

"I am relieved that the royal line of Thulor hasn't weakened."

"Who are you?"

The silvery figure, now definitely man-shaped, grew brighter and seemed to be wearing a suit of armour. "Call me Freddie."

Freddie? "You are Frederick," Maeven blurted, recognising Exconidor's chosen human. "But you're dead!"

The figure bowed again. This time holding out a ghostly box. "Here. Take this."

When her hand brushed the silver glow, a box solidified in her hands.

"Sprinkle the stuff on the fire – it will seal that section of the earth, and protect this whole cave."

"I wasn't planning on staying…"

"You should stay. Here you are safe. That demon will believe that you are fleeing to the far ends of the kingdom." Lifting her smouldering jerkin, Maeven gave herself time to think by sprinkling most of the crushed dragon shells on the embers. She saved a little to leave in the hut of her son's foster parents, sometime soon.

"You met Petulor then?" she asked.

"Thulor's successor, I assume? Yes. And you are Thulor's chosen one?" Frederick smiled.

"If you mean was I elected to try to feed that eating machine – seems so."

"You should not stay away from her for too long…"

"I came here to get some stuff. I didn't expect that damn demon to find me."

"Are you a sorceress?"

"What? No. I can do some magic, and I steal the spells."

A chuckle. "Ah, that explains the stuff you have following you. Some of it is demon-made – it will attract them."

"You mean this bracelet?"

"That… and something in your pocket."

"I have a few more portal stones."

"How did you activate them?"

"The damn bracelet that I can't remove."

"Thulor did choose well."

"Huh?"

"The dragon mages who have chosen to protect the realm, choose a human to help when their successor hatches. I can't recall it ever being a girl before, just someone as sneaky and secretive as they are. The demons have a fair idea of how most humans react, and are not prepared for the ones who think differently."

"Like you?"

"Well, yes. And you, it seems."

Maeven considered this. "Frederick?"

"Freddie," the apparition corrected. "I was only ever Frederick when the old tyrant, my father-in-law, was around. Even my wife, Princess Wilhelmia called me Freddie."

"Why did you end up staying here?" Maeven asked, curious.

"Long story, but Willie, I mean my wife Wilhelmia, went off to start up some sort of priestess sect. I do believe that was Thulor's idea. Anyway, I was getting very tired of things, and when it was my time, I chose to come back to guard Exconidor's crypt."

"From any demons?" Maeven asked.

"And to protect Thulor's mage egg. As soon as they are mature, they find a mate and produce an egg. The first one is a mage egg, and their successor. At least, that was my thought, but Thulor hid it somewhere and didn't tell me. I thought the safest place for it would be her dam's crypt."

"Freddie? Do you think that demon, that calls himself the Serpent, is gone… for good?"

The apparition seemed to be thinking for a while. "We can hope, but I doubt it. That demon is an old one – not easy to kill. If you had not doused the fire, he may have been able to rebound. Now, if he is stuck between fires, sort of in limbo, he will gradually get weaker. Faster, because you tricked him into the dragon cesspit, and that stuff is as inimical to him as these dragon shells. The longer he takes to recover – if he does – the stronger the young dragon mage will be."

"Any other advice?" Maeven found herself asking.

"Only, look after the young dragon as best you can."

"Because she's the last dragon mage?"

"Yes, demons like that one have killed all the others, and any dragon they find, and have turned the minds of men against dragons, too," Freddie explained. "But dragons are all that stand between humankind and demonkind. In your case, she will soon be strong enough to neutralise that bracelet, which is a sink for magic that demons can use. It won't take long to recharge. It still has some of that creature's magic in it."

"And if I don't have anything with Thulor's magic in it, I can't do spells. I left my amulet back at the palace. That stored Thulor's magic."

"You will be safe here. You might be able to use the dragon magic emanating from the crypt."

The apparition began to fade, and Maeven was sorry to sense Freddie leaving, but shortly after, three loud pops heralded the return of the three dragons.

EPILOGUE

The sun shone brightly on the mountain. No trace of the unnatural haze that had dulled the kingdom remained.

Maeven stared at the landscape beyond the cave, from the broken ground known locally as the 'Slide' and on down to the village below.

Petulor followed her, butted her legs and looked up at her human friend. Maeven laughed and patted the dragon's smooth head.

"I sure put a knot in the Serpent's tail!" she said aloud. "I told him I'd steal what he wanted most. I wonder if he is still in a bodiless limbo or found a distant fire to crawl out of."

Petulor butted her again.

"All that effort to stop you being born. If he isn't dead, he'll be really annoyed."

Maeven sobered.

"Did I thank you for getting me out of the Palace? I may be stuck here with you for a few years, but once you are big enough – I'm off, out of here. I've got places to go, things to do, money to spend…"

Maeven's eyes caught sight of a movement near the stream below the village, a woman, holding the hand of a blonde haired toddler.

"… a child to raise…"

The End

OTHER NOVELS by MARGARET GREGORY

WANDA: FROM BAD TO WORSE

If she was going to die young, like her mother, Gwen Willard was determined to die rich and she had very few years to do it. Her first step was to leave home. She met Hooch, who taught her some exciting and illegal skills. She was the Dracos lucky mascot until she came to the attention of the police.

Then her uncanny knack for predicting trouble, warned her to flee to the city and change her name. Life wasn't easy. She was 15, had little money and no regular job. Then she crossed the path of an evil and unscrupulous man and she didn't want him to have his way.

WANDA: CHOOSING CRIME

Wanda was free. She was never going back to jail. But she was homeless, almost penniless and Harrison Franklin had a long and vengeful memory. Jim Phillips had a long memory too, and Wanda had saved his life. Could he save her from Franklin?

WANDA: RISKING LIFE TO LIVE

The euphoria of successful heists were what kept Wanda Dean alive. At 23, she was crime boss Harrison Franklin's top agent – well paid for absolute obedience. That's all that mattered. Until she met Mike Johnston and her boss ordered him killed. For that, the Franklins were going to pay. In Risking Life to Live, justice conflicts with loyalty and the penalty for betrayal is death.

KORVU: THE BEGINNING
The prequel to The Wild One

Jai Ansuni was the first female Atapi sorcerer for thousands of years, but she dare not reveal it. However, when tribal sorcerer, Stacion Ansuni escalates the enmity between Atapi and Kumatan to an ominous level. Jai and her womb mate, Con, try to mitigate his atrocities but can two young Atapi, not even a score of years old, win against the powerful sorcerer?

THE WILD ONE

Sixteen year old Jai Cassidy thought she was finally free of her family until she is discovered by her other relatives…the ones that aren't human. Jai uses her natural perversity and cunning to escape their control, but catapults herself into the middle of a deadly feud between two alien races.

ATAPI SORCERESS
The sequel to The Wild One

Jai Cassidy is beginning her mission of reversing the decline of the non-humanoid Atapi. As a sorceress and an Atapi-Human hybrid, she is vehemently disliked by the male Atapi sorcerers and the humanoid rulers of Korvu. Her task is complicated by the treachery of a group of alien engineers, who are inciting insurrection and harsh reprisals.

THE TYMOREAN TRUST BOOK 1 - POWER RISING

The Tymorean Trust - When peace rules Tymorea - Peace reigns in the universe.

Chosen to be the Advocates of the mystical and incorporeal Guardians of Peace, twins Tymos and Kryslie must first learn to control and use the power rising in them - or it will destroy them.

On Tymorea, only the ruling Triumvirate Governors are powerful enough to guide the strong-willed alien-bred twins until they have mastered their power.

THE TYMOREAN TRUST BOOK 2 - GREAT ONES

The peace of the Guardian Planet, Tymorea, is in deadly peril. War there will create ripples of unrest and destruction throughout the settled universe.

Tymos and Kryslie, still adolescents, have barely mastered their power and Llaimos is still less than a year old, but they are the three chosen to be Advocates of the mystical Guardians of Peace, to safeguard the Tymorean Trust.

THE TYMOREAN TRUST BOOK 3 - RETURN TO EARTH

Even before the war on Tymorea, the Elders foresaw that Great Ones Tymos and Kryslie would have an imperative mission on Earth.

But as the Tymoreans prepare to build an Earthbase to support them, they discover that specifications for two vital protective shields are missing.

Now, nearly a century later, Tymos and Kryslie must find his work and build the generator before the base is found.

THE TYMOREAN TRUST BOOK 4 - EARTH MISSION

Just before their graduation from the prestigious WSRA Washington University, Tymos and Kryslie Ward deliberately disappear.

The Great Ones have foreseen the capture and death of the new Tymorean missionaries and discovered that the leader of the Eastern Imperium plans to undermine the United World Nations. Tymos and Kryslie must protect their kin and prevent a potentially devastating world war.

THE TYMOREAN TRUST BOOK 5 – ALIEN CONTACT

Tymos and Kryslie Ward, hide their Tymorean intelligence and abilities while working as low ranked technicians at the WSRA's lunar base. When an alien ship arrives at Lunar One, pursued by a powerful enemy who will stop at nothing to get what he wants, only the two Tymorean Great Ones have the knowledge and abilities to overcome him, but to do so they must risk their sanity, and their souls.

THE TYMOREAN TRUST BOOK 6 – INVASION

Great Ones Tymos and Kryslie go to rescue the crew of Earth's first deep space mission – and discover that Ciriot space pirates have discovered Earth's location. When the Ciriot invade in force, the Great Ones reveal themselves so that Earth can gain vital help. However, Kryslie becomes the victim of Ciriot, who want to control her mind and make her betray the people of Earth.

TRICKS

Tom and Jo Dwyer had a reputation for playing tricks – and getting detention. They didn't seem to care about that, so long as they made their class laugh. That was until someone began to turn their tricks against them, and it was no longer funny.

SHORT STORIES:

GRAFFITI GIRL

Valerie has become known as "The Graffiti Girl" but she is more than just a street artist. She sees and paints life her way.

In Valkyrie, the second story, Valerie, blinded by an explosion, must learn to paint and see again.

GHOST WRITER

Edwina is a ghost with a mission - to find out why she died.

Only to do so, she must first help another girl.

RATTLING CHAINS

I slammed the phone to my ear, "Colin! Where are you?" I was yelling.

"I haven't time for that. I need your help."

"What? Where?"

"Grab the chain, Hetty! Grab it, and don't let go."

"What chain? Colin? What chain?"

He was gone.

CRAZY TAILS

Three of these stories are based on real creatures I have known, but their names have been changed to protect the not so innocent. The incidents are real, the events happened, but the telling is tempered by nostalgia and the POV – that's where the fantasy comes in.

Spend some moments as a mouse, a possum, a cat and a rabbit.

Connect to Margaret Gregory

Friend me on Facebook:
http://www.facebook.com/margaret.gregory.399